The Depot Master

Other Cape Cod Classics include

Cape Cod
Henry David Thoreau

Cape Cod Folks
Sarah P. McLean

The Depot Master
Joseph C. Lincoln

A Little Maid of Province Town
Alice Turner Curtis

Shifting Sands
Sara Ware Bassett

The Woman-Haters
Joseph C. Lincoln

A Cape Cod Classic

Joseph C. Lincoln

The Depot
Master

Parnassus Book Service

Originally published May 1910 by D. Appleton and Co

First Cape Cod Classics Edition 2021
Published in the United States by Parnassus Book Service
https://www.parnassusbooks.com/imprint

ISBN: 9781732762633

Table of Contents

Chapter I
At the Depot

MR. SIMEON PHINNEY emerged from the side door of his residence and paused a moment to light his pipe in the lee of the lilac bushes. Mr. Phinney was a man of various and sundry occupations, and his sign, nailed to the big silver-leaf in the front yard, enumerated a few of them. "Carpenter, Well Driver, Building Mover, Cranberry Bogs Seen to with Care and Dispatch, etc., etc.," so read the sign. The house was situated in "Phinney's Lane," the crooked little byway off "Cross Street," between the "Shore Road" at the foot of the slope and the "Hill Boulevard"—formerly "Higgins's Roost"—at the top. From the Phinney gate the view was extensive and, for the most part, wet. The hill descended sharply, past the "Shore Road," over the barren fields and knolls covered with bayberry bushes and "poverty grass," to the yellow sand of the beach and the gray, weather-beaten fishhouses scattered along it. Beyond was the bay, a glimmer in the sunset light.

Mrs. Phinney, in the kitchen, was busy with the supper dishes. Her husband, wheezing comfortably at his musical pipe, drew an ancient silver watch from his pocket and looked at its dial. Quarter past six. Time to be getting down to the depot and the post office. At least a dozen male citizens of East Harniss were thinking that very thing at that very moment. It was a community habit of long standing to see the train come in and go after the mail. The facts that the train bore no passengers in whom you were intimately interested, and that you expected no mail made little difference. If you were a man of thirty or older, you went to the depot or the "club," just as your wife or sisters went to the sewing circle, for sociability and mild excitement. If you were a single young man you went to the post office for the same reason that you attended prayer meeting. If you were a single young lady you went to the post office and prayer meeting to furnish a reason for the young man.

Mr. Phinney, replacing his watch in his pocket, meandered to the sidewalk and looked down the hill and along the length of the "Shore Road." Beside the latter highway stood a little house, painted a spotless white, its window blinds a vivid green. In that house dwelt, and dwelt alone, Captain Solomon Berry, Sim Phinney's particular friend. Captain Sol was the East Harniss depot master and, from long acquaintance, Mr. Phinney knew that he should be through supper and ready to return to the depot, by this time. The pair usually walked thither together when the evening meal was over.

But, except for the smoke curling lazily from the kitchen chimney, there was no sign of life about the Berry house. Either Captain Sol had already gone, or he was not yet ready to go. So Mr. Phinney decided that waiting was chancey, and set out alone.

He climbed Cross Street to where the "Hill Boulevard," abiding place of East Harniss's summer aristocracy, bisected it, and there, standing on the corner, and consciously patronizing the spot where he so stood, was Mr. Ogden Hapworth Williams, no less.

Mr. Williams was the village millionaire, patron, and, in a gentlemanly way, "boomer." His estate on the Boulevard was the finest in the county, and he, more than any one else, was responsible for the "buying up" by wealthy people from the city of the town's best building sites, the spots commanding "fine marine sea views," to quote from Abner Payne, local real estate and insurance agent. His own estate was fine enough to be talked about from one end of the Cape to the other and he had bought the empty lot opposite and made it into a miniature park, with flower beds and gravel walks, though no one but he or his might pick the flowers or tread the walks. He had brought on a wealthy friend from New York and a cousin from Chicago, and they, too, had bought acres on the Boulevard and erected palatial "cottages" where once were the houses of country people. Local cynics suggested that the sign on the East Harniss railroad station should be changed to read "Williamsburg." "He owns the place, body and soul," said they.

As Sim Phinney climbed the hill the magnate, pompous, portly, and imposing, held up a signaling finger. "Just as if he was hailin' a horse car," described Simeon afterward.

"Phinney," he said, "come here, I want to speak to you."

The man of many trades obediently approached.

"Good evenin', Mr. Williams," he ventured.

"Phinney," went on the great man briskly, "I want you to give me your figures on a house moving deal. I have bought a house on the Shore Road, the one that used to belong to the—er—Smalleys, I believe."

Simeon was surprised. "What, the old Smalley house?" he exclaimed. "You don't tell me!"

"Yes, it's a fine specimen—so my wife says—of the pure Colonial, whatever that is, and I intend moving it to the Boulevard. I want your figures for the job."

The building mover looked puzzled. "To the Boulevard?" he said. "Why, I didn't know there was a vacant lot on the Boulevard, Mr. Williams."

"There isn't now, but there will be soon. I have got hold of the hundred feet left from the old Seabury estate."

Mr. Phinney drew a long breath. "Why!" he stammered, "that's where Olive Edwards—her that was Olive Seabury—lives, ain't it?"

"Yes," was the rather impatient answer. "She has been living there. But the place was mortgaged up to the handle and—ahem—the mortgage is mine now."

For an instant Simeon did not reply. He was gazing, not up the Boulevard in the direction of the "Seabury place" but across the slope of the hill toward the home of Captain Sol Berry, the depot master. There was a troubled look on his face.

"Well?" inquired Williams briskly, "when can you give me the figures? They must be low, mind. No country skin games, you understand."

"Hey?" Phinney came out of his momentary trance. "Yes, yes,

3

Mr. Williams. They'll be low enough. Times is kind of dull now and I'd like a movin' job first-rate. I'll give 'em to you to-morrer. But—but Olive'll have to move, won't she? And where's she goin'?"

"She'll have to move, sure. And the eyesore on that lot now will come down."

The "eyesore" was the four room building, combined dwelling and shop of Mrs. Olive Edwards, widow of "Bill Edwards," once a promising young man, later town drunkard and ne'er-do-well, dead these five years, luckily for himself and luckier—in a way—for the wife who had stuck by him while he wasted her inheritance in a losing battle with John Barleycorn. At his death the fine old Seabury place had dwindled to a lone hundred feet of land, the little house, and a mortgage on both. Olive had opened a "notion store" in her front parlor and had fought on, proudly refusing aid and trying to earn a living. She had failed. Again Phinney stared thoughtfully at the distant house of Captain Sol.

"But Olive," he said, slowly. "She ain't got no folks, has she? What'll become of her? Where'll she move to?"

"That," said Mr. Williams, with a wave of a fat hand, "is not my business. I am sorry for her, if she's hard up. But I can't be responsible if men will drink up their wives' money. Look out for number one; that's business. I sha'n't be unreasonable with her. She can stay where she is until the new house I've bought is moved to that lot. Then she must clear out. I've told her that. She knows all about it. Well, good-by, Phinney. I shall expect your bid to-morrow. And, mind, don't try to get the best of me, because you can't do it."

He turned and strutted back up the Boulevard. Sim Phinney, pondering deeply and very grave, continued on his way, down Cross Street to Main—naming the village roads was another of the Williams' "improvements"—and along that to the crossing, East Harniss's business and social center at train times.

The station—everyone called it "deepo," of course—was then a small red building, old and out of date, but scrupulously neat because of Captain Berry's rigid surveillance. Close beside it was the "Boston Grocery, Dry Goods and General Store," Mr. Beriah

Higgins, proprietor. Beriah was postmaster and the post office was in his store. The male citizen of middle age or over, seeking opportunity for companionship and chat, usually went first to the depot, sat about in the waiting room until the train came in, superintended that function, then sojourned to the post office until the mail was sorted, returning later, if he happened to be a particular friend of the depot master, to sit and smoke and yarn until Captain Sol announced that it was time to "turn in."

When Mr. Phinney entered the little waiting room he found it already tenanted. Captain Sol had not yet arrived, but official authority was represented by "Issy" McKay—his full name was Issachar Ulysses Grant McKay—a long-legged, freckled-faced, tow-headed youth of twenty, who, as usual, was sprawled along the settee by the wall, engrossed in a paper covered dime novel. "Issy" was a lover of certain kinds of literature and reveled in lurid fiction. As a youngster he had, at the age of thirteen, after a course of reading in the "Deadwood Dick Library," started on a pedestrian journey to the Far West, where, being armed with home-made tomahawk and scalping knife, he contemplated ex-termination of the noble red man. A wrathful pursuing parent had collared the exterminator at the Bayport station, to the huge delight of East Harniss, young and old. Since this adventure Issy had been famous, in a way.

He was Captain Sol Berry's assistant at the depot. Why an as-sistant was needed was a much discussed question. Why Cap-tain Sol, a retired seafaring man with money in the bank, should care to be depot master at ten dollars a week was another. The Captain himself said he took the place because he wanted to do something that was "half way between a loaf and a job." He em-ployed an assistant at his own expense because he "might want to stretch the loafin' half." And he hired Issy because—well, be-cause "most folks in East Harniss are alike and you can always tell about what they'll say or do. Now Issy's different. The Lord only knows what *he's* likely to do, and that makes him interestin' as a conundrum, to guess at. He kind of keeps my sense of re-sponsibility from gettin' mossy, Issy does."

"Issy," hailed Mr. Phinney, "has the Cap'n got here yet?"

Issy answered not. The villainous floorwalker had just prof-
fered matrimony or summary discharge to "Flora, the Beautiful
Shop Girl," and pending her answer, the McKay mind had no
room for trifles.

"Issy!" shouted Simeon. "I say, Is', Wake up, you foolhead! Has
Cap'n Sol—"

"No, he ain't, Sim," volunteered Ed Crocker. He and his chum,
Cornelius Rowe, were seated in two of the waiting room chairs,
their feet on two others. "He ain't got here yet. We was just
talkin' about him. You've heard about Olive Edwards, I s'pose
likely, ain't you?"

Phinney nodded gloomily.

"Yes," he said, "I've heard."

"Well, it's too bad," continued Crocker. "But, after all, it's
Olive's own fault. She'd ought to have married Sol Berry when
she had the chance. What she ever gave him the go-by for, after
the years they was keepin' comp'ny, is more'n I can understand."

Cornelius Rowe shook his head, with an air of wisdom. Captain Sol, himself, remarked once: "I wonder sometimes the
Almighty ain't jealous of Cornelius, he knows so much and is so
responsible for the runnin' of all creation."

"Humph!" grunted Mr. Rowe. "There's more to that business
than you folks think. Olive didn't notice Bill Edwards till Sol
went off to sea and stayed two years and over. How do you know
she shook Sol? You might just as well say he shook her. He always was stubborn as an off ox and cranky as a windlass. I wonder how he feels now, when she's lost her last red and is goin' to
be drove out of house and home. And all on account of that fool
'mountain and Mahomet' business."

"*Which?*" asked Mr. Crocker.

"Never mind that, Cornelius," put in Phinney, sharply. "Why
don't you let other folks' affairs alone? That was a secret that
Olive told your sister and you've got no right to go blabbin'.'"

"Aw, hush up, Sim! I ain't tellin' no secrets to anybody but Ed
here, and he ain't lived in East Harniss long or he'd know it already. The mountain and Mahomet? Why, them was the last

words Sol and Olive had. 'Twas Sol's stubbornness that was most to blame. That was his one bad fault. He would have his own way and he wouldn't change. Olive had set her heart on goin' to Washin'ton for their weddin' tower. Sol wanted to go to Niagara. They argued a long time, and finally Olive says, 'No, Solomon, I'm not goin' to give in this time. I have all the others, but it's not fair and it's not right, and no married life can be happy where one does all the sacrificin'. If you care for me you'll do as I want now.'

"And he laughs and says, 'All right, I'll sacrifice after this, but you and me must see Niagara.' And she was sot and he was sotter, and at last they quarreled. He marches out of the door and says: 'Very good. When you're ready to be sensible and change your mind, you can come to me. And says Olive, pretty white but firm: 'No, Solomon, I'm right and you're not. I'm afraid this time the mountain must come to Mahomet.' That ended it. He went away and never come back, and after a long spell she give in to her dad and married Bill Edwards. Foolish? 'Well, now, *wa'nt* it!"

"Humph!" grunted Crocker. "She must have been a born gump to let a smart man like him get away just for that."

"There's a good many born gumps not so far from here as her house," interjected Phinney. "You remember that next time you look in the glass, Ed Crocker. And—and—well, there's no better friend of Sol Berry's on earth than I am, but, so fur as their quarrel was concerned, if you ask me I'd have to say Olive was pretty nigh right."

"Maybe—maybe," declared the allwise Cornelius, "but just the same if I was Sol Berry, and knew my old girl was likely to go to the poorhouse, I'll bet my conscience—"

"S-ssh!" hissed Crocker, frantically. Cornelius stopped in the middle of his sentence, whirled in his chair, and looked up. Behind him in the doorway of the station stood Captain Sol himself. The blue cap he always wore was set back on his head, a cigar tipped upward from the corner of his mouth, and there was a grim look in his eye and about the smooth shaven lips above the short, grayish-brown beard.

"Issy" sprang from his settee and jammed the paper novel into his pocket. Ed Crocker's sunburned face turned redder yet. Sim Phinney grinned at Mr. Rowe, who was very much embarrassed.

"Er—er—evenin', Cap'n Sol," he stammered. "Nice, seasonable weather, ain't it? Been a nice day."

"Um," grunted the depot master, knocking the ashes from his cigar.

"Just right for workin' outdoor," continued Cornelius.

"I guess it must be. I saw your wife rakin' the yard this mornin'."

Phinney doubled up with a chuckle. Mr. Rowe swallowed hard. "I—I *told* her I'd rake it myself soon's I got time," he sputtered.

"Um. Well, I s'pose she realized your time was precious. Evenin', Sim, glad to see you."

He held out his hand and Phinney grasped it.

"Issy," said Captain Sol, "you'd better get busy with the broom, hadn't you. It's standin' over in that corner and I wouldn't wonder if it needed exercise. Sim, the train ain't due for twenty minutes yet. That gives us at least three quarters of an hour afore it gets here. Come outside a spell. I want to talk to you."

He led the way to the platform, around the corner of the station, and seated himself on the baggage truck. That side of the building, being furthest from the street, was out of view from the post office and "general store."

"What was it you wanted to talk about, Sol?" asked Simeon, sitting down beside his friend on the truck.

The Captain smoked in silence for a moment. Then he asked a question in return.

"Sim," he said, "have you heard anything about Williams buying the Smalley house? Is it true?"

Phinney nodded. "Yup," he answered, "it's true. Williams was just talkin' to me and I know all about his buyin' it and where it's goin'."

He repeated the conversation with the great man. Captain Sol did not interrupt. He smoked on, and a frown gathered and deepened as he listened.

"Humph!" he said, when his friend had concluded. "Humph!

Sim, do you have any idea what—what Olive Seabury will do when she has to go?"

Phinney glanced at him. It was the first time in twenty years that he had heard Solomon Berry mention the name of his former sweetheart. And even now he did not call her by her married name, the name of her late husband.

"No," replied Simeon. "No, Sol, I ain't got the least idea. Poor thing!"

Another interval. Then: "Well, Sim, find out if you can, and let me know. And," turning his head and speaking quietly but firmly, "don't let anybody *else* know I asked."

"Course I won't, Sol, you know that. But don't it seem awful mean turnin' her out so? I wouldn't think Mr. Williams would do such a thing."

His companion smiled grimly; "I would," he said. "'Business is business,' that's his motto. That and 'Look out for number one.'"

"Yes, he said somethin' to me about lookin' out for number one."

"Did he? Humph!" The Captain's smile lost a little of its bitterness and broadened. He seemed to be thinking and to find amusement in the process.

"What you grinnin' at?" demanded Phinney.

"Oh, I was just rememberin' how he looked out for number one the first—no, the second time I met him. I don't believe he's forgot it. Maybe that's why he ain't quite so high and mighty to me as he is to the rest of you fellers. Ha! ha! He tried to patronize me when I first came back here and took this depot and I just smiled and asked him what the market price of johnny-cake was these days. He got red clear up to the brim of his tall hat. Humph! 'twas funny."

"The market price of *Johnny-cake*! He must have thought you was loony."

"No. I'm the last man he'd think was loony. You see I met him a fore he came here to live at all."

"You did? Where?"

"Oh, over to Wellmouth. 'Twas the year afore I come back to

East Harniss, myself, after my long stretch away from it. I never intended to see the Cape again, but I couldn't stay away somehow. I've told you that much—how I went over to Wellmouth and boarded a spell, got sick of that, and, just to be doin' somethin' and not for the money, bought a catboat and took out sailin' parties from Wixon and Wingate's summer hotel."

"And you met Mr. Williams? Well, I snum! Was he at the hotel?"

"No, not exactly. I met him sort of casual this second time."

"*Second* time? Had you met him afore that?"

"Don't get ahead of the yarn, Sim. It happened this way: You see, I was comin' along the road between East Wellmouth and the Center when I run afoul of him. He was fat and shiny, and drivin' a skittish horse hitched to a fancy buggy. When he sighted me he hove to and hailed.

"'Here you!' says he, in a voice as fat as the rest of him. 'Your name's Berry, ain't it.'

"'Yup,' says I.

"'Methusalum Berry or Jehoshaphat Berry or Sheba Berry, or somethin' like that? Hey?' he says.

"'Well,' says I, 'the last shot you fired comes nighest the bull's eye. They christened me Solomon, but 'Twa'n't my fault; I was young at the time and they took advantage.'

"He grinned a kind of lopsided grin, like he had a lemon in his mouth, and commenced to cuss the horse for tryin' to climb a pine tree.

"'I knew 'twas some Bible outrage or other,' he says. 'There's more Bible names in this forsaken sand heap than there is Christians, a good sight. When I meet a man with a Bible name and chin whiskers I hang on to my watch. The feller that sets out to do me has got to have a better make up than that, you bet your life. 'Well, see here, King Sol; can you run a gasoline launch?'

"'Why, yes, I guess I can run 'most any of the everyday kinds,' says I, pullin' thoughtful at my own chin whiskers. This fat man had got me interested. He was so polite and folksy in his remarks. Didn't seem to stand on no ceremony, as you might say. Likewise there was a kind of familiar somethin' about his face. I knew mighty well I'd never met him afore, and yet I seemed to have a floatin' memory of him, same as a chap remembers the taste of the senna and salts his ma made him take when he was little.

"'All right,' says he, sharp. 'Then you come around to my landin' to-morrer mornin' at eight o'clock prompt and take me out in my launch to the cod-fishin' grounds. I'll give you ten dollars to take me out there and back.'

"'Well,' says I, 'ten dollars is a good price enough. Do I furnish—'

"'You furnish nothin' except your grub,' he interrupts. 'The launch'll be ready and the lines and hooks and bait'll be ready. My own man was to do the job, but he and I had a heart-to-heart talk just now and I told him where he could go and go quick. No smart Alec gets the best of me, even if he has got a month's contract. You run that launch and put me on the fishin' grounds. I pay you for that and bringin' me back again. And I furnish my own extras and you can furnish yours. I don't want any of your Yankee bargainin'. See?'

"I saw. There wa'n't no real reason why I couldn't take the job. 'Twas well along into September; the hotel was closed for the season; and about all I had on my hands just then was time.

"'All right,' says I, 'it's a deal. If you'll guarantee to have your launch ready, I—'

"'That's my business,' he says. 'It'll be ready. If it ain't you'll get your pay just the same. To-morrer mornin' at eight o'clock. And don't you forget and be late. Gid-dap, you blackguard!' says he to the horse.

"'Hold on, just a minute,' I hollers, runnin' after him. 'I don't want to be curious nor nosey, you understand, but seems's if it might help me to be on time if I knew where your launch was goin' to be and what your name was.'

"He pulled up then. 'Humph!' he says, 'if you don't know my name and more about my private affairs than I do myself, you're the only one in this county that don't. My name's Williams, and I live in what you folks call the Lathrop place over here toward Trumet. The launch is at my landin' down in front of the house.'

"He drove off then and I walked along thinkin'. I knew who he was now, of course. There was consider'ble talk when the Lathrop place was rented, and I gathered that the feller who hired it answered to the hail of Williams and was a retired banker, sufferin' from an enlarged income and the diseases that go along with it. He lived alone up there in the big house, except for a cranky housekeeper and two or three servants. This was afore he got married, Sim; his wife's tamed him a little. Then the yarns about his temper and language would have filled a log book.

"But all this was way to one side of the mark-buoy, so fur as I was concerned. I'd cruised with cranks afore and I thought I could stand this one—ten dollars' worth of him, anyhow. Bluster and big talk may scare some folks, but to me they're like Aunt Hepsy Parker's false teeth, the further off you be from 'em the more real they look. So the next mornin' I was up bright and early and on my way over to the Lathrop landin'.

"The launch was there, made fast alongside the little wharf. Nice, slick-lookin' craft she was, too, all varnish and gilt gorgeousness. I'd liked her better if she'd carried a sail, for it's my experience that canvas is a handy thing to have aboard in case of need; but she looked seaworthy enough and built for speed.

"While I was standin' on the pier lookin' down at her I heard footsteps and brisk remarks from behind the bushes on the bank, and here comes Williams, puffin' and blowin', followed by a sulky-lookin' hired man totin' a deckload of sweaters and ileskins, with a lunch basket on top. Williams himself wan't carryin' anything but his temper, but he hadn't forgot none of that.

"'Hello, Berry,' says he to me. 'You are on time, ain't you. Blessed if it ain't a comfort to find somebody who'll do what I tell 'em. Now you,' he says to the servant, 'put them things aboard and clear out as quick as you've a mind to. You and I are through; understand? Don't let me find you hangin' around the place when I get back. Cast off, Sol.'

"The man dumped the dunnage into the launch, pretty average ugly, and me and the boss climbed aboard. I cast off.

"'Mr. Williams,' says the man, kind of pleadin', 'ain't you goin' to pay me the rest of my month's wages?'

"Williams told him he wa'n't, and added trimmin's to make it emphatic.

"I started the engine and we moved out at a good clip. All at once that hired man runs to the end of the wharf and calls after us.

"'All right for you, you fat-head!' he yells. 'You'll be sorry for what you done to me.'

"I cal'late the boss would have liked to go back and lick him, but I was hired to go a-fishin', not to watch a one-sided prize fight, and I thought 'twas high time we started.

"The name of that launch was the Shootin' Star, and she certainly lived up to it. 'Twas one of them slick, greasy days, with no sea worth mentionin' and we biled along fine. We had to, because the cod ledge is a good many mile away, 'round Sandy P'int out to sea, and, judgin' by what I'd seen of Fatty so fur, I wa'n't hankerin' to spend more time with him than was necessary. More'n that, there was fog signs showin'.

"'When was you figgerin' on gettin' back, Mr. Williams?' I asked him.

"'When I've caught as many fish as I want to,' he says. 'I told that housekeeper of mine that I'd be back when I got good and ready; it might be to-night and it might be ten days from now. "If I ain't back in a week you can hunt me up," I told her; "but not before. And that goes." I've got *her* trained all right. She knows me. It's a pity if a man can't be independent of females.'

"I knew consider'ble many men that was subjects for pity, 'cordin' to that rule. But I wa'n't in for no week's cruise, and I told him so. He said of course not; we'd be home that evenin'.

"The Shootin' Star kept slippin' along. 'Twas a beautiful mornin' and, after a spell, it had its effect, even on a crippled disposition like that banker man's. He lit up a cigar and begun to get more sociable, in his way. Commenced to ask me questions about myself.

"By and by he says: 'Berry, I suppose you figger that it's a smart thing to get ten dollars out of me for a trip like this, hey?'

"'Not if it's to last a week, I don't,' says I.

"'It's your lookout if it does,' he says prompt. 'You get ten for takin' me out and back. If you ain't back on time 'Tain't my fault.'

"'Unless this craft breaks down,' I says.

"''Twon't break down. I looked after that. My motto is to look out for number one every time, and it's a mighty good motto. At any rate, it's made my money for me.'

"He went on, preachin' about business shrewdness and how it paid, and how mean and tricky in little deals we Rubes was, and yet we didn't appreciate how to manage big things, till I got kind of sick of it.

"'Look here, Mr. Williams,' says I, 'you know how I make my money—what little I do make—or you say you do. Now, if it ain't a sassy question, how did you make yours?'

"Well, he made his by bein' shrewd and careful and always lookin' out for number one. 'Number one' was his hobby. I gathered that the heft of his spare change had come from dickers in stocks and bonds.

"'Humph!' says I. 'Well, speakin' of tricks and meanness, I've allers heard tell that there was some of them things hitched to the tail of the stock market. What makes the stock market price of—well, of wheat, we'll say?'

"That was regulated, so he said, by the law of supply and demand. If a feller had all the wheat there was and another chap had to have some or starve, why, the first one had a right to gouge t'other chap's last cent away from him afore he let it go.

"'That's legitimate,' he says. 'That's cornerin' the market. Law of supply and demand exemplified.'

"''Cordin' to that law,' says I, 'when you was so set on fishin' to-day and hunted me up to run your boat here—'cause I was about the only chap who could run it and wa'n't otherwise busy—I'd ought to have charged you twenty dollars instead of ten.'

"'Sure you had,' he says, grinnin'. 'But you weren't shrewd enough to grasp the situation and do it. Now the deal's closed and it's too late.'

"He went on talkin' about 'pools' and deals' and such. How prices of this stock and that was shoved up a-purpose till a lot of folks had put their money in it and then was smashed flat so's all hands but the 'poolers' would be what he called 'squeezed out,' and the gang would get their cash. That was legitimate, too—'high finance,' he said.

"'But how about the poor folks that had their savin's in them stocks,' I asks, 'and don't know high financin'? Where's the law of supply and demand come in for them?'

"He laughed. 'They supply the suckers and the demand for money,' says he.

"By eleven we was well out toward the fishin' grounds. 'Twas the bad season now; the big fish had struck off still further and there wa'n't another boat in sight. The land was just a yeller and green smooch along the sky line and the waves was runnin' bigger. The Shootin' Star was seaworthy, though, and I wa'n't worried about her. The only thing that troubled me was the fog, and that was pilin' up to wind'ard. I'd called Fatty's attention to it when we fust started, but he said he didn't care a red for fog. Well, I didn't much care nuther, for we had a compass aboard and the engine was runnin' fine. What wind there was was blowin' offshore.

"And then, all to once, the engine *stopped* runnin'. I give the wheel a whirl, but she only coughed, consumptive-like, and quit again. I went for'ard to inspect, and, if you'll believe it, there wa'n't a drop of gasoline left in the tank. The spare cans had ought to have been full, and they was—but 'twas water they was filled with.

"'Is *this* the way you have your boat ready for me?' I remarks, sarcastic.

"'That—that man of mine told me he had everything filled,' he stammers, lookin' scart.

"'Yes,' says I, 'and I heard him hint likewise that he was goin' to make you sorry. I guess he's done it.'

"Well, sir! the brimstone names that Fatty called that man was somethin' surprisin' to hear. When he'd used up all he had in stock he invented new ones. When the praise service was over he turns to me and says: 'But what are we goin' to do?'

"'Do?' says I. 'That's easy. We're goin' to drift.'

"And that's what we done. I tried to anchor, but we wa'n't over

15

the ledge and the iron wouldn't reach bottom by a mile, more or less. I rigged up a sail out of the oar and the canvas spray shield, but there wa'n't wind enough to give us steerageway. So we drifted and drifted, out to sea. And by and by the fog come down and shut us in, and that fixed what little hope I had of bein' seen by the life patrol on shore.

"The breeze died out flat about three o'clock. In one way this was a good thing. In another it wa'n't, because we was well out in deep water, and when the wind did come it was likely to come harder'n we needed. However, there wa'n't nothin' to do but wait and hope for the best, as the feller said when his wife's mother was sick.

"It was gettin' pretty well along toward the edge of the evenin' when I smelt the wind a-comin'. It came in puffs at fust, and every puff was healthier than the one previous. Inside of ten minutes it was blowin' hard, and the seas were beginnin' to kick up. I got up my jury rig—the oar and the spray shield—and took the helm. There wa'n't nothin' to do but run afore it, and the land knows where we would fetch up. At any rate, if the compass was right, we was drivin' back into the bay again, for the wind had hauled clear around.

"The Shootin' Star jumped and sloshed. Fatty had on all the ile-skins and sweaters, but he was shakin' like a custard pie.

"'Oh, oh, heavens!' he chatters. 'What will we do? Will we drown?'

"'Don't know,' says I, tuggin' at the wheel and tryin' to sight the compass. 'You've got the best chance of the two of us, if it's true that fat floats.'

"I thought that might cheer him up some, but it didn't. A big wave heeled us over then and a keg or two of salt water poured over the gunwale. He give a yell and jumped up.

"'My Lord!' he screams. 'We're sinkin'. Help! help!'

"'Set down!' I roared. 'Thought you knew how to act in a boat. Set down! d'you hear me? *Set down and set still!*'

"He set. Likewise he shivered and groaned. It got darker all the time and the wind freshened every minute. I expected to see that jury mast go by the board at any time. Lucky for us it held.

"No use tellin' about the next couple of hours. 'cordin' to my reckonin' they was years and we'd ought to have sailed plumb through the broadside of the Cape, and be makin' a quick run for Africy. But at last we got into smoother water, and then, right acrost our bows, showed up a white strip. The fog had pretty well blowed clear and I could see it.

"'Land, ho!' I yells. 'Stand by! *We're* goin' to bump.'"

Captain Sol stopped short and listened. Mr. Phinney grasped his arm.

"For the dear land sakes, Sol," he exclaimed, "don't leave me hangin' in them breakers no longer'n you can help! Heave ahead! *Did* you bump?"

The depot master chuckled.

"*Did* we?" he repeated. "Well, I'll tell you that by and by. Here comes the train and I better take charge of the ship. Anything so responsible as seein' the cars come in without me to help would give Issy the jumpin' heart disease."

He sprang from the truck and hastened toward the door of the station. Phinney, rising to follow him, saw, over the dark green of the swamp cedars at the head of the track, an advancing column of smoke. A whistle sounded. The train was coming in.

Chapter II
Supply and Demand

AND NOW LIFE in East Harniss became temporarily fevered. Issy McKay dashed out of the station and rushed importantly up and down the platform. Ed Crocker and Cornelius Rowe emerged and draped themselves in statuesque attitudes against the side of the building. Obed Gott came hurrying from his paint and oil shop, which was next to the "general store." Mr. Higgins, proprietor of the latter, sauntered easily across to receive, in his official capacity as postmaster, the mail bag. Ten or more citizens, of both sexes, and of various ages, gathered in groups to inspect and supervise.

The locomotive pulled its string of cars, a "baggage," a "smoker," and two "passengers," alongside the platform. The sliding door of the baggage car was pushed back and the baggage master appeared in the opening. "Hi! Cap'n!" he shouted. "Hi, Cap'n Sol! Here's some express for you."

But unfortunately the Captain was in conversation with the conductor at the other end of the train. Issy, willing and officious, sprang forward. "I'll take it, Bill," he volunteered. "Here, give it to me."

The baggage master handed down the package, a good sized one marked "Glass. With Care." Issy received it, clutched it to his bosom, turned and saw Gertie Higgins, pretty daughter of Beriah Higgins, stepping from the first car to the platform. Gertie had been staying with an aunt in Trumet and was now returning home for a day or two.

Issy stopped short and gazed at her. He saw her meet and kiss her father, and the sight roused turbulent emotions in his bosom. He saw her nod and smile at acquaintances whom she passed. She approached, noticed him, and—oh, rapture!—said laughingly, "Hello, Is." Before he could recover his senses and re-member to do more than grin she had disappeared around the corner of the station. Therefore he did not see the young man who stepped forward to shake her hand and whisper in her ear. This young man was Sam Bartlett, and, as a "city dude," Issy loathed and hated him.

No, Issy did not see the hurried and brief meeting between Bartlett and Gertie Higgins, but he had seen enough to cause for-getfulness of mundane things. For an instant he stared after the vanished vision. Then he stepped blindly forward, tripped over something—"his off hind leg," so Captain Sol afterwards vowed—and fell sprawling, the express package beneath him.

The crash of glass reached the ears of the depot master. He broke away from the conductor and ran toward his prostrate "assistant." Pushing aside the delighted and uproarious by-standers, he forcibly helped the young man to rise.

"What in time?" he demanded.

Issy agonizingly held the package to his ear and shook it.

"I—I'm afraid somethin's cracked," he faltered.

The crowd set up a whoop. Ed Crocker appeared to be in dan-ger of strangling.

"Cracked!" repeated Captain Sol. "Cracked!" he smiled, in spite of himself. "Yes, somethin's cracked. It's that head of yours, Issy. Here, let's see!"

He snatched the package from the McKay hands and in-spected it.

"Smashed to thunder!" he declared. "Who's the lucky one it belongs to? Humph!" He read the inscription aloud, "Major Cuthbertson S. Hardee. The Major, hey! ... Well, Is, you take the remains inside and you and I'll hold services over it later."

"I—I didn't go to do it," protested the frightened Issy.

"Course you didn't. If you had you wouldn't. You're like the feller in Scriptur', you leave undone the things you ought to do and do them that—All right, Jim! Let her go! Cast off!"

The conductor waved his hand, the engine puffed, the bell rang, and the train moved onward. For another twelve hours East Harniss was left marooned by the outside world.

Beriah Higgins and the mail bag were already in the post office. Thither went the crowd to await the sorting and ultimate distribution. A short, fat little man lingered and, walking up to the depot master, extended his hand.

"Hello, Sol!" he said, smiling. "Thought I'd stop long enough to say 'Howdy,' anyhow."

"Why, Bailey Stitt!" cried the Captain. "How are you? Glad to see you. Thought you was down to South Orham, takin' out seasick parties for the Ocean House, same kind of a job I used to have in Wellmouth."

"I am," replied Captain Stitt. "That is, I was. Just now I've run over here to see about contractin' for a supply of clams and quahaugs for our boarders. You never see such a gang to eat as them summer folks, in your life. Barzilla Wingate, he says the same about his crowd. He's comin' on the mornin' train from Wellmouth."

"You don't tell me. I ain't seen Barzilla for a long spell. Where you stoppin'? Come up to the house, won't you?"

"Can't. I'm goin' to put up over to Obed Gott's. His sister, Polena Ginn, is a relation of mine by marriage. So long! Obed's gone on ahead to tell Polena to put the kettle on. Maybe Obed and I'll be back again after I've had supper."

"Do. I'll be round here for two or three hours yet."

He entered the depot. Except the forlorn Issy, who sat in a corner, holding the express package in his lap, Simeon Phinney was the only person in the waiting room.

"Come on now, Sol!" pleaded Sim. "I want to hear the rest of that about you and Williams. You left off in the most ticklish place possible, out of spite, I do believe. I'm hangin' on to that boat in the breakers until I declare I believe I'm catchin' cold just from imagination."

"Wait a minute, Sim," said the depot master. Then he turned to his assistant.

"Issy," he said, "this is about the nineteenth time you've done just this sort of thing. You're no earthly use and I ought to give you your clearance papers. But I can't, you're too—well—ornamental. You've got to be punished somehow and I guess the best way will be to send you right up to Major Hardee's and let you give him the remnants. He'll want to know how it happened, and you tell him the truth. The *truth*, understand? If you invent any fairy tales out of those novels of yours I'll know it by and by and—well, *you'll* know I know. No remarks, please. Git!"

Issy hesitated, seemed about to speak, thought better of it, took up package and cap, and "got."

"Let's see," said the Captain, sitting down in one of the station chairs and lighting a fresh cigar; "where was Williams and I in that yarn of mine? Oh, yes, I could see land and cal'lated we was goin' to bump. Well, we did. Steerin' anyways but dead ahead was out of the question, and all I could do was set my teeth and trust in my bein' a member of the church. The Shootin' Star hit that beach like she was the real article. Overboard went oar and canvas and grub pails, and everything else that wa'n't nailed down, includin' Fatty and me. I grabbed him by the collar and wallowed ashore.

"'Awk! hawk!' he gasps, chokin', 'I'm drownded.'

"I let him *be* drownded, for the minute. I had the launch to think of, and somehow or 'nother I got hold of her rodin' and hauled the anchor up above tide mark. Then I attended to my passenger.

"'Where are we?' he asks.

"I looked around. Close by was nothin' but beach-grass and seaweed and sand. A little ways off was a clump of scrub pines and bayberry bushes that looked sort of familiar. And back of them was a little board shanty that looked more familiar still. I rubbed the salt out of my eyes.

"'*Well*!' says I. 'I swan to man!'

"'What is it?' he says. 'Do you know where we are? Whose house is that?'

"I looked hard at the shanty.

"'Humph!' I grunted. 'I do declare! Talk about a feller's comin' back to his own. Whose shanty is that? Well, it's mine, if you want to know. The power that looks out for the lame and the lazy has hove us ashore on Woodchuck Island, and that's a piece of real estate I own.'

"It sounds crazy enough, that's a fact; but it was true. Woodchuck Island is a little mite of a sand heap off in the bay, two mile from shore and ten from the nighest town. I'd bought it and put up a shanty for a gunnin' shack; took city gunners down there, once in a while, the fall before. That summer I'd leased it to a friend of mine, name of Darius Baker, who used it while he was lobsterin'. The gale had driven us straight in from sea, 'way past Sandy P'int and on to the island. 'Twas like hittin' a nail head in a board fence, but we'd done it. Shows what Providence can do when it sets out.

"I explained some of this to Williams as we waded through the sand to the shanty.

"'But is this Baker chap here now?' he asks.

"'I'm afraid not,' says I. 'The lobster season's about over, and he was goin' South on a yacht this week. Still, he wa'n't to go till Saturday and perhaps—'

"But the shanty was empty when we got there. I fumbled around in the tin matchbox and lit the kerosene lamp in the bracket on the wall. Then I turned to Williams.

"'Well,' says I, 'we're lucky for once in—'

"Then I stopped. When he went overboard the water had washed off his hat. Likewise it had washed off his long black hair—which was a wig—and his head was all round and shiny and bald, like a gull's egg out in a rain storm."

"I knew he wore a wig," interrupted Phinney.

"Of course you do. Everybody does now. But he wa'n't such a prophet in Israel then as he's come to be since, and folks wa'n't acquainted with his personal beauties.

"'What are you starin' at?' he asks.

"I fetched a long breath. 'Nothin',' says I. 'Nothin'.'

"But for the rest of that next ha'f hour I went around in a kind of daze, as if *my* wig had gone and part of my head with it. When a feller has been doin' a puzzle it kind of satisfies him to find out the answer. And I'd done my puzzle.

"I knew where I'd met Mr. Williams afore."

"You did?" cried Simeon.

"Um-hm. Wait a while. Well, Fatty went to bed, in one of the

hay bunks, pretty soon after that. He stripped to his under-
clothes and turned in under the patchwork comforters. He was
too beat out to want any supper, even if there'd been any in
sight. I built a fire in the rusty cook stove and dried his duds and
mine. Then I set down in the busted chair and begun to think.
After a spell I got up and took account of stock, as you might say,
of the eatables in the shanty. Darius had carted off his own grub
and what there was on hand was mine, left over from the gunnin' season—a hunk of salt pork in the pickle tub, some corn
meal in a tin pail, some musty white flour in another pail, a little
coffee, a little sugar and salt, and a can of condensed milk. I took
these things out of the locker they was in, looked 'em over, put
'em back again and sprung the padlock. Then I put the key into
my pocket and went back to my chair to do some more thinkin'.

"Next mornin' I was up early and when the banker turned out
I was fryin' a couple of slices of the pork and had some coffee
b'ilin'. Likewise there was a pan of johnnycake in the oven. The
wind had gone down consider'ble, but 'twas foggy and thick
again, which was a pleasin' state of things for yours truly.

"Williams smelt the cookin' almost afore he got his eyes open.

"'Hurry up with that breakfast,' he says to me. 'I'm hungry as a
wolf.'

"I didn't say nothin' then; just went ahead with my cookin'. He
got into his clothes and went outdoor. Pretty soon he comes
back, cussin' the weather.

"'See here, Mr. Williams,' says I, 'how about them orders to
your housekeeper? Are they straight? Won't she have you
hunted up for a week?'

"He colored pretty red, but from what he said I made out that
she wouldn't. I gathered that him and the old lady wa'n't real
chummy. She give him his grub and her services, and he give her
the Old Harry and her wages. She wouldn't hunt for him, not until she was ordered to. She'd be only too glad to have him out of
the way.

"'Humph!' says I. 'Then I cal'late we'll enjoy the scenery on this
garden spot of creation until the week's up.'

"'What do you mean?' says he. '

23

"'Well,' I says, 'the launch is out of commission, unless it should rain gasoline, and at this time of year there ain't likely to be a boat within hailin' distance of this island; 'specially if the weather holds bad.'

"He swore a blue streak, payin' partic'lar attention to the housekeeper for her general stupidness and to me because I'd got him, so he said, into this scrape. I didn't say nothin'; set the table, with one plate and one cup and sasser and knife and fork, hauled up a chair and set down to my breakfast. He hauled up a box and set down, too.

"'Pass me that corn bread,' says he. 'And why didn't you fry more pork?'

"He was reachin' out for the johnnycake, but I pulled it out of his way.

"'Wait a minute, Mr. Williams,' says I. 'While you was snoozin' last night I made out a kind of manifest of the vittles aboard this shanty. 'cordin' to my figgerin' here's scursely enough to last one husky man a week, let along two husky ones. I paid consider'ble attention to your preachin' yesterday and the text seemed to be to look out for number one. Now in this case I'm the one and I've got to look out for myself. This is my shanty, my island, and my grub. So please keep your hands off that johnnycake.'

"For a minute or so he set still and stared at me. Didn't seem to sense the situation, as you might say. Then the red biled up in his face and over his bald head like a Fundy tide.

"'Why, you dummed villain!' he shouts. 'Do you mean to starve me?'

"'You won't starve in a week,' says I, helpin' myself to pork. 'A feller named Tanner, that I read about years ago, lived for forty days on cold water and nothin' else. There's the pump right over in the corner. It's my pump, but I'll stretch a p'int and not charge for it this time.'

"'You—you—' he stammers, shakin' all over, he was so mad. 'Didn't I hire you—'

"'You hired me to take you out to the fishin' grounds and back, provided the launch was made ready by *you*. It wa'n't ready, so *that* contract's busted. And you was to furnish your extrys and I was to furnish mine. Here they be and I need 'em. It's as legiti- mate a deal as ever I see; perfect case of supply and demand— supply for one and demand for two. As I said afore, I'm the one.'

"'By thunder!' he growls, standin' up, 'I'll show you—'

"I stood up, too. He was fat and flabby and I was thin and wiry. We looked each other over.

"'I wouldn't,' says I. 'You're under the doctor's care, you know.'

"So he set down again, not havin' strength even to swear, and watched me eat my breakfast. And I ate it slow.

"'Say,' he says, finally, 'you think you're mighty smart, don't you. Well, I'm It, I guess, for this time. I suppose you'll have no objection to *sellin'* me a breakfast?'

"'No—o,' says I, 'not a mite of objection. I'll sell you a couple of slices of pork for five dollars a slice and—'

"'*Five dollars* a—!' His mouth dropped open like a main hatch.

"'Sartin,' I says. 'And two slabs of johnnycake at five dollars a slab. And a cup of coffee at five dollars a cup. And—'

"'You're crazy!' he sputters, jumpin' up.

"'Not much, I ain't. I've been settin' at your feet larnin' high fi- nance, that's all. You don't seem to be onto the real inwardness of this deal. I've got the grub market cornered, that's all. The market price of necessaries is five dollars each now; it's likely to rise at any time, but now it's five.'

"He looked at me steady for at least two more minutes. Then he got up and banged out of that shanty. A little later I see him down at the end of the sand spit starin' out into the fog; lookin' for a sail, I presume likely.

"I finished my breakfast and washed up the dishes. He come in by and by. He hadn't had no dinner nor supper, you see, and the salt air gives most folks an almighty appetite.

"'Say,' he says, 'I've been thinkin'. It's usual in the stock and provision market to deal on a margin. Suppose I pay you a one per cent margin now and—'

"'All right,' says I, cheerful. 'Then I'll give you a slip of paper sayin' that you've bought such and such slices of pork and hunks of johnnycake and I'm carryin' 'em for you on a margin. Of course there ain't no delivery of the goods now because—'

"'Humph!' he interrupts, sour. 'You seem to know more'n I thought you did. Now are you goin' to be decent and make me a fair price or ain't you?'

"'Can't sell under the latest quotations,' says I. 'That's five now; and spot cash.'

"'But hang it all!'he says, 'I haven't got money enough with me. Think I carry a national bank around in my clothes?'

"'You carry a Wellmouth Bank check book,' says I, 'because I see it in your jacket pocket last night when I was dryin' your duds. I'll take a check.'

"He started to say somethin' and then stopped. After a spell he seemed to give in all to once.

"'Very good,'he says. 'You get my breakfast ready and I'll make out the check.'

"That breakfast cost him twenty-five dollars; thirty really, because he added another five for an extry cup of coffee. I told him to make the check payable to 'Bearer,' as 'twas quicker to write than 'Solomon.'

"He had two more meals that day and at bedtime I had his checks amountin' to ninety-five dollars. The fog stayed with us all the time and nobody come to pick us up. And the next mornin's outlook was just as bad, bein' a drizzlin' rain and a high wind. The mainland beach was in sight but that's all except salt water and rain.

"He was surprisin'ly cheerful all that day, eatin' like a horse and givin' up his meal checks without a whimper. If things had been different from what they was I'd have felt like a mean sneak thief. *Bein'* as they was, I counted up the hundred and ten I'd made that day without a pinch of conscience.

"This was a Wednesday. On Thursday, the third day of our Robinson Crusoe business, the weather was still thick, though there was signs of clearin'. Fatty come to me after breakfast—which cost him thirty-five, payable, as usual, to 'Bearer'—with almost a grin on his big face.

"'Berry, 'he says, 'I owe you an apology. I thought you was a green Rube, like the rest down here, but you're as sharp as they make 'em. I ain't the man to squeal when I get let in on a bad deal, and the chap who can work me for a sucker is entitled to all he can make. But this pay-as-you-go business is too slow and troublesome. What'll you take for the rest of the grub in the locker there, spot cash? Be white, and make a fair price.'

"I'd been expectin' somethin' like this, and I was ready for him.

"'Two hundred and sixty-five dollars,' says I, prompt.

"He done a little figgerin'. 'Well, allowin' that I have to put up on this heap of desolation for the better part of four days more, that's cheap, accordin' to your former rates,' he says. 'I'll go you. But why not make it two fifty, even?'

"'Two hundred and sixty-five's my price,' says I. So he handed over another 'Bearer' check, and his board bill was paid for a week.

"Friday was a fine day, clear as a bell. Me and Williams had a real picnicky, sociable time. Livin' outdoor this way had made him forget his diseases and the doctor, and he showed signs of bein' ha'fway decent. We loafed around and talked and dug clams to help out the pork—that is, I dug 'em and Fatty superintended. We see no less'n three sailin' craft go by down the bay and tried our best to signal 'em, but they didn't pay attention—thought we was gunners or somethin', I presume likely.

"At breakfast on Saturday, Williams begun to ask questions again.

"'Sol,' says he, 'it surprised me to find that you knew what a "margin" was. You didn't get that from anything I said. Where did you get it?'

"I leaned back on my box seat.

"'Mr. Williams,' says I, 'I cal'late I'll tell you a little story, if you want to hear it. 'Tain't much of a yarn, as yarns go, but maybe it'll interest you. The start of it goes back to consider'ble many year ago, when I was poorer'n I be now, and a mighty sight younger. At that time me and another feller, a partner of mine, had a fish weir out in the bay here. The mackerel struck in and we done well, unusual well. At the end of the season, not countin' what we'd spent for livin' and expenses, we had a balance owin' us at our fish dealer's up to Boston of five hundred dollars—two fifty apiece. My partner was goin' to be married in the spring and was cal'latin' to use his share to buy furniture for the new house with. So we decided we'd take a trip up to Boston and collect the money, stick it into some savin's bank where 'twould draw interest until spring and then haul it out and use it. 'Twas about every cent we had in the world.

"'So to Boston we went, collected our money, got the address of a safe bank and started out to find it. But on the way my partner's hat blowed off and the bank address, which was on a slip of paper inside of it, got lost. So we see a sign on a buildin', along with a lot of others, that kind of suggested bankin', and so we stepped into the buildin' and went upstairs to ask the way again.

"'The place wa'n't very big, but 'twas fixed up fancy and there was a kind of blackboard along the end of the room where a boy was markin' up figgers in chalk. A nice, smilin' lookin' man met us and, when we told him what we wanted, he asked us to set down. Then, afore we knowed it almost, we'd told him the whole story—about the five hundred and all. The feller said to hold on a spell and he'd go along with us and show us where the savin's bank was himself.

"'So we waited and all the time the figgers kept goin' up on the board, under signs of "Pork" and "Wheat" and "Cotton" and such, and we'd hear how so and so's account was makin' a thousand a day, and the like of that. After a while the nice man, who it turned out was one of the bosses of the concern, told us what it meant. Seemed there was a big "rise" in the market and them that bought now was bound to get rich quick. Consequent we said we wished we could buy and get rich, too. And the smilin' chap says, "Let's go have some lunch."'

"Williams laughed. 'Ho, ho!' says he. 'Expensive lunch, was it?'

"'Most extravagant meal of vittles ever I got away with,' I says. 'Cost me and my partner two hundred and fifty apiece, that lunch did. We stayed in Boston two days, and on the afternoon of the second day we was on our way back totin' a couple of neat but expensive slips of paper signifyin' that we'd bought December and May wheat on a one per cent margin. We was a hundred ahead already, 'cordin' to the blackboard, and was figgerin' what sort of palaces we'd build when we cashed in.'

"'Ain't no use preachin' a long sermon over the remains. 'Twas a simple funeral and nobody sent flowers. Inside of a month we was cleaned out and the wheat place had gone out of business— failed, busted, you understand. Our fish dealer friend asked some questions, and found out the shebang wa'n't a real stock dealer's at all. 'Twas what they call a "bucket shop," and we'd bought nothin' but air, and paid a commission for buyin' it. And the smilin', nice man that run the swindle had been hangin' on the edge of bust for a long while and knowed 'twas comin'. Our five hundred had helped pay his way to a healthier climate, that's all.'

"'Hold on a minute,' says Fatty, lookin' more interested. 'What was the name of the firm that took you greenhorns in?'

"" 'twas the Empire Bond, Stock and Grain Exchange,' says I. 'And 'twas on Derbyshire Street.'

"He give a little jump. Then he says, slow, Hu-u-m! I—see.'

"'Yes,' says I. 'I thought you would. You had a mustache then and your name was diff'rent, but you seemed familiar just the same. When your false hair got washed off I knew you right away.'

"He took out his pocket pen and his check book and done a little figgerin'.

"'Humph!' he says, again. 'You lost five hundred and I've paid you five hundred and five. What's the five for?'

"'That's my commission on the sales,' I says.

"And just then comes a hail from outside the shanty. Out we bolted and there was Sam Davis, just steppin' ashore from his power boat. Williams's housekeeper had strained a p'int and had shaded her orders by a couple of days.

"Williams and Sam started for home right off. I followed in the Shootin' Star, havin' borrered gasoline enough for the run. I reached the dock ha'f an hour after they did, and there was Fatty waitin' for me.

"'Berry,' says he, 'I've got a word or two to say to you. I ain't kickin' at your givin' me tit for tat, or tryin' to. Turn about's fair play, if you can call the turn. But it's against my principles to allow anybody to beat me on a business deal. Do you suppose, 'he says, 'that I'd have paid your robber's prices without a word if I hadn't had somethin' up my sleeve? Why, man,' says he, 'I gave you my *checks*, not cash. And I've just telephoned to the Wellmouth Bank to stop payment on those checks. They're no earthly use to you; see? There's one or two things about high finance that you don't know even yet. Ho, ho!'

"And he rocked back and forth on his heels and laughed.

"I held up my hand. 'Wait a jiffy, Mr. Williams,' says I. 'I guess these checks are all right. When we fust landed on Woodchuck, I judged by the looks of the shanty that Baker hadn't left it for good. I cal'lated he'd be back. And sure enough he come back, in his catboat, on Thursday evenin', after you'd turned in. Them checks was payable to "Bearer," you remember, so I give 'em to him. He was to cash 'em in the fust thing Friday mornin', and I guess you'll find he's done it.'"

"Well, I swan to *man*!" interrupted the astonished and delighted Phinney. "So you had him after all! And I was scart you'd lost every cent."

Captain Sol chuckled. "Yes," he went on, "I had him, and his eyes and mouth opened together.

"'*What?*' he bellers. 'Do you mean to say that a boat stopped at that dummed island and *didn't take us off?*'

"'Oh,' says I, 'Darius didn't feel called on to take you off, not after I told him who you was. You see, Mr. Williams,' I says, 'Darius Baker was my partner in that wheat speculation I was tellin' you about.'"

The Captain drew a long breath and re-lit his cigar, which had gone out. His friend pounded the settee ecstatically.

"There!" he cried. "I knew the name 'Darius Baker' wa'n't so strange to me. When was you and him in partners, Sol?"

"Oh, 'way back in the old days, afore I went to sea at all, and afore mother died. You wouldn't remember much about it. Mother and I was livin' in Trumet then and our house here was shut up. I was only a kid, or not much more, and Williams was young, too."

"And that's the way he made his money! *Him*! Why, he's the most respected man in this neighborhood, and goes to church, and—"

"Yes. Well, if you make money *enough* you can always be respected—by some kinds of people—and find some church that'll take you in. Ain't that so, Bailey?"

Captain Stitt and his cousin, Obed Gott, the paint dealer, were standing in the doorway of the station. They now entered.

"I guess it's so," replied Stitt, pulling up a chair, "though I don't know what you was talkin' about. However, it's a pretty average safe bet that what you say is so, Sol, 'most any time. What's the special 'so,' this time?"

"We was talkin' about Mr. Williams," began Phinney.

"The Grand Panjandrum of East Harniss," broke in the depot master. "East Harniss is blessed with a great man, Bailey, and, like consider'ble many blessin's he ain't entirely unmixed."

Obed and Simeon looked puzzled, but Captain Stitt bounced in his chair like a good-natured rubber ball. "Ho! ho!" he chuckled, "you don't surprise me, Sol. We had a great man over to South Orham three years ago and he begun by blessin's and ended with—with t'other thing. Ho! ho!"

"What do you mean?" demanded Sim.

"Why, I mean Stingy Gabe. You've heard of Stingy Gabe, ain't you?"

"I guess we've all heard somethin' about him," laughed Captain Sol; "but we're willin' to hear more. He was a reformer, wa'n't he?"

"He sartin was! Ho! ho!"

"For the land sakes, tell it, Bailey," demanded Mr. Gott impatiently. "Don't sit there bouncin' and gurglin' and gettin' purple in the face. Tell it, or you'll bust tryin' to keep it in."

"Oh, it's a great, long—" began Captain Bailey protestingly.

"Go on," urged Phinney. "We've got more time than anything else, the most of us. Who was this Stingy Gabe?"

"Yes," urged Gott, "and what did he reform?"

Captain Stitt held up a compelling hand. "It's all of a piece," he interrupted. "It takes in everything, like an eatin'-house stew. And, as usual in them cases, the feller that ordered it didn't know what was comin' to him.

"Stingy Gabe was that feller. His Sunday name was Gabriel

Atkinson Holway, and his dad used to peddle fish from Orham to Denboro and back. The old man was christened Gabriel, likewise. He owed 'most everybody, and, besides, was so mean that he kept the scales and trimmin's of the fish he sold to make chowder for himself and family. All hands called him 'Stingy Gabe,' and the boy inherited the name along with the fifteen hundred dollars that the old man left when he died. He cleared out—young Gabe did—soon as the will was settled and afore the outstandin' debts was, and nobody in this latitude see hide nor hair of him till three years ago this comin' spring.

"Then, lo and behold you! he drops off the parlor car at the Orham station and cruises down to South Orham, bald-headed and bay-windowed, sufferin' from pomp and prosperity. Seems he'd been spendin' his life cornerin' copper out West and then copperin' the corners in Wall Street. The folks in his State couldn't put him in jail, so they sent him to Congress. Now, as the Honorable Atkinson Holway, he'd come back to the Cape to rest his wrist, which had writer's cramp from signin' stock certificates, and to ease his eyes with a sight of the dear old home of his boyhood.

"Bill Nickerson comes postin' down to me with the news.

"'Bailey,' says he, 'what do you think's happened? Stingy Gabe's struck the town.'

"'For how much?' I asks, anxious. 'Don't let him have it, whatever 'tis.'

"Then he went on to explain. Gabe was rich as all get out, and 'twas his intention to buy back his old man's house and fix it up for a summer home. He was delighted to find how little change there was in South Orham.

"'No matter if 'tain't but fifteen cents he'll get it, if the s'lectmen don't watch him,' I says; and the bills, too. I know *his* tribe.'

"'You don't understand,' says Nickerson. 'He ain't no thief. He's rich, I tell you, and he's cal'latin' to do the town good.'

"'Course he is,' I says. 'It runs in the family. His dad done it good, too—good as 'twas ever done, I guess.'

"But next day Gabe himself happens along, and I see right off that I'd made a mistake in my reckonin'. The Honorable Atkinson Holway wa'n't figgerin' to borrow nothin'. When a chap has been skinnin' halibut, minnows are too small for him to bother with. Gabe was full of fried clams and philanthropy.

"'By Jove! Stitt, 'he says, 'livin' here has been the dream of my life.'

"'You'll be glad to wake up, won't you?' says I. 'I wish I could.'

"'I tell you, 'he says, 'this little old village is all right! All it needs is a public-spirited resident to help it along. I propose to be the P. S. R.'

"And on that program he started right in. Fust off he bought his dad's old place, built it over into the eight-sided palace that's there now, fetched down a small army of servants skippered by an old housekeeper, and commenced to live simple but complicated. Then, havin' provided the needful charity for himself, he's ready to scatter manna for the starvin' native.

"He had a dozen schemes laid out. One was to build a free but expensive library; another was to pave the main road with brick; third was to give stained-glass windows and velvet cushions to the meetin' house, so's the congregation could sleep comfortable in a subdued light. The stained-glass idee put him in close touch with the minister, Reverend Edwin Fisher, and the minister suggested the men's club. And he took to that men's club scheme like an old maid to strong tea; the rest of the improvements went into dry dock to refit while Admiral Gabe got his men's club off the ways.

"'Twas the billiard room that made the minister hanker for a men's club. That billiard room was the worry of his life. Old man Jotham Gale run it and had run it sence the Concord fight, in a way of speakin'. You remember his sign, maybe: 'Jotham W. Gale. Billiard, Pool, and Sipio Saloon. Cigars and Tobacco. Tonics and Pipes. Minors under Ten Years of Age not Admitted.' Jotham's customers was called, by the outsiders, 'the billiard-room gang.'

"The billiard room gang wa'n't the best folks in town, I'll own right up to that. Still, they wa'n't so turrible wicked. Jotham never sold rum, and he'd never allow no rows in his place. But, just the same, his saloon was reckoned a bad influence. Young men hadn't ought to go there—most of us said that. If there was a nicer place *to* go, argues the minister, 'twould help the moral tone of the community consider'ble. 'Why not,' says he to Stingy Gabe, 'start a free club for men that'll make the billiard room look like the tail boat in a race?' And says Gabe: 'Bully! I'll do it.'"

Captain Stitt paused long enough to enjoy a chuckle all by himself. Before he had quite finished his laugh, slow and reluctant steps were heard on the back platform and Issy appeared on the threshold. He was without the package, but did not look happy.

"Well, Is," inquired the depot master, "did you give the remains to the Major?"

"Yes, sir," answered Issy.

"Did you tell him how the shockin' fatality happened? How the thing got broken?"

"Yes, sir, I told him."

"What did he say? Didn't let his angry passions rise, did he?"

"No-o; no, sir, he didn't rise nothin'. He didn't get mad neither. But you could see he felt pretty bad. Talked about 'old family glass' and 'priceless airloons' or some such. Said much as he regretted to, he should feel it no more'n justice to have somebody pay damages."

"Humph!" Captain Sol looked very grave. "Issy, I can see your finish. You'll have to pay for somethin' that's priceless, and how are you goin' to do that? 'Old family glass,' hey? Hum! And I thought I saw the label of a Boston store on that package."

Obed Gott leaned forward eagerly.

"Is that Major Hardee you're talkin' about?" he asked.

"Yes, sir. He's the only Major we've got. Cap'ns are plenty as June bugs, but Majors and Gen'rals are scarce. Why?"

"Oh, nothin'. Only—" Mr. Gott muttered the remainder of the sentence under his breath. However, the depot master heard it and his eye twinkled.

"You're glad of it!" he exclaimed. "Why, Obed! Major Cuthbertson Scott Hardee! I'm surprised. Better not let the women folks hear you say that."

"Look here!" cried Captain Stitt, rather tartly, "am I goin' to finish that yarn of mine or don't you want to hear it?"

"*Beg* your pardon, Bailey. Go on. The last thing you said was what Stingy Gabe said, and that was—"

Chapter III
"Stingy Gabe"

A ND THAT," SAID Captain Bailey, mollified by the renewed inter-est of his listeners, "was, 'Bully! I'll do it!'

"So he calls a meetin' of everybody interested, at his new house. About every respectable man in town was there, includin' me. Most of the billiard-room gang was there, likewise. Jotham, of course, wa'n't invited.

"Gabe calls the meetin' to order and the minister makes a speech tellin' about the scheme. 'Our generous and public-spir-ited citizen, Honorable Atkinson Holway,' had offered to build a suitable clubhouse, fix it up, and donate it to the club, them and their heirs forever, Amen. 'Twas to belong to the members to do what they pleased with—no strings tied to it at all. Dues would be merely nominal, a dollar a year or some such matter. Now, who favored such a club as that?

"Well, 'most everybody did. Daniel Bassett, chronic politician, justice of the peace, and head of the 'Conservatives' at town meetin', he made a talk, and in comes him and his crew. Gaius Ellis, another chronic, who is postmaster and skipper of the 'Progressives,' had been fidgetin' in his seat, and now up he bobs and says he's for it; then every 'Progressive' jines immediate. But the billiard-roomers; they didn't jine. They looked sort of sheep-ish, and set still. When Mr. Fisher begun to hint p'inted in their direction, they got up and slid outdoor. And right then I'd ought to have smelt trouble, but I didn't; had a cold in my head, I guess likely.

"Next thing was to build the new clubhouse, and Gabe went at it hammer and tongs. He had a big passel of carpenters down from the city, and inside of three months the buildin' was up, and she was a daisy, now I tell you. There was a readin' room and a meetin' room and an 'amusement room.' The amusements was crokinole and parchesi and checkers and the like of that. Also there was a gymnasium and a place where you could play the pianner and sing—till the sufferin' got acute and somebody come along and abated you.

"When I fust went inside that clubhouse I see 'twas bound to be 'Good-by, Bill,' for Jotham. His customers would shake his ratty old shanty for sartin, soon's they see them elegant new rooms. I swan, if I didn't feel sorry for the old reprobate, and, thinks I, I'll drop around and sympathize a little. Sympathy don't cost nothin', and Jotham's pretty good company.

"I found him settin' alongside the peanut roaster, watchin' a couple of patients cruelize the pool table.

"'Hello, Bailey!' says he. 'You surprise me. Ain't you 'fraid of catchin' somethin' in this ha'nt of sin? Have a chair, anyhow. And a cigar, won't you?'

"I took the chair, but I steered off from the cigar, havin' had experience. Told him I guessed I'd use my pipe. He chuckled.

"'Fur be it from me to find fault with your judgment,' he says. 'Terbacker does smoke better'n anything else, don't it.'

"We set there and puffed for five minutes or so. Then he sort of jumped.

"'What's up?' says I.

"'Oh, nothin'!' he says. 'Bije Simmons got a ball in the pocket, that's all. Don't do that too often, Bije; I got a weak heart. Well, Bailey,' he adds, turnin' to me, 'Gabe's club's fixed up pretty fine, ain't it?'

"'Why, yes,' I says; ''tis.'

"'Finest ever I see,' says he. 'I told him so when I was in there.'

"'What?' says I. 'You don't mean to say *you've* been in that clubroom?'

"'Sartin. Why not? I want to take in all the shows there is—'specially the free ones. Make a good billiard room, that clubhouse would.'

"I whistled. 'Whew!' says I. 'Didn't tell Gabe *that*, did you?'

"He nodded. 'Yup,' says he. 'I told him.'

"I whistled again. 'What answer did he make?' I asked.

"'Oh, he wa'n't enthusiastic. Seemed to cal'late I'd better shut up my head and my shop along with it, afore he knocked off one and his club knocked out t'other.'

"I pitied the old rascal; I couldn't help it.

"'Jotham,' says I, 'I ain't the wust friend you've got in South Orham, even if I don't play pool much. If I was you I'd clear out of here and start somewheres else. You can't fight all the best folks in town.'

"He didn't make no answer. Just kept on a-puffin'. I got up to go. Then he laid his hand on my sleeve.

"'Bailey,' says he, 'when Betsy Mayo was ailin', her sister's tribe was all for the Faith Cure and her husband's relations was high for patent medicine. When the Faith Curists got to workin', in would come some of the patent mediciners and give 'em the bounce. And when *they* went home for the night, the Faithers would smash all the bottles. Finally they got so busy fightin' 'mong themselves that Betsy see she was gettin' no better fast, and sent for the reg'lar doctor. *He* done the curin', and got the pay.'

"'Well,' says I, 'what of it?'

"'Nothin',' says he. 'Only I've been practisin' a considerable spell. So long. Come in again some time when it's dark and the respectable element can't see you.'

"I went away thinkin' hard. And next mornin' I hunted up Gabe, and says I:

"'Mr. Holway,' I says, 'what puzzles me is how you're goin' to elect the officers for the new club. Put up a Conservative and the Progressives resign. H'ist the Progressive ensign and the Conservatives'll mutiny. As for the billiard-roomers—providin' any jine—they've never been known to vote for anybody but themselves. I can't see no light yet—nothin' but fog.'

"He winks, sly and profound. 'That's all right,' says he. 'Fisher and I have planned that. You watch!'

"Sure enough, they had. The minister was mighty popular, so, when 'twas out that he was candidate to be fust president of the club, all hands was satisfied. Two vice presidents was named— one bein' Bassett and t'other Ellis. Secretary was a leadin' Conservative; treasurer a head Progressive. Officers and crew was happy and mutiny sunk ten fathoms. *Only* none of the billiard-room gang had jined, and they was the fish we was really tryin' for.

"'Twas next March afore one of 'em did come into the net, though we'd have on all kinds of bait—suppers and free ice cream Saturday nights, and the like of that. And meantime things had been happenin'.

"The fust thing of importance was Gabe's leavin' town. Our Cape winter weather was what fixed him. He stood the no'th-easters and Scotch drizzles till January, and then he heads for Key West and comfort. Said his heart still beat warm for his native village, but his feet was froze—or words similar. He cal'lated to be back in the spring. Then the Reverend Fisher got a call to somewheres in York State, and felt he couldn't afford not to hear it. Nobody blamed him; the salary paid a minister in South Orham is enough to make any feller buy patent ear drums. But that left our men's club without either skipper or pilot, as you might say.

"One week after the farewell sermon, Daniel Bassett drops in casual on me. He was passin' around smoking material lavish and regardless.

"'Stitt,' says he, 'you've always voted for Conservatism in our local affairs, haven't you?'

"'Well,' says I, 'I didn't vote to roof the town hall with a new mortgage, if that's what you mean.'

"'Exactly,' he says. 'Now, our men's club, while not as yet the success we hoped for, has come to be a power for good in our community. It needs for its president a conservative, thoughtful man. Bailey,' he says, 'it has come to my ears that Gaius Ellis intends to run for that office. You know him. As a taxpayer, as a sober, thoughtful citizen, my gorge rises at such insolence. I protest, sir! I protest against—'

"He was standin' up, makin' gestures with both arms, and he had his town-meetin' voice iled and runnin'. I was too busy to hanker for a stump speech, so I cut across his bows.

"'All right, all right,' says I. 'I'll vote for you, Dan.'

"He fetched a long breath. 'Thank you,' says he. 'Thank you. That makes ten. Ellis can count on no more than nine. My election is assured.'

"Seein' that there wa'n't but nineteen reg'lar voters who come to the club meetin's, if Bassett had ten of 'em it sartin did look as if he'd get in. But on election night what does Gaius Ellis do but send a wagon after old man Solomon Peavey, who'd been dry docked with rheumatiz for three months, and Sol's vote evened her up. 'Twas ten to ten, a deadlock, and the election was postponed for another week.

"This was of a Tuesday. On Wednesday I met Bije Simmons, the chap who was playin' pool at Jotham's.

"'Hey, Bailey!' says he. 'Shake hands with a brother. I'm goin' to jine the men's club.'

"'You *be*?' says I, surprised enough, for Simmons was a billiard-roomer from 'way back.

"'Yup,' he says. 'I'll be voted in at next meetin', sure. I'm studyin' up on parchesi now.'

"'Hum!' I says, thinkin'. 'How you goin to vote?'

"'Me?' says he. 'Me? Why, man, I wonder at you! Can't you see the fires of Conservatism blazin' in my eyes? I'm Conservative bred and Conservative born, and when I'm dead there'll be a Conservative gone. By, by. See you Tuesday night.'

"He went off, stoppin' everybody he met to tell 'em the news. And on Thursday Ed Barnes dropped in to pay me the seventy-five cents he'd borrowed two years ago come Fourth of July. When I'd got over the fust shock and had counted the money three times, I commenced to ask questions.

"'Somebody die and will you a million, Ed?' I wanted to know.

"'No,' says he. 'It's the reward of virtue. I'm goin' to be a better man. I'm jinin' the men's club.'

"'*No!*' says I, for Ed was as strong a billiard-roomer as Bije.

"'Sure!' he answers. 'I'm filled full of desires for crokinole and progressiveness. See you Tuesday night at the meetin'.'

"And, would you b'lieve it, at that meetin' no less'n six confirmed members of the billiard-room gang was voted into the men's club. 'Twas a hallelujah gatherin'. I couldn't help thinkin' how glad and proud Gabe and Mr. Fisher would have been to see their dreams comin' true. But Bassett and Ellis looked more worried than glad, and when the votin' took place I understood the reason. Them new members had divided even, and the ballots stood Bassett thirteen and Ellis thirteen. The tie was still on and the election was put off for another week.

"In that week, surprisin' as it may seem, two more billiard-roomers seen a light and jined with us. However, one was for Bassett and t'other for Ellis, so the deadlock wa'n't broken. Jotham had only a couple of his reg'lars left, and I swan to man if *they* didn't catch the disease inside of the follerin' fortni't and hand in their names. The 'Billiard, Pool, and Sipio Saloon,' from bein' the liveliest place in town, was now the deadest. Through the window you could see poor Jotham mopin' lonesome among his peanuts and cigars. The sayin' concernin' the hardness of the transgressor's sleddin' was workin' out for *him*, all right. But the conversions had come so sudden that I couldn't understand it, though I did have some suspicions.

"'Look here, Dan,' says I to Bassett, 'are you goin' to keep this up till judgment? There ain't but thirty votin' names in this place—except the chaps off fishin', and they won't be back till fall. Fifteen is for you and fifteen for Gaius. Most astonishin' agreement of difference ever I see. We'll never have a president, at this rate.'

"He winked. 'Won't, hey?' he says. 'Sure you've counted right? I make it thirty-one.'

"'I don't see how,' says I, puzzled. 'Nobody's left outside the club but Jotham himself, and he—'

"'That's all right,' he interrupts, winkin' again. 'You be on hand next Tuesday night. You can't always tell, maybe somethin'll happen.'

"I was on hand, all right, and somethin' did happen, two somethin's, in fact. We hadn't much more'n got in our seats afore the door opened, and in walked Gaius Ellis, arm in arm with a man; and the man was the Honorable Stingy Gabe Atkinson Holway.

"'Gentlemen,' sings out Gaius, bubblin' over with joy, 'I propose three cheers for our founder, who has returned to us after his long absence.'

"We give the cheers—that is, some of the folks did. Bassett and our gang wa'n't cheerin' much; they looked as if somebody had passed 'em a counterfeit note. You see, Gabe Holway was one of the hide-boundest Progressives afloat, and a blind man could see who'd got him back again and which way he'd vote. It sartinly looked bad for Bassett now.

"Gaius proposes that, out of compliment, as founder of the club, Mr. Holway be asked to preside. So he was asked, though the Conservatives wa'n't very enthusiastic. Gabe took the chair, preached a little sermon about bein' glad to see his native home once more, and raps for order.

"'If there's no other business afore the meetin',' says he, 'we will proceed to ballot for president.'

"But it turned out that there was other business. Dan Bassett riz to his feet and commenced one of the most feelin' addresses ever I listened to.

"Fust he congratulated all hands upon the success of Mr. Holway's philanthropic scheme for the betterment of South Orham's male citizens. Jeered at at fust by the unregenerate, it had gone on, winnin' its way into the hearts of the people, until one by one the said unregenerate had regenerated, and now the club numbered thirty souls and the Honorable Atkinson.

"'But,' says Dan, wavin' his arms, 'one man yet remains outside. One lone man! The chief sinner, you say? Yes, I admit it. But, gentlemen, a repentant sinner. Alone he sits amid the wreck of his business—a business wrecked by us, gentlemen—without a customer, without a friend. Shall it be said that the free and open-handed men's club of South Orham turned its back upon one man, merely because he *has* been what he was? Gentlemen, I have talked with Jotham Gale; he is old, he is friendless, he no longer has a means of livelihood—we have taken it from him. We have turned his followers' steps to better paths. Shall we not turn his, also? Gentlemen and friends, Jotham Gale is repentant, he feels his ostrichism'—whatever he meant by that—'he desires to become self-respecting, and he asks us to help him. He wishes to join this club. Gentlemen, I propose for membership in our association the name of Jotham W. Gale.'

"He set down and mopped his face. And the powwow that broke loose was somethin' tremendous. Of course 'twas plain enough what Dan's game was. This was the 'somethin'' that was goin' to happen.

"Ellis see the way the land lay, and he bounces up to protest. 'Twas an outrage; a scandal; ridiculous; and so forth, and so on. Poor Gabe didn't know what to do, and so he didn't do nothin'. A head Conservative seconds Jotham's nomination. 'Twas put to a vote and carried easy. Dan's speech had had its effect and a good many folks voted out of sympathy. How did I vote? *I'll* never tell you.

"And then Bassett gets up, smilin', goes to the outside door, opens it, and leads in the new member. He'd been waitin' on the steps, it turned out. Jotham looked mighty quiet and meek. I pitied the poor old codger more'n ever. Snaked in, he was, out of the wet, like a yeller dog, by the club that had kicked him out of his own shop.

"Chairman Gabe pounds for order, and suggests that the votin' can go on. But Ellis jumps up, and says he:

"'What's the sense of votin' now?' he asks sarcastic. 'Will the lost lamb we've just yanked into the fold have the face to stand up and bleat that he hasn't promised to vote Conservative? Dan Bassett, of all the contemptible tricks that ever—'

"Bassett's face was redder'n a ripe tomatter. He shakes his fist in Gaius's face and yells opinions and comments.

"'Don't you talk to me about tricks, you ward-heeler!' he hollers. 'Why did you fetch Mr. Holway back home? Why did you, hey? That was the trickiest trick that I—'

"Gabe pretty nigh broke his mallet thumpin'.

"'Gentlemen! gentlemen!' says he. 'This is most unseemly. Sit down, if you *please*. Mr. Ellis, when the purpose of this association is considered, it seems to me very wrong to find fault because the chief of our former antagonists has seen the error of his ways and become one of us. Mr. Bassett, I do not understand your intimation concernin' myself. I shall adjourn this meetin' until next Friday evenin', gentlemen. Meanwhile, let us remember that we *are* gentlemen.'

"He thumped the desk once, and parades out of the buildin', dignified as Julius Caesar. The rest of us toddled along after him, all talkin' at once. Bassett and Ellis glowered at each other and hove out hints about what would happen afore they got through. 'Twas half-past ten afore I got to bed that night, and Sarah J.—that's Mrs. Stitt—kept me awake another hour explainin' whys and wherefores.

"For the next three days nobody done anything but knock off work and talk club politics. You'd see 'em on the corners and in the post office and camped on the meetin'-house steps, arguin' and jawin'. Dan and Gaius was hurryin' around, moppin' their foreheads and lookin' worried. On Thursday there was all sorts of rumors afloat. Finally they all simmered down to one, and that one was what made me stop Stingy Gabe on the street and ask for my bearin's.

"'Mr. Holway,' says I, 'is it true that Dan and Gaius have resigned and agreed to vote for somebody else?'

"He nodded, grand and complacent.

"'Then who's the somebody?' says I. 'For the land sakes! tell me. It's as big a miracle as the prodigal son.'

"I remember now that the prodigal son ain't a miracle, but I was excited then.

"'Stitt,' says he, 'I am the "somebody," as you call it. I have decided to let my own wishes and inclinations count for nothin' in this affair, and to accept the office of president myself. It will be announced at the meetin'.'

"I whistled. 'By gum!' says I. 'You've got a great head, Mr. Holway, and I give you public credit for it. It's the only course that ain't full of breakers. Did you think of it yourself?'

"He colored up a little. 'Why, no, not exactly,' he says. 'The fact is, the credit belongs to our new member, Mr. Gale.'

"'To *Jotham*?' says I, astonished.

"'Yes. He suggested my candidacy, as a compromise. Said that he, for one, would be proud to vote for me. Mr. Gale seems thoroughly repentant, a changed man. I am counting on him for great things in the future.'

"So the fuss seemed settled, thanks to the last person on earth you'd expect would be peacemaker. But that afternoon I met Darius Tompkins, Bassett's right-hand man.

"'Bailey,' says he, 'you're a Conservative, ain't you? You're for Dan through thick and thin?'

"'Why!' says I, 'I understand Dan and Gaius are both out of it now, and it's settled on Holway. Dan's promised to vote for him.'

"'*He* has,' says Tompkins, with a wink, 'but the rest of us ain't. We pledged our votes to Dan Bassett, and we ain't the kind to go back on our word. Dan himself'll vote for Gabe; so'll Gaius and his reg'lar tribe. That'll make twelve, countin' Holway's own.'

"'Make seventeen, you mean,' says I. 'Gaius and his crowd's fifteen and Dan's sixteen and Gabe's seven—'

"He winked again, and interrupted me. 'You're countin' wrong, my boy,' says he. 'Five of Gaius's folks come from the old billiard-room gang. Just suppose somethin' happened to make that five vote, on the quiet, for Bassett. Then—'

"A customer come in then, and Tompkins had to leave; but afore he went he got me to one side and whispers:

"'Keep mum, old man, and vote straight for Dan. We'll show old Holway that we can't be led around by the nose.'

"'Tompkins,' says I, 'I know your head well enough to be sartin that it didn't work this out by itself. And why are you so sure of the billiard roomers? Who put you up to this?'

"He rapped the side of his nose. 'The smartest politician in this town,' says he, 'and the oldest—J. W. Gale, Esq.! S-s-sh-h! Don't say nothin'.'

"I didn't say nothin'. I was past talk. And that evenin' as I went past the billiard room on my way home, who should come out of it but Gaius Ellis, and *he* looked as happy as Tompkins had.

"Friday night that clubroom was filled. Every member was there, and most of 'em had fetched their wives and families along to see the fun. There was whisperin' and secrecy everywheres. Honorable Gabe took the chair and makes announcements that the shebang is open for business.

"Up gets Dave Bassett and all but sheds tears. He says that he made up his mind to vote, not for himself, but for the founder and patron of the club, the Honorable Atkinson Holway. He spread it over Gabe thick as sugar on a youngster's cake. And when he set down all hands applauded like fury. But I noticed that he hadn't spoke for nary Conservative but himself.

"Then Gaius Ellis rises and sobs similar. He's stopped votin' for himself, too. His ballot is for that grand and good man, Gabriel Atkinson Holway, Esq. More applause and hurrahs.

"And then who should get up but Jotham Gale. He talks humble, like a has-been that knows he's a back number, but he says it's his privilege to cast his fust vote in that club for Mr. Holway, South Orham's pride. Nobody was expectin' him to say anything, and the cheers pretty nigh broke the winders.

"Gabe was turrible affected by the soft soap, you could see that. He fairly sobbed as he sprinkled gratitude and acceptances. When the agony was over, he says the votin' can begin.

"I cal'lated he expected somebody'd move to make it unanimous, but they didn't. So the blank ballots was handed around, and the pencils got busy. Gabe app'ints three tellers, Bassett and Ellis, of course, for two—and the third, Jotham Gale.

"'As a compliment to our newest member,' says the chairman, smilin' philanthropic.

"When the votes was in the hat, the tellers retired to the amusement room to count up. It took a long time. I see the Conservatives and Progressives nudgin' each other and winkin' back and forth. Five minutes, then ten, then fifteen.

"And all of a sudden the biggest row bu'st loose in that amusement room that ever you heard. Rattlety—bang! Biff! Smash! The door flew open, and in rolled Bassett and Ellis, all legs and arms. Gabe and some of the rest hauled 'em apart and held 'em so, but the language them two hove at each other was enough to bring down a judgment.

"'Gentlemen! gentlemen!' hollers poor Gabe. 'What in the world? I am astounded! I—'

"'You miserable traitor!' shrieks Gaius, wavin' a fist at Dan.

"'You low-down hound!' whoops Dan back at him.

"'Silence!' bellers Gabe, poundin' thunder storms on the desk. 'Will some one explain why these maniacs are—Ah, Mr. Gale—

thank goodness, *you* at least are sane!'

"Jotham walks to the front of the platform. He was holdin' the hat and a slip of paper with the result set down on it.

"'Ladies and feller members,' says he, 'there's been some surprisin' votin' done in this election. Things ain't gone as we cal'lated they would, somehow. Mr. Holway, your election wa'n't unanimous, after all.'

"The way he said it made most everybody think Gabe was elected, anyhow, and I guess Holway thought so himself, for he smiled forgivin' and says:

"'Never mind, Mr. Gale,' says he. 'A unanimous vote was perhaps too much to expect. Go on.'

"'Yes,' says Jotham. 'Well, here's the way it stands. I'll read it to you.'

"He fixes his specs and reads like this:

"'Number of votes cast, 32.'

"'Honorable Atkinson Holway has 4.'

"'*What*?' gasps Stingy Gabe, fallin' into his chair.

"'Yes, sir,' says Jotham. 'It's a shame, I know, but it looks as nobody voted for you, Mr. Holway, but yourself and me and Dan and Gaius. To proceed:

"'Daniel Bassett has 9.'

"The Conservatives and their women folks fairly groaned out loud. Tompkins jumped to his feet, but Jotham held up a hand.

"'Just a moment, D'rius,'he says. 'I ain't through yet.'

"'Gaius Ellis has 9.'

"Then 'twas the Progressives' turn to groan. The racket and hubbub was gettin' louder all the time.

"'There's ten votes left,' goes on Jotham, 'and they bear the name of Jotham W. Gale. I can't understand it, but it does appear that I'm elected president of this 'ere club. Gentlemen, I thank you for the honor, which is as great as 'tis unexpected.'

"Gabe and the Progressives and the Conservatives set and looked at each other. And up jumps 'Bije Simmons, and calls for three cheers for the new president.

"Nobody jined in them cheers but the old billiard room gang; they did, though, every one of 'em, and Jotham smiled fatherly down on his flock.

"I s'pose there ain't no need of explainin'. Jotham had worked it all, from the very fust. When the tie business begun and Gaius and Dan was bribin' the billiard roomers to jine the club, 'twas him that fixed how they should vote so's to keep the deadlock goin'. 'Twas him that put Bassett up to proposin' him as a member. 'Twas him that suggested Gabe's comin' back to Gaius. 'Twas him that—But what's the use? 'twas him all along. He was it.

"That night everybody but the billiard-room gang sent in their resignation to that club. We refused to be bossed by such people. Gabe resigned, too. He was disgusted with East Harniss and all hands in it. He'd have took back the clubhouse, but he couldn't, as the deed of gift was free and clear. But he swore he'd never give it another cent.

"Folks thought that would end the thing, because it wouldn't be self-supportin', but Jotham had different idees. He simply moved his pool tables and truck up from the old shop, and now he's got the finest place of the kind on the Cape, rent free.

"'I told you 'twould make a good billiard saloon, didn't I, Bailey?' he says, chucklin'.

"'Jotham,' says I, 'of your kind you're a perfect wonder.'

"'Well,' says he, 'I diagnosed that men's club as sufferin' from acute politics. I've been doctorin' that disease for a long time. The trouble with you reformers,' he adds, solemn, 'is that, when it comes to political doin's, you ain't practical.'

"As for Stingy Gabe, he shut up his fine house and moved to New York. Said he was through with helpin' the moral tone.

"'When I die,' he says to me, 'if I go to the bad place I may start in reformin' that. It don't need it no more'n South Orham does, but' 'twilltwill be enough sight easier job.'

"And," concluded Captain Stitt, as soon as he could be heard above the "Haw! haws!" caused by the Honorable Holway's final summing-up of his native town, "I ain't so sure that he was greatly mistook. What do you think, Sol?"

The depot master shook his head. "Don't know, Bailey," he answered, dryly. "I'll have to visit both places 'fore I give an opinion. I *have* been to South Orham, but the neighborhood that your friend Gabe compared it to I ain't seen—yet. I put on that 'yet,'" he added, with a wink, "'cause I knew Sim Phinney would if I didn't."

Captain Bailey rose and covered a yawn with a plump hand.

"I believe I'll go over to Obed's and turn in," he said. "I'm sleepy as a minister's horse tonight. You don't mind, do you, Obed?"

"No-o," replied Mr. Gott, slowly. "No, I don't, 'special. I kind of thought I'd run into the club a few minutes and see some of the other fellers. But it ain't important—not very."

The "club" was one of the rooms over Mr. Higgins's store and post office. It had been recently fitted up with chairs and tables from its members' garrets and, when the depot and store were closed, was a favorite gathering place of those reckless ones who cared to "set up late"—that is, until eleven o'clock. Most of the men in town belonged, but many, Captain Berry among them, visited the room but seldom.

"Checkers," said the depot master, referring to the "club's" favorite game, "is too deliberately excitin' for me. To watch Beriah Higgins and Ezra Weeks fightin' out a game of checkers is like gettin' your feet froze in January and waitin' for spring to come and thaw 'em out. It's a numbin' kind of dissipation."

But Obed Gott was a regular attendant at the "club," and to-night he had a particular reason for wishing to be there. His cousin noticed his hesitation and made haste to relieve his mind.

"That's all right, Obed," he said, "go to the club, by all means. I ain't such a stranger at your house that I can't find my way to bed without help. Good-night, Sim. Good-night, Issy. Cheer up; maybe the Major's glassware *is* priceless. So long, Cap'n Sol. See you again some time tomorrer."

He and Mr. Gott departed. The depot master rose from his chair. "Issy," he commanded, "shut up shop."

Issy obeyed, closing the windows and locking the front door. Captain Sol himself locked the ticket case and put the cash till into the small safe.

"That'll do, Is," said the Captain. "Good-night. Don't worry too much over the Major's glass. I'll talk with him, myself. You dream about pleasanter things—your girl, if you've got one."

That was a chance shot, but it struck Issy in the heart. Even during his melancholy progress to and from Major Hardee's, the vision of Gertie Higgins had danced before his greenish-blue eyes. His freckles were engulfed in a surge of blushes as, with a stammered "Night, Cap'n Berry," he hurried out into the moon-light.

The depot master blew out the lamps. "Come on, Sim," he said, briefly. "Goin' to walk up with me, or was *you* goin' to the club?"

"Cal'late I'll trot along with you, if you don't mind. I'd just as soon get home early and wrastle with the figures on that Williams movin' job."

They left the depot, locked and dark, passed the "general store," where Mr. Higgins was putting out his lights prior to ad-journment to the "club" overhead, walked up Main Street to Cross Street, turned and began climbing the hill. Simeon spoke several times but his friend did not answer. A sudden change had come over him. The good spirits with which he told of his adventure with Williams and which had remained during Phin-ney's stay at the depot, were gone, apparently. His face, in the moonlight, was grave and he strode on, his hands in his pockets.

At the crest of the hill he stopped.

"Good-night, Sim," he said, shortly, and, turning, walked off.

The building mover gazed after him in surprise. The nearest way to the Berry home was straight down Cross Street, on the other side of the hill, to the Shore Road, and thence along that road for an eighth of a mile. The Captain's usual course was just that. But to-night he had taken the long route, the Hill Boule-vard, which made a wide curve before it descended to the road below.

Sim, who had had a shrewd suspicion concerning his friend's silence and evident mental disturbance, stood still, looking and wondering. Olive Edwards, Captain Berry's old sweetheart, lived on the Boulevard. She was in trouble and the Captain knew it. He had asked, that very evening, what she was going to do when forced to move. Phinney could not tell him. Had he gone to find out for himself? Was the mountain at last coming to Mohammed?

For some minutes Simeon remained where he was, thinking and surmising. Then he, too, turned and walked cautiously up the Boulevard. He passed the Williams mansion, its library windows ablaze. He passed the twenty-five room "cottage" of the gentleman from Chicago. Then he halted. Opposite him was the little Edwards dwelling and shop. The curtains were up and there was a lamp burning on the small counter. Beside the lamp, in a rocking chair, sat Olive Edwards, the widow, sewing. As he gazed she dropped the sewing in her lap, and raised her head.

Phinney saw how worn and sad she looked. And yet, how young, considering her forty years and all she had endured and must endure. She put her hand over her eyes, then removed it wearily. A lump came in Simeon's throat. If he might only help her; if *some one* might help her in her lonely misery.

And then, from where he stood in the shadow of the Chicago gentleman's hedge, he saw a figure step from the shadows fifty feet farther on. It was Captain Solomon Berry. He walked to the middle of the road and halted, looking in at Olive. Phinney's heart gave a jump. Was the Captain going into that house, going to *her*, after all these years? *was* the mountain—

But no. For a full minute the depot master stood, looking in at the woman by the lamp. Then he jammed his hands into his pockets, wheeled, and tramped rapidly off toward his home. Simeon Phinney went home, also, but it was with a heavy heart that he sat down to figure the cost of moving the Williams "pure Colonial" to its destined location.

Chapter IV
The Major

THE DEPOT MASTER and his friend, Mr. Phinney, were not the only ones whose souls were troubled that evening. Obed Gott, as he stood at the foot of the stairs leading to the meeting place of the "club," was vexed and worried. His cousin, Captain Stitt, had gone into the house and up to his room, and Obed, after seeing him safely on his way, had returned to the club. But, instead of entering immediately, he stood in the Higgins doorway, thinking, and frowning as he thought. And the subject of his thought was the idol of feminine East Harniss, the "old-school gentleman," Major Cuthbertson Scott Hardee.

The Major first came to East Harniss one balmy morning in March—came, and created an immediate sensation. "Redny" Blount, who drives the "depot wagon," was wrestling with a sample trunk belonging to the traveling representative of Messrs. Braid & Gimp, of Boston, when he heard a voice—and such a voice—saying:

"Pardon me, my dear sir, but may I trouble you for one moment?"

Now "Redny" was not used to being addressed as "my dear sir." He turned wonderingly, and saw the Major, in all his glory, standing beside him. "Redny's" gaze took in the tall, slim figure in the frock coat tightly buttoned; took in the white hair, worn just long enough to touch the collar of the frock coat; the long, drooping white mustache and imperial; the old-fashioned stock and open collar; the black and white checked trousers; the gaiters; and, last of all, the flat brimmed, carefully brushed, old-fashioned silk hat. Mr. Blount gasped.

"Huh?" he said.

"Pardon me, my dear sir," repeated the Major, blandly,

smoothly, and with an air of—well, not condescension, but gracious familiarity. "Will you be so extremely kind as to inform me concerning the most direct route to the hotel or boarding house?"

The word "hotel" was the only part of this speech that struck home to "Redny's" awed mind.

"Hotel?" he repeated, slowly. "Why, yes, sir. I'm goin' right that way. If you'll git right into my barge I'll fetch you there in ten minutes."

There was enough in this reply, and the manner in which it was delivered, to have furnished the station idlers, in the ordinary course of events, with matter for gossip and discussion for a week. Mr. Blount had not addressed a person as "sir" since he went to school. But no one thought of this; all were too much overcome by the splendor of the Major's presence.

"Thank you," replied the Major. "Thank you. I am obliged to you, sir. Augustus, you may place the baggage in this gentleman's conveyance."

Augustus was an elderly negro, very black as to face and a trifle shabby as to clothes, but with a shadow of his master's gentility, like a reflected luster, pervading his person. He bowed low, departed, and returned dragging a large, old style trunk, and carrying a plump valise.

"Augustus," said the Major, "you may sit upon the seat with the driver. That is," he added, courteously, "if Mr.—Mr.—"

"Blount," prompted the gratified "Redny."

"If Mr. Blount will be good enough to permit you to do so."

"Why, sartin. Jump right up. Giddap, you!"

There was but one passenger, besides the Major and Augustus, in the "depot wagon" that morning. This passenger was Mrs. Polena Ginn, who had been to Brockton on a visit. To Mrs. Polena the Major, raising his hat in a manner that no native of East Harniss could acquire by a lifetime of teaching, observed that it was a beautiful morning. The flustered widow replied that it "was so." This was the beginning of a conversation that lasted until the "Central House" was reached, a conversation that left Polena impressed with the idea that her new acquaintance was as near the pink of perfection as mortal could be.

"It wa'n't his clothes, nuther," she told her brother, Obed Gott, as they sat at the dinner table. "I don't know what 'twas, but you could jest see that he was a gentleman all over. I wouldn't wonder if he was one of them New York millionaires, like Mr. Williams—but *so* different. 'Redny' Blount says he see his name onto the hotel register and 'twas 'Cuthbertson Scott Hardee.' Ain't that a tony name for you? And his darky man called him 'Major.' I never see sech manners on a livin' soul! Obed, I *do* wish you'd stop eatin' pie with a knife."

Under these pleasing circumstances did Major Cuthbertson Scott Hardee make his first appearance in East Harniss, and the reputation spread abroad by Mr. Blount and Mrs. Ginn was confirmed as other prominent citizens met him, and fell under the spell. In two short weeks he was the most popular and respected man in the village. The Methodist minister said, at the Thursday evening sociable, that "Major Hardee is a true type of the old-school gentleman," whereupon Beriah Higgins, who was running for selectman, and therefore felt obliged to be interested in all educational matters, asked whereabouts that school was located, and who was teaching it now.

It was a treat to see the Major stroll down Main Street to the post office every pleasant spring morning. Coat buttoned tight, silk hat the veriest trifle on one side, one glove on and its mate carried with the cane in the other hand, and the buttonhole bouquet—always the bouquet—as fresh and bright and jaunty as its wearer himself.

It seemed that every housekeeper whose dwelling happened to be situated along that portion of the main road had business in the front yard at the time of the Major's passing. There were steps to be swept, or rugs to be shaken, or doorknobs to be polished just at that particular time. Dialogues like the following interrupted the triumphal progress at three minute intervals:

"Good-morning, Mrs. Sogberry. *Good*-morning. A delightful morning. Busy as the proverbial bee once more, I see. I can never cease to admire the industry and model neatness of the Massachusetts housekeeper. And how is your charming daughter this morning? Better, I trust?"

"Well, now, Major Hardee, I don't know. Abbie ain't so well's I wish she was. She set up a spell yesterday, but the doctor says she ain't gittin' along the way she'd ought to. I says to him, s'I, 'Abbie ain't never what you'd call a reel hearty eater, but, my land! when she don't eat *nothn'*,' I says—"

And so on and so on, with the Major always willing to listen, always sympathetic, and always so charmingly courteous.

The Central House, East Harniss's sole hotel, and a very small one at that, closed its doors on April 10th. Mr. Godfrey, its proprietor, had come to the country for his health. He had been inveigled, by an advertisement in a Boston paper, into buying the Central House at East Harniss. It would afford him, so he reasoned, light employment and a living. The employment was light enough, but the living was lighter. He kept the Central House for a year. Then he gave it up as a bad job and returned to the city. "I might keep my health if I stayed," he admitted, in explaining his position to Captain Berry, "but if I want to keep to what little money I have left, I'd better go. Might as well die of disease as starvation."

Everyone expected that the "gentleman of the old school" would go also, but one evening Abner Payne, whose business is "real estate, fire and life insurance, justice of the peace, and houses to let and for sale," rushed into the post office to announce that the Major had leased the "Gorham place," furnished, and intended to make East Harniss his home.

"He likes the village so well he's goin' to stay here always," explained Abner. "Says he's been all 'round the world, but he never see a place he liked so well's he does East Harniss. How's that for high, hey? And you callin' it a one-horse town, Obed Gott!"

The Major moved into the "Gorham place" the next morning. It—the "place"—was an old-fashioned house on the hill, though not on Mr. Williams' "Boulevard." It had been one of the finest mansions in town once on a time, but had deteriorated rapidly since old Captain Elijah Gorham died. Augustus carried the Major's baggage from the hotel to the house. This was done very early and none of the natives saw the transfer. There was some speculation as to how the darky managed to carry the big trunk single-handed; one of two persons asked Augustus this very question, but they received no satisfactory answer. Augustus was habitually close-mouthed. Mr. Godfrey left town that same morning on the first train.

The Major christened his new home "Silver-leaf Hall," because of two great "silver-leaf" trees that stood by the front door. He had some repairing, paper hanging and painting done, ordered a big stock of groceries from the local dealer, and showed by his every action that his stay in East Harniss was to be a lengthy one. He hired a pew in the Methodist church, and joined the "club." Augustus did the marketing for "Silver-leaf Hall," and had evidently been promoted to the position of housekeeper.

The Major moved in April. It was now the third week in June and his popularity was, if possible, more pronounced than ever. On this particular, the evening of Captain Bailey Stitt's unexpected arrival, Obed had been sitting by the tea table in his dining room after supper, going over the account books of his paint, paper, and oil store. His sister, Mrs. Polena Ginn, was washing dishes in the kitchen.

"Wat's that letter you're readin', Obed?" she called from her post by the sink.

"Nothin'," said her brother, gruffly, crumpling up the sheet of note paper and jamming it into his pocket.

"My sakes! you're shorter'n pie crust to-night. What's the matter? Anything gone wrong at the store?"

"No."

Silence again, only broken by the clatter of dishes. Then Polena said:

"Obed, when are you goin' to take me up to the clubroom so's I can see that picture of Major Hardee that he presented the club with? Everybody says it's just lovely. Sarah T. says it's perfectly elegant, only not quite so handsome as the Major reelly is. She says it don't flatter him none."

"Humph! Anybody'd think Hardee was some kind of a wonder, the way you women folks go on 'bout him. How do you know but what he might be a reg'lar fraud? Looks ain't everything."

"Well, I never! Obed Gott, I should think you'd be 'shamed of yourself, talkin' that way. I shan't speak another word to you to-night. I never see you act so unlikely. An old fraud! The idea! That grand, noble man!"

Obed tried to make some sort of half-hearted apology, but his sister wouldn't listen to it. Polena's dignity was touched. She was a woman of consequence in East Harniss, was Polena. Her husband had, at his death, left her ten thousand dollars in her own right, and she owned bonds and had money in the Well-mouth Bank. Nobody, not even her brother, was allowed to talk to her in that fashion.

To tell the truth, Obed was sorry he had offended his sister. He had been throwing out hints of late as to the necessity of build-ing an addition to the paint and oil store, and had cast a longing look upon a portion of Polena's ten thousand. The lady had not promised to extend the financial aid, but she had gone so far as to say she would think about it. So Obed regretted his insinua-tions against the Major's integrity.

After a while he threw the account books upon the top of the chest of drawers, put on his hat and coat and announced that he was going over to the depot for a "spell." Polena did not deign to reply, so, after repeating the observation, he went out and slammed the door.

Now, two hours later, as he stood in the doorway of the club, he was debating what he should do in a certain matter. That matter concerned Major Hardee and was, therefore, an ex-tremely delicate one. At length Mr. Gott climbed the narrow stairs and entered the clubroom. It was blue with tobacco smoke.

The six or eight members present hailed him absently and went on with their games of checkers or "seven-up." He at-tempted a game of checkers and lost, which did not tend to make his temper any sweeter. His ill nature was so apparent that Beriah Higgins, who suffered from dyspepsia and consequent ill temper, finally commented upon it.

"What's the matter with you, Obed?" he asked tartly. "Too

much of P'lena's mince pie?"

"No," grunted Mr. Gott shortly.

"What is it, then? Ain't paint sellin' well?"

"Sellin' well 'nough. I could sell a hundred ton of paint to-morrow, more'n likely, but when it come to gittin' the money for it, that would be another story. If folks would pay their bills there wouldn't be no trouble."

"Who's stuck you now?"

"I don't s'pose anybody has, but it's just as bad when they don't pay up. I've got to have money to keep a-goin' with. It don't make no diff'rence if it's as good a customer as Major Hardee; he ought to remember that we ain't all rich like him and—"

A general movement among all the club members interrupted him. The checker players left their boards and came over; the "seven-up" devotees dropped their cards and joined the circle.

"What was that you said?" asked Higgins, uneasily. "The Major owin' you money, was it?"

"Oh, course I know he's all right and a fine man and all that," protested Obed, feeling himself put on the defensive. "But that ain't it. What's a feller goin' to do when he needs the money and gets a letter like that?"

He drew the crumpled sheet of note paper from his pocket, and threw it on the table. Higgins picked it up and read it aloud, as follows:

SILVERLEAF HALL, JUNE 20TH.

MY DEAR MR GOTT: I am in receipt of your courteous communication of recent date. I make it an unvarying rule to keep little ready money here in East Harniss, preferring rather to let it remain at interest in the financial institutions of the cities. Another rule of mine, peculiar, I dare say—even eccentric, if you like—is never to pay by check. I am expecting remittances from my attorneys, however, and will then bear you in mind. Again thanking you for your courtesy, and begging you to extend to your sister my kindest regards, I remain, my dear sir,
Yours very respectfully,
CUTHBERTSON SCOTT HARDEE.
P. S.—I shall be delighted to have the pleasure of entertaining your

*sister and yourself at dinner at the hall on any date agreeable to
you. Kindly let me hear from you regarding this at your earliest
convenience. I must insist upon this privilege, so do not disappoint
me, I beg.*

The reception accorded this most gentlemanly epistle was peculiar. Mr. Higgins laid it upon the table and put his hand into
his own pocket. So did Ezra Weeks, the butcher; Caleb Small, the
dry goods dealer; "Hen" Leadbetter, the livery stable keeper;
"Bash" Taylor, the milkman, and three or four others. And, wonder of wonders, each produced a sheet of note paper exactly like
Obed's.

They spread them out on the table. The dates were, of course,
different, and they differed in other minor particulars, but in the
main they were exactly alike. And each one of them ended with
an invitation to dinner.

The members of the club looked at each other in amazement.
Higgins was the first to speak.

"Godfrey mighty!" he exclaimed. "Say, this is funny, ain't it? It's
more'n funny; it's queer! By jimmy, it's more'n that—it's serious! Look here, fellers; is there anybody in this crowd that the
Major's paid for anything any time?"

They waited. No one spoke. Then, with one impulse, every
face swung about and looked up to where, upon the wall, hung
the life-size photograph of the Major, dignified, gracious, and
gilt-framed. It had been presented to the club two months before by Cuthbertson Scott Hardee, himself.

"Ike—Ike Peters," said Higgins. "Say, Ike—has he ever paid you
for havin' that took?"

Mr. Peters, who was the town photographer, reddened, hesitated, and then stammered, "Why, no, he ain't, yet."

"Humph!" grunted Higgins. No one else said anything. One or
two took out pocket memorandum books and went over some
figures entered therein. Judging by their faces the results of
these calculations were not pleasing. Obed was the first to break
the painful silence:

"Well!" he exclaimed, sarcastically; "ain't nobody got nothin'
to say? If they ain't, I have. Or, at any rate, I've got somethin' to

do." And he rose and started to put on his coat.

"Hi! hold on a minute, Obed, you loon!" cried Higgins. "Where are you goin'?"

"I'm goin' to put my bill in Squire Baker's hands for c'lection, and I'm goin' to do it tonight, too."

He was on his way to the door, but two or three ran to stop him.

"Don't be a fool, Obed," said Higgins. "Don't go off ha'f cocked. Maybe we're gittin' scared about nothin'. We don't know but we'll get every cent that's owed us."

"Don't *know*! Well, I ain't goin' to wait to find out. What makes me b'ilin' is to think how we've set still and let a man that we never saw afore last March, and don't know one blessed thing about, run up bills and *run* 'em up. How we come to be such everlastin' fools I don't see! What did we let him have the stuff for? Why didn't we make him pay? I—"

"Now see here, Obed Gott," broke in Weeks, the butcher, "you know why just as well as we do. Why, blast it!" he added earnestly, "if he was to come into my shop to-morrow and tip that old high hat of his, and smile and say 'twas a fine mornin and 'How's the good lady to-day?' and all that, he'd get ha'f the meat there was in the place, and I wouldn't say 'Boo'! I jest couldn't, that's all."

This frank statement was received with approving nods and a chorus of muttered "That's so's."

"It looks to me this way," declared Higgins. "If the Major's all right, he's a mighty good customer for all of us. If he ain't all right, we've got to find it out, but we're in too deep to run resks of gettin' him mad 'fore we know for sure. Let's think it over for a week. Inside of that time some of us'll hint to him, polite but firm, you understand, that we've got to have something on account. A week from to-night we'll meet in the back room of my store, talk it over and decide what to do. What do you say?"

Everybody but Obed agreed. He declared that he had lost money enough and wasn't going to be a fool any longer. The others argued with him patiently for a while and then Leadbetter, the livery stable keeper, said sharply:

"See here, Obe! You ain't the only one in this. How much does the Major owe you?"

"Pretty nigh twenty dollars."

"Humph! You're lucky. He owes me over thirty, and I guess Higgins is worse off than any of us. Ain't that so, Beriah?"

"About seventy, even money," answered the grocer, shortly. "No use, Obed, we've got to hang together. Wait a week and then see. And, fellers," he added, "don't tell a soul about this business, 'specially the women folks. There ain't a woman nor girl in this town that don't think Major Hardee's an A1, gold-plated saint, and twouldn't be safe to break the spell on a guess."

Obed reached home even more disgruntled than when he left it. He sat up until after twelve, thinking and smoking, and when he went to bed he had a brilliant idea. The next morning he wrote a letter and posted it.

Chapter V
A Baby and a Robbery

THE MORNING TRAIN for Boston, at that season of the year, reached East Harniss at five minutes to six, an "ungodly hour," according to the irascible Mr. Ogden Williams, who, in company with some of his wealthy friends, the summer residents, was petitioning the railroad company for a change in the time-table. When Captain Sol Berry, the depot master, walked briskly down Main Street the morning following Mr. Gott's eventful evening at the club, the hands of the clock on the Methodist church tower indicated that the time was twenty minutes to six.

Issy McKay was already at the depot, the doors of which were open. Captain Sol entered the waiting room and unlocked the ticket rack and the little safe. Issy, languidly toying with the broom on the front platform, paused in his pretense of sweeping and awaited permission to go home for breakfast. It came, in characteristic fashion.

"How's the salt air affectin' your appetite, Is?" asked the Captain, casually.

Issy, who, being intensely serious by nature, was uneasy when he suspected the presence of a joke, confusedly stammered that he cal'lated his appetite was all right.

"Payin' for the Major's glass ain't kept you awake worryin', has it?"

"No-o, sir. I—"

"P'r'aps you thought he was the one to 'do the worryin', hey?"

"I—I don't know."

"Well, what's your folks goin' to have to eat this mornin'?"

Issy admitted his belief that fried clams were to be the breakfast.

"So? Clams? Is, did you ever read the soap advertisement about not bein' a clam?"

"I—I don't know's I ever did. No, sir."

"All right; I only called your attention to it as a warnin', that's all. When anybody eats as many clams as you do there's a fair chance of his turnin' into one. Now clear out, and don't stay so long at breakfast that you can't get back in time for dinner. Trot!"

Issy trotted. The depot master seated himself by the door of the ticket office and fell into a reverie. It was interrupted by the entrance of Hiram Baker. Captain Hiram was an ex-fishing skipper, fifty-five years of age, who, with his wife, Sophronia, and their infant son, Hiram Joash Baker, lived in a small, old-fashioned house at the other end of the village, near the shore. Captain Hiram, having retired from the sea, got his living, such as it was, from his string of fish traps, or "weirs."

The depot master hailed the new arrival heartily.

"Hello, there, Hiram!" he cried, rising from his chair. "Glad to see you once in a while. Ain't goin' to leave us, are you? Not goin' abroad for your health, or anything of that kind, hey?"

Captain Baker laughed.

"No," he answered. "No further abroad than Hyannis. And I'll be back from there tonight, if the Lord's willin' and the cars don't get off the track. Give me a round trip ticket, will you, Sol?"

The depot master retired to the office, returning with the desired ticket. Captain Hiram counted out the price from a confused mass of coppers and silver, emptied into his hand from a blackened leather purse, tied with a string.

"How's Sophrony?" asked the depot master. "Pretty smart, I hope."

"Yup, she's smart. Has to be to keep up with the rest of the family—'specially the youngest."

He chuckled. His friend laughed in sympathy.

"The youngest is the most important of all, I s'pose," he observed. "How *is* the junior partner of H. Baker and Son?"

"He ain't a silent partner, I'll swear to that. Honest, Sol, I b'lieve my 'Dusenberry' is the cutest young one outside of a show. I said so only yesterday to Mr. Hilton, the minister. I did, and I meant it."

"Well, we're all gettin' ready to celebrate his birthday. Ho, ho!"

This was a standard joke and was so recognized and honored. A baby born on the Fourth of July is sure of a national celebration of his birthday. And to Captain Baker and his wife, no celebration, however widespread, could do justice to the importance of the occasion. When, to answer the heart longings of the child-loving couple married many years, the baby came, he was accepted as a special dispensation of Providence and valued accordingly.

"He's got a real nice voice, Hiram," said Sophronia, gazing proudly at the prodigy, who, clutched gingerly in his father's big hands, was screaming his little red face black. "I shouldn't wonder if he grew up to sing in the choir."

"That's the kind of voice to make a fo'mast hand step lively!" declared Hiram. "You'll see this boy on the quarter deck of a clipper one of these days."

Naming him was a portentous proceeding and one not to be lightly gone about. Sophronia, who was a Methodist by descent and early confirmation, was of the opinion that the child should have a Bible name.

The Captain respected his wife's wishes, but put in an ardent plea for his own name, Hiram.

"There's been a Hiram Baker in our family ever since Noah h'isted the main-r'yal on the ark," he declared. "I'd kinder like to keep the procession a-goin'."

They compromised by agreeing to make the baby's Christian name Hiram and to add a middle name selected at random from the Scriptures. The big, rickety family Bible was taken from the center table and opened with shaking fingers by Mrs. Baker. She read aloud the first sentence that met her eye: "The son of Joash."

"Joash!" sneered her husband. "You ain't goin' to cruelize him with that name, be you?"

"Hiram Baker, do you dare to fly in the face of Scriptur'?"

"All right! Have it your own way. Go to sleep now, Hiram Joash, while I sing 'Storm along, John,' to you."

Little Hiram Joash punched the minister's face with his fat fist when he was christened, to the great scandal of his mother and the ill-concealed delight of his father.

"Can't blame the child none," declared the Captain. "I'd punch anybody that christened a middle name like that onto me."

But, in spite of his name, the baby grew and prospered. He fell out of his crib, of course, the moment that he was able, and barked his shins over the big shells by the what-not in the parlor the first time that he essayed to creep. He teethed with more or less tribulation, and once upset the household by an attack of the croup.

They gave up calling him by his first name, because of the Captain's invariably answering when the baby was wanted and not answering when he himself was wanted. Sophronia would have liked to call him Joash, but her husband wouldn't hear of it. At length the father took to calling him "Dusenberry," and this nickname was adopted under protest.

Captain Hiram sang the baby to sleep every night. There were three songs in the Captain's repertoire. The first was a chanty with a chorus of

> John, storm along, storm along, John,
> Ain't I glad my day's work's done.
> The second was the "Bowline Song."

> Haul on the bowline, the 'Phrony is a-rollin',
> Haul on the bowline! the bowline *haul!*

At the "haul!" the Captain's foot would come down with a thump. Almost the first word little Hiram Joash learned was "haul!" He used to shout it and kick his father vigorously in the vest.

These were fair-weather songs. Captain Hiram sang them when everything was going smoothly. The "Bowline Song" indicated that he was feeling particularly jubilant. He had another that he sang when he was worried. It was a lugubrious ditty, with a refrain beginning:

Oh, sailor boy, sailor boy, 'neath the wild billow,
Thy grave is yawnin' and waitin' for thbald headee.

He sang this during the worst of the teething period, and, later, when the junior partner wrestled with the whooping cough. You could always tell the state of the baby's health by the Captain's choice of songs.

Meanwhile Dusenberry grew and prospered. He learned to walk and to talk, after his own peculiar fashion, and, at the mature age of two years and six months, formally shipped as first mate aboard his father's dory. His duties in this responsible position were to sit in the stern, securely fastened by a strap, while the Captain and his two assistants rowed out over the bar to haul the nets of the deep water fish weir.

The first mate gave the orders, "All hands on deck! 'Tand by to det ship under way!" There was no "sogerin'" aboard the Hiram Junior—that was the dory's name—while the first officer had command.

Captain Hiram, always ready to talk of the wonderful baby, told the depot master of the youngster's latest achievement, which was to get the cover off the butter firkin in the pantry and cover himself with butter from head to heel.

"Ho, ho, ho!" he roared, delightedly, "when Sophrony caught him at it, what do you s'pose he said? Said he was playin' he was a slice of bread and was spreadin' himself. Haw! haw!"

Captain Sol laughed in sympathy.

"But he didn't mean no harm by it," explained the proud father. "He's got the tenderest little heart in the world. When he found his ma felt bad he bust out cryin' and said he'd scrape it all off again and when it come prayer time he'd tell God who did it, so He'd know 'Twa'n't mother that wasted the nice butter. What do you think of that?"

"No use talkin', Hiram," said the depot master, "that's the kind of boy to have."

"You bet you! Hello! here's the train. On time, for a wonder. See you later, Sol. You take my advice, get married and have a boy of your own. Nothin' like one for solid comfort."

The train was coming and they went out to meet it. The only

passenger to alight was Mr. Barzilla Wingate, whose arrival had been foretold by Bailey Stitt the previous evening. Barzilla was part owner of a good-sized summer hotel at Wellmouth Neck. He and the depot master were old friends.

After the train had gone Wingate and Captain Sol entered the station together. The Captain had insisted that his friend come home with him to breakfast, instead of going to the hotel. After some persuasion Barzilla agreed. So they sat down to await Issy's arrival. The depot master could not leave the station until the "assistant" arrived.

"Well, Barzilla," asked Captain Sol, "what's the newest craze over to the hotel?"

"The newest," said Wingate, with a grin, "is automobiles."

"Automobiles? Why, I thought 'twas baseball."

"Baseball was last summer. We had a championship team then. Yes, sir, we won out, though for a spell it looked pretty dubious. But baseball's an old story. We've had football since, and now—"

"Wait a minute! Football? Why, now I do remember. You had a football team there and—and wa'n't there somethin' queer, some sort of a—a robbery, or stealin', or swindlin' connected with it? Seems's if I'd heard somethin' like that."

Mr. Wingate looked his friend over, winked, and asked a question.

"Sol," he said, "you ain't forgot how to keep a secret?"

The depot master smiled. "I guess not," he said.

"Well, then, I'm goin' to trust you with one. I'm goin' to tell you the whole business about that robbin'. It's all mixed up with football and millionaires and things—and it's a dead secret, the truth of it. So when I tell you it mustn't go no further.

"You see," he went on, "it was late into August when Peter T. was took down with the inspiration. Not that there was anything 'specially new in his bein' took. He was subject to them seizures, Peter was, and every time they broke out in a fresh place. The Old Home House itself was one of his inspirations, so was the hirin' of college waiters, the openin' of the two 'Annex' cottages, the South Shore Weather Bureau, and a whole lot more. Sometimes, as in the weather-bureau foolishness, the disease left him and t'other two patients—meanin' me and Cap'n Jonadab—pretty weak in the courage, and wasted in the pocketbook; but gen'rally they turned out good, and our systems and bank accounts was more healthy than normal. One of Peter T.'s inspirations was consider'ble like typhoid fever—if you did get over it, you felt better for havin' had it.

"This time the attack was in the shape of a 'supplementary season.' 'twas Peter's idea that shuttin' up the Old Home the fust week in September was altogether too soon.

"'What's the use of quittin',' says he, 'while there's bait left and the fish are bitin'? Why not keep her goin' through September and October? Two or three ads—*my* ads—in the papers, hintin' that the ducks and wild geese are beginnin' to keep the boarders awake by roostin' in the back yard and hollerin' at night—two or three of them, and we'll have gunners here by the regiment. Other summer hotels do it, the Wapatomac House and the rest, so why not us? It hurts my conscience to see good money gettin' past the door 'count of the "Not at Home" sign hung on the knob. What d'you say, partners?' says he.

"Well, we had consider'ble to say, partic'lar Cap'n Jonadab. 'Twas too risky and too expensive. Gunnin' was all right except for one thing—that is, that there wa'n't none wuth mentionin'.

"'Ducks are scurser round here than Democrats in a Vermont town-meetin',' growled the Cap'n. 'And as for geese! How long has it been since you see a goose, Barzilla?'

"'Land knows!' says I. 'I can remember as fur back as the fust time Washy Sparrow left off workin', but I can't—'

"Brown told us to shut up. Did we cal'late he didn't know what he was talkin' about?

"'I can see two geese right now,' he snaps; 'but they're so old and leather-headed you couldn't shoot an idea into their brains with a cannon. Gunnin' ain't the whole thing. My makin' a noise like a duck is only to get the would-be Teddy Roosevelts headed for this neck of the woods. After they get here, it's up to us to keep 'em. And I can think of as many ways to do that as the Cap'n can of savin' a quarter. Our baseball team's been a success, ain't it? Sure thing! Then why not a football team? Parker says he'll get it together, and coach and cap'n it, too. And Robinson and his daughter have agreed to stay till October fifteenth. So there's a start, anyhow.'

"'Twas a start, and a pretty good one. The Robinsons had come to the Old Home about the fust of August, and they was our star boarders. 'G. W. Robinson' was the old man's name as entered on the hotel log, and his daughter answered to the hail of 'Grace'—that is, when she took a notion to answer at all. The Robinsons was what Peter T. called 'exclusive.' They didn't mix much with the rest of the bunch, but kept to themselves in their rooms, partic'lar when a fresh net full of boarders was hauled aboard. Then they seemed to take an observation of every arrival afore they mingled; questioned the pedigree and statistics of all hands, and acted mighty suspicious.

"The only thing that really stirred Papa Robinson up and got him excited and friendly was baseball and boat racin'. He was an old sport, that was plain, the only real plain thing about him; the rest was mystery. As for Grace, she wa'n't plain by a good sight, bein' what Brown called a 'peach.' She could have had every single male in tow if she'd wanted 'em. Apparently she didn't want em, preferrin' to be lonesome and sad and interestin'. Yes, sir, there was a mystery about them Robinsons, and even Peter T. give in to that.

"'If 'twas anybody else,' says he, 'I'd say the old man was a crook, down here hidin' from the police. But he's too rich for that, and always has been. He ain't any fly-by-night. I can tell the real article without lookin' for the "sterlin'" mark on the handle. But I'll bet all the cold-storage eggs in the hotel against the henyard—and that's big odds—that he wa'n't christened Robinson. And his face is familiar to me. I've seen it somewhere, either in print or in person. I wish I knew where.'

"So if the Robinsons had agreed to stay—them and their two servants—that was a big help, as Brown said. And Parker would help, too, though we agreed there wa'n't no mystery about him. He was a big, broad-shouldered young feller just out of college somewheres, who had drifted our way the fortni't after the

Robinsons came, with a reputation for athletics and a leanin' toward cigarettes and Miss Grace. She leaned a little, too, but hers wa'n't so much of a bend as his was. He was dead gone on her, and if she'd have decided to stay under water, he'd have ducked likewise. 'Twas easy enough to see why *he* believed in a 'supplementary season.'

"Me and Jonadab argued it out with Peter, and finally we met halfway, so's to speak. We wouldn't keep the whole shebang open, but we'd shut up everything but one Annex cottage, and advertise that as a Gunner's Retreat. So we done it.

"And it worked. Heavens to Betsy—yes! It worked so well that by the second week in September we had to open t'other Annex. The gunnin' was bad, but Peter's ads fetched the would-be's, and his 'excursions' and picnics and the football team held 'em. The football team especial. Parker cap'ned that, and, from the gunnin' crew and the waiters and some fishermen in the village, he dug up an eleven that showed symptoms of playin' the game. We played the Trumet High School, and beat it, thanks to Parker, and that tickled Pa Robinson so that he bought a two-handled silver soup tureen—'lovin' cup,' he called it—and agreed to give it to the team round about that won the most of the series. So the series was arranged, the Old Home House crowd and the Wapatomac House eleven and three high-school gangs bein' in it. And 'twas practice, practice, practice, from then on.

"When we opened the second Annex, the question of help got serious. Most of our college waiters had gone back to school, and we was pretty shy of servants. So we put some extry advertisin' in the Cape weeklies, and trusted in Providence.

"The evenin' follown' the ad in the weeklies, I was settin' smokin' on the back piazza of the shut-up main hotel, when I heard the gate click and somebody crunchin' along the clam-shell path. I sung out: 'Ahoy, there!' and the cruncher, whoever he was, come my way. Then I made out that he was a tall young chap, with his hands in his pockets.

"'Good evenin',' says he. 'Is this Mr. Brown?'

"'Thankin' you for the compliment, it ain't,' I says. 'My name's Wingate.'

"'Oh!' says he. 'Is that so? I've heard father speak of you, Mr. Wingate. He is Solomon Bearse, of West Ostable. I think you know him slightly.'

"Know him? Everybody on the Cape knows Sol Bearse; by reputation, anyhow. He's the richest, meanest old cranberry grower and coastin'-fleet owner in these parts.

"'Is Sol Bearse your dad?' I asks, astonished. 'Why, then, you must be Gus?'

"'No, 'he says. 'I'm the other one—Fred.'

"'Oh, the college one. The one who's goin' to be a lawyer.'

"'Well, yes—and no,' says he. 'I *was* the college one, as you call it, but I'm not goin' to be a lawyer. Father and I have had some talk on that subject, and I think we've settled it. I—well, just at present, I'm not sure what I'm goin' to be. That's what I've come to you for. I saw your ad in the Item, and—I want a job.'

"I was set all aback, and left with my canvas flappin', as you might say. Sol Bearse's boy huntin' a job in a hotel kitchen! Soon's I could fetch a whole breath, I wanted partic'lars. He give 'em to me.

"Seems he'd been sent out to one of the colleges in the Middle West by his dad, who was dead set on havin' a lawyer in the family. But the more he studied, the less he hankered for law. What he wanted to be was a literature—a book-agent or a poet, or some such foolishness. Old Sol, havin' no more use for a poet than he had for a poor relation, was red hot in a minute. Was this what he'd been droppin' good money in the education collection box for? Was this—etcetery and so on. He'd be—what the church folks say he will be—if Fred don't go in for law. Fred, he comes back that he'll be the same if he does. So they disowned each other by mutual consent, as the Irishman said, and the boy marches out of the front door, bag and baggage. And, as the poetry market seemed to be sort of overly supplied at the present time, he decided he must do somethin' to earn a dollar, and, seein' our ad, he comes to Wellmouth Port and the Old Home.

"'But look here,' says I, 'we ain't got no job for a literary. We need fellers to pass pie and wash dishes. And *that* ain't no poem.'

"Well, he thought perhaps he could help make up advertisin'.

"'You can't,' I told him. 'One time, when Peter T. Brown was away, me and Cap'n Jonadab cal'lated that a poetry advertisement would be a good idee and we managed to shake out ten lines or so. It begun:

"When you're feelin' tired and pale
To the Old Home House you ought to come without fail."

"'We thought 'twas pretty slick, but we never got but one answer, and that was a circular from one of them correspondence schools of authors, sayin' they'd let us in on a course at cut rates. And the next thing we knew we see that poem in the joke page of a Boston paper. I never—'

"He laughed, quiet and sorrowful. He had the quietest way of speakin', anyhow, and his voice was a lovely tenor. To hear it purrin' out of his big, tall body was as unexpected as a hymn tune in a cent-in-the-slot talkin' machine.

"'Too bad,' he says. 'As a waiter, I'm afraid—'

"Just then the door of one of the Annex houses opened sudden, and there stood Grace Robinson. The light behind her showed her up plain as could be. I heard Fred Bearse make a kind of gaspin' noise in his throat.

"'What a lovely night!' she says, half to herself. Then she calls: 'Papa, dear, you really ought to see the stars.'

"Old man Robinson, who I judged was in the settin' room, snarled out somethin' which wa'n't no compliment to the stars. Then he ordered her to come in afore she catched cold. She sighed and obeyed orders, shuttin' the door astern of her. Next thing I knew that literary tenor grabbed my arm—'twa'n't no canary-bird grip, neither.

"'Who was that?' he whispers, eager.

"I told him. 'That's the name they give,' says I, 'but we have doubts about its bein' the real one. You see, there's some mystery about them Robinsons, and—'

"'I'll take that waiter's place,' he says, quick. 'Shall I go right in and begin now? Don't stop to argue, man; I say I'll take it.'

"And he did take it by main strength, pretty nigh. Every time I'd open my mouth he'd shut it up, and at last I give in, and showed him where he could sleep.

"'You turn out at five sharp,' I told him. 'And you needn't bother to write no poems while you're dressin', neither.'

"'Good night,' he answers, brisk. 'Go, will you, please? I want to think.'

"I went. 'Tain't until an hour later that I remembered he hadn't asked one word concernin' the wages. And next mornin' he comes to me and suggests that perhaps 'twould be as well if I didn't tell his real name. He was pretty sure he'd been away schoolin' so long that he wouldn't be recognized. 'And incognitos seem to be fashionable here,' he purrs, soft and gentle.

"I wouldn't know an incognito if I stepped on one, but the tenor voice of him kind of made me sick.

"'All right,' I snaps, sarcastic. 'Suppose I call you "Willie." How'll that do?'

"'Do as well as anything, I guess,' he says. Didn't make no odds to him. If I'd have called him 'Maud,' he'd have been satisfied.

"He waited in Annex Number Two, which was skippered by Cap'n Jonadab. And, for a poet, he done pretty well, so the Cap'n said.

"'But say, Barzilla,' asks Jonadab, 'does that Willie thing know the Robinsons?'

"'Guess not,' I says. But, thinkin' of the way he'd acted when the girl come to the door: 'Why?'

"'Oh, nothin' much. Only when he come in with the doughnuts the fust mornin' at breakfast, I thought Grace sort of jumped and looked funny. Anyhow, she didn't eat nothin' after that. P'r'aps that was on account of her bein' out sailin' the day afore, though.'

"I said I cal'lated that was it, but all the same I was interested. And when, a day or so later, I see Grace and Willie talkin' together earnest, out back of the kitchen, I was more so. But I never said nothin'. I've been seafarin' long enough to know when to keep my main hatch closed.

"The supplementary season dragged along, but it wa'n't quite the success it looked like at the start. The gunnin' that year was even worse than usual, and excursions and picnics in late September ain't all joy, by no manner of means. We shut up the second Annex at the end of the month, and transferred the help to Number One. Precious few new boarders come, and a good many of the old ones quit. Them that did stay, stayed on account of the football. We was edgin' up toward the end of the series, and our team and the Wapatomac crowd was neck and neck. It looked as if the final game between them and us, over on their grounds, would settle who'd have the soup tureen.

"Pa Robinson and Parker had been quite interested in Willie when he fust come. They thought he might play with the eleven, you see. But he wouldn't. Set his foot right down.

"'I don't care for athletics,' he says, mild but firm. 'They used to interest me somewhat, but not now.'

"The old man was crazy. He'd heard about Willie's literature leanin's, and he give out that he'd never see a writer yet that wa'n't a 'sissy.' Wanted us to fire Bearse right off, but we kept him, thanks to me. If he'd seen the 'sissy' kick the ball once, same as I did, it might have changed his mind some. He was passin' along the end of the field when the gang was practicin', and the ball come his way. He caught it on the fly, and sent it back with his toe. It went a mile, seemed so, whirlin' and whizzin'. Willie never even looked to see where it went; just kept on his course for the kitchen.

"The big sensation hit us on the fifth of October, right after supper. Me and Peter T. and Jonadab was in the office, when down comes Henry, old Robinson's man servant, white as a sheet and wringin' his hands distracted.

"'Oh, I say, Mr. Brown!' says he, shakin' all over like a quick-sand. 'Oh, Mr. Brown, sir! Will you come right up to Mr. Sterz—I mean Mr. Robinson's room, please, sir! 'E wants to see you gentlemen special. 'Urry, please! 'Urry!'

"So we ''urried,' wonderin' what on earth was the matter. And when we got to the Robinson rooms, there was Grace, lookin' awful pale, and the old man himself ragin' up and down like a horse mack'rel in a fish weir.

"Soon as papa sees us, he jumped up in the air, so's to speak, and when he lit 'twas right on our necks. His daughter, who seemed to be the sanest one in the lot, run and shut the door.

"'Look here, you!' raved the old gent, shakin' both fists under Peter T.'s nose. 'Didn't you tell me this was a respectable hotel? And ain't we payin' for respectability?'

"Peter admitted it, bein' too much set back to argue, I cal'late.

"'Yes!' rages Robinson. 'We pay enough for all the respectability in this state. And yet, by the livin' Moses! I can't go out of my room to spoil my digestion with your cussed dried-apple pie, but what I'm robbed!'

"'Robbed!' the three of us gurgles in chorus.

"'Yes, sir! Robbed! Robbed! *Robbed*! What do you think I came here for? And why do I stay here all this time? 'Cause I *like* it? 'Cause I can't afford a better place? No, sir! By the great horn spoon! I come here because I thought in this forsaken hole I could get lost and be safe. And now—'

"He tore around like a water spout, Grace trying to calm him, and Henry and Suzette, the maid, groanin' and sobbin' accompaniments in the corner. I looked at the dresser. There was silver-backed brushes and all sorts of expensive doodads spread out loose, and Miss Robinson's watch and a di'mond ring, and a few other knickknacks. I couldn't imagine a thief's leavin' all that truck, and I said so.

"'Them?' sputters Pa, frantic. 'What the brimstone blazes do you think I care for them? I could buy that sort of stuff by the carload, if I wanted to. But what's been stole is—Oh, get out and leave me alone! You're no good, the lot of you!'

"'Father has had a valuable paper stolen from him,' explains Grace. 'A very valuable paper.'

"'Valuable!' howls her dad. '*Valuable*! Why, if Gordon and his gang get that paper, they've got *me*, that's all. Their suit's as good as won, and I know it. And to think that I've kept it safe up to within a month of the trial, and now—Grace Sterzer, you stop pattin' my head. I'm no pussy-cat! By the—' And so on, indefinite.

"When he called his daughter Sterzer, instead of Robinson, I cal'lated he was loony, sure enough. But Peter T. slapped his leg.

"'Oh!' he says, as if he'd seen a light all to once. 'Ah, *now* I begin to get wise. I knew your face was—See here, Mr. Sterzer—Mr.

Gabriel Sterzer—don't you think we'd better have a real, plain talk on this matter? Let's get down to tacks. Was the paper you lost something to do with the Sterzer-Gordon lawsuit? The Aluminum Trust case, you know?'

"The old man stopped dancin', stared at him hard, and then set down and wiped his forehead.

"'Something to *do* with it?' he groans. 'Why, you idiot, it was *it*! If Gordon's lawyers get that paper—and they've been after it for a year—then the fat's all in the fire. There's nothin' left for me to do but compromise.'

"When Peter T. mentioned the name of Gabriel Sterzer, me and Jonadab begun to see a light, too. 'Course you remember the bust-up of the Aluminum Trust—everybody does. The papers was full of it. There'd been a row among the two leadin' stock-holders, Gabe Sterzer and 'Major' Gordon. Them two double-back-action millionaires practically owned the trust, and the state 'twas in, and the politics of that state, and all the politicians. Each of 'em run three or four banks of their own, and a couple of newspapers, and other things, till you couldn't rest. Then they had the row, and Gabe had took his playthings and gone home, as you might say. Among the playthings was a majority of the stock, and the Major had sued for it. The suit, with pictures of the leadin' characters and the lawyers and all, had been spread-eagled in the papers everywheres. No wonder 'Robinson's' face was familiar.

"But it seemed that Sterzer had held the trump card in the shape of the original agreement between him and Gordon. And he hung on to it like the Old Scratch to a fiddler. Gordon and his crowd had done everything, short of murder, to get it; hired folks to steal it, and so on, because, once they *did* get it, Gabe hadn't a leg to stand on—he'd have to divide equal, which wa'n't his desires, by a good sight. The Sterzer lawyers had wanted him to leave it in their charge, but no—he knew too much for that. The pig-headed old fool had carted it with him wherever he went, and him and his daughter had come to the Old Home House because he figgered nobody would think of their bein' in such an out-of-the-way place as that. But they *had* thought of it. Anyhow, the paper was gone.

"'But Mr. Robinzer—Sterson, I mean—' cut in Cap'n Jonadab, 'you could have 'em took up for stealin', couldn't you? They wouldn't dare—'

"'Course they'd dare! S'pose they don't know I wouldn't have that agreement get in the papers? Dare! They'd dare anything. If they get away with it, by hook or crook, all I can do is haul in my horns and compromise. If they've got that paper, the suit never comes to trial.'

"'Well, they ain't got it yet,' says Peter, decided. 'Whoever stole the thing is right here in this boardin'-house, and it's up to us to see that they stay here. Barzilla, you take care of the mail. No letters must go out to-night. Jonadab, you set up and watch all hands, help and all. Nobody must leave this place, if we have to tie em. And I'll keep a gen'ral overseein' of the whole thing, till we get a detective. And—if you'll stand the waybill, Mr. Sterzer—we'll have the best Pinkerton in Boston down here in three hours by special train. By the way, are you sure the thing *is* lifted? Where was it?'

"Old Gabe kind of colored up, and give in that 'twas under his pillow. He always kept it there after the beds was made.

"'Humph!' grunts Brown. 'Why didn't you hang it on the door-knob? Under the pillow! If I was a sneak thief, the first place I'd look would be under the pillow; after that I'd tackle the jewelry box and the safe.'

"There was consider'ble more talk. Seems the Sterzers had left Henry on guard, same as they always done, when they went to supper. They could trust him and Suzette absolute, they said. But Henry had gone down the hall after a drink of water, and when he had got back everything apparently was all right. 'Twa'n't till Gabe himself come up that he found the paper gone. I judged he'd made it interestin' for Henry; the poor critter looked that way.

"All hands agreed to keep mum for the present and to watch. Peter hustled to the office and called up the Pinkertons over the long distance."

Mr. Wingate paused. Captain Sol was impatient.

"Go on," he said. "Don't stop now, I'm gettin' anxious."

Barzilla rose to his feet. "Here's your McKay man back again," he said. "Let's go up to your house and have breakfast. We can talk while we're eatin'. I'm empty as a poorhouse boarder's pocketbook."

Chapter VI
Aviation and Avarice

B REAKFAST AT CAPT. Sol Berry's was a bountiful meal. The depot master employed a middle-aged woman who came in each day, cooked his meals and did the housework, returning to her own home at night. After Mr. Wingate had mowed a clean swath through ham and eggs, cornbread and coffee, and had reached the cooky and doughnut stage, he condescended to speak further concerning the stolen paper.

"Well," he said, "Brown give me and Jonadab a serious talkin' to when he got us alone."

"'Now, fellers, 'he says, 'we know what we've got to do. Nothin'll be too good for this shebang and us if we get that agreement back. Fust place, the thing was done a few minutes after the supper-bell rung. That is, unless that 'Enry is in on the deal, which ain't unlikely, considerin' the price he could get from the Gordon gang. Was anybody late at the tables?'

"Why, yes; there were quite a few late. Two of the 'gunners,' who'd been on a forlorn-hope duck hunt; and a minister and his wife, out walkin' for their health; and Parker and two fellers from the football team, who'd been practicin'.

"'Any of the waiters or the chambermaids?' asked Peter.

"I'd been expectin' he'd ask that, and I hated to answer.

"'One of the waiters was a little late,' says I. 'Willie wa'n't on hand immediate. Said he went to wash his hands.'

"Now the help gen'rally washed in the fo'castle—the servants' quarters, I mean—but there was a wash room on the floor where the Sterzer-Robinsons roomed. Peter looked at Jonadab, and the two of 'em at me. And I had to own up that Willie had come downstairs from that wash room a few minutes after the bell rung.

"'Hum!' says Peter T. 'Hum!'he says. 'Look here, Barzilla, didn't you tell me you knew that feller's real name, and that he had been studying law?'

"'No,' says I, emphatic. 'I said 'twas law he was tryin' to get away from. His tastes run large to literation and poetry.'

"'Hum!' says Peter again. 'All papers are more or less literary— even trust agreements. Hum!'

"'All the same,' says I, 'I'll bet my Sunday beaver that *he* never took it.'

"They didn't answer, but looked solemn. Then the three of us went on watch.

"Nobody made a move to go out that evenin'. I kept whatever mail was handed in, but there was nothin' that looked like any agreements, and nothin' addressed to Gordon or his lawyers. At twelve or so, the detective come. Peter drove up to the depot to meet the special. He told the whole yarn on the way down.

"The detective was a nice enough chap, and we agreed he should be 'Mr. Snow,' of New York, gunnin' for health and ducks. He said the watch must be kept up all night, and in the mornin' he'd make his fust move. So said, so done.

"And afore breakfast that next mornin' we called everybody into the dinin' room, boarders, help, stable hands, every last one. And Peter made a little speech. He said that a very valuable paper had been taken out of Mr. Robinson's room, and 'twas plain that it must be on the premises somewhere. 'Course, nobody was suspicioned, but, speakin' for himself, he'd feel better if his clothes and his room was searched through. How'd the rest feel about it?

"Well, they felt diff'rent ways, but Parker spoke up like a brick, and said he wouldn't rest easy till *his* belongin's was pawed over, and then the rest fell in line. We went through everybody and every room on the place. Found nothin', of course. Snow—the detective—said he didn't expect to. But I tell you there was some talkin' goin' on, just the same. The minister, he hinted that he had some doubts about them dissipated gunners; and the gunners cal'lated they never see a parson yet wouldn't bear watchin'. As for me, I felt like a pickpocket, and, judgin' from

Jonadab's face, he felt the same.

"The detective man swooped around quiet, bobbin' up in un-expected places, like a porpoise, and askin' questions once in a while. He asked about most everybody, but about Willie, espe-cial. I judged Peter T. had dropped a hint to him and to Gabe. Anyhow, the old critter give out that he wouldn't trust a poet with the silver handles on his grandmarm's coffin. As for Grace, she acted dreadful nervous and worried. Once I caught her swabbin' her eyes, as if she'd been cryin'; but I'd never seen her and Willie together but the one time I told you of.

"Four days and nights crawled by. No symptoms yet. The Pinkertons was watchin' the Gordon lawyers' office in New York, and they reported that nothin' like that agreement had reached there. And our own man—Snow—said he'd go bail it hadn't been smuggled off the premises sense *he* struck port. So 'twas safe so far; but where was it, and who had it?

"The final football game, the one with Wapatomac, was to be played over on their grounds on the afternoon of the fifth day. Parker, cap'n of the eleven, give out that, considerin' everything, he didn't know but we'd better call it off. Old Robinson—Sterzer, of course—wouldn't hear of it.

"'Not much,' says he. 'I wouldn't chance your losin' that game for forty papers. You sail in and lick 'em!' or words to that effect.

"So the eleven was to cruise across the bay in the Greased Lightnin', Peter's little motor launch, and the rooters was to go by train later on. 'Twas Parker's idee, goin' in the launch. 'Twould be more quiet, less strain on the nerves of his men, and they could talk over plays and signals on the v'yage.

"So at nine o'clock in the forenoon they was ready, the whole team—three waiters, two fishermen, one carpenter from up to Wellmouth Center, a stable hand, and Parker and three reg'lar boarders. These last three was friends of Parker's that he'd had come down some time afore. He knew they could play football, he said, and they'd come to oblige him.

"The eleven gathered on the front porch, all in togs and sweaters, principally provided and paid for by Sterzer. Cap'n Parker had the ball under his arm, and the launch was waitin' ready at the landin'. All the boarders—except Grace, who was upstairs in her room—and most of the help was standin' round to say good luck and good-by.

"Snow, the detective, was there, and I whispered in his ear.

"'Say,' I says, 'do you realize that for the fust time since the robbery here's a lot of folks leavin' the house? How do you know but what—'

"He winked and nodded brisk. 'I'll attend to that,' he says.

"But he didn't have to. Parker spoke fust, and took the wind out of his sails.

"'Gentlemen,' says he, 'I don't know how the rest of you feel, but, as for me, I don't start without clear skirts. I suggest that Mr. Brown and Mr. Wingate here search each one of us, thoroughly. Who knows,' says he, laughin', 'but what I've got that precious stolen paper tucked inside my sweater? Ha! ha! Come on, fellers! I'll be first.'

"He tossed the ball into a chair and marched into the office, the rest of the players after him, takin' it as a big joke. And there the searchin' was done, and done thorough, 'cause Peter asked Mr. Snow to help, and he knew how. One thing was sure; Pa Gabe's agreement wa'n't hid about the persons of that football team. Everybody laughed—that is, all but the old man and the detective. Seemed to me that Snow was kind of disappointed, and I couldn't see why. 'Twa'n't likely any of *them* was thieves.

"Cap'n Parker picked up his football and started off for the launch. He'd got about ha'fway to the shore when Willie—who'd been stand-in' with the rest of the help, lookin' on—stepped for'ard pretty brisk and whispered in the ear of the Pinkerton man. The detective jumped, sort of, and looked surprised and mighty interested.

"'By George!' says he. 'I never thought of that.' Then he run to the edge of the piazza and called.

"'Mr. Parker!' he sings out. 'Oh, Mr. Parker!'

"Parker was at the top of the little rise that slopes away down to the landin'. The rest of the eleven was scattered from the shore to the hotel steps. He turns, without stoppin', and answers.

"'What is it?' he sings out, kind of impatient.

"'There's just one thing we forgot to look at,' shouts Snow. 'Merely a matter of form, but just bring that—Hey! Stop him! Stop him!'

"For Parker, instead of comin' back, had turned and was leggin' it for the launch as fast as he could, and that was some.

"'Stop!' roars the Pinkerton man, jumpin' down the steps. 'Stop, or—'

"'Hold him, Jim!' screeched Parker, over his shoulder. One of the biggest men on the eleven—one of the three 'friends' who'd been so obligin' as to come down on purpose to play football—made a dive, caught the detective around the waist, and threw him flat.

"'Go on, Ed!' he shouts. 'I've got him, all right.'

"Ed—meanin' Parker—was goin' on, and goin' fast. All hands seemed to be frozen stiff, me and Jonadab and Peter T. included. As for me, I couldn't make head nor tail of the doin's; things was comin' too quick for *my* understandin'.

"But there was one on that piazza who wa'n't froze. Fur from it! Willie, the poet waiter, made a jump, swung his long legs over the porch-rail, hit the ground, and took after that Parker man like a cat after a field mouse.

"Run! I never see such runnin'! He fairly flashed across that lawn and over the rise. Parker was almost to the landin'; two more jumps and he'd been aboard the launch. If he'd once got aboard, a turn of the switch and that electric craft would have had him out of danger in a shake. But them two jumps was two too many. Willie riz off the ground like a flyin' machine, turned his feet up and his head down, and lapped his arms around Parker's knees. Down the pair of 'em went 'Ker-wallop!' and the football flew out of Parker's arms.

"In an eyewink that poet was up, grabs the ball, and comes tearin' back toward us.

"'Stop him!' shrieks Parker from astern.

"'Head him off! Tackle him!' bellers the big chap who was hangin' onto the detective.

"They tell me that discipline and obeyin' orders is as much in football as 'tis aboard ship. If that's so, every one of the Old Home House eleven was onto their jobs. There was five men between Willie and the hotel, and they all bore down on him like bats on a June bug.

"'Get him!' howls Parker, racin' to help.

"'Down him!' chimes in big Jim, his knee in poor Snow's back.

"'Run, Bearse! Run!' whoops the Pinkerton man, liftin' his mouth out of the sand.

"He run—don't you worry about that! Likewise he dodged. One chap swooped at him, and he ducked under his arms. Another made a dive, and he jumped over him. The third one he pushed one side with his hand. 'Pushed!' did I say? 'Knocked' would be better, for the feller—the carpenter 'twas—went over and over like a barrel rollin' down hill. But there was two more left, and one of 'em was bound to have him.

"Then a window upstairs banged open.

"'Oh, Mr. Bearse!' screamed a voice—Grace Sterzer's voice. 'Don't let them get you!'

"We all heard her, in spite of the shoutin' and racket. Willie heard her, too. The two fellers, one at each side, was almost on him, when he stopped, looked up, jumped back, and, as cool as a rain barrel in January, he dropped that ball and kicked it.

"I can see that picture now, like a tableau at a church sociable. The fellers that was runnin', the others on the ground, and that literary pie passer with his foot swung up to his chin.

"And the ball! It sailed up and up in a long curve, began to drop, passed over the piazza roof, and out of sight.

"'Lock your door, Miss Sterzer,' sung out Fred Bearse—'Willie' for short. 'Lock your door and keep that ball. I think your father's paper is inside it.'

"As sure as my name is Barzilla Wingate, he had kicked that football straight through the open window into old Gabe's room."

The depot master whooped and slapped his knee. Mr. Wingate grinned delightedly and continued:

"There!" he went on, "the cat's out of the bag, and there ain't much more to tell. Everybody made a bolt for the room, old Gabe and Peter T. in the lead. Grace let her dad in, and the ball was ripped open in a hurry. Sure enough! Inside, between the leather and the rubber, was the missin' agreement. Among the jubilations and praise services nobody thought of much else until Snow, the Pinkerton man, come upstairs, his clothes tore and his eyes and nose full of sand.

"'Humph!' says he. 'You've got it, hey? Good! Well, you haven't got friend Parker. Look!'

"Such of us as could looked out of the window. There was the launch, with Parker and his three 'friends' in it, headin' two-forty for blue water.

"'Let 'em go,' says old Gabe, contented. 'I wouldn't arrest 'em if I could. This is no police-station job.'

"It come out afterwards that Parker was a young chap just from law school, who had gone to work for the firm of shysters who was attendin' to the Gordon interests. They had tracked Sterzer to the Old Home House, and had put their new hand on the job of gettin' that agreement. Fust he'd tried to shine up to Grace, but the shine—her part of it—had wore off. Then he decided to steal it; and he done it, just how nobody knows. Snow, the detective, says he cal'lates Henry, the servant, is wiser'n most folks thinks, fur's that's concerned.

"Snow had found out about Parker inside of two days. Soon's he got the report as to who he was, he was morally sartin that he was the thief. He'd looked up Willie's record, too, and that was clear. In fact, Willie helped him consider'ble. 'Twas him that recognized Parker, havin' seen him play on a law-school team. Also 'twas Willie who thought of the paper bein' in the football.

"Land of love! What a hero they made of that waiter!

"'By the livin' Moses!' bubbles old Gabe, shakin' both the boy's hands. 'That was the finest run and tackle and the finest kick I ever saw anywhere. I've seen every big game for ten years, and I never saw anything half so good.'

"The Pinkerton man laughed. 'There's only one chap on earth who can kick like that. Here he is,' layin' his hand on 'Willie's' shoulder. 'Bearse, the All-American half-back last year.'

"Gabe's mouth fell open. 'Not "Bung" Bearse, of Yarvard!' he sings out. 'Why! *Why!*'

"'Of course, father!' purrs his daughter, smilin' and happy. 'I knew him at once. He and I were—er—slightly acquainted when I was at Highcliffe.'

"'But—but "Bung" Bearse!' gasps the old gent. 'Why, you rascal! I saw you kick the goal that beat Haleton. Your reputation is worldwide.'

"Willie—Fred Bearse, that is—shook his head, sad and regretful.

"'Thank you, Mr. Sterzer,' says he, in his gentle tenor. 'I have no desire to be famous in athletics. My aspirations now are entirely literary.'

"Well, he's got his literary job at last, bein' engaged as sportin' editor on one of Gabe's papers. His dad, old Sol Bearse, seems to be pretty well satisfied, partic'lar as another engagement between the Bearse family and the Sterzers has just been given out."

Barzilla helped himself to another doughnut. His host leaned back in his chair and laughed uproariously.

"Well, by the great and mighty!" he exclaimed, "that Willie chap certainly did fool you, didn't he. You can't always tell about these college critters. Sometimes they break out unexpected, like chickenpox in the 'Old Men's Home.' Ha! ha! Say, do you know Nate Scudder?"

"Know him? Course I know him! The meanest man on the Cape, and livin' right in my own town, too! Well, if I didn't know him I might trust him, and that would be the beginnin' of the end—for me."

"It sartin would. But what made me think of him was what he told me about his nephew, who was a college chap, consider'ble like your 'Willie,' I jedge. Nate and this nephew, Augustus Tolliver, was mixed up in that flyin'-machine business, you remember."

"I know they was. Mixed up with that Professor Dixland the papers are makin' such a fuss over. Wellmouth's been crazy over it all, but it happened a year ago and nobody that I know of has got the straight inside facts about it yet. Nate won't talk at all.

Whenever you ask him he busts out swearin' and walks off. His wife's got such a temper that nobody dared ask her, except the minister. He tried it, and ain't been the same man since."

"Well," the depot master smilingly scratched his chin, "I cal'late I've got those inside facts."

"You *have*?"

"Yes. Nate gave 'em to me, under protest. You see, I know Nate pretty well. I know some things about him that ... but never mind that part. I asked him and, at last, he told me. I'll have to tell you in his words, 'cause half the fun was the way he told it and the way he looked at the whole business. So you can imagine I'm Nate, and—"

"'Twill be a big strain on my imagination to b'lieve you're Nate Scudder, Sol Berry."

"Thanks. However, you'll have to do it for a spell. Well, Nate said that it really begun when the Professor and Olivia landed at the Wellmouth depot with the freight car full of junk. Of course, the actual beginnin' was further back than that, when that Harmon man come on from Philadelphy and hunted him up, makin' proclamation that a friend of his, a Mr. Van Brunt of New York, had said that Scudder had a nice quiet island to let and maybe he could hire it.

"Course Nate had an island—that little sun-dried sandbank a mile or so off shore, abreast his house, which we used to call 'Horsefoot Bar.' That crazy Van Brunt and his chum, Hartley, who lived there along with Sol Pratt a year or so ago, re-christened it 'Ozone Island,' you remember. Nate was willin' to let it. He'd let Tophet, if he owned it, and a fool come along who wanted to hire it and could pay for the rent and heat.

"So Nate and this Harmon feller rowed over to the Bar—to Ozone Island, I mean—and the desolation and loneliness of it seemed to suit him to perfection. So did the old house and big barn and all the tumbledown buildin's stuck there in the beach-grass and sand. Afore they'd left they made a dicker. He wa'n't the principal in it. He was the private secretary and fust mate of Mr. Professor Ansel Hobart Dixland, the scientist—perhaps Scudder'd heard of him?

"Perhaps he had, but if so, Nate forgot it, though he didn't tell him that. Harmon ordered a fifteen-foot-high board fence built all around the house and barn, and made Nate swear not to tell a soul who was comin' nor anything. Dixland might want the island two months, he said, or he might want it two years. Nate didn't care. He was in for good pickin's, and begun to pick by slicin' a liberal commission off that fencebuildin' job. There was a whole passel of letters back and forth between Nate and Harmon, and finally Nate got word to meet the victims at the depot.

"There was the professor himself, an old dried-up relic with whiskers and a temper; and there was Miss Olivia Dixland, his niece and housekeeper, a slim, plain lookin' girl, who wore eyeglasses and a straight up and down dress. And there was a freight car full of crates and boxes and land knows what all. But nary sign was there of a private secretary and assistant. The professor told Nate that Mr. Harmon's health had suddenly broke down and he'd had to be sent South.

"'It's a calamity,' says he; 'a real calamity! Harmon has been with me in my work from the beginnin'; and now, just as it is approachin' completion, he is taken away. They say he may die. It is very annoyin'.'

"'Humph!' says Nate. 'Well, maybe it annoys *him* some, too; you can't tell. What you goin' to do for a secretary?'

"'I understand,' says the professor, 'that there is a person of consider'ble scientific attainment residin' with you, Mr. Scudder, at present. Harmon met him while he was here; they were in the same class at college. Harmon recommended him highly. Olivia,' he says to the niece, 'what was the name of the young man whom Harmon recommended?'

"'Tolliver, Uncle Ansel,' answers the girl, lookin' kind of disdainful at Nate. Somehow he had the notion that she didn't take to him fust rate.

"'Hey?' sings out Nate. 'Tolliver? Why, that's Augustus! *Augustus*! well, I'll be switched!'

"Augustus Tolliver was Nate's nephew from up Boston way. Him and Nate was livin' together at that time. Huldy Ann, Mrs. Scudder, was out West, in Omaha, takin' care of a cousin of hers who was a chronic invalid and, what's more to the purpose, owned a lot of stock in copper mines.

"Augustus was a freckle-faced, spindle-shanked little critter, with spectacles and a soft, polite way of speakin' that made you want to build a fire under him to see if he could swear like a Christian. He had a big head with consider'ble hair on the top of it and nothin' underneath but what he called 'science' and 'sociology.' His science wa'n't nothin' but tommy-rot to Nate, and the 'sociology' was some kind of drivel about everybody bein' equal to everybody else, or better. 'Seemed to think 'twas wrong to get a good price for a thing when you found a feller soft enough to pay it. Did you ever hear the beat of that in your life?' says Nate.

"However, Augustus had soaked so much science and sociology into that weak noddle of his that they kind of made him drunk, as you might say, and the doctor had sent him down to board with the Scudders and sleep it off. 'Nervous prostration' was the way he had his symptoms labeled, and the nerve part was all right, for if a hen flew at him he'd holler and run. Scart! you never see such a scart cat in your born days. Scart of a boat, scart of being seasick, scart of a gun, scart of everything! Most special he was scart of Uncle Nate. The said uncle kept him that way so's he wouldn't dast to kick at the grub him and Huldy Ann give him, I guess.

"'Augustus Tolliver,' says old Dixland, noddin'. 'Yes, that is the name. Has he had a sound scientific trainin'?'

"'Scientific trainin'!' says Nate. 'Scientific trainin'? Why, you bet he's had it! That's the only kind of trainin' he *had* had. He'll be just the feller for you, Mr. Dixland.'

"So that was settled, all but notifyin' Augustus. But Scudder sighted another speculation in the offin', and hove alongside of it.

"'Mr. Harmon, when he was here,' says he, 'he mentioned you needin' a nice, dependable man to live on the island and be sort of general roustabout. My wife bein' away just now, and all, it struck me that I might as well be that man. Maybe my terms'll seem a little high, at fust mention, but—'

"'Very good,' says the professor, 'very good. I'm sure you'll be satisfactory. Now please see to the unloading of that car. And be careful, *very* careful.'

"Nate broke the news to Augustus that afternoon. He had his nose stuck in a book, as usual, and never heard, so Nate yelled at him like a mate on a tramp steamer, just to keep in trainin'.

"'Who? Who? Who? What? What?' squeals Augustus, jumpin' out of the chair as if there was pins in it. 'What is it? Who did it? Oh, my poor nerves!'

"'Drat your poor nerves!' Nate says. 'I've got a good promisin' job for you. Listen to this.'

"Then he told about the professor's wantin' Gus to be assistant and help do what the old man called 'experiments.'

"'Dixland?' says Gus, 'Ansel Hobart Dixland, the great scientist! And I'm to be *his* assistant? Assistant to the man who discovered *dixium* and invented—'

"'Oh, belay there!' snorts Nate, impatient. Tell me this—he's awful rich, ain't he?'

"'Why, I believe—yes, Harmon said he was. But to think of *my* bein'—'

"'Now, nephew,' Nate cut in, 'let me talk to you a minute. Me and your Aunt Huldy Ann have been mighty kind to you sence you've been here, and here's your chance to do us a good turn. You stick close to science and the professor and let me attend to the finances. If this family ain't well off pretty soon it won't be your Uncle Nate's fault. Only don't you put your oar in where 'Tain't needed.'

"Lord love you, Gus didn't care about finances. He was so full of joy at bein' made assistant to the great Ansel Whiskers Dixland that he forgot everything else, nerves and all.

"So in another day the four of 'em was landed on Ozone Island and so was the freight-car load of crates and boxes. Grub and necessaries was to be provided by Scudder—for salary as stated and commission understood.

"It took Nate less than a week to find out what old Dixland was up to. When he learned it, he set down in the sand and fairly snorted disgust. The old idiot was cal'latin' to *fly*. Seems that for years he'd been experimentin' with what he called 'aeroplanes,' and now he'd reached the stage where he b'lieved he could flap his wings and soar. 'Thinks I,' says Nate, 'your life work's cut out for you, Nate Scudder. You'll spend the rest of your days as gen'ral provider for the Ozone private asylum.' Well, Scudder wa'n't complainin' none at the outlook. He couldn't make a good livin' no easier.

"The aeroplane was in sections in them boxes and crates. Nate and Augustus and the professor got out the sections and fitted 'em together. The buildin's on Ozone was all joined together—first the house, then the ell, then the wash-rooms and big sheds, and, finally, the barn. There was doors connectin', and you could go from house to barn, both downstairs and up, without steppin' outside once.

"'Twas in the barn that they built what Whiskers called the 'flyin' stage.' 'twas a long chute arrangement on trestles, and the idea was that the aeroplane was to get her start by slidin' down the chute, out through the big doors and off by the atmosphere route to glory. I say that was the *idea*. In practice she worked different.

"Twice the professor made proclamations that everything was ready, and twice they started that flyin' machine goin'. The fust time Dixland was at the helm, and him and the aeroplane dropped headfust into the sandbank just outside the barn. The machine was underneath, and the pieces of it acted as a fender, so all the professor fractured was his temper. But it took ten days to get the contraption ready for the next fizzle. Then poor, shaky, scart Augustus was pilot, and he went so deep into the bank that Nate says he wondered whether 'twas wuth while doin' anything but orderin' the gravestone. But they dug him out at last, whole, but frightened blue, and his nerves was worse than ever after that.

"Then old Dixland announces that he has discovered somethin' wrong in the principle of the thing, and they had to wait while he ordered some new fittin's from Boston.

"Meanwhile there was other complications settin' in. Scudder was kept busy providin' grub and such like and helpin' the niece,

Olivia, with the housework. Likewise he had his hands full keepin' the folks alongshore from findin' out what was goin' on. All this flyin' foolishness had to be a dead secret.

"But, busy as he was, he found time to notice the thick acquaintance that was developin' between Augustus and Olivia. Them two was what the minister calls 'kindred sperrits.' Seems she was sufferin' from science same as he was and, more'n that, she was loaded to the gunwale with 'social reform.' To hear the pair of 'em go on about helpin' the poor and 'settlement work' and such was enough, accordin' to Nate, to make you leave the table. But there! He couldn't complain. Olivia was her uncle's only heir, and Nate could see a rainbow of promise ahead for the Scudder family.

"The niece was a nice, quiet girl. The only thing Nate had against her, outside of the sociology craziness and her not seemin' to take a shine to him, was her confounded pets. Nate said he never had no use for pets—lazy critters, eatin' up the victuals and costin' money—but Olivia was dead gone on 'em. She adopted an old reprobate of a tom-cat, which she labeled 'Galileo,' after an Eyetalian who invented spyglasses or somethin' similar, and a great big ugly dog that answered to the hail of 'Phillips Brooks'; she named him that because she said the original Phillips was a distinguished parson and a great philanthropist.

"That dog was a healthy philanthropist. When Nate kicked him the first time, he chased him the whole length of the barn. After that they had to keep him chained up. He was just pinin' for a chance to swaller Scudder whole, and he showed it.

"Well, as time went on, Olivia and Augustus got chummier and chummier. Nate give 'em all the chance possible to be together, and as for old Professor Whiskers, all he thought of, anyway, was his blessed flyin' machine. So things was shapin' themselves well, 'cordin' to Scudder's notion.

"One afternoon Nate come, unexpected, to the top of a sand hill at t'other end of the island, and there, below, set Olivia and Augustus. He had a clove hitch 'round her waist, and they was lookin' into each other's spectacles as if they was windows in the pearly gates. Thinks Nate: 'They've signed articles,' and he tiptoed away, feelin' that life wa'n't altogether an empty dream.

"They was lively hours, them that followed. To begin with, when Nate got back to the barn he found the professor layin' on the floor, under the flyin' stage, groanin' soulful but dismal. He'd slipped off one of the braces of the trestles and sprained both wrists and bruised himself till he wa'n't much more than one big lump. He hadn't bruised his tongue none to speak of, though, and his language wa'n't sprained so that you'd notice it. What broke him up most of all was that he'd got his aeroplane ready to 'fly' again, and now he was knocked out so's he couldn't be aboard when she went off the ways.

"'It is the irony of fate,' says he.

"'I got it off the blacksmith over to Wellmouth Centre,' Nate told him; 'but *he* might have got it from Fate, or whoever you mean. 'Twas slippery iron, I know that, and I warned you against steppin' on it yesterday.'

"The professor more'n hinted that Nate was a dunderhead idiot, and then he commenced to holler for Tolliver; he wanted to see Tolliver right off. Scudder thought he'd ought to see a doctor, but he wouldn't, so Nate plastered him up best he could, got him into the big chair in the front room, and went huntin' Augustus. Him and Olivia was still camped in the sand bank. Gus's right arm had got tired by this time, I cal'late, but he had a new hitch with his left. Likewise they was still starin' into each other's specs.

"'Excuse me for interruptin' the mesmerism,' says Nate, 'but the professor wants to see you.'

"They jumped and broke away. But it took more'n that to bring 'em down out of the clouds. They'd been flyin' a good sight higher than the old aeroplane had yet.

"'Uncle Nathan,' says Augustus, gettin' up and shakin' hands, 'I have the most wonderful news for you. It's hardly believable. You'll never guess it.'

"'Give me three guesses and I'll win on the fust,' says Nate. 'You two are engaged.'

"They looked at him as if he'd done somethin' wonderful. 'But,

93

Uncle,' says Gus, shakin' hands again, 'just think! she's actually consented to marry me.'

"'Well, that's gen'rally understood to be a part of engagin', ain't it?' says Nate. 'I'm glad to hear it. Miss Dixland, I congratulate you. You've got a fine, promisin' young man.'

"That, to Nate's notion, was about the biggest lie he ever told, but Olivia swallered it for gospel. She seemed to thaw toward Scudder a little mite, but 'Twa'n't at a permanent melt, by no means.

"'Thank you, Mr. Scudder,' says she, still pretty frosty. 'I am full aware of Mr. Tolliver's merits. I'm glad to learn that *you* recognize them. He has told some things concernin' his stay at your home which—'

"'Yes, yes,' says Nate, kind of hurried. 'Well, I'm sorry to dump bad news into a puddle of happiness like this, but your Uncle Ansel, Miss Dixland, has been tryin' to fly without his machine, and he's sorry for it.'

"Then he told what had happened to the professor, and Olivia started on the run for the house. Augustus was goin', too, but Nate held him back.

"'Wait a minute, Gus,' says he. 'Walk along with me; I want to talk with you. Now, as an older man, your nighest relation, and one that's come to love you like a son—yes, sir, like a son—I think it's my duty just now to say a word of advice. You're goin' to marry a nice girl that's comin' in for a lot of money one of these days. The professor, he's kind of old, his roof leaks consider'ble, and this trouble is likely to hurry the end along.

"'Now, then,' Nate goes on, 'Augustus, my boy, what are you and that simple, childlike girl goin' to do with all that money? How are you goin' to take care of it? You and 'Livia—you mustn't mind my callin' her that 'cause she's goin' to be one of the family so soon—you'll want to be fussin' with science and such, and you won't have no time to attend to the finances. You'll need a good, safe person to be your financial manager. Well, you know me and you know your Aunt Huldy Ann. *We* know all about financin'; *We've* had experience. You just let us handle the bonds and coupons and them trifles. We'll invest 'em for you. We'll be yours and 'Livia's financial managers. As for our wages, maybe they'll seem a little high, but that's easy arranged. And—'

"Gus interrupted then. 'Oh, that's all settled, 'he says. 'Olivia and I have planned all that. When we're married we shall devote our lives to social work—to settlement work. All the money we ever get we shall use to help the poor. *We* don't want any of it. We shall live *Among* the poor, live just as frugally as they do. Our money we shall give—every cent of it—to charity and—'

"'Lord sakes!' yells Nate, '*Don't* talk that way! Don't! Be you crazy, too? Why—'

"But Gus went on, talkin' a steady streak about livin' in a little tenement in what he called the 'slums' and chuckin' the money to this tramp and that, till Nate's head was whirlin'. 'Twa'n't no joke. He meant it and so did she, and they was just the pair of loons to do it, too.

"Afore Nate had a chance to think up anything sensible to say, Olivia comes hollerin' for Gus to hurry. Off he went, and Nate followed along, holdin' his head and staggerin' like a voter comin' home from a political candidate's picnic. All he could think of was: '*This* the end of all my plannin'! What—*what'll* Huldy Ann say to *this*?'

"Nate found the professor bolstered up in his chair, with the other two standin' alongside. He was layin' down the law about that blessed aeroplane.

"'No! no! *no*! I tell you!' he roars, 'I'll see no doctor. My invention is ready at last, and, if I'm goin' to die, I'll die successful. Tolliver, you've been a faithful worker with me, and yours shall be the privilege of makin' the first flight. Wheel me to the window, Olivia, and let me see my triumph.'

"But Olivia didn't move. Instead, she looked at Augustus and he at her. 'Wheel me to the window!' yells Dixland. 'Tolliver, what are you waitin' for? The doors are open, the aeroplane is ready. Go this instant and fly.'

"Augustus was a bird all right, 'cordin' to Nate's opinion, but he didn't seem anxious to spread his wings. He was white, and them nerves of his was all in a twitter. If ever there was a scart critter, 'twas him then.

"'Go out and fly,' says Nate to him, pretty average ugly. 'Don't you hear the boss's order? Here, professor, I'll push you to the window.'

"'Thank you, Scudder,' says Dixland. And then turnin' to Gus: 'Well, sir, may I ask why you wait?'

"'Twas Olivia that answered. 'Uncle Ansel,' says she, 'I must tell you somethin'. I should have preferred tellin' you privately,' she puts in, glarin' at Nate, 'but it seems I can't. Mr. Tolliver and I are engaged to be married.'

"Old Whiskers didn't seem to care a continental. All he had in his addled head was that flyin' contraption.

"'All right, all right,' he snaps, fretty, 'I'm satisfied. He appears to be a decent young man enough. But now I want him to start my aeroplane.'

"'No, Uncle Ansel,' goes on Olivia, 'I cannot permit him to risk his life in that way. His nerves are not strong and neither is his heart. Besides, the aeroplane has failed twice. Luckily no one was killed in the other trials, but the chances are that the third time may prove fatal.'

"'Fatal, you imbecile!' shrieks the professor. 'It's perfected, I tell you! I—'

"'It makes no difference. No, uncle, Augustus and I have made up our minds. His life and health are too precious; he must be spared for the grand work that we are to do together. No, Uncle Ansel, he shall *not* fly.'

"Did you ever see a cat in a fit? That was the professor just then, so Nate said. He tried to wave his sprained wrists and couldn't; tried to stamp his foot and found it too lame. But his eyeglasses flashed sparks and his tongue spit fire.

"'Are you goin' to start that machine?' he screams at the blue-white, shaky Augustus.

"'No, Professor Dixland,' stammers Gus. 'No, sir, I'm sorry, but—'

"'Why don't you ask Mr. Scudder to make the experiment, uncle?' suggests that confounded niece, smilin' the spitefullest smile.

"'Scudder,' says the professor, 'I'll give you five thousand dollars cash to start in that aeroplane this moment.'

"For a jiffy Nate was staggered. Five thousand dollars *cash*—whew! But then he thought of how deep Gus had been shoved into that sandbank. And there was a new and more powerful motor aboard the thing now. Five thousand dollars ain't much good to a telescoped corpse. He fetched a long breath.

"'Well, now, Mr. Dixland,' he says, 'I'd like to, fust rate, but you see I don't know nothin' about mechanics.'

"'Professor—' begins Augustus. 'Twas the final straw. Old Whiskers jumped out of the chair, lameness and all.

"'Out of this house, you ingrate!' he bellers. 'Out this instant! I discharge you. Go! go!'

"He was actually frothin' at the mouth. I cal'late Olivia thought he was goin' to die, for she run to him.

"'You'd better go, I think,' says she to her shakin' beau. 'Go, dear, now. I must stay with him for the present, but we will see each other soon. Go now, and trust me.'

"'I disown you, you ungrateful girl,' foams her uncle. 'Scudder, I order you to put that—that creature off this island.'

"'Yes, sir,' says Nate, polite; 'in about two shakes of a heifer's tail.'

"He started for Augustus, and Gus started for the door. I guess Olivia might have interfered, but just then the professor keels over in a kind of faint and she had to tend to him. Gus darts out of the door with Nate after him. Scudder reached the beach just as his nephew was shovin' off in the boat, bound for the mainland.

"'Consarn your empty head!' Nate yelled after him. 'See what you get by not mindin' me, don't you? I'm runnin' things on this island after this. I'm boss here; understand? When you're ready to sign a paper deedin' over ha'f that money your wife's goin' to get to me and Huldy Ann, maybe I'll let you come back. And perhaps then I'll square things for you with Dixland. But if you dare to set foot on these premises until then I'll murder you; I'll drown you; I'll cut you up for bait; I'll feed you to the dog.'

"He sculled off, his oars rattlin' 'Hark from the tomb' in the rowlocks. He b'lieved Nate meant it all. Oh, Scudder had *him* trained all right."

Chapter VII
Captain Sol Decides to Move

Trust Nate for that," interrupted Wingate. "He's just as much a born bully as he is a cheat and a skinflint."

"Yup," went on Captain Sol. "Well, when Nate got back to the house the professor was alone in the chair, lookin' sick and weak. Olivia was up in her room havin' a cryin' fit. Nate got the old man to bed, made him some clam soup and hot tea, and fetched and carried for him like he was a baby. The professor's talk was mainly about the ungrateful desertion, as he called it, of his assistant.

"'Keep him away from this island,' he says. 'If he comes, I shall commit murder; I know it.'

"Scudder promised that Augustus shouldn't come back. The professor wanted guard kept night and day. Nate said he didn't know's he could afford so much time, and Dixland doubled his wages on the spot. So Nate agreed to stand double watches, made him comfort'ble for the night, and left him.

"Olivia didn't come downstairs again. She didn't seem to want any supper, but Nate did and had it, a good one. Galileo, the cat, came yowlin' around, and Nate kicked him under the sofy. Phillips Brooks was howlin' starvation in the woodshed, and Scudder let him howl. If he starved to death Nate wouldn't put no flowers on his grave. Take it altogether, he was havin' a fairly good time.

"And when, later on, he set alone up in his room over the kitchen, he begun to have a better one. Prospects looked good. Maybe old Dixland *would* disown his niece. If he did, Nate figgered he was as healthy a candidate for adoption as anybody.

And Augustus would have to come to terms or stay single. That is, unless him and Olivia got married on nothin' a week, paid yearly. Nate guessed Huldy Ann would think he'd managed pretty well.

"He set there for a long while, thinkin', and then he says he cal'lates he must have dozed off. At any rate, next thing he knew he was settin' up straight in his chair, listenin'. It seemed to him that he'd heard a sound in the kitchen underneath.

"He looked out of the window, and right away he noticed somethin'. 'Twas a beautiful, clear moonlight night, and the high board fence around the buildin's showed black against the white sand. And in that white strip was a ten-foot white gape. Nate had shut that gate afore he went upstairs. Who'd opened it? Then he heard the noise in the kitchen again. Somebody was talkin' down there.

"Nate got up and tiptoed acrost the room. He was in his stockin' feet, so he didn't make a sound. He reached into the corner and took out his old duck gun. It was loaded, both barrels. Nate cocked the gun and crept down the back stairs.

"There was a lamp burnin' low on the kitchen table, and there, in a couple of chairs hauled as close together as they could be, set that Olivia niece and Augustus. They was in a clove hitch again and whisperin' soft and slushy.

"My! but Scudder was b'ilin'! He give one jump and landed in the middle of that kitchen floor.

"'You—you—you!' he yelled, wavin' the shotgun. 'You're back here, are you? You know what I told you I'd do to you? Well, now, I'll do it.'

"The pair of 'em had jumped about as far as Nate had, only the opposite way. Augustus was a paralyzed statue, but Olivia had her senses with her.

"'Run, Augustus!' she screamed. 'He'll shoot you. Run!'

"And then, with a screech like a siren whistle, Augustus commenced to run. Nate was between him and the outside door, so he bolted headfirst into the dining room. And after him went Nate Scudder, so crazy mad he didn't know what he was doin'.

"'Twas pitch dark in the dining room, but through it they went rattlety bang! dishes smashin', chairs upsettin' and 'hurrah, boys!' to pay gen'rally. Then through the best parlor and into the front hall.

"I cal'late Nate would have had him at the foot of the front stairs if it hadn't been for Galileo. That cat had been asleep on the sofy, and the noise and hullabaloo had stirred him up till he was as crazy as the rest of 'em. He run right under Nate's feet and down went Nate sprawlin' and both barrels of the shotgun bust loose like a couple of cannon.

"Galileo took for tall timber, whoopin' anthems. Up them front stairs went Augustus, screechin' shrill, like a woman; he was *sure* Nate meant to murder him now. And after him his uncle went on all fours, swearin' tremendous.

"Then 'twas through one bedroom after another, and each one more crowded with noisy, smashable things than that previous. Nate said he could remember the professor roarin' 'Fire!' and 'Help!' as the two of 'em bumped into his bed, but they didn't stop—they was too busy. The whole length of the house upstairs they traveled, then through the ell, then the woodshed loft, and finally out into the upper story of the barn. And there Nate knew he had him. The ladder was down.

"'Now!' says Nate. 'Now, you long-legged villain, if I don't give you what's comin' to you, then—Oh, there ain't no use in your climbin' out there; you can't get down.'

"The big barn doors was open, and, in the moonlight, Nate could see Gus scramblin' up and around on the flyin' stage where the professor's aeroplane was perched, lookin' like some kind of magnified June bug.

"'Come back, you fool!' Scudder yelled at him. 'Come back and be butchered. You might as well; it's too high for you to drop. You won't? Then I'll come after you.'

"Nate says he never shall forget Augustus's face in the blue light when he see his uncle climbin' out on that stage after him. He was simply desperate—that's it, desperate. And the next thing he did was jump into the saddle of the machine and pull the startin' lever.

"There was the buzz of the electric motor, a slippery, slidin'

sound, one awful hair-raisin' whoop from Augustus, and then—
'F-s-s-s-t!'—down the flyin' stage whizzed that aeroplane and
out through the doors.

"Nate set down on the trestles and waited for the sound of the
smash. I guess he actually felt conscience stricken. Of course,
he'd only done his duty, and yet—

"But no smash came. Instead, there was a long scream from the
kitchen—Olivia's voice that was. And then another yell that for
pure joy beat anything ever heard.

"'It flies!' screamed Professor Ansel Hobart Whiskers Dixland,
from his bedroom window. 'At last! At last! It *flies!*'

"It took Nate some few minutes to paw his way back through
the shed loft and the ell over the things him and Gus knocked
down on the fust lap, until he got to his room where the trouble
had started. Then he went down to the kitchen and outdoor.

"Olivia, a heavenly sort of look on her face, was standin' in the
moonlight, with her hands clasped, lookin' up at the sky.

"'It flies!' says she, in a kind of whisper over and over again.
'Oh! it *flies!*'

"Alongside of her was old Dixland, wrapped in a bedquilt, for-
gettin' all about sprains and lameness; and he likewise was star-
ing at the sky and sayin' over and over:

"'It flies! It really *flies!*'

"And Nate looked up, and there, scootin' around in circles, now
up high and now down low, tippin' this way and tippin' that,
was that aeroplane. And in the stillness you could hear the buzz
of the motor and the yells of Augustus.

"Down flopped Scudder in the sand. 'Great land of love, 'he
says, 'it *flies!*'

"Well, for five minutes or so they watched that thing swoop
and duck and sail up there overhead. And then, slow and easy as
a feather in a May breeze, down she flutters and lands soft on a
hummock a little ways off. And that Augustus—a fool for luck—
staggers out of it safe and sound, and sets down and begins to
cry.

"The fust thing to reach him was Olivia. She grabbed him
around the neck, and you never heard such goin's on as them

two had. Nate come hurryin' up.

"'Here you!' he says, pullin' 'em apart. 'That's enough of this. And you,' he adds to Gus, 'clear right out off this island. I won't make shark bait of you this time, but—'

"And then comes Dixland, hippity-hop over the hummocks. 'My noble boy!' he sings out, fallin' all of a heap onto Augustus's round shoulders. 'My noble boy! My hero!'

"Nate looked on for a full minute with his mouth open. Olivia went away toward the house. The professor and Gus was sheddin' tears like a couple of waterin' pots.

"'Come! come!' says Scudder finally; 'get up, Mr. Dixland; you'll catch cold. Now then, you Tolliver, toddle right along to your boat. Don't you worry, professor, I'll fix him so's he won't come here no more.'

"But the professor turned on him like a flash.

"'How dare you interfere?' says he. 'I forgive him everything. He is a hero. Why, man, he *flew*!'

"Olivia came up behind and touched Nate on the shoulders. 'Don't you think you'd better go, Mr. Scudder?' she purred. 'I've unchained Phillips Brooks.'

"Nate swears he never made better time than he done gettin' to the shore and the boat Augustus had come over in. But that philanthropist dog only missed the supper he'd been waitin' for by about a foot and a half, even as 'twas.

"And that was the end of it, fur's Nate was concerned. Olivia was boss from then on, and Scudder wa'n't allowed to land on his own island. And pretty soon they all went away, flyin' machine and all, and now Gus and Olivia are married."

"Well, by gum!" cried Wingate. "Say, that must have broke Nate's heart completely. All that good money goin' to the poor. Ha! ha!"

"Yes," said Captain Sol, with a broad grin. "Nate told me that every time he realized that Gus's flyin' at all was due to his scarin' him into it, it fairly made him sick of life."

"What did Huldy Ann say? I'll bet the fur flew when *she* heard of it!"

"I guess likely it did. Scudder says her jawin's was the worst of all. Her principal complaint was that he didn't take up with the professor's five-thousand offer and try to fly. 'What if 'twas risky?' she says. 'If anything happened to you the five thousand would have come to your heirs, wouldn't it? But no! you never think of no one but yourself.'"

Mr. Wingate glanced at his watch. "Good land!" he cried, "I didn't realize 'twas so late. I must trot along down and meet Stitt. He and I are goin' to corner the clam market."

"I must be goin', too," said the depot master, rising and moving toward the door, picking up his cap on the way. He threw open the door and exclaimed, "Hello! here's Sim. What you got on your mind, Sim?"

Mr. Phinney looked rather solemn. "I wanted to speak with you a minute, Sol," he began. "Hello! Barzilla, I didn't know you was here."

"I shan't be here but one second longer," replied Mr. Wingate, as he and Phinney shook hands. "I'm late already. Bailey'll think I ain't comin'. Good-by, boys. See you this afternoon, maybe."

"Yes, do," cried Berry, as his guest hurried down to the gate. "I want to hear about those automobiles over your way. You ain't bought one, have you, Barzilla?"

Wingate grinned over his shoulder. "No," he called, "I ain't. But other folks you know have. It's the biggest joke on earth. You and Sim'll want to hear it."

He waved a big hand and walked briskly up the Shore Road. The depot master turned to his friend.

"Well, Sim?" he asked.

"Well, Sol," answered the building mover gravely, "I've just met Mr. Hilton, the minister, and he told me somethin' about Olive Edwards, somethin' I thought you'd want to know. You said for me to find out what she was cal'latin' to do when she had to give up her home and—"

"I know what I said," interrupted the depot master rather sharply. "What did Hilton say?"

"Mr. Hilton told me not to tell," continued Phinney, "and I shan't tell nobody but you, Sol. I know you wont t mention it. The minister says that Olive's hard up as she can be. All she's got in the world is the little furniture and store stuff in her house. The store stuff don't amount to nothin', but the furniture belonged to her pa and ma, and she set a heap by it. Likewise, as everybody knows, she's awful proud and self-respectin'. Anything like charity would kill her. Now out West—in Omaha or somewheres—she's got a cousin who owed her dad money. Old Cap'n Seabury lent this Omaha man two or three thousand dollars and set him up in business. Course, the debt's outlawed, but Olive don't realize that, or, if she did, it wouldn't count with her. She couldn't understand how law would have any effect on payin' money you honestly owe. She's written to the Omaha cousin, tellin' him what a scrape she's in and askin' him to please, if convenient, let her have a thousand or so on account. She figgers if she gets that, she can go to Bayport or Orham or somewheres and open another notion store."

Captain Berry lit a cigar. "Hum!" he said, after a minute. "You say she's written to this chap. Has she got an answer yet?"

"No, not any definite one. She heard from the man's wife sayin' that her husband—the cousin—had gone on a fishin' trip somewheres up in Canady and wouldn't be back afore the eighth of next month. Soon's he does come he'll write her. But Mr. Hilton thinks, and so do I—havin' heard a few things about this cousin—that it's mighty doubtful if he sends any money."

"Yes, I shouldn't wonder. Where's Olive goin' to stay while she's waitin' to hear?"

"In her own house. Mr. Hilton went to Williams and pleaded with him, and he finally agreed to let her stay there until the 'Colonial' is moved onto the lot. Then the Edwardses house'll be tore down and Olive'll have to go, of course."

The depot master puffed thoughtfully at his cigar.

"She won't hear before the tenth, at the earliest," he said. "And if Williams begins to move his 'Colonial' at once, he'll get it to her lot by the seventh, sure. Have you given him your figures for the job?"

"Handed 'em in this very mornin'. One of his high-and-mighty servants, all brass buttons and braid, like a feller playin' in the band, took my letter and condescended to say he'd pass it on to

Williams. I'd liked to have kicked the critter, just to see if he *could* unbend; but I jedged 'twouldn't be good business."

"Probably not. If the 'Colonial' gets to Olive's lot afore she hears from the Omaha man, what then?"

"Well, that's the worst of it. The minister don't know what she'll do. There's plenty of places where she'd be more'n welcome to visit a spell, but she's too proud to accept. Mr. Hilton's afraid she'll start for Boston to hunt up a job, or somethin'. You know how much chance she stands of gettin' a job that's wuth anything."

Phinney paused, anxiously awaiting his companion's reply. When it came it was very unsatisfactory.

"I'm goin' to the depot," said the Captain, brusquely. "So long, Sim."

He slammed the door of the house behind him, strode to the gate, flung it open, and marched on. Simeon gazed in astonishment, then hurried to overtake him. Ranging alongside, he endeavored to reopen the conversation, but to no purpose. The depot master would not talk. They turned into Cross Street.

"Well!" exclaimed Mr. Phinney, panting from his unaccustomed hurry, "what be we, runnin' a race? Why! ... Oh, how d'ye do, Mr. Williams, sir? Want to see me, do you?"

The magnate of East Harniss stepped forward.

"Er—Phinney," he said, "I want a moment of your time. Morning, Berry."

"Mornin', Williams," observed Captain Sol brusquely. "All right, Sim. I'll wait for you farther on."

He continued his walk. The building mover stood still. Mr. Williams frowned with lofty indignation.

"Phinney," he said, "I've just looked over those figures of yours, your bid for moving my new house. The price is ridiculous."

Simeon attempted a pleasantry. "Yes," he answered, "I thought 'twas ridic'lous myself; but I needed the money, so I thought I could afford to be funny."

The Williams frown deepened.

"I didn't mean ridiculously low," he snapped; "I meant ridiculously high. I'd rather help out you town fellows if I can, but you can't work me for a good thing. I've written to Colt and Adams, of Boston, and accepted their offer. You had your chance and didn't see fit to take it. That's all. I'm sorry."

Simeon was angry; also a trifle skeptical.

"Mr. Williams," he demanded, "do you mean to tell me that *them* people have agreed to move you cheaper'n I can?"

"Their price—their actual price may be no lower; but considering their up-to-date outfit and—er—progressive methods, they're cheaper. Yes. Morning, Phinney."

He turned on his heel and walked off. Mr. Phinney, crestfallen and angrier than ever, moved on to where the depot master stood waiting for him. Captain Sol smiled grimly.

"You don't look merry as a Christmas tree, Sim," he observed. "What did his Majesty have to say to you?"

Simeon related the talk with Williams. The depot master's grim smile grew broader.

"Sim," he asked, with quiet sarcasm, "don't you realize that progressive methods are necessary in movin' a house?"

Phinney tried to smile in return, but the attempt was a failure.

"Yes," went on the Captain. "Well, if you can't take the Grand Panjandrum home, you can set on the fence and see him go by. That ought to be honor enough, hadn't it? However, I may need some of your ridiculous figgers on a movin' job of my own, pretty soon. Don't be *too* comical, will you?"

"What do you mean by that, Sol Berry?"

"I mean that I may decide to move my own house."

"Move your *own* house? Where to, for mercy sakes?"

"To that lot on Main Street that belongs to Abner Payne. Abner has wanted to buy my lot here on the Shore Road for a long time. He knows it'll make a fine site for some rich bigbug's summer 'cottage.' He would have bought the house, too, but I think too much of that to sell it. Now Abner's come back with another offer. He'll swap my lot for the Main Street one, pay my movin' expenses and a fair 'boot' besides. He don't really care for my *house*, you understand; it's my *land* he's after."

"Are you goin' to take it up?"

"I don't know. The Main Street lot's a good one, and my

house'll look good on it. And I'll make money by the deal."

"Yes, but you've always swore by that saltwater view of yours. Told me yourself you never wanted to live anywheres else."

Captain Sol took the cigar from his lips, looked at it, then threw it violently into the gutter.

"What difference does it make where I live?" he snarled. "Who in blazes cares where I live or whether I live at all?"

"Sol Berry, what on airth—"

"Shut up! Let me alone, Sim! I ain't fit company for anybody just now. Clear out, there's a good feller."

The next moment he was striding down the hill. Mr. Phinney drew a long breath, scratched his head and shook it solemnly. *What* did it all mean?

Chapter VIII
The Obligations
of a Gentleman

THE METHODS OF Messrs. Colt and Adams, the Boston firm of building movers, were certainly progressive, if promptness in getting to work is any criterion. Two days after the acceptance of their terms by Mr. Williams, a freight car full of apparatus arrived at East Harniss. Then came a foreman and a gang of laborers. Horses were hired, and within a week the "pure Colonial" was off its foundations and on its way to the Edwards lot. The moving was no light task. The big house must be brought along the Shore Road to the junction with the Hill Boulevard, then swung into that aristocratic highway and carried up the long slope, around the wide curve, to its destination.

Mr. Phinney, though he hated the whole operation, those having it in charge, and the mighty Williams especially, could not resist stealing down to see how his successful rivals were progressing with the work he had hoped to do. It caused him much chagrin to see that they were getting on so very well. One morning, after breakfast, as he stood at the corner of the Boulevard and the Shore Road, he found himself engaged in a mental calculation.

Three days more and they would swing into the Boulevard; four or five days after that and they would be abreast the Edwards lot. Another day and ... Poor Olive! She would be homeless. Where would she go? It was too early for a reply from the Omaha cousin, but Simeon, having questioned the minister, had little hope that that reply would be favorable. Still it was a chance, and if the money *should* come before the "pure Colonial" reached the Edwards lot, then the widow would at least not be driven penniless from her home. She would have to leave that home in any event, but she could carry out her project of opening another shop in one of the neighboring towns. Otherwise ... Mr. Phinney swore aloud.

"Humph!" said a voice behind him. "I agree with you, though I don't know what it's all about. I ain't heard anything better put for a long while."

Simeon spun around, as he said afterwards, "like a young one's pinwheel." At his elbow stood Captain Berry, the depot master, hands in pockets, cigar in mouth, the personification of calmness and imperturbability. He had come out of his house, which stood close to the corner, and walked over to join his friend.

"Land of love!" exclaimed Simeon. "Why don't you scare a fellow to death, tiptoein' around? I never see such a cat-foot critter!"

Captain Sol smiled. "Jumpin' it, ain't they?" he said, nodding toward the "Colonial." "Be there by the tenth, won't it?"

"Tenth!" Mr. Phinney sniffed disgust. "It'll be there by the sixth, or I miss my guess."

"Yup. Say, Sim, how soon could you land that shanty of mine in the road if I give you the job to move it?"

"I couldn't get it up to the Main Street lot inside of a fortnight," replied Sim, after a moment's reflection. "Fur's gettin' it in the road goes, I could have it here day after to-morrow if I had gang enough."

The depot master took the cigar out of his mouth and blew a ring of smoke. "All right," he drawled, "get gang enough."

Phinney jumped. "You mean you've decided to take up with Payne's offer and swap your lot for his?" he gasped. "Why, only two or three days ago you said—"

"Ya-as. That was two or three days ago, and I've been watchin' the 'Colonial' since. I cal'late the movin' habit's catchin'. You have your gang here by noon to-day."

"Sol Berry, are you crazy? You ain't seen Abner Payne; he's out of town—"

"Don't have to see him. He's made me an offer and I'll write and accept it."

"But you've got to have a selectmen's permit to move—"

"Got it. I went up and saw the chairman an hour ago. He's a friend of mine. I nominated him town-meetin' day."

"But," stammered Phinney, very much upset by the suddenness of it all, "you ain't got my price nor—"

"Drat your price! Give it when I ask it. See here, Sim, are you goin' to have my house in the middle of the road by day after tomorrer? Or was that just talk?"

"'Twa'n't talk. I can have it there, but—"

"All right," said Captain Sol coolly, "then have it."

Hands in pockets, he strolled away. Simeon sat down on a rock by the roadside and whistled.

However, whistling was a luxurious and time-wasting method of expressing amazement, and Mr. Phinney could not afford luxuries just then. For the rest of that day he was a busy man. As Bailey Stitt expressed it, he "flew round like a sand flea in a mitten," hiring laborers, engaging masons, and getting his materials ready. That very afternoon the masons began tearing down the chimneys of the little Berry house. Before the close of the following day it was on the rollers. By two of the day after that it was in the middle of the Shore Road, just when its mover had declared it should be. They were moving it, furniture and all, and Captain Sol was, as he said, going to "stay right aboard all the voyage." No cooking could be done, of course, but the Captain arranged to eat at Mrs. Higgins's hospitable table during the transit. His sudden freak was furnishing material for gossip throughout the village, but he did not care. Gossip concerning his actions was the last thing in the world to trouble Captain Sol Berry.

The Williams's "Colonial" was moving toward the corner at a rapid rate, and the foreman of the Boston moving firm walked over to see Mr. Phinney.

"Say," he observed to Simeon, who, the perspiration streaming down his face, was resting for a moment before recommencing his labor of arranging rollers; "say," observed the foreman, "we'll be ready to turn into the Boulevard by tomorrer night and you're blockin' the way."

"That's all right," said Simeon, "we'll be past the Boulevard corner by that time."

He thought he was speaking the truth, but next morning, before work began, Captain Berry appeared. He had had breakfast and strolled around to the scene of operations.

"Well," asked Phinney, "how'd it seem to sleep on wheels?"

"Tiptop," replied the depot master. "Like it fust rate. S'pose my next berth will be somewheres up there, won't it?"

He was pointing around the corner instead of straight ahead. Simeon gaped, his mouth open.

"Up *there?*" he cried. "Why, of course not. That's the Boulevard. We're goin' along the Shore Road."

"That so? I guess not. We're goin' by the Boulevard. Can go that way, can't we?"

"Can?" repeated Simeon aghast. "Course we *can!* But it's like boxin' the whole compass backward to get ha'f a p'int east of no'th. It's way round Robin Hood's barn. It'll take twice as long and cost—"

"That's good," interrupted the Captain. "I like to travel, and I'm willin' to pay for it. Think of the view I'll get on the way."

"But your permit from the selectmen—" began Phinney. Berry held up his hand.

"My permit never said nothin' about the course to take," he answered, his eye twinkling just a little. "There, Sim, you're wastin' time. I move by the Hill Boulevard."

And into the Boulevard swung the Berry house. The Colt and Adams foreman was an angry man when he saw the beams laid in that direction. He rushed over and asked profane and pointed questions.

"Thought you said you was goin' straight ahead?" he demanded.

"Thought I was," replied Simeon, "but, you see, I'm only navigator of this craft, not owner."

"Where is the blankety blank?" asked the foreman.

"If you're referrin' to Cap'n Berry, I cal'late you'll find him at the depot," answered Phinney. To the depot went the foreman.

Receiving little satisfaction there, he hurried to the home of his employer, Mr. Williams. The magnate, red-faced and angry, returned with him to the station. Captain Sol received them blandly. Issy, who heard the interview which followed, declared that the depot master was so cool that "an iceberg was a bonfire 'longside of him." Issy's description of this interview, given to a dozen townspeople within the next three hours, was as follows:

"Mr. Williams," said the wide-eyed Issy, "he comes postin' into the waitin' room, his foreman with him. Williams marches over to Cap'n Sol andhe says, 'Berry, 'he says, 'are you responsible for the way that house of yours is moved?'

"Cap'n Sol bowed and smiled. 'Yes,' says he, sweet as a fresh scallop.

"'You're movin' it to Main Street, aren't you? I so understood.'

"'You understood correct. That's where she's bound.'

"'Then what do you mean by turning out of your road and into mine?'

"'Oh, I don't own any road. Have you bought the Boulevard? The selectmen ought to have told us that. I s'posed it was town thoroughfare.'

"Mr. Williams colored up a little. 'I didn't mean my road in that sense, 'he says. 'But the direct way to Main Street is along the shore, and everybody knows it. Now why do you turn from that into the Boulevard?'

"Cap'n Sol took a cigar from his pocket. 'Have one?' says he, passin' it toward Mr. Williams. 'No? Too soon after breakfast, I s'pose. Why do I turn off?' he goes on. 'Well, I'll tell you. I'm goin' to stay right aboard my shack while it's movin', and it's so much pleasanter a ride up the hill that I thought I'd go that way. I always envied them who could afford a house on the Boulevard, and now I've got the chance to have one there—for a spell. I'm sartin I shall enjoy it.'

"The foreman growled, disgusted. Mr. Williams got redder yet.

"'Don't you understand?' he snorts. 'You're blockin' the way of the house I'M movin'. I have capable men with adequate apparatus to move it, and they would be able to go twice as fast as your one-horse country outfit. You're blockin' the road. Now they must follow you. It's an outrage!'

"Cap'n Sol smiled once more. 'Too bad,' says he. 'It's a pity such a nice street ain't wider. If it was my street in my town—I b'lieve that's what you call East Harniss, ain't it?—seems to me I'd widen it.'

"The boss of 'my town' ground his heel into the sand. 'Berry,' he snaps, 'are you goin' to move that house over the Boulevard ahead of mine?'

"The Cap'n looked him square in the eye. 'Williams,' says he, 'I am.'

"The millionaire turned short and started to go.

"'You'll pay for it,' he snarls, his temper gettin' free at last.

"'I cal'late to,' purrs the Cap'n. 'I gen'rally do pay for what I want, and a fair price, at that. I never bought in cheap mortgages and held 'em for clubs over poor folks, never in my life. Good mornin'.'

"And right to Mr. Williams's own face, too," concluded Issy. "*What* do you think of that?"

Here was defiance of authority and dignity, a sensation which should have racked East Harniss from end to end. But most of the men in the village, the tradespeople particularly, had another matter on their minds, namely, Major Cuthbertson Scott Hardee, of "Silverleaf Hall." The Major and his debts were causing serious worriment.

The creditors of the Major met, according to agreement, on the Monday evening following their previous gathering at the club. Obed Gott, one of the first to arrive, greeted his fellow members with an air of gloomy triumph and a sort of condescending pity.

Higgins, the "general store" keeper, acting as self-appointed chairman, asked if anyone had anything to report. For himself, he had seen the Major and asked point-blank for payment of his bill. The Major had been very polite and was apparently much concerned that his fellow townsmen should have been inconvenienced by any neglect of his. He would write to his attorneys at once, so he said.

"He said a whole lot more, too," added Higgins. "Said he had never been better served than by the folks in this town, and that I kept a fine store, and so on and so forth. But I haven't got any money yet. Anybody else had any better luck?"

No one had, although several had had similar interviews with the master of "Silverleaf Hall."

"Obed looks as if he knew somethin'," remarked Weeks. "What is it, Obed?"

Mr. Gott scornfully waved his hand.

"You fellers make me laugh," he said. "You talk and talk, but you don't do nothin'. I b'lieve in doin', myself. When I went home t'other night, thinks I: 'There's one man that might know somethin' 'bout old Hardee, and that's Godfrey, the hotel man.' So I wrote to Godfrey up to Boston and I got a letter from him. Here 'tis."

He read the letter aloud. Mr. Godfrey wrote that he knew nothing about Major Hardee further than that he had been able to get nothing from him in payment for his board.

"So I seized his trunk," the letter concluded. "There was nothing in it worth mentioning, but I took it on principle. The Major told me a lot about writing to his attorneys for money, but I didn't pay much attention to that. I'm afraid he's an old fraud, but I can't help liking him, and if I had kept on running my hotel I guess he would have got away scot-free."

"There!" exclaimed the triumphant Obed, with a sneer, "I guess that settles it, don't it? Maybe you'd be willin' to turn your bills over to Squire Baker now."

But they were not willing. Higgins argued, and justly, that although the Major was in all probability a fraud, not even a lawyer could get water out of a stone, and that when a man had nothing, suing him was a waste of time and cash.

"Besides," he said, "there's just a chance that he may have attorneys and property somewheres else. Let's write him a letter and every one of us sign it, tellin' him that we'll call on him Tuesday night expectin' to be paid in full. If we call and don't get any satisfaction, why, we ain't any worse off, and then we can— well, run him out of town, if nothin' more."

So the letter was written and signed by every man there. It

was a long list of signatures and an alarming total of indebtedness. The letter was posted that night.

The days that followed seemed long to Obed. He was ill-natured at home and ugly at the shop, and Polena declared that he was "gettin' so a body couldn't live with him." Her own spirits were remarkably high, and Obed noticed that, as the days went by, she seemed to be unusually excited. On Thursday she announced that she was going to Orham to visit her niece, one Sarah Emma Cahoon, and wouldn't be back right off. He knew better than to object, and so she went.

That evening each of the signers of the letter to Major Hardee received a courteous note saying that the Major would be pleased to receive the gentlemen at the Hall. Nothing was said about payment.

So, after some discussion, the creditors marched in procession across the fields and up to "Silverleaf Hall."

"Hardee's been to Orham to-day," whispered the keeper of the livery stable, as they entered the yard. "He drove over this mornin' and come back to-night."

"*Drove* over!" exclaimed Obed, halting in his tracks. "He did? Where'd he get the team? I'll bet five dollars you was soft enough to let him have it, and never said a word. Well, if you ain't—By jimmy! you wait till I get at him! I'll show you that he can't soft soap me."

Augustus met them at the door and ushered them into the old-fashioned parlor. The Major, calm, cool, and imperturbably polite, was waiting to receive them. He made some observation concerning the weather.

"The day's fine enough," interrupted Obed, pushing to the front, "but that ain't what we come here to talk about. Are you goin' to pay us what you owe? That's what we want to know."

The "gentleman of the old school" did not answer immediately. Instead he turned to the solemn servant at his elbow.

"Augustus," he said, "you may make ready." Then, looking serenely at the irate Mr. Gott, whose clenched fist rested under the center table, which he had thumped to emphasize his demands, the Major asked:

"I beg your pardon, my dear sir, but what is the total of my indebtedness to you?"

"Nineteen dollars and twenty-eight cents, and I want you to understand that—"

Major Hardee held up a slim, white hand.

"One moment, if you please," he said. "Now, Augustus."

Augustus opened the desk in the corner and produced an imposing stack of bank notes. Then he brought forth neat piles of halves, quarters, dimes, and pennies, and arranged the whole upon the table. Obed's mouth and those of his companions gaped in amazement.

"Have you your bill with you, Mr. Gott?" inquired the Major.

Dazedly Mr. Gott produced the required document.

"Thank you. Augustus, nineteen twenty-eight to this gentleman. Kindly receipt the bill, Mr. Gott, if you please. A mere formality, of course, but it is well to be exact. Thank you, sir. And now, Mr. Higgins."

One by one the creditors shamefacedly stepped forward, received the amount due, receipted the bill, and stepped back again. Mr. Peters, the photographer, was the last to sign.

"Gentlemen," said the Major, "I am sorry that my carelessness in financial matters should have caused you this trouble, but now that you are here, a representative gathering of East Harniss's men of affairs, upon this night of all nights, it seems fitting that I should ask for your congratulations. Augustus."

The wooden-faced Augustus retired to the next room and reappeared carrying a tray upon which were a decanter and glasses.

"Gentlemen," continued the Major, "I have often testified to my admiration and regard for your—perhaps I may now say *our*—charming village. This admiration and regard has extended to the fair daughters of the township. It may be that some of you have conscientious scruples against the use of intoxicants. These scruples I respect, but I am sure that none of you will refuse to at least taste a glass of wine with me when I tell you that I have this day taken one of the fairest to love and cherish during life."

He stepped to the door of the dining room, opened it, and said quietly, "My dear, will you honor us with your presence?"

There was a rustle of black silk and there came through the doorway the stately form of her who had been Mrs. Polena Ginn.

"Gentlemen," said the Major, "permit me to present to you my wife, the new mistress of 'Silverleaf Hall.'"

The faces of the ex-creditors were pictures of astonishment. Mr. Gott's expressive countenance turned white, then red, and then settled to a mottled shade, almost as if he had the measles. Polena rushed to his side.

"O Obed!" she exclaimed. "I know we'd ought to have told you, but 'twas only Tuesday the Major asked me, and we thought we'd keep it a secret so's to s'prise you. Mr. Langworthy over to Orham married us, and—"

"My dear," her husband blandly interrupted, "we will not intrude our private affairs upon the patience of these good friends. And now, gentlemen, let me propose a toast: To the health and happiness of the mistress of 'Silverleaf Hall'! Brother Obed, I—"

The outside door closed with a slam; "Brother Obed" had fled.

A little later, when the rest of the former creditors of the Major came out into the moonlight, they found their companion standing by the gate gazing stonily into vacancy. "Hen" Leadbetter, who, with Higgins, brought up the rear of the procession, said reflectively:

"When he fust fetched out that stack of money I couldn't scarcely b'lieve my eyes. I begun to think that we fellers had put our foot in it for sartin, and had lost a mighty good customer; but, of course, it's all plain enough *now*."

"Yes," remarked Weeks with a nod; "I allers heard that P'lena kept a mighty good balance in the bank."

"It looks to me," said Higgins slyly, "as if we owed Obed here a vote of thanks. How 'bout that, Obed?"

And then Major Hardee's new brother-in-law awoke with a jump.

"Aw, you go to grass!" he snarled, and tramped savagely off down the hill.

Chapter IX
The Widow Bassett

THESE DEVELOPMENTS, MAJOR Hardee's marriage and Mr. Gott's discomfiture, overshadowed, for the time, local interest in the depot master's house moving. This was, in its way, rather fortunate, for those who took the trouble to walk down to the lower end of the Boulevard were astonished to see how very slowly the moving was progressing.

"Only one horse, Sim?" asked Captain Hiram Baker. "Only one! Why, it'll take you forever to get through, won't it?"

"I'm afraid it'll take quite a spell," admitted Mr. Phinney.

"Where's your other one, the white one?"

"The white horse," said Simeon slowly, "ain't feelin' just right and I've had to lay him off."

"Humph! that's too bad. How does Sol act about it? He's such a hustler, I should think—"

"Sol," interrupted Sim, "ain't unreasonable. He understands."

He chuckled inwardly as he said it. Captain Sol did understand. Also Mr. Phinney himself was beginning to understand a little.

The very day on which Williams and his foreman had called on the depot master and been dismissed so unceremoniously, that official paid a short visit to his mover.

"Sim," he said, the twinkle still in his eye, "his Majesty, Williams the Conqueror, was in to see me just now and acted real peevish. He was pretty disrespectful to you, too. Called your outfit 'one horse.' That's a mistake, because you've got two horses at work right now. It seems a shame to make a great man like that lie. Hadn't you better lay off one of them horses?"

"Lay one *off*?" exclaimed Simeon. "What for? Why, we'll be slow enough, as 'tis. With only one horse we wouldn't get through for I don't know how long."

"That's so," murmured the Captain. "I s'pose with one horse you'd hardly reach the middle of the Boulevard by—well, before the tenth of the month. Hey?"

The tenth of the month! The *tenth*! Why, it was on the tenth that that Omaha cousin of Olive Edwards was to—Mr. Phinney began to see—to see and to grin, slow but expansive.

"Hm-m-m!" he mused.

"Yes," observed Captain Sol. "That white horse of yours looks sort of ailin' to me, Sim. I think he needs a rest."

And, sure enough, next day the white horse was pronounced unfit and taken back to the stable. The depot master's dwelling moved, but that is all one could say truthfully concerning its progress.

At the depot the Captain was quieter than usual. He joked with his assistant less than had been his custom, and for the omission Issy was duly grateful. Sometimes Captain Sol would sit for minutes without speaking. He seemed to be thinking and to be pondering some grave problem. When his friends, Mr. Wingate, Captain Stitt, Hiram Baker, and the rest, dropped in on him he cheered up and was as conversational as ever. After they had gone he relapsed into his former quiet mood.

"He acts sort of blue, to me," declared Issy, speaking from the depths of sensational-novel knowledge. "If he was a younger man I'd say he was most likely in love. Ah, hum! I s'pose bein' in love does get a feller mournful, don't it?"

Issy made this declaration to his mother only. He knew better than to mention sentiment to male acquaintances. The latter were altogether too likely to ask embarrassing questions.

Mr. Wingate and Captain Stitt were still in town, although their stay was drawing to a close. One afternoon they entered the station together. Captain Sol seemed glad to see them.

"Set down, fellers," he ordered. "I swan I'm glad to see you. I ain't fit company for myself these days."

"Ain't Betsy Higgins feedin' you up to the mark?" asked Stitt. "Or is house movin' gettin' on your vitals?"

"No," growled the depot master, "grub's all right and so's

movin', I cal'late. I'm glad you fellers come in. What's the news to Orham, Barzilla? How's the Old Home House boarders standin' it? Hear from Jonadab regular, do you?"

Mr. Wingate laughed. "Nothin' much," he said. "Jonadab's too busy to write these days. Bein' a sport interferes with letter writing consider'ble."

"Sport!" exclaimed Captain Bailey. "Land of Goshen! Cap'n Jonadab is the last one I'd call a sport."

"That's 'cause you ain't a good judge of human nature, Bailey," chuckled Barzilla. "When ancient plants like Jonadab Wixon *do* bloom, they're gay old blossoms, I tell you!"

"What do you mean?" asked the depot master.

"I mean that Jonadab's been givin' me heart disease, that's what; givin' it to me in a good many diff'rent ways, too. We opened the Old Home House the middle of April this year, because Peter T. Brown thought we might catch some spring trade. We did catch a little, though whether it paid to open up so early's a question. But 'twas June 'fore Jonadab got his disease so awful bad. However, most any time in the last part of May the reg'lar programme of the male boarders was stirrin' him up.

"Take it of a dull day, for instance. Sky overcast and the wind aidgin' round to the sou'east, so's you couldn't tell whether 'twould rain or fair off; too cold to go off to the ledge cod fishin' and too hot for billiards or bowlin'; a bunch of the younger women folks at one end of the piazza playin' bridge; half a dozen men, includin' me and Cap'n Jonadab, smokin' and tryin' to keep awake at t'other end; amidships a gang of females—all 'fresh air fiends'—and mainly widows or discards in the matrimony deal, doin' fancywork and gossip. That would be about the usual layout.

"Conversation got to you in homeopath doses, somethin' like this:

"'Did you say "Spades"? *Well*! if I'd known you were going to make us lose our deal like that, I'd never have bridged it—not with *this* hand.'

"'Oh, Miss Gabble, have you heard what people are sayin' about—' The rest of it whispers.

"'A—oo—*ow*! By George, Bill! this is dead enough, isn't it? Shall we match for the cigars or are you too lazy?'

"Then, from away off in the stillness would come a drawn-out 'Honk! honk!' like a wild goose with the asthma, and pretty soon up the road would come sailin' a big red automobile, loaded to the guards with goggles and grandeur, and whiz past the hotel in a hurricane of dust and smell. Then all hands would set up and look interested, and Bill would wink acrost at his chum and drawl:

"'That's the way to get over the country! Why, a horse isn't one—two—three with that! Cap'n Wixon, I'm surprised that a sportin' man like you hasn't bought one of those things long afore this.'

"For the next twenty minutes there wouldn't be any dullness. Jonadab would take care of that. He'd have the floor and be givin' his opinions of autos and them that owned and run 'em. And between the drops of his language shower you'd see them boarders nudgin' each other and rockin' back and forth contented and joyful.

"It always worked. No matter what time of day or night, all you had to say was 'auto' and Cap'n Jonadab would sail up out of his chair like one of them hot-air balloons the youngsters nowadays have on Fourth of July. And he wouldn't come down till he was empty of remarks, nuther. You never see a man get so red faced and eloquent.

"It wa'n't because he couldn't afford one himself. I know that's the usual reason for them kind of ascensions, but 'Twa'n't his. No, sir! the summer hotel business has put a considerable number of dollars in Jonadab's hands, and the said hands are like a patent rat trap, a mighty sight easier to get into than out of. He could have bought three automobiles if he'd wanted to, but he didn't want to. And the reason he didn't was named Tobias Loveland and lived over to Orham."

"I know Tobias," interrupted Captain Bailey Stitt.

"Course you do," continued Barzilla. "So does Sol, I guess. Well, anyhow, Tobias and Cap'n Jonadab never did hitch. When they was boys together at school they was always rowin' and fightin', and when they grew up to be thirty and courted the same girl—ten years younger than either of 'em, she was—twa'n't much better. Neither of 'em got her, as a matter of fact; she married a tin peddler named Bassett over to Hyannis. But both cal'lated they would have won if t'other hadn't been in the race, and consequently they loved each other with a love that passed understandin'. Tobias had got well to do in the cranberry-raisin' line and drove a fast horse. Jonadab, durin' the last prosperous year or two, had bought what he thought was some horse, likewise. They met on the road one day last spring and trotted alongside one another for a mile. At the end of that mile Jonadab's craft's jib boom was just astern of Tobias's rudder. Inside of that week the Cap'n had swapped his horse for one with a two-thirty record, and the next time they met Tobias was left with a beautiful, but dusty, view of Jonadab's back hair. So *he* bought a new horse. And that was the beginnin'.

"It went along that way for twelve months. Fust one feller's nag would come home freighted with perspiration and glory, and then t'other's. One week Jonadab would be so bloated with horse pride that he couldn't find room for his vittles, and the next he'd be out in the stable growlin' 'cause it cost so much for hay to stuff an old hide rack that wa'n't fit to put in a museum. At last it got so that neither one could find a better horse on the Cape, and the two they had was practically an even match. I begun to have hopes that the foolishness was over. And then the tin peddler's widow drifts in to upset the whole calabash.

"She made port at Orham fust, this Henrietta Bassett did, and the style she slung killed every female Goliath in the Orham sewin' circle dead. Seems her husband that was had been an inventor, as a sort of side line to peddlin' tinware, and all to once he invented somethin' that worked. He made money—nobody knew how much, though all hands had a guess—and pretty soon afterwards he made a will and Henrietta a widow. She'd been livin' in New York, so she said, and had come back to revisit the scenes of her childhood. She was a mighty well-preserved woman—artificial preservatives, I cal'late, like some kinds of tomatter ketchup—and her comin' stirred Orham way down to the burnt places on the bottom of the kettle."

"I guess I remember *her*, too," put in Captain Bailey.

"Say!" queried Mr. Wingate snappishly, "do you want to tell about her? If you do, why—"

"Belay, both of you!" ordered the depot master. "Heave ahead, Barzilla."

"The news of her got over to Wellmouth, and me and Jonadab heard of it. He was some subject to widows—most widower men are, I guess—but he didn't develop no alarmin' symptoms in this case and never even hinted that he'd like to see his old girl. Fact is, his newest horse trade had showed that it was afraid of automobiles, and he was beginnin' to get rabid along that line. Then come that afternoon when him and me was out drivin' together, and we—Well, I'll have to tell you about that.

"We was over on the long stretch of wood road between Trumet and Denboro, nice hard macadam, the mare—her name was Celia, but Jonadab had re-christened her Bay Queen after a boat he used to own—skimmin' along at a smooth, easy gait, when, lo and behold you! we rounds a turn and there ahead of us is a light, rubber-tired wagon with a man and woman on the seat of it. I heard Jonadab give a kind of snort.

"'What's the matter?' says I.

"'Nothin',' says he, between his teeth. 'Only, if I ain't some mistaken, that's Tobe Loveland's rig. Wonder if he's got his spunk with him? The Queen's feelin' her oats to-day, and I cal'late I can show him a few things.'

"'Rubbish!' says I, disgusted. 'Don't be foolish, Jonadab. I don't know nothin' about his spunk, but I do know there's a woman with him. 'Tain't likely he'll want to race you when he's got a passenger aboard.'

"'Oh, I don't know!' says he. 'I've got you, Barzilla; so 'twill be two and two. Let's heave alongside and see.'

"So he clucked to the Queen, and in a jiffy we was astern of t'other rig. Loveland looked back over his shoulder.

"'Ugh!' he grunts, 'bout as cordial as a plate of ice cream. ''Lo, Wixon, that you?'

"'Um-hm,' begins Jonadab. 'How's that crowbait of yours to-day, Tobe? Got any go in him? 'Cause if he has, I—'

"He stopped short. The woman in Loveland's carriage had turned her head and was starin' hard.

"'Why!' she gasps. 'I do believe—Why, Jonadab!'

"'*Hettie!*' says the Cap'n.

"Well, after that 'twas pull up, of course, and shake hands and talk. The widow, she done most of the talkin'. She was *so* glad to see him. How had he been all these years? She knew him instantly. He hadn't changed a mite—that is, not so *very* much. She was plannin' to come over to the Old Home House and stay a spell later on; but now she was havin' *such* a good time in Orham, Tobias—Mr. Loveland—was makin' it *so* pleasant for her. She did enjoy drivin' so much, and Mr. Loveland had the fastest horse in the county—did we know that?

"Tobias and Jonadab glowered back and forth while all this gush was bein' turned loose, and hardly spoke to one another. But when 'twas over and we was ready to start again, the Cap'n says, says he:

"'I'll be mighty glad to see you over to the hotel, when you're ready to come, Hettie. I can take you ridin', too. Fur's horse goes, I've got a pretty good one myself.'

"'Oh!' squeals the widow. 'Really? Is that him? It's awful pretty, and he looks fast.'

"'She is,' says Jonadab. 'There's nothin' round here can beat her.'

"'Humph!' says Loveland. 'Git dap!'

"'Git dap!' says Jonadab, agreein' with him for once.

"Tobias started, and we started. Tobias makes his horse go a little faster, and Jonadab speeded up some likewise. I see how 'twas goin' to be, and therefore I wa'n't surprised to death when the next ten minutes found us sizzlin' down that road, neck and neck with Loveland, dust flyin', hoofs poundin', and the two drivers leanin' way for'ard over the dash, reins gripped and teeth sot. For a little ways 'twas an even thing, and then we commenced to pull ahead a little.

"'Loveland,' yells Jonadab, out of the port corner of his mouth, 'if I ain't showin' you my tailboard by the time we pass the fust house in Denboro, I'll eat my Sunday hat.'

"I cal'late he would 'a' beat, too. We was drawin' ahead all the time and had a three-quarter length lead when we swung clear of the woods and sighted Denboro village, quarter of a mile away. And up the road comes flyin' a big auto, goin' to beat the cars.

"Let's forget the next few minutes; they wa'n't pleasant ones for me. Soon's the Bay Queen sot eyes on that auto, she stopped trottin' and commenced to hop; from hoppin' she changed to waltzin' and high jumpin'. When the smoke had cleared, the auto was out of sight and we was in the bushes alongside the road, with the Queen just gettin' ready to climb a tree. As for Tobias and Henrietta, they was roundin' the turn by the fust house in Denboro, wavin' by-bys to us over the back of the seat.

"We went home then; and every foot of the way Cap'n Jonadab called an automobile a new kind of name, and none complimentary. The boarders, they got wind of what had happened and begun to rag him, and the more they ragged, the madder he got and the more down on autos.

"And, to put a head on the whole business, I'm blessed if Tobias Loveland didn't get in with an automobile agent who was stoppin' in Orham and buy a fifteen-hundred-dollar machine off him. And the very next time Jonadab was out with the Queen on the Denboro road, Tobias and the widow whizzed past him in that car so fast he might as well have been hove to. And, by way of rubbin' it in, they come along back pretty soon and rolled alongside of him easy, while Henrietta gushed about Mr. Loveland's beautiful car and how nice it was to be able to go just as swift as you wanted to. Jonadab couldn't answer back, nuther, bein' too busy keepin' the Queen from turnin' herself into a flyin' machine.

"'Twas then that he got himself swore in special constable to arrest auto drivers for overspeedin'; and for days he wandered round layin' for a chance to haul up Tobias and get him fined. He'd have had plenty of game if he'd been satisfied with strangers, but he didn't want them anyhow, and, besides, most of 'em was on their way to spend money at the Old Home House.

'Twould have been poor business to let any of *that* cash go for fines, and he realized it.

"'Twas in early June, only a few weeks ago, that the widow come to our hotel. I never thought she meant it when she said she was comin', and so I didn't expect her. Fact is, I was expectin' to hear that she and Tobe Loveland was married or engaged. But there was a slip up somewheres, for all to once the depot wagon brings her to the Old Home House, she hires a room, and settles down to stay till the season closed, which would be in about a fortn't.

"From the very fust she played her cards for Jonadab. He meant to be middlin' average frosty to her, I imagine—her bein' so thick with Tobias prejudiced him, I presume likely. But land sakes! she thawed him out like hot toddy thaws out some folks' tongues. She never took no notice of his coldness, but smiled and gushed and flattered, and looked her prettiest—which was more'n average, considerin' her age—and by the end of the third day he was hangin' round her like a cat round a cook.

"It commenced to look serious to me. Jonadab was a pretty old fish to be caught with soft soap and a set of false crimps; but you can't never tell. When them old kind do bite, they gen'rally swallow hook and sinker, and he sartinly did act hungry. I wished more'n once that Peter T. Brown, our business manager, was aboard to help me with advice, but Peter is off tourin' the Yosemite with his wife and her relations, so whatever pilotin' there was I had to do. And every day fetched Jonadab's bows nigher the matrimonial rocks.

"I'd about made up my mind to sound the fog horn by askin' him straight out what he was cal'latin' to do; but somethin' I heard one evenin', as I set alone in the hotel office, made me think I'd better wait a spell.

"The office window was open and the curtain drawed down tight. I was settin' inside, smokin' and goin' over the situation, when footsteps sounded on the piazza and a couple come to anchor on the settee right by that window. Cap'n Jonadab and Henrietta! I sensed that immediate.

"She was laughin' and actin' kind of queer, and he was talkin' mighty earnest.

"'Oh, no, Cap'n! Oh, no!' she giggles. 'You mustn't be so serious on such a beautiful night as this. Let's talk about the moon.'

"'Drat the moon!' says Jonadab. 'Hettie, I—'

"'Oh, just see how beautiful the water looks! All shiny and—"

"'Drat the water, too! Hettie, what's the reason you don't want to talk serious with me? If that Tobe Loveland—'

"'Really, I don't see why you bring Mr. Loveland's name into the conversation. He is a perfect gentleman, generous and kind; and as for the way in which he runs that lovely car of his—'

"The Cap'n interrupted her. He ripped out somethin' emphatic.

"'Generous!' he snarls. ''Bout as generous as a hog in the feed trough, he is. And as for runnin' that pesky auto, if I'd demean myself to own one of them things, I'll bet my other suit I could run it better'n he does. If I couldn't, I'd tie myself to the anchor and jump overboard.'

"The way she answered showed pretty plain that she didn't believe him. 'Really?' she says. 'Do you think so? Good night, Jonadab.'

"I could hear her walkin' off acrost the piazza. He went after her. 'Hettie,' he says, 'you answer me one thing. Are you engaged to Tobe Loveland?'

"She laughed again, sort of teasin' and slow. 'Really,' says she, 'you are—Why, no, I'm not.'

"That was all, but it set me to thinkin' hard. She wa'n't engaged to Loveland; she said so, herself. And yet, if she wanted Jonadab, she was actin' mighty funny. I ain't had no experience, but it seemed to me that then was the time to bag him and she'd put him off on purpose. She was ages too ancient to be a flirt for the fun of it. What was her game?"

Chapter X
Captain Jonadab Goes

M R. Wingate stopped and roared a greeting to Captain Hiram Baker, who was passing the open door of the waiting room.

"Hello, there, Hime!" he shouted. "Come up in here! What, are you too proud to speak to common folks?"

Captain Hiram entered. "Hello!" he said. "You look like a busy gang, for sure. What you doin'—seatin' chairs?"

"Just now we're automobilin'," observed Captain Sol. "Set down, Hiram."

"Automobilin'?" repeated the new arrival, evidently puzzled.

"Sartin. Barzilla's takin' us out. Go on, Barzilla."

Mr. Wingate smiled broadly. "Well," he began, "we *have* just about reached the part where I went autoin'. The widow and me and Jonadab."

"Jonadab!" shouted Stitt. "I thought you said—"

"I know what I said. But we went auto ridin' just the same.

"'Twas Henry G. Bradbury that took us out, him and his brannew big tourin' car. You see, he landed to board with us the next day after Henrietta come—this Henry G. did—and he was so quiet and easy spoken and run his car so slow that even a pizen auto hater like Jonadab couldn't take much offense at him. He wa'n't very well, he said, subject to some kind of heart attacks, and had come to the Old Home for rest.

"Him and the Cap'n had great arguments about the sins of automobilin'. Jonadab was sot on the idee that nine folks out of ten hadn't machine sense enough to run a car. Bradbury, he declared that that was a fact with the majority of autos, but not with his. 'Why, a child could run it,' says he. 'Look here, Cap'n: To start it you just do this. To stop it you do so and so. To make her go slow you haul back on this lever. To make her go faster you shove down this one. And as for steerin'—well, a man that's handled the wheels of as many catboats as you have would simply have a picnic. I'm in entire sympathy with your feelin's against speeders and such—I'd be a constable if I was in your shoes—but this is a gentleman's car and runs like one.'

"All Jonadab said was 'Bosh!' and 'Humph!' but he couldn't help actin' interested, particular as Mrs. Bassett kept him alongside of the machine and was so turrible interested herself. And when, this partic'lar afternoon, Henry G. invites us all to go out with him for a little 'roll around,' the widow was so tickled and insisted so that he just *had* to go; he didn't dast say no.

"Somehow or 'nother—I ain't just sure yet how it happened— the seatin' arrangements was made like this: Jonadab and Bradbury on the front seat, and me and Henrietta in the stuffed cockpit astern. We rolled out and purred along the road, smooth as a cat trottin' to dinner. No speedin', no joltin', no nothin'. *'Twas* a 'gentleman's car'; there wa'n't no doubt about that.

"We went 'way over to Bayport and Orham and beyond. And all the time Bradbury kept p'intin' out the diff'rent levers to Jonadab and tellin' him how to work 'em. Finally, after we'd headed back, he asked Jonadab to take the wheel and steer her a spell. Said his heart was feelin' sort of mean and 'twould do him good to rest.

"Jonadab said no, emphatic and more'n average ugly, but Henry G. kept beggin' and pleadin', and pretty soon the widow put in her oar. He must do it, to please her. He had *said* he could do it—had told her so—and now he must make good. Why, when Mr. Loveland—

"'All right,' snarls Jonadab. 'I'll try. But if ever—'

"'Hold on!' says I. 'Here's where I get out.'

"However, they wouldn't let me, and the Cap'n took the wheel. His jaw was set and his hands shakin', but he done it. Hettie had give her orders and she was skipper.

"For a consider'ble spell we just crawled. Jonadab was steerin' less crooked every minute and it tickled him; you could see that.

"'Answers her hellum tiptop, don't she?' he says.

"'Bet your life!' says Bradbury. 'Better put on a little more speed, hadn't we?'"

He put it on himself, afore the new pilot could stop him, and we commenced to move.

"'When you want to make her jump,' he says, you press down on that with your foot, and you shove the spark back.'

"'Shut up!' howls Jonadab. 'Belay! Don't you dast to touch that. I'm scart to death as 'tis. Here! you take this wheel.'

"But he wouldn't, and we went on at a good clip. For a green hand the Cap'n was leavin' a pretty straight wake.

"'Gosh!' he says, after a spell; 'I b'lieve I'm kind of gettin' the hang of the craft.'

"'Course you are,' says Bradbury. 'I told—Oh!'

"He straightens up, grabs at his vest, and slumps down against the back of the seat.

"'What *is* it?' screams the widow. 'Oh, what *is* it, Mr. Bradbury?'

"He answers, plucky, but toler'ble faintlike. My heart!' he gasps. 'I—I'm afraid I'm goin' to have one of my attacks. I must get to a doctor quick.'

"'Doctor!' I sings out. 'Great land of love! there ain't a doctor nigher than Denboro, and that's four mile astern.'

"'Never mind,' cries the Bassett woman. 'We must go there, then. Turn around, Jonadab! Turn around at once! Mr. Bradbury—'

"But poor Henry G. was curled up against the cushions and we couldn't get nothin' out of him but groans. And all the time we was sailin' along up the road.

"'Turn around, Jonadab!' orders Henrietta. 'Turn around and go for the doctor!'

"Jonadab's hands was clutched on that wheel, and his face was white as his rubber collar.

"'Jerushy!' he groans desperate, 'I—I don't know *how* to turn around.'

"'Then stop, you foolhead!' I bellers. 'Stop where you be!'

"And he moans—almost cryin' he was: 'I—I've forgotten how to *stop*.'

"Talk about your situations! If we wa'n't in one then I miss my guess. Every minute we was sinkin' Denboro below the horizon.

"'We *must* get to a doctor,' says the widow. 'Where is there another one, Mr. Wingate?'

"'The next one's in Bayport,' says I, 'and that's ten mile ahead if it's a foot.'

"However, there wa'n't nothin' else for it, so toward Bayport we put. Bradbury groaned once in a while, and Mrs. Bassett got nervous.

"'We'll never get there at this rate,' says she. 'Go faster, Jonadab. Faster! Press down on—on that thing he told you to. Please! for *my* sake.'

"'Don't you—' I begun; but 'twas too late. He pressed, and away we went. We was eatin' up the road now, I tell you, and though I was expectin' every minute to be my next, I couldn't help admirin' the way the Cap'n steered. And, as for him, he was gettin' more and more set up and confident.

"'She handles like a yacht, Barzilla,' he grunts, between his teeth. 'See me put her around the next buoy ahead there. Hey! how's that?'

"The next 'buoy' was a curve in the road, and we went around it beautiful. So with the next and the next and the next. Bayport wa'n't so very fur ahead. All to once another dreadful thought struck me.

"'Look here!' I yells. 'How in time are we goin' to stop when we—*ow*!'

"The Bassett woman had pinched my arm somethin' savage. I looked at her, and she was scowlin' and shakin' her head.

"'S-sh-sh!' she whispers. 'Don't disturb him. He'll be frightened and—'

"'Frightened! Good heavens to Betsy! I cal'late he won't be the only one that's fri—'

"But she looked so ugly that I shut up prompt, though I done a heap of thinkin'. On we went and, as we turned the next 'buoy,' there, ahead of us, was another auto, somethin' like ours, with only one person in it, a man, and goin' in the same direction we was, though not quite so fast.

"Then I *was* scart. 'Hi, Jonadab!' I sings out. 'Heave to! Come about! Shorten sail! Do you want to run him down? Look *out!*'

"I might as well have saved my breath. Heavin' to and the rest of it wa'n't included in our pilot's education. On we went, same as ever. I don't know what might have happened if the widow hadn't kept her head. She leaned over the for'ard rail of the after cockpit and squeezed a rubber bag that was close to Jonadab's starboard arm. It was j'ined to the fog whistle, I cal'late, 'cause from under our bows sounded a beller like a bull afoul of a barb-wire fence.

"The feller in t'other car turned his head and looked. Then he commenced to sheer off to wind'ard so's to let us pass. But all the time he kept lookin' back and starin' and, as we got nigher, and I could see him plainer through the dust, he looked more and more familiar. 'Twas somebody I knew.

"Then I heard a little grunt, or gasp, from Cap'n Jonadab. He was leanin' for'ard over the wheel, starin' at the man in the other auto. The nigher we got, the harder he stared; and the man in front was actin' similar in regards to him. And, all to once, the head car stopped swingin' off to wind'ard, turned back toward the middle of the road, and begun to go like smoke. The next instant I felt our machine fairly jump beneath me. I looked at Jonadab's foot. 'Twas pressed hard down on the speed lever.

"'You crazy loon!' I screeched. 'You—you—you—Stop it! Take your foot off that! Do you want to—!'

"I was climbin' over the back of the front seat, my knee pretty nigh on Bradbury's head. But, would you believe it, that Jonadab man let go of the wheel with one hand—let *go* of it, mind you—and give me a shove that sent me backward in Henrietta Bassett's lap.

"'Barzilla!' he growled, between his teeth, 'you set where you be and keep off the quarterdeck. I'm runnin' this craft. I'll beat that Loveland this time or run him under, one or t'other!'

"As sure as I'm alive this minute, the man in the front car was Tobias Loveland!

"And from then on—Don't talk! I dream about it nights and wake up with my arms around the bedpost. I ain't real sure, but I kind of have an idee that the bedpost business comes from the fact that I was huggin' the widow some of the time. If I did, 'Twa'n't knowin'ly, and she never mentioned it afterwards. All I can swear to is clouds of dust, and horns honkin', and telegraph poles lookin' like teeth in a comb, and Jonadab's face set as the Day of Judgment.

"He kept his foot down on the speed place as if 'twas glued. He shoved the 'spark'—whatever that is—'way back. Every once in a while he yelled, yelled at the top of his lungs. What he yelled hadn't no sense to it. Sometimes you'd think that he was drivin' a horse and next that he was handlin' a schooner in a gale.

"'Git dap!' he'd whoop. 'Go it, you cripples! Keep her nose right in the teeth of it! She's got the best of the water, so let her bile! Whe-E-E!'

"We didn't stop at Bayport. Our skipper had made other arrangements. However, the way I figgered it, we was long past needin' a doctor, and you can get an undertaker 'most anywhere. We went through the village like a couple of shootin' stars, Tobias about a length ahead, his hat blowed off, his hair—what little he's got—streamin' out behind, and that blessed red buzz wagon of his fairly skimmin' the hummocks and jumpin' the smooth places. And right astern of him comes Jonadab, hangin' to the wheel, *his* hat gone, his mouth open, and fillin' the dust with yells and coughs.

"You could see folks runnin' to doors and front gates; but you never saw 'em reach where they was goin'—time they done that we was somewheres round the next bend. A pullet run over us once—yes, I mean just that. She clawed the top of the widow's bunnit as we slid underneath her, and by the time she lit we was so fur away she wa'n't visible to the naked eye. Bradbury—who'd got better remarkable sudden—was pawin' at Jonadab's arm, tryin' to make him ease up; but he might as well have pawed the wind. As for Henrietta Bassett, she was acrost the back of the front seat tootin' the horn for all she was wuth. And curled down in a heap on the cockpit floor was a fleshy, seafarin' person by the name of Barzilla Wingate, sufferin' from chills and fever.

"I think 'twas on the long stretch of the Trumet road that we beat Tobias. I know we passed somethin' then, though just what I ain't competent to testify. All I'm sure of is that, t'other side of Bayport village, the landscape got some less streaked and you could most gen'rally separate one house from the next.

"Bradbury looked at Henrietta and smiled, a sort of sickly smile. She was pretty pale, but she managed to smile back. I got up off the floor and slumped on the cushions. As for Cap'n Jonadab Wixon, he'd stopped yellin', but his face was one broad, serene grin. His mouth, through the dust and the dirt caked around it, looked like a rain gully in a sand-bank. And, occasional, he crowed, hoarse but vainglorious.

"'Did you see me?' he barked. 'Did you notice me lick him? He'll laugh at me, will he?—him and his one-horse tin cart! Ho! *Ho!* Why, you'd think he was settin' down to rest! I've got him where I want him now! Ho, ho! Say, Henrietta, did you go swift as you—? Land sakes! Mr. Bradbury, I forgot all about you. And I— I guess we must have got a good ways past the doctor's place.'

"Bradbury said never mind. He felt much better, and he cal'lated he'd do till we fetched the Old Home dock. He'd take the wheel, now, he guessed.

"But, would you b'lieve it, that fool Jonadab wouldn't let him! He was used to the ship now, he said, and, if 'twas all the same to Henry G. and Hettie, he'd kind of like to run her into port.

"'She answers her hellum fine, 'he says. 'After a little practice I cal'late I could steer—'

"'Steer!' sings out Bradbury. '*Steer!* Great Caesar's ghost! I give you my word, Cap'n Wixon, I never saw such handlin' of a machine as you did goin' through Bayport, in my life. You're a wonder!'

"'Um-hm,' says Jonadab contented. 'I've steered a good many vessels in my time, through traffic and amongst the shoals, and never run afoul of nothin' yet. I don't see much diff'rence on shore—'cept that it's a little easier.'

"*Easier!* Wouldn't that—Well, what's the use of talkin'?

"We got to the Old Home House safe and sound; Jonadab, actin' under Bradbury's orders, run her into the yard, slowin' up and stoppin' at the front steps slick as grease. He got out, his chest swelled up like a puffin' pig, and went struttin' in to tell everybody what he'd done to Loveland. I don't know where Bradbury and the widow went. As for me, I went aloft and turned in. And 'twas two days and nights afore I got up again. I had a cold, anyway, and what I'd been through didn't help it none.

"The afternoon of the second day, Bradbury come up to see me. He was dressed in his city clothes and looked as if he was goin' away. Sure enough, he was; goin' on the next train.

"'Where's Jonadab?' says I.

"'Oh, he's out in his car, 'he says. 'Huntin' for Loveland again, maybe.'

"'*His* car? You mean yours.'

"'No, I mean his. I sold my car to him yesterday mornin' for twenty-five hundred dollars cash.'

"I set up in bed. 'Go 'long!' I sings out. 'You didn't nuther!'

"'Yes, I did. Sure thing. After that ride, you couldn't have separated him from that machine with blastin' powder. He paid over the money like a little man.'

"I laid down again. Jonadab Wixon payin' twenty-five hundred dollars for a plaything! Not promisin', but actually *payin'* it!

"'Has—has the widow gone with him?' I asked, soon's I could get my breath.

"He laughed sort of queer. 'No, 'he says, 'she's gone out of town for a few days. Ha, ha! Well, between you and me, Wingate, I doubt if she comes back again. She and I have made all we're likely to in this neighborhood, and she's too good a business woman to waste her time. Good-by; glad to have met you.'

"But I smelt rat strong and wouldn't let him go without seein' the critter.

"'Hold on!' I says. 'There's somethin' underneath all this. Out with it. I won't let on to the Cap'n if you don't want me to.'

"'Well,' says he, laughin' again, 'Mrs. Bassett *won't* come back and I know it. She and I have sold four cars on the Cape in the last five weeks, and the profits'll more'n pay vacation expenses. Two up in Wareham, one over in Orham, to Loveland—'

"'Did *you* sell Tobias his?' I asks, settin' up again.

"'Hettie and I did—yes. Soon's we landed him, we come over to bag old Wixon. I thought one time he'd kill us before we got him, but he didn't. How he did run that thing! He's a game sport.'

"'See here!' says I. '*You* and Hettie sold—What do you mean by that?'

"'Mrs. Bassett is my backer in the auto business,' says he. 'She put in her money and I furnished the experience. We've got a big plant up in—' namin' a city in Connecticut.

"I fetched a long breath. '*Well*!' says I. 'And all this makin' eyes at Tobe and Jonadab was just—just—'

"'Just bait, that's all,' says he. 'I told you she was a good business woman.'

"I let this sink in good. Then says I, 'Humph! I swan to man! And how's your heart actin' now?'

"'Fine!' he says, winkin'. 'I had that attack so's the Cap'n would learn to run on his own hook. I didn't expect quite so much of a run, but I'm satisfied. Don't you worry about my heart disease. That twenty-five hundred cured it. 'Twas all in the way of business,' says Henry G. Bradbury."

"Whew!" whistled Captain Hiram as Barzilla reached into his pocket for pipe and tobacco. "Whew! I should say your partner had a narrer escape. Want to look out sharp for widders. They're dangerous, hey, Sol?"

The depot master did not answer. Captain Hiram asked another question. "How'd Jonadab take Hettie's leavin'?" he inquired.

"Oh," said Barzilla, "I don't think he minded so much. He was too crazy about his new auto to care for anything else. Then, too, he was b'ilin' mad 'cause Loveland swore out a warrant against him for speedin'.

"'Nice trick, ain't it?'he says. 'I knew Tobe was a poor loser, but I didn't think he'd be so low down as all that. Says I was goin' fifty mile an hour. He! he! Well, I *was* movin', that's a fact. I don't care. 'Twas wuth the twenty-dollar fine.'

"'Maybe so,' I says, 'but 'twon't look very pretty to have a special auto constable hauled up and fined for breakin' the law he's s'posed to protect.'

"He hadn't thought of that. His face clouded over.

"'No use, Barzilla,' says he; 'I'll have to give it up.'

"'Guess you will,' says I. 'Automobilin' is—'

"'I don't mean automobilin',' he snorts disgusted. 'Course not! I mean bein' constable.'

"So there you are! From cussin' automobiles he's got so that he can't talk enough good about 'em. And every day sence then he's out on the road layin' for another chance at Tobias. I hope he gets that chance pretty soon, because—well, there's a rumor goin' round that Loveland is plannin' to swap his car for a bigger and faster one. If he does ..."

"If he does," interrupted Captain Sol, "I hope you'll fix the next race for over here. I'd like to see you go by, Barzilla."

"Guess you'd have to look quick to see him," laughed Stitt. "Speakin' about automobiles—"

"By gum!" ejaculated Wingate, "you'd have to look somewheres else to find *me*. I've got all the auto racin' I want!"

"Speakin' of automobiles," began Captain Bailey again. No one paid the slightest attention.

"How's Dusenberry, your baby, Hiram?" asked the depot master, turning to Captain Baker. "His birthday's the Fourth, and that's only a couple of days off."

The proud parent grinned, then looked troubled.

"Why, he ain't real fust-rate," he said. "Seems to be some under the weather. Got a cold and kind of sore throat. Dr. Parker says he cal'lates it's a touch of tonsilitis. There's consider'ble fever, too. I was hopin' the doctor'd come again to-day, but he's gone away on a fishin' cruise. Won't be home till late to-morrer. I s'pose me and Sophrony hadn't ought to worry. Dr. Parker seems to know about the case."

"Humph!" grunted the depot master, "there's only two bein's in creation that know it all. One's the Almighty and t'other's young Parker. He's right out of medical school and is just as fresh as his diploma. He hadn't any business to go fishin' and leave his patients. We lost a good man when old Dr. Ryder died. He ... Oh, well! you mustn't worry, Hiram. Dusenberry'll pull out in time for his birthday. Goin' to celebrate, was you?"

Captain Baker nodded. "Um-hm," he said. "Sophrony's goin'

to bake a frosted cake and stick three candles on it—he's three year old, you know—and I've made him a 'twuly boat with sails,' that's what he's been beggin' for. Ho! ho! he's the cutest little shaver!"

"Speakin' of automobiles," began Bailey Stitt for the third time.

"That youngster of yours, Hiram," went on the depot master, "is the right kind. Compared with some of the summer young ones that strike this depot, he's a saint."

Captain Hiram grinned. "That's what I tell Sophrony," he said. "Sometimes when Dusenberry gets to cuttin' up and she is sort of provoked, I say to her, 'Old lady,' I say, 'if you think *that's* a naughty boy, you ought to have seen Archibald.'"

"Who was Archibald?" asked Barzilla.

"He was a young rip that Sim Phinney and I run across four years ago when we went on our New York cruise together. The weir business had been pretty good and Sim had been teasin' me to go on a vacation with him, so I went. Sim ain't stopped talkin' about our experiences yet. Ho! ho!"

"You bet he ain't!" laughed the depot master. "One mix-up you had with a priest, and a love story, and land knows what. He talks about that to this day."

"What was it? He never told me," said Wingate.

"Why, it begun at the Golconda House, the hotel where Sim and I was stayin'. We—"

"Did *you* put up at the Golconda?" interrupted Barzilla. "Why, Cap'n Jonadab and me stayed there when we went to New York."

"I know you did. Jonadab recommended it to Sim, and Sim took the recommendation. That Golconda House is the only grudge I've got against Jonadab Wixon. It sartin is a tough old tavern."

"I give in to that. Jonadab's so sot on it account of havin' stopped there on his honeymoon, years and years ago. He's too stubborn to own it's bad. It's a matter of principle with him, and he's sot on principle."

"Yes," continued Baker. "Well, Sim and me had been at that Golconda three days and nights. Mornin' of the fourth day we walked out of the dinin' room after breakfast, feelin' pretty average chipper. Gettin' safe past another meal at that hotel was enough of itself to make a chap grateful.

"We walked out of the dinin' room and into the office. And there, by the clerk's desk, was a big, tall man, dressed up in clothes that was loud enough to speak for themselves, and with a shiny new tall hat, set with a list to port, on his head. He was smooth-faced and pug-nosed, with an upper lip like a camel's.

"He didn't pay much attention to us, nor to anybody else, for the matter of that. He was as mournful as a hearse, for all his joyful togs.

"'Fine day, ain't it?' says Sim, social.

"The tall chap looked up at him from under the deck of the beaver hat.

"'Huh!' he growls out, and looks down again.

"'I say it's a fine day,' said Phinney again.

"'I was after hearin' yez say it,' says the man, and walks off, scowlin' like a meat ax. We looked after him.

"'Who was that murderer?' asks Sim of the clerk. 'And when are they going to hang him?'

"'S-sh-sh!' whispers the clerk, scart. ''Tis the boss. The bloke what runs the hotel. He's a fine man, but he has troubles. He's blue.'

"'So that's the boss, hey?' says I. 'And he's blue. Well, he looks it. What's troublin' him? Ain't business good?'

"'Never better. It ain't that. He has things on his mind. You see—'

"I cal'late he'd have told us the yarn, only Sim wouldn't wait to hear it. We was goin' sight-seein' and we had 'aquarium' and 'Stock Exchange' on the list for that afternoon. The hotel clerk had made out a kind of schedule for us of things we'd ought to see while we was in New York, and so fur we'd took in the zoological menagerie and the picture museum, and Central Park and Brooklyn Bridge.

"On the way downtown in the elevated railroad Sim done some preachin'. His text was took from the Golconda House sign, which had 'T. Dempsey, Proprietor,' painted on it.

"'It's that Dempsey man's conscience that makes him so blue,

Hiram,' says Sim. 'It's the way he makes his money. He sells liquor.'

"'Oh!' says I. 'Is *that* it? I thought maybe he'd been sleepin' on one of his own hotel beds. *They're* enough to make any man blue—black and blue.'

"The 'aquarium' wa'n't a success. Phinney was disgusted. He give one look around, grabbed me by the arm, and marched me out of that building same as Deacon Titcomb, of the Holiness Church at Denboro, marched his boy out of the Universalist sociable.

"'It's nothin' but a whole passel of fish,' he snorts. 'The idea of sendin' two Cape Codders a couple of miles to look at *fish*. I've looked at 'em and fished for 'em, and et 'em all the days of my life,' he says, 'and when I'm on a vacation I want a change. I'd forgot that "aquarium" meant fish, or you wouldn't have got me within smellin' distance of it. Necessity's one thing and pleasure's another, as the boy said about takin' his ma's spring bitters.'

"So we headed for the Stock Exchange. We got our gallery tickets at the bank where the Golconda folks kept money, and in a little while we was leanin' over a kind of marble bulwarks and starin' down at a gang of men smokin' and foolin' and carryin' on. 'Twas a dull day, so we found out afterward, and I guess likely that was true. Anyway, I never see such grown-up men act so much like children. There was a lot of poles stuck up around with signs on 'em, and around every pole was a circle of bedlamites hollerin' like loons. Hollerin' was the nighest to work of anything I see them fellers do, unless 'twas tearin' up papers and shovin' the pieces down somebody's neck or throwin' 'em in the air like a play-actin' snowstorm.

"'What's the matter with 'em?' says I. 'High finance taken away their brains?'

"But Phinney was awful interested. He dumped some money in a mine once. The mine caved in on it, I guess, for not a red cent ever come to the top again, but he's been a kind of prophet concernin' finances ever sence.

"'I want to see the big fellers,' says he. 'S'pose that fat one is Morgan?'

"'I don't know,' says I. 'Me and Pierpont ain't met for ever so long. Don't lean over and point so; you're makin' a hit.'

"He was, too. Some of the younger crew on the floor was lookin' up and grinnin', and more kept stoppin' and joinin' in all the time. I cal'late we looked kind of green and soft, hangin' over that marble rail, like posies on a tombstone; and green is the favorite color to a stockbroker, they tell me. Anyhow, we had a good-sized congregation under us in less than no time. Likewise, they got chatty, and commenced to unload remarks.

"'Land sakes!' says one. 'How's punkins?'

"'How's crops down your way?' says another.

"Now there wa'n't nothin' real bright and funny about these questions—more fresh than new, they struck me—but you'd think they was gems from the comic almanac, jedgin' by the haw-haws. Next minute a little bald-headed smart Alec, with clothes that had a tailor's sign hull down and out of the race, steps to the front and commences to make a speech.

"'Gosh t'mighty, gents,' says he. 'With your kind permission, I'll sing "When Reuben Comes to Town."'

"And he did sing it, too, in a voice that needed cultivatin' worse'n a sandy front yard. And with every verse the congregation whooped and laughed and cheered. When the anthem was concluded, all hands set up a yell and looked at us to see how we took it.

"As for me, I was b'ilin' mad and mortified and redhot all over. But Sim Phinney was as cool as an October evenin'. Once in a while old Sim comes out right down brilliant, and he done it now. He smiled, kind of tolerant and easy, same as you might at the tricks of a hand-organ monkey. Then he claps his hands, applaudin' like, reaches into his pocket, brings up a couple of pennies, and tosses 'em down to little baldhead, who was standin' there blown up with pride.

"For a minute the crowd was still. And *then* such a yell as went up! The whole floor went wild. Next thing I knew the gallery was filled with brokers, grabbin' us by the hands, poundin' us on the back, beggin' us to come have a drink, and generally goin' crazy. We was solid with the 'system' for once in our lives. We could have had that whole buildin', from marble decks to gold main-truck, if we'd said the word. Fifty yellin' lunatics was on hand to give it to us; the other two hundred was joyfully mutilatin' the baldhead.

"Well, I wanted to get away, and so did Sim, I guess; but the crowd wouldn't let us. We'd got to have a drink; hogsheads of drinks. That was the best joke on Eddie Lewisburg that ever was. Come on! We *must* come on! Whee! Wow!

"I don't know how it would have ended if some one hadn't butted head first through the mob and grabbed me by the shoulder. I was ready to fight by this time, and maybe I'd have begun to fight if the chap who grabbed me hadn't been a few inches short of seven foot high. And, besides that, I knew him. 'Twas Sam Holden, a young feller I knew when he boarded here one summer. His wife boarded here, too, only she wa'n't his wife then. Her name was Grace Hargrave and she was a fine girl. Maybe you remember 'em, Sol?"

The depot master nodded.

"I remember 'em well," he said. "Liked 'em both—everybody did."

"Yes. Well, he knew us and was glad to see us.

"'It *is* you!' he sings out. 'By George! I thought it was when I came on the floor just now. My! but I'm glad to see you. And Mr. Phinney, too! Bully! Clear out and let 'em alone, you Indians.'

"The crowd didn't want to let us alone, but Sam got us clear somehow, and out of the Exchange Buildin' and into the back room of a kind of restaurant. Then he gets chairs for us, orders cigars, and shakes hands once more.

"'To think of seein' you two in New York!' he says, wonderin'. 'What are you doin' here? When did you come? Tell us about it.'

"So we told him about our pleasure cruise, and what had happened to us so fur. It seemed to tickle him 'most to death.

"'Grace and I are keepin' house, in a modest way, uptown,' says Sam, 'and she'll be as glad to see you as I am. You're comin' up to dinner with me to-night, and you're goin' to make us a visit, you know,' he says.

"Well, if we didn't know it then, we learned it right away.

Nothin' that me or Simeon could say would make him change the course a point. So Phinney went up to the Golconda House and got our bags, and at half-past four that afternoon the three of us was in a hired hack bound uptown.

"On the way Sam was full of fun as ever. He laughed and joked, and asked questions about East Harniss till you couldn't rest. All of a sudden he slaps his knee and sings out:

"'There! I knew I'd forgotten somethin'. Our butler left yesterday, and I was to call at the intelligence office on my way home and see if they'd scared up a new one.'

"I looked at Simeon, and he at me.

"'Hum!' says I, thinkin' about that 'modest' housekeepin'. 'Do you keep a butler?'

"'Not long,' says he, dry as a salt codfish. And that's all we could get out of him.

"I s'pose there's different kinds of modesty. We hadn't more'n got inside the gold-plated front door of that house when I decided that the Holden brand of housekeepin' wa'n't bashful enough to blush. If I'D been runnin' that kind of a place, the only time I'd felt shy and retirin' was when the landlord came for the rent.

"One of the fo'mast hands—hired girls, I mean—went aloft to fetch Mrs. Holden, and when Grace came down she was just as nice and folksy and glad to see us as a body could be. But she looked sort of troubled, just the same.

"'I'm ever so glad you're here,' says she to me and Simeon. 'But, oh, Sam! it's a shame the way things happen. Cousin Harriet and Archie came this afternoon to stay until to-morrow. They're on their way South. And I have promised that you and I shall take Harriet to see Marlowe to-night. Of course we won't do it now, under any consideration, but you know what she is.'

"Sam seemed to know. He muttered somethin' that sounded like a Scripture text. Simeon spoke up prompt.

"'Indeed you will,' says he, decided. 'Me and Hiram ain't that kind. We've got relations of our own, and we know what it means when they come a-visitin'. You and Mr. Holden'll take your comp'ny and go to see—whatever 'tis you want to see, and

143

we'll make ourselves to home till you get back. Yes, you will, or we clear out this minute.'

"They didn't want to, but we was sot, and so they give in finally. It seemed that this Cousin Harriet was a widow relation of the Holdens, who lived in a swell country house over in Connecticut somewhere, and was rich as the rest of the tribe. Archie was her son. 'Hers and the Evil One's,' Sam said.

"We didn't realize how much truth there was in this last part until we run afoul of Archie and his ma at dinner time. Cousin Harriet was tall and middlin' slim, thirty-five years old, maybe, at a sale for taxes, but discounted to twenty at her own valuation. She was got up regardless, and had a kind of chronic, tired way of talkin', and a condescendin' look to her, as if she was on top of Bunker Hill monument, and all creation was on its knees down below. She didn't warm up to Simeon and me much; eyed us over through a pair of gilt spyglasses, and admitted that she was 'charmed, I'm sure.' Likewise, she was afflicted with 'nerves,' which must be a divil of a disease—for everybody but the patient, especial.

"Archie—his ma hailed him as 'Archibald, dear'—showed up pretty soon in tow of his 'maid,' a sweet-faced, tired-out Irish girl named Margaret. 'Archibald, dear,' was five years old or so, sufferin' from curls and the lack of a lickin'. I never see a young one that needed a strap ile more.

"'How d'ye do Archie?' says Simeon, holdin' out his hand.

"Archie didn't take the hand. Instead of that he points at Phinney and commences to laugh.

"'Ho, ho!' says he, dancin' and pointin'. 'Look at the funny whiskers.'

"Sim wa'n't expectin' that, and it set him all aback, like he'd run into a head squall. He took hold of his beard and looked foolish. Sam and Grace looked ashamed and mad. Cousin Harriet laughed one of her lazy laughs.

"'Archibald, de-ar,' she drawls, 'you mustn't speak that way. Now be nice, and play with Margaret durin' dinner, that's a good boy.'

"'I won't,' remarks Archie, cheerful. 'I'm goin' to dine with you, mama.'

"'Oh, no, you're not, dear. You'll have your own little table, and—'

"Then 'twas' Hi, yi!' 'Bow, wow!' Archibald wa'n't hankerin' for little tables. He was goin' to eat with us, that's what. His ma, she argued with him and pleaded, and he yelled and stamped and hurrahed. When Margaret tried to soothe him he went at her like a wild-cat, and kicked and pounded her sinful. She tried to take him out of the room, and then Cousin Harriet come down on her like a scow load of brick.

"'Haven't I told you,' says she, sharp and vinegary, 'not to oppose the child in that way? Archibald has such a sensitive nature,' she says to Grace, 'that opposition arouses him just as it did me at his age. Very well, dear; you *may* dine with us to-night, if you wish. Oh, my poor nerves! Margaret, why don't you place a chair for Master Archibald? The creature is absolutely stupid at times,' she says, talkin' about that poor maid afore her face with no more thought for her feelin's than if she was a wooden image. 'She has no tact whatever. I wouldn't have Archibald's spirit broken for anything.'

"'Twas his neck that needed breakin' if you asked *me*. That was a joyful meal, now I tell you.

"There was more joy when 'twas over. Archie didn't want to go to bed, havin' desires to set up and torment Simeon with questions about his whiskers; askin' if they growed or was tied on, and things like that. Course he didn't know his ma was goin' to the show, or he wouldn't have let her. But finally he was coaxed upstairs by Margaret and a box of candy, and, word havin' been sent down that he was asleep, Sam got out his plug hat, and Grace and Cousin Harriet got on their fur-lined dolmans and knit clouds, and was ready for the hack.

"'I feel mighty mean to go off and leave you this way,' says Sam to me and Simeon. 'But you make yourself at home, won't you? This is your house to-night, you know; servants and all.'

"'How about that boy's wakin' up?' says I.

"'Oh, his maid'll attend to him. If she needs any help you can give it to her,' he says, winkin' on the side.

"But Cousin Harriet was right at his starboard beam, and she

145

heard him. She flew up like a settin' hen.

"'Indeed they will *not!*' she sings out. 'If anyone but Margaret was to attempt to control Archibald, I don't dare think what might happen. I shall not stir from this spot until these persons promise not to interfere in *any* way; Archibald, dear, is such a sensitive child.'

"So we promised not to interfere, although Sim Phinney looked disappointed when he done it. I could see that he'd had hopes afore he give that promise."

Chapter XI
In the Great Metropolis

So THEY LEFT you and Sim Phinney to keep house, did they, Hiram?" observed Wingate.

"They did. And, for a spell, we figgered on bein' free from too much style.

"After they'd gone we loafed into the settin' room or libr'ry, or whatever you call it, and come to anchor in a couple of big lazy chairs.

"'Now,' says I, takin' off my coat, 'we can be comf'table.'

"But we couldn't. In bobs a servant girl to know if we 'wanted anything.' We didn't, but she looked so shocked when she see me in my shirt sleeves that I put the coat on again, feelin' as if I'd ought to blush. And in a minute back she comes to find out if we was *sure* we didn't want anything. Sim was hitchin' in his chair. Between 'nerves' and Archibald, his temper was raw on the edges.

"'Say,' he bursts out, 'you look kind of pale to me. What you need is fresh air. Why don't you go take a walk?'

"The girl looked at him with her mouth open.

"'Oh,' says she, 'I couldn't do that, thank you, sir. That would leave no one but the cook and the kitchen girl. And the master said you was to be made perfectly comf'table, and—'

"'Yes,' says Sim, dry, 'I heard him say it. And we can't be comf'table with you shut up in the house this nice evenin'. Go and take a walk, and take the cook and stewardess with you. Don't argue about it. I'm skipper here till the boss gets back. Go, the three of you, and go *now*. D'ye hear?'

"There was a little more talk, but not much. In five minutes or so the downstairs front door banged, and there was gigglin' outside.

"'There,' says Simeon, peelin' off *his* coat and throwin' himself back in one chair with his feet on another one. 'Now, by Judas, I'm goin' to be homey and happy like poor folks. I don't wonder that Harriet woman's got nerves. Darn style, anyhow! Pass over that cigar box, Hiram.'

"'Twas half an hour later or so when Margaret, the nursemaid, came downstairs. I'd almost forgot her. We was tame and toler'ble contented by that time. Phinney called to her as she went by the door.

"'Is that young one asleep?' he asked.

"'Yes, sir,' says she, 'he is. Is there anything I can do? Did you want anything?'

"Simeon looks at me. 'I swan to man, it's catchin'!'he says. 'They've all got it. No, we don't want anything, except—What's the matter? *You* don't need fresh air, do you?'

"The girl looked as if she'd lost her last friend. Her pretty face was pale and her eyes was wet, as if she'd been cryin'.

"'No, sir,' says she, puzzled. 'No, sir, thank you, sir.'

"'She's tired out, that's all,' says I. I swan, I pitied the poor thing. 'You go somewheres and take a nap,' I told her. 'Me and my friend won't tell.'

"Oh, no, she couldn't do that. It wa'n't that she was tired—no more tired than usual—but she'd been that troubled in her mind lately, askin' our pardon, that she was near to crazy.

"We was sorry for that, but it didn't seem to be none of our business, and she was turnin' away, when all at once she stops and turns back again.

"'Might I ask you gintlemen a question?' she says, sort of pleadin'. 'Sure I mane no harm by it. Do aither of you know a man be the name of Michael O'Shaughnessy?'

"Me and Sim looked at each other. 'Which?' says I. 'Mike O' who?' says Simeon.

"'Aw, don't you know him?' she begs. '*Don't* you know him? Sure I hoped you might. If you'd only tell me where he is I'd git on me knees and pray for you. O Mike, Mike! why did you leave me like this? What'll become of me?'

"And she walks off down the hall, coverin' her face with her hands and cryin' as if her heart was broke.

"'There! there!' says Simeon, runnin' after her, all shook up. He's a kind-hearted man—especially to nice-lookin' females. 'Don't act so, 'he says. 'Be a good girl. Come right back into the settin' room and tell me all about it. Me and Cap'n Baker ain't got nerves, and we ain't rich, neither. You can talk to us. Come, come!'

"She didn't know how to act, seemingly. She was like a dog that's been kicked so often he's suspicious of a pat on the head. And she was cryin' and sobbin' so, and askin' our pardon for doin' it, that it took a good while to get at the real yarn. But we did get it, after a spell.

"It seems that the girl—her whole name was Margaret Sullivan—had been in this country but a month or so, havin' come from Ireland in a steamboat to meet the feller who'd kept comp'ny with her over there. His name was Michael O'Shaughnessy, and he'd been in America for four years or more, livin' with a cousin in Long Island City. And he'd got a good job at last, and he sent for her to come on and be married to him. And when she landed 'twas the cousin that met her. Mike had drawn a five-thousand-dollar prize in the Mexican lottery a week afore, and hadn't been seen sence.

"So poor Margaret goes to the cousin's to stay. And she found them poor as Job's pet chicken, and havin' hardly grub enough aboard to feed the dozen or so little cousins, let alone free boarders like her. And so, havin' no money, she goes out one day to an intelligence office where they deal in help, and puts in a blank askin' for a job as servant girl. 'Twas a swell place, where bigbugs done their tradin', and there she runs into Cousin Harriet, who was a chronic customer, always out of servants, owin' to the complications of Archibald and nerves. And Harriet hires her, because she was pretty and would work for a shavin' more'n nothin', and carts her right off to Connecticut. And when Margaret sets out to write for her trunk, and to tell where she is, she finds she's lost the cousin's address, and can't remember whether it's Umpty-eighth Street or Tin Can Avenue.

"'And, oh,' says she, 'what *shall* I do? The mistress is that hard to please, and the child is that wicked till I want to die. And I have no money and no friends. O Mike! Mike!' she says. 'If you only knew you'd come to me. For it's a good heart he has, although the five thousand dollars carried away his head,' says she.

"I don't believe I ever wanted to make a feller's acquaintance more than I done that O'Shaughnessy man's. The mean blackguard, to leave his girl that way. And 'twas easy to see what she'd been through with Cousin Harriet and that brat. We tried to comfort her all we could; promised to have a hunt through Long Island and the directory, and to help get her another place when she got back from the South, and so on. But 'twas kind of unsatisfactory. 'Twas her Mike she wanted.

"'I told the Father about it at the church up there,' she says, 'and he wrote, but the letters was lost, I guess. And I thought if I might see a priest here in New York he might help me. But the mistress is to go at noon to-morrer, and I'll have no time. What *shall* I do?' says she, and commenced to cry again.

"Then I had an idea. 'Priest?' says I. 'There's a fine big church, with a cross on the ridgepole of it, not five minutes' walk from this house. I see it as we was comin' up. Why don't you run down there this minute?' I says.

"No, she didn't want to leave Archibald. Suppose he should wake up.

"'All right,' says I. 'Then I'll go myself. And I'll fetch a priest up here if I have to tote him on my back, like the feller does the codfish in the advertisin' picture.'

"I didn't have to tote him. He lived in a mighty fine house, hitched onto the church, and there was half a dozen assistant parsons to help him do his preachin'. But he was big and fat and gray-haired and as jolly and as kind-hearted a feller as you'd want to meet. He said he'd come right along; and he done it.

"Phinney opened the door for us. 'What's the row?' says I, lookin' at his face.

"'Row?' he snorts; 'there's row enough for six. That da—excuse me, mister—that cussed Archibald has woke up.'

"He had; there wa'n't no doubt about it. And he was raisin' hob, too. The candy, mixed up with the dinner, had put his works in line with his disposition, and he was poundin' and yellin' upstairs enough to wake the dead. Margaret leaned over the balusters.

"'Is it the Father?' she says. 'Oh, dear! what'll I do?'

"'Send some of the other servants to the boy,' says the priest, 'and come down yourself.'

"Simeon, lookin' kind of foolish, explained what had become of the other servants. Father McGrath—that was his name— laughed and shook all over.

"'Very well,' says he. 'Then bring the young man down. Perhaps he'll be quiet here.'

"So pretty soon down come Margaret with Archibald, full of the Old Scratch, as usual, dressed up gay in a kind of red blanket nighty, with a rope around the middle of it. The young one spotted Simeon, and set up a whoop.

"'Oh! there's the funny whiskers,' he sings out.

"'Good evenin', my son,' says the priest.

"'Who's the fat man?' remarks Archibald, sociable. 'I never saw such a red fat man. What makes him so red and fat?'

"These questions didn't make Father McGrath any paler. He laughed, of course, but not as if 'twas the funniest thing he ever heard.

"'So you think I'm fat, do you, my boy?' says he.

"'Yes, I do,' says Archibald. 'Fat and red and funny. Most as funny as the whisker man. I never saw such funny-lookin' people.'

"He commenced to point and holler and laugh. Poor Margaret was so shocked and mortified she didn't know what to do.

"'Stop your noise, sonny,' says I. 'This gentleman wants to talk to your nurse.'

"The answer I got was some unexpected.

"'What makes your feet so big?' says Archie, pointin' at my Sunday boots. 'Why do you wear shoes like that? Can't you help it? You're funny, too, aren't you? You're funnier than the rest of 'em.'

"We all went into the library then, and Father McGrath tried to ask Margaret some questions. I'd told him the heft of the yarn on the way from the church, and he was interested. But the questionin' was mighty unsatisfyin'. Archibald was the whole team, and the rest of us was yeller dogs under the wagon.

"'Can't you keep that child quiet?' asks the priest, at last, losin' his temper and speakin' pretty sharp.

"'O Archie, dear! *Do* be a nice boy,' begs Margaret, for the eight hundredth time.

"'Why don't you punish him as he deserves?'

"'Father, dear, I can't. The mistress says he's so sensitive that he has to have his own way. I'd lose my place if I laid a hand on him.'

"'Come on into the parlor and see the pictures, Archie,' says I.

"'I won't,' says Archibald. 'I'm goin' to stay here and see the fat man make faces.'

"'You see,' says Sim, apologizin' 'we can't touch him, 'cause we promised his ma not to interfere. And my right hand's got cramps in the palm of it this minute,' he adds, glarin' at the young one.

"Father McGrath stood up and reached for his hat. Margaret began to cry. Archibald, dear, whooped and kicked the furniture. And just then the front-door bell rang.

"For a minute I thought 'twas Cousin Harriet and the Holdens come back, but then I knew it was hours too early for that. Margaret was too much upset to be fit for company, so I answered the bell myself. And who in the world should be standin' on the steps but that big Dempsey man, the boss of the Golconda House, where me and Simeon had been stayin'; the feller we'd spoke to that very mornin'.

"'Good evenin', sor,' says he, in a voice as deep as a well. 'I'm glad to find you to home, sor. There's a telegram come for you at my place, 'he says, 'and as your friend lift the address when he come for the baggage this afternoon, I brought it along to yez. I was comin' this way, so 'twas no trouble.'

"'That's real kind of you,' I says. 'Step inside a minute, won't you?'

"So in he comes, and stands, holdin' his shiny beaver in his hand, while I tore open the telegram envelope. 'Twas a message from a feller I knew with the Clyde Line of steamboats. He had found out, somehow, that we was in New York, and the telegram was an order for us to come and make him a visit.

"'I hope it's not bad news, sor,' says the big chap.

"'No, no,' says I. 'Not a bit of it, Mr. Dempsey. Come on in and have a cigar, won't you?'

"'Thank you, sor,' says he. 'I'm glad it's not the bad news. Sure, I ax you and your friend's pardon for bein' so short to yez this mornin', but I'm in that throuble lately that me timper is all but gone.'

"'That so?' says I. 'Trouble's thick in this world, ain't it? Me and Mr. Phinney got a case of trouble on our hands now, Mr. Dempsey, and—'

"'Excuse me, sor,' he says. 'My name's not Dempsey. I suppose you seen the sign with me partner's name on it. I only bought into the business a while ago, and the new sign's not ready yit. Me name is O'Shaughnessy, sor.'

"'What?' says I. And then: '*What?*'

"'O'Shaughnessy. Michael O'Shaughnessy. I—'

"'Hold on!' I sung out. 'For the land sakes, hold on! *What's* your name?'

"He bristled up like a cat.

"'Michael O'Shaughnessy,' he roars, like the bull of Bashan. 'D'yez find any fault with it? 'twas me father's before me—Michael Patrick O'Shaughnessy, of County Sligo. I'll have yez know—what's that?'

"'Twas a scream from the libr'ry. Next thing I knew, Margaret, the nurse girl, was standin' in the hall, white as a Sunday shirt, and swingin' back and forth like a wild-carrot stalk in a gale.

"'Mike!' says she, kind of low and faint. 'Mary be good to us! *Mike!*'

"And the big chap dropped his tall hat on the floor and turned as white as she was.

"'*Maggie!*' he hollers. And then they closed in on one another.

"Sim and the priest and Archie had followed the girl into the hall. Me and Phinney was too flabbergasted to do anything, but big Father McGrath was cool as an ice box. When Archibald, like the little imp he was, sets up a whoop and dives for them two, the priest grabs him by the rope of the blanket nighty and swings him into the libr'ry, and shuts the door on him.

"'And now,' says he, takin' Sim and me by the arms and leadin' us to the parlor, 'we'll just step in here and wait a bit.'

"We waited, maybe, ten minutes. Archibald, dear, shut up in the libr'ry, was howlin' blue murder, but nobody paid any attention to him. Then there was a knock on the door between us and the hall, and Father McGrath opened it. There they was, the two of 'em—Mike and Maggie—lookin' red and foolish—but happy, don't talk!

"'You see, sor,' says the O'Shaughnessy man to me, ''twas the five-thousand-dollar prize that done it. I'd been workin' at me trade, sor—larnin' to tind bar it was—and I'd just got a new job where the pay was pretty good, and I'd sint over for Maggie, and was plannin' for the little flat we was to have, and the like of that, when I drew that prize. And the joy of it was like handin' me a jolt on the jaw. It put me out for two weeks, sor, and when I come to I was in Baltimore, where I'd gone to collect the money; and two thousand of the five was gone, and I knew me job in New York was gone, and I was that shamed and sick it took me three days more to make up me mind to come to me Cousin Tim's, where I knew Maggie'd be waitin' for me. And when I did come back she was gone, too.'

"'And then,' says Father McGrath, sharp, 'I suppose you went on another spree, and spent the rest of the money.'

"'I did not, sor—axin' your pardon for contradictin' your riverence. I signed the pledge, and I'll keep it, with Maggie to help me. I put me three thousand into a partnership with me friend Dempsey, who was runnin' the Golconda House—'tis over on the East Side, with a fine bar trade—and I'm doin' well, barrin' that I've been crazy for this poor girl, and advertisin' and—'

"'And look at the clothes of him!' sings out Margaret, reverent-like. 'And is that *your* tall hat, Mike? To think of you with a tall hat! Sure it's a proud girl I am this day. Saints forgive me, I've forgot Archie!'

"And afore we could stop her she'd run into the hall and unfastened the libr'ry door. It took her some time to smooth down the young one's sensitive feelin's, and while she was gone, me and Simeon told the O'Shaughnessy man a little of what his girl had had to put up with along of Cousin Harriet and Archibald. He was mad.

"'Is that the little blackguard?' he asks, pointin' to Archibald, who had arrived by now.

"'That's the one,' says I.

"Archibald looked up at him and grinned, sassy as ever.

"'Father McGrath,' asks O'Shaughnessy, determined like, 'can you marry us this night?'

"'I can,' says the Father.

"'And will yez?'

"'I will, with pleasure.'

"'Maggie,' says Mike, 'get your hat and jacket on and come with the Father and me this minute. These gintlemen here will explain to your lady when she comes back. But *you'll* come back no more. We'll send for your trunk to-morrer.'

"Even then the girl hesitated. She'd been so used to bein' a slave that I suppose she couldn't realize she was free at last.

"'But, Mike, dear,' she says. 'I—oh, your lovely hat! Put it down, Archie, darlin'. Put it down!'

"Archibald had been doin' a little cruisin' on his own hook, and he'd dug up Mike's shiny beaver where it had been dropped in the hall. Now he was dancin' round with it, bangin' it on the top as if it was a drum.

"'Put it down, *please!*' pleads Margaret. 'Twas plain that that plug was a crown of glory to her.

"'Drop it, you little thafe!' yells O'Shaughnessy, makin' a dive for the boy.

"'I won't!' screams Archibald, and starts to run. He tripped over the corner of a mat, and fell flat. The plug hat was underneath him, and it fell flat, too.

"'Oh! oh! oh!' wails Margaret, wringin' her hands. 'Your beautiful hat, Mike!'

"Mike's face was like a sunset.

"'Your reverence,' says he, 'tell me this; don't the wife promise to "obey" in the marriage service?'

"'She does,' says Father McGrath.

"'D'ye hear that, you that's to be Margaret O'Shaughnessy? You do? Well, then, as your husband that's to be in tin minutes, I order you to give that small divil what's comin' to him. D'ye hear me? Will yez obey me, or will yez not?'

"She didn't know what to do. You could see she wanted to— her fingers was itchin' to do it, but—And then Archie held up the ruins of the hat and commenced to laugh.

"That settled it. Next minute he was across her knee and gettin' what he'd been sufferin' for ever sence he was born; and gettin' all the back numbers along with it, too.

"And in the midst of the performance Sim Phinney leans over to me with the most heavenly, resigned expression on his face, and says he:

"'It ain't *our* fault, Hiram. We promised not to interfere.'"

"What did Sam Holden and his wife say when they got home?" asked Captain Sol, when the triumphant whoops over Archibald's righteous chastisement had subsided.

"We didn't give him much of a chance to say anything. I laid for him in the hall when he arrived and told him that Phinney had got a telegram and must leave immediate. He wanted to know why, and a whole lot more, but I told him we'd write it. Neither Sim nor me cared to face Cousin Harriet after her darlin' son had spun his yarn. Ha! ha! I'd like to have seen her face—from a safe distance."

Captain Bailey Stitt cleared his throat. "Referrin' to them automobiles," he said, "I—"

"Say, Sol," interrupted Wingate, "did I ever tell you of Cap'n Jonadab's and my gettin' took up by the police when *we* was in New York?"

"No," replied the astounded depot master. "Took up by the *police*?"

"Um—hm. Surprises you, don't it? Well, that whole trip was a surprise to me.

"When Laban Thorp set out to thrash his son and the boy

licked him instead, they found the old man settin' in the barn-
yard, holdin' on to his nose and grinnin' for pure joy.

"'Hurt?' says he. 'Why, some. But think of it! Only think of it! I
didn't believe Bill had it in him.'

"Well, that's the way I felt when Cap'n Jonadab sprung the
New York plan on to me. I was pretty nigh as much surprised as
Labe. The idea of a man with a chronic case of lockjaw of the
pocketbook, same as Jonadab had worried along under ever
sence I knew him, suddenly breakin' loose with a notion to go to
New York on a pleasure cruise! 'twas too many for me. I set and
looked at him.

"'Oh, I mean it, Barzilla,' he says. 'I ain't been to New York
sence I was mate on the Emma Snow, and that was 'way back in
the eighties. That is, to stop I ain't. That time we went through
on the way to Peter T.'s weddin' don't count, 'cause we only went
in the front door and out the back, like Squealer Wixon went
through high school. Let's you and me go and stay two or three
days and have a real high old time,' says he.

"I fetched a long breath. 'Jonadab,' I says, don't scare a feller
this way; I've got a weak heart. If you're goin' to start in and be
divilish in your old age, why, do it kind of gradual. Let's go over
to the billiard room and have a bottle of sass'parilla and a five-
cent cigar, just to break the ice.'

"But that only made him mad.

"'You talk like a fish,' he says. 'I mean it. Why can't we go? It's
September, the Old Home House is shut up for the season, you
and me's done well—fur's profits are concerned—and we ought
to have a change, anyway. We've got to stay here in Orham all
winter.'

"'Have you figgered out how much it's goin' to cost?' I asked
him.

"Yes, he had. 'It won't be so awful expensive,' he says. 'I've got
some stock in the railroad and that'll give me a pass fur's Fall
River. And we can take a lunch to eat on the boat. And a stateroom's a dollar; that's fifty cents apiece. And my daughter's goin'
to Denboro on a visit next week, so I'd have to pay board if I
stayed to home. Come on, Barzilla! don't be so tight with your

money.'

"So I said I'd go, though I didn't have any pass, nor no daughter to feed me free gratis for nothin' when I got back. And when we started, on the followin' Monday, nothin' would do but we must be at the depot at two o'clock so's not to miss the train, which left at quarter past three.

"I didn't sleep much that night on the boat. For one thing, our stateroom was a nice lively one, alongside of the paddle box and just under the fog whistle; and for another, the supper that Jonadab had brought, bein' mainly doughnuts and cheese, wa'n't the best cargo to take to bed with you. But it didn't make much diff'rence, 'cause we turned out at four, so's to see the scenery and git our money's worth. What was left of the doughnuts and cheese we had for breakfast.

"We made the dock on time, and the next thing was to pick out a hotel. I was for cruisin' along some of the main streets until we hove in sight of a place that looked sociable and not too expensive. But no; Jonadab had it all settled for me. We was goin' to the 'Wayfarer's Inn,' a boardin' house where he'd put up once when he was mate of the Emma Snow. He said 'twas a fine place and you could git as good ham and eggs there as a body'd want to eat.

"So we set sail for the 'Wayfarer's,' and of all the times gittin' to a place—don't talk! We asked no less than nine policemen and one hundred and two other folks, and it cost us thirty cents in car fares, which pretty nigh broke Jonadab's heart. However, we found it, finally, 'way off amongst a nest of brick houses and peddler carts and children, and it wa'n't the 'Wayfarer's Inn' no more, but was down in the shippin' list as the 'Golconda House.' Jonadab said the neighborhood had changed some sence he was there, but he guessed we'd better chance it, 'cause the board was cheap.

"We had a nine-by-ten room up aloft somewheres, and there we set down on the edge of the bed and a chair to take account of stock, as you might say.

"'Now, I tell you, Jonadab,' says I, 'we don't want to waste no time, and we've got the day afore us. What do you say if we cruise along the water front for a spell? There's ha'f a dozen Orham folks aboard diff'rent steamers that hail from this port, and 'twouldn't be no more'n neighborly to call on 'em. There's Silas Baker's boy, Asa—he's with the Savannah Line and he'd be mighty glad to see us. And there's—'

"But Jonadab held up his hand. He'd been mysterious as a baker's mince pie ever sence we started, hintin' at somethin' he'd got to do when we'd got to New York. And now he out with it.

"'Barzilla,' he says, 'I ain't sayin' but what I'd like to go to the wharves with you, first rate. And we will go, too. But afore we do anything else I've got an errand that must be attended to. 'Twas give to me by a dyin' man,' he says, 'and I promised him I'd do it. So that comes first of all.'

"He got his wallet out of his inside vest pocket, where it had been pinned in tight to keep it safe from robbers, unwound a foot or so of leather strap, and dug up a yeller piece of paper that looked old enough to be Methusalem's will, pretty nigh.

"'Do you remember Patrick Kelly in Orham?' he asks.

"'Who?' says I. 'Pat Kelly, the Irishman, that lived in the little old shack back of your barn? Course I do. But he's been dead for I don't know how long.'

"'I know he has. Do you remember his boy Jim that run away from home?'

"'Let's see,' I says. 'Seems to me I do. Freckled, red-headed rooster, wa'n't he? And of all the imps of darkness that ever—'

"'S-sh-sh!' he interrupted solemn. 'Don't say that now, Barzilla. Sounds kind of irreverent. Well, me and old Pat was pretty friendly, in a way, though he did owe me rent. When he was sick with the pleurisy he sends for me and he says, "Cap'n 'Wixon," says he, "you're pretty close with the money," he says— he was kind of out of his head at the time and liable to say foolish things—"you're pretty close," he says, "but you're a man of your word. My boy Jimmie, that run away, was the apple of my eye."'

"'That's what he said about his girl Maggie that was took up for stealin' Mrs. Elkanah Higgins's spoons,' I says. 'He had a healthy crop of apples in *his* orchard.'

"'S-sh-h! *Don't* talk so! I feel as if the old man's spirit was with us this minute. "He's the apple of my eye," he says, "and he run away, after me latherin' the life out of him with a wagon spoke. 'Twas all for his good, but he didn't understand, bein' but a child. And now I've heard," he says, "that he's workin' at 116 East Blank Street in the city of New York. Cap'n Wixon, you're a man of money and a travelin' man," he says (I was fishin' in them days). "When you go to New York," he says, "I want you to promise me to go to the address on this paper and hunt up Jimmie. Tell him I forgive him for lickin' him," he says, "and die happy. Will you promise me that, Cap'n, on your word as a gentleman?" And I promised him. And he died in less than ten months afterwards, poor thing.'

"'But that was sixteen—eighteen—nineteen years ago,' says I. 'And the boy run away three years afore that. You've been to New York in the past nineteen years, once anyhow.'

"'I know it. But I forgot. I'm ashamed of it, but I forgot. And when I was goin' through the things up attic at my daughter's last Friday, seein' what I could find for the rummage sale at the church, I come across my old writin' desk, and in it was this very piece of paper with the address on it just as I wrote it down. And me startin' for New York in three days! Barzilla, I swan to man, I believe something *sent* me to that attic.'

"I knew what sent him there and so did the church folks, judgin' by their remarks when the contribution came in. But I was too much set back by the whole crazy business to say anything about that.

"'Look here, Jonadab Wixon,' I sings out, 'do you mean to tell me that we've got to put in the whole forenoon ransackin' New York to find a boy that run off twenty-two years ago?'

"'It won't take the forenoon, 'he says. 'I've got the number, ain't I?'

"'Yes, you've got the number where he *was*. If you want to know where I think he's likely to be now, I'd try the jail.'

"But he said I was unfeelin' and disobligin' and lots more, so, to cut the argument short, I agreed to go. And off we put to hunt up 116 East Blank Street. And when we located it, after a good hour of askin' questions, and payin' car fares and wearin' out shoe leather, 'twas a Chinese laundry.

"'Well,' I says, sarcastic, 'here we be. Which one of the heathen do you think is Jimmie? If he had an inch or so more of upper lip, I'd gamble on that critter with the pink nighty and the baskets on his feet. He has a kind of familiar chicken-stealin' look in his eye. Oh, come down on the wharves, Jonadab, and be sensible.'

"Would you believe it, he wa'n't satisfied. We must go into the wash shop and ask the Chinamen if they knew Jimmie Kelly. So we went in and the powwow begun.

"'Twas a mighty unsatisfyin' interview. Jonadab's idea of talkin' to furriners is to yell at 'em as if they was stone deef. If they don't understand what you say, yell louder. So between his yells and the heathen's jabber and grunts the hullabaloo was worse than a cat in a hen yard. Folks begun to stop outside the door and listen and grin.

"'What did he say?' asks the Cap'n, turnin' to me.

"'I don't know,' says I, 'but I cal'late he's gettin' ready to send a note up to the crazy asylum. Come on out of here afore I go loony myself.'

"So he done it, finally, cross as all get out, and swearin' that all Chinese was no good and oughtn't to be allowed in this country. But he wouldn't give up, not yet. He must scare up some of the neighbors and ask them. The fifth man that we asked was an old chap who remembered that there used to be a liquor saloon once where the laundry was now. But he didn't know who run it or what had become of him.

"'Never mind,' I says. 'You're as warm as you're likely to be this trip. A rum shop is just about the place I'd expect that Kelly boy *would* be in. And, if he's like the rest of his relations on his dad's side, he drank himself to death years ago. *Now* will you head for the Savannah Line?'

"Not much, he wouldn't. He had another notion. We'd look in the directory. That seemed to have a glimmer of sense some-wheres in its neighborhood, so we found an apothecary store and the clerk handed us out a book once again as big as a church Bible.

"'Kelly,' says Jonadab. 'Yes, here 'tis. Now, "James Kelly." Land of Love! Barzilla, look here.'

"I looked, and there wa'n't no less than a dozen pages of James Kellys beginning with fifty James A.'s and endin' with four James Z.'s. The Y in 'New York' ought to be a C, judgin' by that directory.

"'Godfrey mighty!' I says. 'This ain't no forenoon's job, Jonadab. If you're goin' through that list you'll have to spend the rest of your life here. Only, unless you want to be lonesome, you'll have to change your name to Kelly.'

"'If I'd only got his middle letter,' says he, mournful, ''twould have been easier. He had four middle names, if I remember right—the old man was great on names—and 'twas too much trouble to write 'em all down. Well, I've done my duty, anyhow. We'll go and call on Ase Baker.'

"But 'twas after eleven o'clock then, and the doughnuts and cheese I had for breakfast was beginnin' to feel as if they wanted company. So we decided to go back to the Golconda and have some dinner first.

"We had ham and eggs for dinner, some that was left over from the last time Jonadab stopped there, I cal'late. Lucky there was hot bread and coffee on the bill or we'd never got a square meal. Then we went up to our room and the Cap'n laid down on the bed. He was beat out, he said, and wanted to rest up a spell afore haulin' anchor for another cruise."

Chapter XII
A Vision Sent

"WHERE'S THE ARRESTIN' come in?" demanded Stitt.

"Comes quick now, Bailey. Plenty quick enough for me and Jonadab, I tell you that! After we got to our room the Cap'n went to sleep pretty soon and I set in the one chair, readin' the newspaper and wishin' I hadn't ate so many of the warm bricks that the Golconda folks hoped was biscuit. They made me feel like a schooner goin' home in ballast. I guess I was drowsin' off myself, but there comes a most unearthly yell from the bed and I jumped ha'f out of the chair. There was Jonadab settin' up and lookin' wild.

"'What in the world?' says I.

"'Oh! Ugh! My soul!' says he.

"'Your soul, hey?' says I. 'Is that all? I thought mebbe you'd lost a quarter.'

"'Barzilla,' he says, comin' to and starin' at me solemn, 'Barzilla, I've had a dream—a wonderful dream.'

"'Well,' I says, 'I ain't surprised. A feller that h'isted in as much fried dough as you did ought to expect—'

"'But I tell you 'twas a *wonderful* dream,' he says. 'I dreamed I was on Blank Street, where we was this mornin', and Patrick Kelly comes to me and p'ints his finger right in my face. I see him as plain as I see you now. And he says to me—he said it over and over, two or three times—Seventeen," says he, "Seventeen." Now what do you think of that?'

"'Humph!' I says. 'I ain't surprised. I think 'twas just seventeen of them biscuits that you got away with. Wonder to me you didn't see somebody worse'n old Pat.'

"But he was past jokin'. You never see a man so shook up by the nightmare as he was by that one. He kept goin' over it and tellin' how natural old Kelly looked and how many times he said 'Seventeen' to him.

"'Now what did he mean by it?'he says. 'Don't tell me that was a common dream, 'cause twa'n't. No, sir, 'twas a vision sent to me, and I know it. But what did he mean?'

"'I think he meant you was seventeen kinds of an idiot,' I snorts, disgusted. 'Get up off that bed and stop wavin' your arms, will you? He didn't mean for you to turn yourself into a windmill, that's sartin sure.'

"Then he hits his knee a slap that sounds like a window blind blowin' to. 'I've got it!' he sings out. 'He meant for me to go to number seventeen on that street. That's what he meant.'

"I laughed and made fun of him, but I might as well have saved my breath. He was sure Pat Kelly's ghost had come hikin' back from the hereafter to tell him to go to 17 Blank Street and find his boy. 'Else why was he *on* Blank Street?'he says. 'You tell me that.'

"I couldn't tell him. It's enough for me to figger out what makes live folks act the way they do, let alone dead ones. And Cap'n Jonadab was a Spiritu'list on his mother's side. It ended by my agreein' to give the Jimmie chase one more try.

"'But it's got to be the last,' I says. 'When you get to number seventeen don't you say you think the old man meant to say "seventy" and stuttered.'

"Number 17 Blank Street was a little combination fruit and paper store run by an Eyetalian with curly hair and the complexion of a molasses cooky. His talk sounded as if it had been run through a meat chopper. All he could say was, 'Nica grape, genta'men? On'y fifteen cent a pound. Nica grape? Nica apple? Nica pear? Nica ploom?'

"'Kelly?' says Jonadab, hollerin' as usual. 'Kelly! d'ye understand? K-E-L-Kel L-Y-ly, Kelly. *You* know, *Kelly*! We want to find him.'

"And just then up steps a feller about six feet high and three foot through. He was dressed in checkerboard clothes, some gone to seed, and you could hardly see the blue tie he had on for the glass di'mond in it. Oh, he was a little wilted now—for the lack of water, I judge—but 'twas plain that he'd been a sunflower in his time. He'd just come out of a liquor store next door to the fruit shop and was wipin' his mouth with the back of his hand.

"'What's this I hear?' says he, fetchin' Jonadab a welt on the back like a mast goin' by the board. 'Is it me friend Kelly you're lookin' for?'

"I was just goin' to tell him no, not likin' his looks, but Jonadab cut in ahead of me, out of breath from the earthquake the feller had landed him, but excited as could be.

"'Yes, yes!' says he. 'It's Mr. Kelly we want. Do you know him?'

"'Do I know him? Why, me bucko, 'tis me old college chum he is. Come on with me and we'll give him the glad hand.'

"He grabs Jonadab by the arm and starts along the sidewalk, steerin' a toler'ble crooked course, but gainin' steady by jerks.

"'I was on me way to Kelly's place now,' says he. 'And here it is. Sure didn't I bate the bookies blind on Rosebud but yesterday— or was it the day before? I don't know, but come on, me lads, and we'll do him again.'

"He turned in at a little narrer entry-like, and went stumblin' up a flight of dirty stairs. I caught hold of Jonadab's coat tails and pulled him back.

"'Where you goin', you crazy loon?' I whispered. 'Can't you see he's three sheets in the wind? And you haven't told him what Kelly you want, nor nothin'.'

"But I might as well have hollered at a stone wall. 'I don't care if he's as fur gone in liquor as Belshazzer's goat,' sputters the Cap'n, all worked up. 'He's takin' us to a Kelly, ain't he? And is it likely there'd be another one within three doors of the number I dreamed about? Didn't I tell you that dream was a vision sent? Don't lay to *now*, Barzilla, for the land sakes! It's Providence a-workin'.'

"''Cording to my notion the sunflower looked more like an agent from t'other end of the line than one from Providence, but just then he commenced to yell for us and upstairs we went, Jonadab first.

"'Whisht!' says the checkerboard, holdin' on to Jonadab's collar and swingin' back and forth. 'Before we proceed to blow in on me friend Kelly, let us come to an understandin' concernin' and touchin' on—and—and—I don't know. But b'ys,' says he, solemn and confidential, 'are you on the square? Are yez dead game sports, hey?'

"'Yes, yes!' says Jonadab. 'Course we be. Mr. Kelly and us are old friends. We've come I don't know how fur on purpose to see him. Now where's—'

"'Say no more,' hollers the feller. 'Say no more. Come on with yez.' And he marches down the dark hall to a door with a 'To let' sign on it and fetches it a bang with his fist. It opens a little ways and a face shows in the crack.

"'Hello, Frank!' hails the sunflower, cheerful. 'Will you take that ugly mug of yours out of the gate and lave me friends in?'

"'What's the matter wid you, Mike?' asks the chap at the door. 'Yer can't bring them two yaps in here and you know it. Gwan out of this.'

"He tried to shut the door, but the checkerboard had his foot between it and the jamb. You might as well have tried to shove in the broadside of an ocean liner as to push against that foot.

"'These gents are friends of mine,' says he. 'Frank, I'll do yez the honor of an introduction to Gin'ral Grant and Dan'l O'Connell. Open that door and compose your face before I'm obliged to break both of 'em.'

"'But I tell you, Mike, I can't,' says the door man, lookin' scared. 'The boss is out, and you know—'

"'*Will* you open that door?' roars the big chap. And with that he hove his shoulder against the panels and jammed the door open by main force, all but flattenin' the other feller behind it. 'Walk in, Gin'ral,' he says to Jonadab, and in we went, me wonderin' what was comin' next, and not darin' to guess.

"There was a kind of partitioned off hallway inside, with another door in the partition. We opened that, and there was a good-sized room, filled with men, smokin' and standin' around. A high board fence was acrost one end of the room, and from behind it comes a jinglin' of telephone bells and the sounds of talk. The floor was covered with torn papers, the window blinds was shut, the gas was burnin' blue, and, between it and the smoke, the smells was as various as them in a fish glue factory. On the fence was a couple of blackboards with 'Belmont' and 'Brighton' and suchlike names in chalk wrote on 'em, and beneath that a whole mess in writin' and figures like, 'Red Tail 4—Wt—108—Jock Smith—5—1,' 'Sourcrout 5—Wt—99—Jock Jones—20—5,' and similar rubbish. And the gang—a mighty mixed lot—was scribblin' in little books and watchin' each other as if they was afraid of havin' their pockets picked; though, to look at 'em, you'd have guessed the biggest part had nothin' in their pockets but holes.

"The six-foot checkerboard—who, it turned out, answered to the hail of 'Mike'—seemed to be right at home with the gang. He called most of 'em by their first names and went sasshayin' around, weltin' 'em on the back and tellin' 'em how he'd 'put crimps in the bookies rolls t'other day,' and a lot more stuff that they seemed to understand, but was hog Greek to me and Jonadab. He'd forgot us altogether which was a mercy the way I looked at it, and I steered the Cap'n over into a corner and we come to anchor on a couple of rickety chairs.

"'What—why—what kind of a place *is* this, Barzilla?' whispers Jonadab, scared.

"'Sh-h-h!' says I. 'Land knows. Just set quiet and hang on to your watch.'

"'But—but I want to find Kelly,' says he.

"'I'd give somethin' to find a back door,' says I. 'Ain't this a collection of dock rats though! If this is a part of your dream, Jonadab, I wish you'd turn over and wake up. Oh land! here's one murderer headin' this way. Keep your change in your fist and keep the fist shut.'

"A more'n average rusty peep, with a rubber collar on and no necktie, comes slinkin' over to us. He had a smile like a crack in a plate.

"'Say, gents, 'he says, 'have you made your bets yet? I've got a dead straight line on the handicap,' says he, 'and I'll put you next for a one spot. It's a sure t'ing at fifteen to three. What do you say?'

"I didn't say nuthin'; but that fool dream was rattlin' round in

Jonadab's skull like a bean in a blowgun, and he sees a chance for a shot.

"'See here, mister,' he says. 'Can you tell me where to locate Mr. Kelly?'

"'Who—Pete?' says the feller. 'Oh, he ain't in just now. But about that handicap. I like the looks of youse and I'll let youse in for a dollar. Or, seein' it's you, we'll say a half. Only fifty cents. I wouldn't do better for my own old man,' he says.

"While the Cap'n was tryin' to unravel one end of this gibberish I spoke up prompt.

"'Say,' says I, 'tell me this, will you? Is the Kelly who owns this—this palace, named Jimmie—James, I mean?'

"'Naw,' says he. 'Sure he ain't. It's Pete Kelly, of course—Silver Pete. But what are you givin' us? Are you bettin' on the race, or ain't you?'

"Well, Jonadab understood that. He bristled up like a brindled cat. If there's any one thing the Cap'n is down on, it's gamblin' and such—always exceptin' when he knows he's won already. You've seen that kind, maybe.

"'Young feller,' he says, perkish, 'I want you to know that me and my friend ain't the bettin' kind. What sort of a hole *is* this, anyway?'

"The rubber collared critter backed off, lookin' worried. He goes acrost the room, and I see him talkin' to two or three other thieves as tough as himself. And they commenced to stare at us and scowl.

"'Come on,' I whispered to Jonadab. 'Let's get out of this place while we can. There ain't no Jimmie Kelly here, or if there is you don't want to find him.'

"He was as willin' to make tracks as I was, by this time, and we headed for the door in the partition. But Rubber Collar and some of the others got acrost our bows.

"'Cut it out,' says one of 'em. 'You can't get away so easy. Hi, Frank! Frank! Who let these turnip pullers in here, anyhow? Who are they?'

"The chap who was tendin' door comes out of his coop. 'You've got me,' he says. 'They come in with Big Mike, and he was loaded and scrappy and jammed 'em through. Said they was pals of his. Where is he?'

"There was a hunt for Mike, and, when they got his bearin's, there he was keeled over on a bench, breathin' like an escape valve. And an admiral's salute wouldn't have woke him up. The whole crew was round us by this time, some ugly, and the rest laffin' and carryin' on.

"'It's the Barkwurst gang,' says one.

"'It's old Bark himself,' says another. 'Look at them lace curtains.' And he points to Jonadab's whiskers.

"'This one's Jacobs in disguise,' sings out somebody else. 'You can tell him by the Rube get-up. Haw! haw!'

"'Soak 'em! Do 'em up! Don't let 'em out!' hollers a ha'f dozen more.

"Jonadab was game; I'll say that for him. And I hadn't been second mate in my time for nothin'.

"'Take your hands off me!' yells the Cap'n. 'I come in here to find a man I'm lookin' for, James Kelly it was, and—You would, would you! Stand by, Barzilla!'

"I stood by. Rubber Collar got one from me that made him remember home and mother, I'll bet. Anyhow, my knuckles ached for two days afterwards. And Jonadab was just as busy. But I cal'late we'd have been ready for the oven in another five minutes if the door hadn't bu'st open with a bang, and a loud dressed chap, with the sweat pourin' down his face, come tearin' in.

"'Beat it, fellers!' he yells. 'The place is goin' to be pinched. I've just had the tip, and they're right on top of me.'

"*Then* there was times. Everybody was shoutin' and swearin' and fallin' over each other to get out. I was kind of lost in the shuffle, and the next thing I remember for sartin is settin' up on Rubber Collar's stomach and lookin' foggy at the door, where the loud dressed man was wrestlin' with a policeman. And there was police at the windows and all around.

"Well, don't talk! I got up, resurrects Jonadab from under a heap of gamblers and furniture, and makes for harbor in our old corner. The police was mighty busy, especially a fat, round-faced, red-mustached man, with gold bands on his cap and arms, that the rest called 'Cap'n.' Him and the loud dressed chap who'd give the alarm was talkin' earnest close to us.

"'I can't help it, Pete,' says the police cap'n. ' 'twas me or the Vice Suppression crowd. They've been on to you for two weeks back. I only just got in ahead of 'em as it was. No, you'll have to go along with the rest and take your chances. Quiet now, everybody, or you'll get it harder,' he roars, givin' orders like the skipper of a passenger boat. 'Stand in line and wait your turns for the wagon.'

"Jonadab grabbed me by the wrist. He was pale and shakin' all over.

"'Oh, Lordy!' says he, 'we're took up. Will we have to go to jail, do you think?'

"'I don't know,' I says, disgusted. 'I presume likely we will. Did you dream anything like this? You'd better see if you can't dream yourself out now.' Twas rubbin' it in, but I was mad.

"'Oh! oh!' says he, flappin' his hands. 'And me a deacon of the church! Will folks know it, do you think?'

"'Will they know it! Sounds as if they knew it already. Just listen to that.'

"The first wagon full of prizes was bein' loaded in down at the front door, and the crowd outside was cheerin' 'em. Judgin' by the whoops and hurrahs there wa'n't no less than a million folks at the show, and they was gettin' the wuth of admission.

"'Oh, dear!' groans Jonadab. 'And it'll be in the papers and all! I can't stand this.'

"And afore I could stop him he'd run over and tackled the head policeman.

"'Mister—Mister Cap'n,' he says, pantin', 'there's been a mistake, an awful mis—take—'

"'That's right,' says the police cap'n, 'there has. Six or eight of you tin horns got clear. But—' Then he noticed who was speakin' to him and his mouth dropped open like a hatch. 'Well, saints above!'he says. 'Have the up-state delegates got to buckin' the ponies, too? Why ain't you back home killin' pertater bugs? You ought to be ashamed.'

"'But we wa'n't gamblin'—me and my friend wa'n't. We was led in here by mistake. We was told that a feller named Kelly lived here and we're huntin' for a man of that name. I've got a message to him from his poor dead father back in Orham. We come all the way from Orham, Mass.—to find him and—'

"The police cap'n turned around then and stared at him hard. 'Humph!' says he, after a spell. 'Go over there and set down till I want you. No, you'll go now and we'll waste no breath on it. Go on, do you hear!'

"So we went, and there we set for ha'f an hour, while the rest of the gang and the blackboards and the paper slips and the telephones and Big Mike and his chair was bein' carted off to the wagon. Once, when one of the constables was beatin' acrost to get us, the police cap'n spoke to him.

"'You can leave these two,' he says. 'I'll take care of them.'

"So, finally, when there was nothin' left but the four walls and us and some of the police, he takes me and Jonadab by the elbows and heads for the door.

"'Now,' says he, 'walk along quiet and peaceable and tell me all about it. Get out of this!' he shouts to the crowd of small boys and loafers on the sidewalk, 'or I'll take you, too.'

"The outsiders fell astern, lookin' heartbroke and disapp'inted that we wa'n't hung on the spot, and the fat boss policeman and us two paraded along slow but grand. I felt like the feller that was caught robbin' the poorhouse, and I cal'late Jonadab felt the same, only he was so busy beggin' and pleadin' and explainin' that he couldn't stop to feel anything.

"He told it all, the whole fool yarn from one end to t'other. How old Pat give him the message and how he went to the laundry, and about his ridiculous dream, every word. And the fat policeman shook all over, like a barrel of cod livers.

"By and by we got to a corner of a street and hove to. I could see the station house loomin' up large ahead. Fatty took a card from his pocketbook, wrote on it with a pencil, and then hailed a hack, one of them stern-first kind where the driver sits up aloft 'way aft. He pushed back the cap with the gilt wreath on it, and I could see his red hair shinin' like a sunset.

"'Here,' says he to the hack driver, 'take these—this pair of salads to the—what d'ye call it?—the Golconda House, wherever on top of the pavement that is. And mind you, deliver 'em safe and don't let the truck horses get a bite at 'em. And at half-past eight to-night you call for 'em and bring 'em here,' handin' up the card he'd written on.

"''Tis the address of my house, I'm givin',' he says, turnin' to Jonadab. 'I'll be off duty then and we'll have dinner and talk about old times. To think of you landin' in Silver Pete's pool room! Dear! dear! Why, Cap'n Wixon, barrin' that your whiskers are a bit longer and a taste grayer, I'd 'a' known you anywheres. Many's the time I've stole apples over your back fence. I'm Jimmie Kelly,' says he."

"Well, by mighty!" exclaimed the depot master, slapping his knee. "So *he* was the Kelly man! Humph!"

"Funny how it turned out, wa'n't it?" said Barzilla. "Course, Cap'n Jonadab was perfectly sat on spiritu'lism and signs and omens and such after that. He's had his fortune told no less'n eight times sence, and, nigh's I can find out, each time it's different. The amount of blondes and brunettes and widows and old maids that he's slated to marry, accordin' to them fortune tellers, is perfectly scandalous. If he lives up to the prophecies, Brigham Young wouldn't be a twospot 'longside of him."

"It's funny about dreams," mused Captain Hiram. "Folks are always tellin' about their comin' true, but none of mine ever did. I used to dream I was goin' to be drowned, but I ain't been yet."

The depot master laughed. "Well," he observed, "once, when I was a youngster, I dreamed two nights runnin' that I was bein' hung. I asked my Sunday school teacher if he believed dreams come true, and he said yes, sometimes. Then I told him my dream, and he said he believed in that one. I judged that any other finish for me would have surprised him. But, somehow or other, they haven't hung me yet."

"There was a hired girl over at the Old Home House who was sat on fortune tellin'," said Wingate. "Her name was Effie, and—"

"Look here!" broke in Captain Bailey Stitt, righteous indignation in his tone, "I've started no less than nineteen different times to tell you about how I went sailin' in an automobile. Now do you want to hear it, or don't you?"

"How you went *sailin'* in an auto?" repeated Barzilla. "Went ridin', you mean."

"I mean sailin'. I went ridin', too, but—"

"You'll have to excuse me, Bailey," interrupted Captain Hiram, rising and looking at his watch. "I've stayed here a good deal longer'n I ought to, already. I must be gettin' on home to see how poor little Dusenberry, my boy, is feelin'. I do hope he's better by now. I wish Dr. Parker hadn't gone out of town."

The depot master rose also. "And I'll have to be excused, too," he declared. "It's most time for the up train. Good-by, Hiram. Give my regards to Sophrony, and if there's anything I can do to help, in case your baby should be sick, just sing out, won't you?"

"But I want to tell about this automobilin' scrape," protested Captain Bailey. "It was one of them things that don't happen every day."

"So was that fortune business of Effie's," declared Wingate. "Honest, the way it worked out was queer enough."

But the train whistled just then and the group broke up. Captain Sol went out to the platform, where Cornelius Rowe, Ed Crocker, Beriah Higgins, Obed Gott, and other interested citizens had already assembled. Wingate and Stitt followed. As for Captain Hiram Baker, he hurried home, his conscience reproving him for remaining so long away from his wife and poor little Hiram Joash, more familiarly known as "Dusenberry."

Chapter XIII
Dusenberry's Birthday

MRS. Baker met her husband at the door.

"How is he?" was the Captain's first question. "Better, hey?"

"No," was the nervous answer. "No, I don't think he is. His throat's terrible sore and the fever's just as bad."

Again Captain Hiram's conscience smote him.

"Dear! dear!" he exclaimed. "And I've been loafin' around the depot with Sol Berry and the rest of 'em instead of stayin' home with you, Sophrony. I *knew* I was doin' wrong, but I didn't realize—"

"Course you didn't, Hiram. I'm glad you got a few minutes' rest, after bein' up with him half the night. I do wish the doctor was home, though. When will he be back?"

"Not until late to-morrer, if then. Did you keep on givin' the medicine?"

"Yes, but it don't seem to do much good. You go and set with him now, Hiram. I must be seein' about supper."

So into the sick room went Captain Hiram to sit beside the crib and sing "Sailor boy, sailor boy, 'neath the wild billow," as a lugubrious lullaby.

Little Hiram Joash tossed and tumbled. He was in a fitful slumber when Mrs. Baker called her husband to supper. The meal was anything but a cheerful one. They talked but little. Over the home, ordinarily so cheerful, had settled a gloom that weighed upon them.

"My! my!" sighed Captain Hiram, "how lonesome it seems without him chatterin' and racketin' sound. Seems darker'n usual, as if there was a shadow on the place."

"Hush, Hiram! don't talk that way. A shadow! Oh, *what* made you say that? Sounds like a warnin', almost."

"Warnin'?"

"Yes, a forewarnin', you know. 'The valley of the shadow—'"

"*Hush!*" Captain Baker's face paled under its sunburn. "Don't say such things, Sophrony. If that happened, the Lord help you and me. But it won't—it won't. We're nervous, that's all. We're always so careful of Dusenberry, as if he was made out of thin china, that we get fidgety when there's no need of it. We mustn't be foolish."

After supper Mrs. Baker tiptoed into the bedroom. She emerged with a very white face.

"Hiram," she whispered, "he acts dreadful queer. Come in and see him."

The "first mate" was tossing back and forth in the crib, making odd little choky noises in his swollen throat. When his father entered he opened his eyes, stared unmeaningly, and said: "'Tand by to det der ship under way."

"Good Lord! he's out of his head," gasped the Captain. Sophronia and he stepped back into the sitting room and looked at each other, the same thought expressed in the face of each. Neither spoke for a moment, then Captain Hiram said:

"Now don't you worry, Sophrony. The Doctor ain't home, but I'm goin' out to—to telegraph him, or somethin'. Keep a stiff upper lip. It'll be all right. God couldn't go back on you and me that way. He just couldn't. I'll be back in a little while."

"But, oh, Hiram! if he should—if he *should* be taken away, what *would* we do?"

She began to cry. Her husband laid a trembling hand on her shoulder.

"But he won't," he declared stoutly. "I tell you God wouldn't do such a thing. Good-by, old lady. I'll hurry fast as I can."

As he took up his cap and turned to the door he heard the voice of the weary little first mate chokily calling his crew to quarters. "All hands on deck!"

The telegraph office was in Beriah Higgins's store. Thither ran the Captain. Pat Sharkey, Mr. Higgins's Irish helper, who acted as telegraph operator during Gertie Higgins's absence, gave

Captain Hiram little satisfaction.

"How can I get Dr. Parker?" asked Pat. "He's off on a cruise and land knows where I can reach him to-night. I'll do what I can, Cap, but it's ten chances out of nine against a wire gettin' to him."

Captain Hiram left the store, dodging questioners who were anxious to know what his trouble might be, and dazedly crossed Main Street, to the railway station. He thought of asking advice of his friend, the depot master.

The evening train from Boston pulled out as he passed through the waiting room. One or two passengers were standing on the platform. One of these was a short, square-shouldered man with gray side whiskers and eyeglasses. The initials on his suit case were J. S. M., Boston, and they stood for John Spencer Morgan. If the bearer of the suit case had followed the fashion of the native princes of India and had emblazoned his titles upon his baggage, the commonplace name just quoted might have been followed by "M.D., LL.D., at Harvard and Oxford; vice president American Medical Society; corresponding secretary Associated Society of Surgeons; lecturer at Harvard Medical College; author of 'Diseases of the Throat and Lungs,' etc., etc."

But Dr. Morgan was not given to advertising either his titles or himself, and he was hurrying across the platform to Redny Blount's depot wagon when Captain Hiram touched him on the arm.

"Why, hello, Captain Baker," exclaimed the Doctor, "how do you do?"

"Dr. Morgan," said the Captain, "I—I hope you'll excuse my presumin' on you this way, but I want to ask a favor of you, a great favor. I want to ask if you'll come down to the house and see the boy; he's on the sick list."

"What, Dusenberry?"

"Yes, sir. He's pretty bad, I'm 'fraid, and the old lady's considerable upset about him. If you just come down and kind of take an observation, so's we could sort of get our bearin's, as you might say, 'twould be a mighty help to all hands."

"But where's your town physician? Hasn't he been called?"

The Captain explained. He had inquired, and he had telegraphed, but could get no word of Dr. Parker's whereabouts.

The great Boston specialist listened to Captain Hiram's story in an absent-minded way. Holidays were few and far between with him, and when he accepted the long-standing invitation of Mr. Ogden Williams to run down for the week end he determined to forget the science of medicine and all that pertained to it for the four days of his outing. But an exacting patient had detained him long enough to prevent his taking the train that morning, and now, on the moment of his belated arrival, he was asked to pay a professional call. He liked the Captain, who had taken him out fishing several times on his previous excursions to East Harniss, and he remembered Dusenberry as a happy little sea urchin, but he simply couldn't interrupt his pleasure trip to visit a sick baby. Besides, the child was Dr. Parker's patient, and professional ethics forbade interference.

"Captain Hiram," he said, "I am sorry to disappoint you, but it will be impossible for me to do what you ask. Mr. Williams expected me this morning, and I am late already. Dr. Parker will, no doubt, return soon. The baby cannot be dangerously ill or he would not have left him."

The Captain slowly turned away.

"Thank you, Doctor," he said huskily. "I knew I hadn't no right to ask."

He walked across the platform, abstractedly striking his right hand into his left. When he reached the ticket window he put one hand against the frame as if to steady himself, and stood there listlessly.

The enterprising Mr. Blount had been hanging about the Doctor like a cat about the cream pitcher; now he rushed up, grasped the suit case, and officiously led the way toward the depot wagon. Dr. Morgan followed more slowly. As he passed the Captain he glanced up into the latter's face, lighted, as it was, by the lamp inside the window.

The Doctor stopped and looked again. Then he took another step forward, hesitated, turned on his heel, and said:

"Wait a moment, Blount. Captain Hiram, do you live far from here?"

The Captain started. "No, sir, only a little ways."

"All right. I'll go down and look at this boy of yours. Mind you, I'll not take the case, simply give my opinion on it, that's all. Blount, take my grip to Mr. Williams's. I'm going to walk down with the Captain."

"Haul on ee bowline, ee bowline, haul!" muttered the first mate, as they came into the room. The lamp that Sophronia was holding shook, and the Captain hurriedly brushed his eyes with the back of his hand.

Dr. Morgan started perceptibly as he bent forward to look at the little fevered face of Dusenberry. Graver and graver he became as he felt the pulse and peered into the swollen throat. At length he rose and led the way back into the sitting room.

"Captain Baker," he said simply, "I must ask you and your wife to be brave. The child has diphtheria and—"

"Diphthery!" gasped Sophronia, as white as her best table-cloth.

"Good Lord above!" cried the Captain.

"Diphtheria," repeated the Doctor; "and, although I dislike extremely to criticize a member of my own profession, I must say that any physician should have recognized it."

Sophronia groaned and covered her face with her apron.

"Ain't there—ain't there no chance, Doctor?" gasped the Captain.

"Certainly, there's a chance. If I could administer antitoxin by to-morrow noon the patient might recover. What time does the morning train from Boston arrive here?"

"Ha'f-past ten or thereabouts."

Dr. Morgan took his notebook from his pocket and wrote a few lines in pencil on one of the pages. Then he tore out the leaf and handed it to the Captain.

"Send that telegram immediately to my assistant in Boston," he said. "It directs him to send the antitoxin by the early train. If nothing interferes it should be here in time."

Captain Hiram took the slip of paper and ran out at the door bareheaded.

Dr. Morgan stood in the middle of the floor absent-mindedly

looking at his watch. Sophronia was gazing at him appealingly. At length he put his watch in his pocket and said quietly:

"Mrs. Baker, I must ask you to give me a room. I will take the case." Then he added mentally: "And that settles my vacation."

Dr. Morgan's assistant was a young man whom nature had supplied with a prematurely bald head, a flourishing beard, and a way of appearing ten years older than he really was. To these gifts, priceless to a young medical man, might be added boundless ambition and considerable common sense.

The yellow envelope which contained the few lines meaning life or death to little Hiram Joash Baker was delivered at Dr. Morgan's Back Bay office at ten minutes past ten. Dr. Payson—that was the assistant's name—was out, but Jackson, the colored butler, took the telegram into his employer's office, laid it on the desk among the papers, and returned to the hall to finish his nap in the armchair. When Dr. Payson came in, at 11:30, the sleepy Jackson forgot to mention the dispatch.

The next morning as Jackson was cleaning the professional boots in the kitchen and chatting with the cook, the thought of the yellow envelope came back to his brain. He went up the stairs with such precipitation that the cook screamed, thinking he had a fit.

"Doctah! Doctah!" he exclaimed, opening the door of the assistant's chamber, "did you git dat telegraft I lef' on your desk las' night?"

"What telegraph?" asked the assistant sleepily. By way of answer Jackson hurried out and returned with the yellow envelope. The assistant opened it and read as follows:

Send 1,500 units Diphtheritic Serum to me by morning train. Don't fail. Utmost importance.
J. S. Morgan.

Dr. Payson sprang out of bed, and running to the table took up the Railway Guide, turned to the pages devoted to the O. C. and C. C. Railroad and ran his finger down the printed tables. The morning train for Cape Cod left at 7:10. It was 6:45 at that moment. As has been said, the assistant had considerable common sense. He proved this by wasting no time in telling the forgetful Jackson what he thought of him. He sent the latter after a cab and proceeded to dress in double-quick time. Ten minutes later he was on his way to the station with the little wooden case containing the precious antitoxin, wrapped and addressed, in his pocket.

It was seven by the Arlington Street Church clock as the cab rattled down Boylston Street. A tangle of a trolley car and a market wagon delayed it momentarily at Harrison Avenue and Essex Street. Dr. Payson, leaning out as the carriage swung into Dewey Square, saw by the big clock on the Union Station that it was 7:13. He had lost the train.

Now, the assistant had been assistant long enough to know that excuses—in the ordinary sense of the word—did not pass current with Dr. Morgan. That gentleman had telegraphed for antitoxin, and said it was important that he should have it; therefore, antitoxin must be sent in spite of time-tables and forgetful butlers. Dr. Payson went into the waiting room and sat down to think. After a moment's deliberation he went over to the ticket office and asked:

"What is the first stop of the Cape Cod express?"

"Brockboro," answered the ticket seller.

"Is the train usually on time?"

"Well, I should smile. That's Charlie Mills's train, and the old man ain't been conductor on this road twenty-two years for nothin'."

"Mills? Does he live on Shawmut Avenue?"

"Dunno. Billy, where does Charlie Mills live?"

"Somewhere at the South End. Shawmut Avenue, I think."

"Thank you," said the assistant, and, helping himself to a timetable, he went back rejoicing to his seat in the waiting room. He had stumbled upon an unexpected bit of luck.

There might be another story written in connection with this one; the story of a veteran railroad man whose daughter had been very, very ill with a dreaded disease of the lungs, and who, when other physicians had given up hope, had been brought back to health by a celebrated specialist of our acquaintance. But this story cannot be told just now; suffice it to say that Conductor Charlie Mills had vowed that he would put his neck beneath the wheels of his own express train, if by so doing he could confer a favor on Dr. John Spencer Morgan.

The assistant saw by his time-table that the Cape Cod express reached Brockboro at 8:05. He went over to the telegraph office and wrote two telegrams. The first read like this:

CALVIN S. WISE, The People's Drug Store, 28 Broad Street, Brockboro, Mass.: *Send package 1,500 units Diphtheritic Serum marked with my name to station. Hand to Conductor Mills, Cape Cod express. Train will wait. Matter life and death.*

The second telegram was to Conductor Mills. It read:

Hold train Brockboro to await arrival C. A. Wise. Great personal favor. Very important.

Both of these dispatches were signed with the magic name, "J. S. Morgan, M.D."

"Well," said the assistant as he rode back to his office, "I don't know whether Wise will get the stuff to the train in time, or whether Mills will wait for him, but at any rate I've done my part. I hope breakfast is ready, I'm hungry."

Mr. Wise, of "The People's Drug Store," had exactly two minutes in which to cover the three-quarters of a mile to the station. As a matter of course, he was late. Inquiring for Conductor Mills, he was met by a red-faced man in uniform, who, watch in hand, demanded what in the vale of eternal torment he meant by keeping him waiting eight minutes.

"Do you realize," demanded the red-faced man, "that I'm liable to lose my job? I'll have you to understand that if any other man than Doc. Morgan asked me to hold up the Cape Cod express, I'd tell him to go right plumb to—"

Here Mr. Wise interrupted to hand over the package and explain that it was a matter of life and death. Conductor Mills only grunted as he swung aboard the train.

"Hump her, Jim," he said to the engineer; "she's got to make up those eight minutes."

And Jim did.

And so it happened that on the morning of the Fourth of July, Dusenberry's birthday, Captain Hiram Baker and his wife sat together in the sitting room, with very happy faces. The Captain had in his hands the "truly boat with sails," which the little first mate had so ardently wished for.

She was a wonder, that boat. Red hull, real lead on the keel, brass rings on the masts, reef points on the main and fore sail, jib, flying jib and topsails, all complete. And on the stern was the name, "Dusenberry. East Harniss."

Captain Hiram set her down in front of him on the floor.

"Gee!" he exclaimed, "won't his eyes stick out when he sees that rig, hey? Wisht he would be well enough to see it to-day, same as we planned."

"Well, Hiram," said Sophrony, "we hadn't ought to complain. We'd ought to be thankful he's goin' to get well at all. Dr. Morgan says, thanks to that blessed toxing stuff, he'll be up and around in a couple of weeks."

"Sophrony," said her husband, "we'll have a special birthday celebration for him when he gets all well. You can bake the frosted cake and we'll have some of the other children in. I *told* you God wouldn't be cruel enough to take him away."

And this is how Fate and the medical profession and the O. C. and C. C. Railroad combined to give little Hiram Joash Baker his birthday, and explains why, as he strolled down Main Street that afternoon, Captain Hiram was heard to sing heartily:

Haul on the bowline, the 'Phrony is a-rollin',
Haul on the bowline, the bowline, *haul*!

Chapter XIV
Effie's Fate

S URELY, BUT VERY, very slowly, the little Berry house moved on its rollers up the Hill Boulevard. Right at its heels—if a house may be said to have heels—came the "pure Colonial," under the guidance of the foreman with "progressive methods." Groups of idlers, male and female, stood about and commented. Simeon Phinney smilingly replied to their questions. Captain Sol himself seemed little interested. He spent most of his daylight time at the depot, only going to the Higginses' house for his meals. At night, after the station was closed, he sought his own dwelling, climbed over the joist and rollers, entered, retired to his room, and went to bed.

Each day also he grew more taciturn. Even with Simeon, his particular friend, he talked little.

"What *is* the matter with you, Sol?" asked Mr. Phinney. "You're as glum as a tongue-tied parrot. Ain't you satisfied with the way I'm doin' your movin'? The white horse can go back again if you say so."

"I'm satisfied," grunted the depot master. "Let you know when I've got any fault to find. How soon will you get abreast the—abreast the Seabury lot?"

"Let's see," mused the building mover. "Today's the eighth. Well, I'll be there by the eleventh, *sure*. Can't drag it out no longer, Sol, even if the other horse is took sick. 'Twon't do. Williams has been complainin' to the selectmen and they're be-ginnin' to pester me. As for that Colt and Adams foreman—whew!"

He whistled. His companion smiled grimly.

"Williams himself drops in to see me occasional," he said. "Tells me what he thinks of me, with all the trimmin's added. I cal'late he gets as good as he sends. I'm always glad to see him; he keeps me cheered up, in his way."

"Ye-es, I shouldn't wonder. Was he in to-day?"

"He was. And somethin' has pleased him, I guess. At any rate he was in better spirits. Asked me if I was goin' to move right onto that Main Street lot soon as my house got there."

"What did you say?"

"I said I was cal'latin' to. Told him I hated to get out of the high-society circles I'd been livin' in lately, but that everyone had their comedowns in this world."

"Ho, ho! that was a good one. What answer did he make to that?"

"Well, he said the 'high society' would miss me. Then he finished up with a piece of advice. 'Berry,' says he, 'don't move onto that lot *too* quick. I wouldn't if I was you.' Then he went away, chucklin'."

"Chucklin', hey? What made him so joyful?"

"Don't know"—Captain Sol's face clouded once more—"and I care less," he added brusquely.

Simeon pondered. "Have you heard from Abner Payne, Sol?" he asked. "Has Ab answered that letter you wrote sayin' you'd swap your lot for the Main Street one?"

"No, he hasn't. I wrote him that day I told you to move me."

"Hum! that's kind of funny. You don't s'pose—"

He stopped, noticing the expression on his friend's face. The depot master was looking out through the open door of the waiting room. On the opposite side of the road, just emerging from Mr. Higgins's "general store," was Olive Edwards, the widow whose home was to be pulled down as soon as the "Colonial" reached its destination. She came out of the store and started up Main Street. Suddenly, and as if obeying an involuntary impulse, she turned her head. Her eyes met those of Captain Sol Berry, the depot master. For a brief instant their glance met, then Mrs. Edwards hurried on.

Sim Phinney sighed pityingly. "Looks kind of tired and worried, don't she?" he ventured. His friend did not speak.

"I say," repeated Phinney, "that Olive looks sort of worn out and—"

"Has she heard from the Omaha cousin yet?" interrupted the depot master.

"No; Mr. Hilton says not. Sol, what *do* you s'pose—"

But Captain Sol had risen and gone into the ticket office. The door closed behind him. Mr. Phinney shook his head and walked out of the building. On his way back to the scene of the house moving he shook his head several times.

On the afternoon of the ninth Captain Bailey Stitt and his friend Wingate came to say good-by. Stitt was going back to Orham on the "up" train, due at 3:30. Barzilla would return to Wellmouth and the Old Home House on the evening (the "down") train.

"Hey, Sol!" shouted Wingate, as they entered the waiting room. "Sol! where be you?"

The depot master came out of the ticket office. "Hello, boys!" he said shortly.

"Hello, Sol!" hailed Stitt. "Barzilla and me have come to shed the farewell tear. As hirelin's of soulless corporations, meanin' the Old Home House at Wellmouth and the Ocean House at Orham, we've engaged all the shellfish along-shore and are goin' to clear out."

"Yes," chimed in his fellow "hireling," "and we thought the pleasantest place to put in our few remainin' hours—as the papers say when a feller's goin' to be hung—was with you."

"I thought so," said Captain Bailey, with a wink. "We've been havin' more or less of an argument, Sol. Remember how Barzilla made fun of Jonadab Wixon for believin' in dreams? Yes, well that was only make believe. He believes in 'em himself."

"I don't either," declared Wingate. "And I never said so. What I said was that sometimes it almost seemed as if there was somethin' *in* fortune tellin' and such."

"There is," chuckled Bailey with another wink at the depot master. "There's money in it—for the fortune tellers."

"I said—and I say again," protested Barzilla, "that I knew a case at our hotel of a servant girl named Effie, and she—"

"Oh, Heavens to Betsy! Here he goes again, I steered him in

here on purpose, Sol, so's he'd get off that subject."

"You never neither. You said—"

The depot master held up his hand. "Don't both talk at once," he commanded. "Set down and be peaceful, can't you. That's right. What about this Effie, Barzilla?"

"Now look here!" protested Stitt.

"Shut up, Bailey! Who was Effie, Barzilla?"

"She was third assistant roustabout and table girl at the Old Home House," said Wingate triumphantly. "Got another cigar, Sol? Thanks. Yes, this Effie had never worked out afore and she was greener'n a mess of spinach; but she was kind of pretty to look at and—"

"Ah, ha!" crowed Captain Bailey, "here comes the heart confessions. Want to look out for these old bachelors, Sol. Fire away, Barzilla; let us know the worst."

"I took a fancy to her, in a way. She got in the habit of tellin' me her troubles and secrets, me bein' old enough to be her dad—"

"Aw, yes!" this from Stitt, the irrepressible. "That's an old gag. We know—"

"*will* you shut up?" demanded Captain Sol. "Go on, Barzilla."

"Me bein' old enough to be her dad," with a glare at Captain Bailey, "and not bein' too proud to talk with hired help. I never did have that high-toned notion. 'Twa'n't so long since I was a fo'mast hand.

"So Effie told me a lot about herself. Seems she'd been over to the Cattle Show at Ostable one year, and she was loaded to the gunwale with some more or less facts that a fortune-tellin' specimen by the name of the 'Marvelous Oriental Seer' had handed her in exchange for a quarter.

"'Yup,' says she, bobbin' her head so emphatic that the sky-blue ribbon pennants on her black hair flapped like a loose tops'l in a gale of wind. 'Yup,' says she, 'I b'lieve it just as much as I b'lieve anything. How could I help it when he told me so much that has come true already? He said I'd seen trouble, and the dear land knows that's so! and that I might see more, and I cal'late that's pretty average likely. And he said I hadn't been brought up in luxury—'

"'Which wa'n't no exaggeration neither,' I put in, thinkin' of the shack over on the Neck Road where she and her folks used to live.

"'No,' says she; 'and he told me I'd always had longin's for better and higher things and that my intellectuals was above my station. Well, ever sence I was knee high to a kitchen chair I'd ruther work upstairs than down, and as for intellectuals, ma always said I was the smartest young one she'd raised yet. So them statements give me consider'ble confidence. But he give out that I was to make a journey and get money, and when *that* come true I held up both hands and stood ready to swaller all the rest of it.'

"'So it come true, did it?' says I.

"'Um-hm,' says she, bouncin' her head again. 'Inside of four year I traveled 'way over to South Eastboro—'most twelve mile—to my Uncle Issy's fun'ral, and there I found that he'd left me nine hundred dollars for my very own. And down I flops on the parlor sofy and says I: "There! don't talk superstition to *me* no more! A person that can foretell Uncle Issy's givin' anybody a cent, let alone nine hundred dollars, is a good enough prophet for *me* to tie to. Now I *know* that I'm going to marry the dark-complected man, and I'll be ready for him when he comes along. I never spent a quarter no better than when I handed it over to that Oriental Seer critter at the Cattle Show." That's what I said then and I b'lieve it yet. Wouldn't you feel the same way?'

"I said sure thing I would. I'd found out that the best way to keep Effie's talk shop runnin' was to agree with her. And I liked to hear her talk.

"'Yup,' she went on, 'I give right in then. I'd traveled same as the fortune teller said, and I'd got more money'n I ever expected to see, let alone own. And ever sence I've been sartin as I'm alive that the feller I marry will be of a rank higher'n mine and dark complected and good-lookin' and distinguished, and that he'll be name of Butler.'

"'Butler?' says I. 'What will he be named Butler for?'

"''Cause the Seer critter said so. He said he could see the word Butler printed out over the top of my head in flamin' letters. Pa used to say 'twas a wonder it never set fire to my crimps, but he was only foolin'. I know that it's all comin' out true. You ain't acquaintanced to any Butlers, are you?'

"'No,' says I. 'I heard Ben Butler make a speech once when he was gov'nor, but he's dead now. There ain't no Butlers on the Old Home shippin' lists.'

"'Oh, I know that!' she says. 'And everybody round here is homelier'n a moultin' pullet. There now! I didn't mean exactly *every*body, of course. But you ain't dark complected, you know, nor—'

"'No,' says I, 'nor rank nor distinguished neither. Course the handsome part might fit me, but I'd have to pass on the rest of the hand. That's all right, Effie; my feelin's have got fire-proofed sence I've been in the summer hotel business. Now you'd better run along and report to Susannah. I hear her whoopin' for you, and she don't light like a canary bird on the party she's mad with.'

"She didn't, that was a fact. Susannah Debs, who was housekeeper for us that year, was middlin' young and middlin' good-lookin', and couldn't forget it. Also and likewise, she had a suit for damages against the railroad, which she had hopes would fetch her money some day or other, and she couldn't forget that neither. She was skipper of all the hired hands and, bein' as Effie was prettier than she was, never lost a chance to lay the poor girl out. She put the other help up to pokin' fun at Effie's green ways and high-toned notions, and 'twas her that started 'em callin' her 'Lady Evelyn' in the fo'castle—servants' quarters, I mean.

"'I'm a-comin', 'screams Effie, startin' for the door. 'Susannah's in a tearin' hurry to get through early to-day,' she adds to me. 'She's got the afternoon off, and her beau's comin' to take her buggy ridin'. He's from over Harniss way somewheres and they say he's just lovely. My sakes! I wisht somebody'd take *me* to ride. Ah hum! cal'late I'll have to wait for my Butler man. Say, Mr. Wingate, you won't mention my fortune to a soul, will you? I never told anybody but you.'

"I promised to keep mum and she cleared out. After dinner, as I was smokin', along with Cap'n Jonadab, on the side piazza, a horse and buggy drove in at the back gate. A young chap with black curly hair was pilotin' the craft. He was a stranger to me, wore a checkerboard suit and a bonfire necktie, and had his hat twisted over one ear. Altogether he looked some like a sunflower goin' to seed.

"'Who's that barber's sign when it's to home?' says I to Jonadab. He snorted contemptuous.

"'That?'he says. 'Don't you know the cut of that critter's jib? He plays pool "for the house" in Web Saunders's place over to Orham. He's the housekeeper's steady comp'ny—steady by spells, if all I hear's true. Good-for-nothin' cub, I call him. Wisht I'd had him aboard a vessel of mine; I'd 'a' squared his yards for him. Look how he cants his hat to starboard so's to show them lovelocks. Bah!'

"'What's his name?' I asks.

"'Name? Name's Butler—Simeon Butler. Don't you remember ... Hey? What in tunket ...?'

"Both of us had jumped as if somebody'd touched off a bomb-shell under our main hatches. The windows of the dining room was right astern of us. We whirled round, and there was Effie. She'd been clearin' off one of the tables and there she stood, with the smashed pieces of an ice-cream platter in front of her, the melted cream sloppin' over her shoes, and her face lookin' like the picture of Lot's wife just turnin' to salt. Only Effie looked as if she enjoyed the turnin'. She never spoke nor moved, just stared after that buggy with her black eyes sparklin' like burnt holes in a blanket.

"I was too astonished to say anything, but Jonadab had his eye on that smashed platter and *he* had things to say, plenty of 'em. I walked off and left Effie playin' congregation to a sermon on the text 'Crockery costs money.' You'd think that ice-cream dish was a genuine ugly, nicked 'antique' wuth any city loon's ten dollars, instead of bein' only new and pretty fifty-cent china. I felt real sorry for the poor girl.

"But I needn't have been. That evenin' I found her on the back steps, all Sunday duds and airs. Her hair had a wire friz on it, and her dress had Joseph's coat in Scriptur' lookin' like a mournin' rig. She'd have been real handsome—to a body that was color blind.

"'My, Effie!' says I, 'you sartin do look fine to-night.'

"'Yup,' she says, contented, 'I guess likely I do. Hope so, 'cause I'm wearin' all I've got. Say, Mr. Wingate,' says she, excited as a cat in a fit, 'did you see him?'

"'Him?' says I. 'Who's him?'

"'Why, *him*! The one the Seer said was comin'. The handsome, dark-complected feller I'm goin' to marry. The Butler one. That was him in the buggy this afternoon.'

"I looked at her. I'd forgot all about the fool prophecy.

"'Good land of love!' I says. 'You don't cal'late he's comin' to marry *you*, do you, just 'cause his name's Butler? There's ten thousand Butlers in the world. Besides, your particular one was slated to be high ranked and distinguished, and this specimen scrubs up the billiard-room floor and ain't no more distinguished than a poorhouse pig.'

"'Ain't?' she sings out. 'Ain't distinguished? With all them beautiful curls, and rings on his fingers, and—'

"'Bells on his toes? No!' says I, emphatic. 'Anyhow, he's signed for the v'yage already. He's Susannah Debs's steady, and they're off buggy ridin' together right now. And if she catches you makin' eyes at her best feller—Whew!'

"Didn't make no difference. He was her Butler, sure. 'Twas Fate—that's what 'twas—Fate, just the same as in storybooks. She was sorry for poor Susannah and she wouldn't do nothin' mean nor underhanded; but couldn't I understand that 'twas all planned out for her by Providence and that everlastin' Seer? Just let me watch and see, that's all.

"What can you do with an idiot like that? I walked off disgusted and left her. But I cal'lated to watch. I judged 'twould be more fun than any 'play-actin' show ever I took in.

"And 'twas, in a way. Don't ask me how they got acquainted, 'cause I can't tell you for sartin. Nigh's I can learn, Susannah and Sim had some sort of lover's row durin' their buggy ride, and when they got back to the hotel they was scurcely on speakin' terms. And Sim, who always had a watch out for'ard for pretty girls, see Effie standin' on the servants' porch all togged up regardless and gay as a tea-store chromo, and nothin' to do but he

must be introduced. One of the stable hands done the intro-
ducin', I b'lieve, and if he'd have been hung afterwards 'twould
have sarved him right.

"Anyhow, inside of a week Butler come round again to take a
lady friend drivin', but this time 'twas Effie, not the housekeeper, that was passenger. And Susannah glared after 'em like
a cat after a sparrow, and the very next day she was for havin'
Effie discharged for incompetentiveness. I give Jonadab the tip,
though, so that didn't go through. But I cal'late there was a parrot and monkey time among the help from then on.

"They all sided with Susannah, of course. She was their boss,
for one thing, and 'Lady Evelyn's' high-minded notions wa'n't
popular, for another. But Effie didn't care—bless you, no! She
and that Butler sport was together more and more, and the next
thing I heard was that they was engaged. I snum, if it didn't look
as if the Oriental man knew his job after all.

"I spoke to the stable hand about it.

"'Look here,' says I, 'is this business betwixt that pool player
and our Effie serious?'

"He laughed. 'Serious enough, I guess,' he says. 'They're goin'
to be married pretty soon, I hear. It's all 'cordin' to the law and
the prophets. Ain't you heard about the fortune tellin' and how
'twas foretold she'd marry a Butler?'

"I'd heard, but I didn't s'pose he had. However, it seemed that
Effie hadn't been able to keep it to herself no longer. Soon as
she'd hooked her man she'd blabbed the whole thing. The
fo'mast hands wa'n't talkin' of nothin' else, so this feller said.

"'Humph!' says I. 'Is it the prophecy that Butler's bankin' on?'

"He laughed again. 'Not so much as on Lady Evelyn's nine hundred, I cal'late,' says he. Sim likes Susannah the best of the two,
so we all reckon, but she ain't rich and Effie is. And yet, if the
Debs woman should win that lawsuit of hers against the railroad she'd have pretty nigh twice as much. Butler's a fool not to
wait, I think,' he says.

"This was of a Monday. On Friday evenin' Effie comes around
to see me. I was alone in the office.

"'Mr. Wingate,' she says, 'I'm goin' to leave to-morrer night.

I'm goin' to be married on Sunday.'

"I'd been expecting it, but I couldn't help feelin' sorry for her.

"'Don't do nothin' rash, Effie,' I told her. 'Are you sure that But-ler critter cares anything about you and not your money?'

"She flared up like a tar barrel. 'The idea!' she says, turnin' red. 'I just come in to give you warnin'. Good-by.'

"'Hold on,' I sung out to her. 'Effie, I've thought consider'ble about you lately. I've been tryin' to help you a little on the sly. I realized that 'twa'n't pleasant for you workin' here under Susan-nah Debs, and I've been tryin' to find a nice place for you. I wrote about you to Bob Van Wedderburn; he's the rich banker chap who stopped here one summer. "Jonesy," we used to call him. I know him and his wife fust rate, and he'd do 'most anything as a favor to me. I told him what a neat, handy girl you was, and he writes that he'll give you the job of second girl at his swell New York house, if you want it. Now you just hand that Sim Butler his clearance papers and go work for Bob's wife. The wages are dou-ble what you get here, and—'

"She didn't wait to hear the rest. Just sailed out of the room with her nose in the air. In a minute, though, back she come and just put her head in the door.

"'I'm much obliged to you, Mr. Wingate,' says she. 'I know you mean well. But you ain't had your fate foretold, same's I have. It's all been arranged for me, and I couldn't stop it no more'n Jonah could help swallerin' the whale. I—I kind of wish you'd be on hand at the back door on Sunday mornin' when Simeon comes to take me away. You—you're about the only real friend I've got,' she says.

"And off she went, for good this time. I pitied her, in spite of her bein' such a dough head. I knew what sort of a husband that pool-room shark would make. However, there wa'n't nothin' to be done. And next day Cap'n Jonadab was round, madder'n a licked pup. Seems Susannah's lawyer at Orham had sent for her to come right off and see him. Somethin' about the suit, it was. And she was goin' in spite of everything. And with Effie's leavin' at the same time, what was we goin' to do over Sunday? and so forth and so on.

"Well, we had to do the best we could, that's all. But that Saturday was busy, now I tell you. Sunday mornin' broke fine and clear and, after breakfast was over, I remembered Effie and that 'twas her weddin' day. On the back steps I found her, dressed in all her grandeur, with her packed trunk ready, waitin' for the bridegroom.

"'Ain't come yet, hey, Effie?' says I.

"'No,' says she, smilin' and radiant. 'It's a little early for him yet, I guess.'

"I went off to 'tend to the boarders. At half past ten, when I made the back steps again, she was still there. T'other servants was peekin' out of the kitchen windows, grinnin' and passin' remarks.

"'Hello!' I calls out. 'Not married yet? What's the matter?'

"She'd stopped smilin', but she was as chipper as ever, to all appearances.

"'I—I guess the horse has gone lame or somethin',' says she. 'He'll be here any time now.'

"There was a cackle from the kitchen windows. I never said nothin'. She'd made her nest; now let her roost on it.

"But at twelve Butler hadn't hove in sight. Every hand, male and female, on the place, that wa'n't busy, was hangin' around the back of the hotel, waitin' and watchin' and ridiculin' and havin' a high time. Them that had errands made it a p'int to cruise past that way. Lots of the boarders had got wind of the doin's, and they was there, too.

"Effie was settin' on her trunk, tryin' hard to look brave. I went up and spoke to her.

"'Come, my girl,' says I. 'Don't set here no longer. Come into the house and wait. Hadn't you better?'

"'No!' says she, loud and defiant like. 'No, sir! It's all right. He's a little late, that's all. What do you s'pose I care for a lot of jealous folks like those up there?' wavin' her flipper scornful toward the kitchen.

"And then, all to once, she kind of broke down, and says to me, with a pitiful sort of choke in her voice:

"'Oh, Mr. Wingate! I can't stand this. Why *don't* he come?'

"I tried hard to think of somethin' comfortin' to say, but afore I could h'ist a satisfyin' word out of my hatches I heard the noise of a carriage comin'. Effie heard it, too, and so did everybody else. We all looked toward the gate. 'Twas Sim Butler, sure enough, in his buggy and drivin' the same old horse; but settin' alongside of him on the seat was Susannah Debs, the housekeeper. And maybe she didn't look contented with things in gen'ral!

"Butler pulled up his horse by the gate. Him and Susannah bowed to all hands. Nobody said anything for a minute. Then Effie bounced off the trunk and down them steps.

"'Simmie' she sung out, breathless like, 'Simeon Butler, what does this mean?'

"The Debs woman straightened up on the seat. 'Thank you, marm,' says she, chilly as the top section of an ice chest, 'I'll request you not to call my husband by his first name.'

"It was so still you could have heard yourself grow. Effie turned white as a Sunday tablecloth.

"'Your—husband?' she gasps. 'Your—your *husband?*'

"'Yes, marm,' purrs the housekeeper. 'My husband was what I said. Mr. Butler and me have just been married.'

"'Sorry, Effie, old girl,' puts in Butler, so sassy I'd love to have preached his fun'ral sermon. 'Too bad, but fust love's strongest, you know. Susie and me was engaged long afore you come to town.'

"*Then* such a haw-haw and whoop bust from the kitchen and fo'castle as you never heard. For a jiffy poor Effie wilted right down. Then she braced up and her black eyes snapped.

"'I wish you joy of your bargain, marm,' says she to Susannah. 'You'd ought to be proud of it. And as for *you*,' she says, swingin' round toward the rest of the help, 'I—'

"'How 'bout that prophet?' hollers somebody.

"'Three cheers for the Oriental!' bellers somebody else.

"'When you marry the right Butler fetch him along and let us see him!' whoops another.

"She faced 'em all, and I gloried in her spunk.

"'When I marry him I *will* come back,' says she. 'And when I do you'll have to get down on your knees and wait on me. You—and you—Yes, and *you*, too!'

"The last two 'yous' was hove at Sim and Susannah. Then she turned and marched into the hotel. And the way them hired hands carried on was somethin' scandalous—till I stepped in and took charge of the deck.

"That very afternoon I put Effie and her trunk aboard the train. I paid her fare to New York and give her directions how to locate the Van Wedderburns.

"'So long, Effie,' says I to her. 'It's all right. You're enough sight better off. All you want to do now is to work hard and forget all that fortune-tellin' foolishness.'

"She whirled on me like a top.

"'Forget it!' she says. 'I *guess* I shan't forget it! It's comin' true, I tell you—same as all the rest come true. You said yourself there was ten thousand Butlers in the world. Some day the right one— the handsome, high-ranked, distinguished one—will come along, and I'll get him. You wait and see, Mr. Wingate—just you wait and see.'"

Chapter XV
The "Hero" and the Cowboy

"So that was the end of it, hey?" said Captain Bailey. "Well, it's what you might expect, but it wa'n't much to be so anxious to tell; and as for *provin'* anything about fortune tellin'—why—"

"It *ain't* the end," shouted the exasperated Barzilla. "Not nigh the end. 'Twas the beginnin'. The housekeeper left us that day, of course, and for the rest of that summer the servant question kept me and Jonadab from thinkin' of other things. Course, the reason for the Butler scamp's sudden switch was plain enough. Susannah's lawyer had settled the case with the railroad and, even after his fee was subtracted, there was fifteen hundred left. That was enough sight better'n nine hundred, so Sim figgered when he heard of it; and he hustled to make up with his old girl.

"Fifteen hundred dollars doesn't last long with some folks. At the beginnin' of the next spring season both of 'em was round huntin' jobs. Susannah was a fust-rate waitress, so we hired her for that—no more housekeeper for hers, and served her right. As for her husband, we took him on in the stable. He wouldn't have been wuth his salt if it hadn't been for her. She said she'd keep him movin' and she did. She nagged and henpecked him till I'd have been sorry if 'twas anybody else; as 'twas, I got consider'ble satisfaction out of it.

"I got one letter from Effie pretty soon after she left, sayin' she liked her new job and that the Van Wedderburns liked her. And that's all I did hear, though Bob himself wrote me in May, sayin' him and Mabel, his wife, had bought a summer cottage in Wapatomac, and me and Jonadab—especially me—must be sure and come to see it and them. He never mentioned his second girl, and I almost forgot her myself.

"But one afternoon in early July a big six-cylinder automobile come sailin' down the road and into the Old Home House yard. A shofer—I b'lieve that's what they call the tribe—was at the helm of it, and on the back seat, lollin' luxurious against the upholstery, was a man and a woman, got up regardless in silk dusters and goggles and veils and prosperity. I never expect to see the Prince of Wales and his wife, but I know how they'd look—after seein' them two.

"Jonadab was at the bottom step to welcome 'em, bowin' and scrapin' as if his middle j'int had just been iled. I wa'n't fur astern, and every boarder on deck was all eyes and envy.

"The shofer opens the door of the after cockpit of the machine, and the man gets out fust, treadin' gingerly but grand, as if he was doin' the ground a condescension by steppin' on it. Then he turns to the woman and she slides out, her duds rustlin' like the wind in a scrub oak. The pair sails up the steps, Jonadab and me backin' and fillin' in front of 'em. All the help that could get to a window to peek had knocked off work to do it.

"'Ahem!' says the man, pompous as Julius Caesar—he was big and straight and fine lookin' and had black side whiskers half mast on his cheeks—ahem!' says he. 'I say, good people, may we have dinner here?'

"Well, they tell us time and tide waits for no man, but prob'ly that don't include the nobility. Anyhow, although 'twas long past our reg'lar dinner time, I heard Jonadab tellin' 'em sure and sartin they could. If they wouldn't mind settin' on the piazza or in the front parlor for a spell, he'd have somethin' prepared in a jiffy. So up to the piazza they paraded and come to anchor in a couple of chairs.

"'You can have your automobile put right into the barn,' I says, 'if you want to.'

"'I don't know as it will be necessary—' began the big feller, but the woman interrupted him. She was starin' through her thick veil at the barn door. Sim Butler, in his overalls and ragged shirt sleeves, was leanin' against that door, interested as the rest of us in what was goin' on.

"'I would have it put there, I think,' says the woman, lofty and superior. 'It is rather dusty, and I think the wheels ought to be washed. Can that man be trusted to wash 'em?' she asks, pointin' kind of scornful at Simeon.

"'Yes, marm, I cal'late so,' I says. 'Here, Sim!' I sung out, callin' Butler over to the steps. 'Can you wash the dust off them wheels?'

"He said course he could, but he didn't act joyful over the job. The woman seemed some doubtful.

"'He looks like a very ignorant, common person,' says she, loud and clear, so that everybody, includin' the 'ignorant person' himself, could hear her. 'However, James'll superintend. James,' she orders the shofer, 'you see that it is well done, won't you? Make him be very careful.'

"James looked Butler over from head to foot. 'Humph!' he sniffs, contemptuous, with a kind of half grin on his face. 'Yes, marm, I'll 'tend to it.'

"So he steered the auto into the barn, and Simeon got busy. Judgin' by the sharp language that drifted out through the door, 'twas plain that the shofer was superintendin' all right.

"Jonadab heaves in sight, bowin', and makes proclamation that dinner is served. The pair riz up majestic and headed for the dinin' room. The woman was a little astern of her man, and in the hall she turns brisk to me.

"'Mr. Wingate,' she whispers, 'Mr. Wingate.'

"I stared at her. Her voice had sounded sort of familiar ever since I heard it, but the veil kept a body from seein' what she looked like.

"'Hey?' I sings out. 'Have I ever—'

"'S-s-h-h!' she whispers. 'Say, Mr. Wingate, that—that Susannah thing is here, ain't she? Have her wait on us, will you, please?'

"And she swept the veil off her face. I choked up and staggered bang! against the wall. I swan to man if it wa'n't Effie! *Effie*, in silks and automobiles and gorgeousness!

"Afore I could come to myself the two of 'em marched into that dining room. I heard a grunt and a 'Land of love!' from just ahead of me. That was Jonadab. And from all around that dinin' room come a sort of gasp and then the sound of whisperin'. That was the help.

"They took a table by the window, which had been made ready. Down they set like a king and a queen perchin' on thrones. One of the waiter girls went over to em.

"But I'd come out of my trance a little mite. The situation was miles ahead of my brain, goodness knows, but the joke of it all was gettin' a grip on me. I remembered what Effie had asked and I spoke up prompt.

"'Susannah,' says I, 'this is a particular job and we're anxious to please. You'd better do the waitin' yourself.'

"I wish you could have seen the glare that ex-housekeeper give me. For a second I thought we'd have open mutiny. But her place wa'n't any too sartin and she didn't dare risk it. Over she walked to that table, and the fun began.

"Jonadab had laid himself out to make that meal a success, but they ate it as if 'twas pretty poor stuff and not by no means what they fed on every day. They found fault with 'most everything, but most especial with Susannah's waitin'. My! how they did order her around—a mate on a cattle boat wa'n't nothin' to it. And when 'twas all over and they got up to go, Effie says, so's all hands can hear:

"'The food here is not so bad, but the service—oh, horrors! However, Albert,' says she to the side-whiskered man, 'you had better give the girl our usual tip. She looks as if she needed it, poor thing!'

"Then they paraded out of the room, and I see Susannah sling the half dollar the man had left on the table clear to Jericho, it seemed like.

"The auto was waitin' by the piazza steps. The shofer and Butler was standin' by it. And when Sim see Effie with her veil throwed back he pretty nigh fell under the wheels he'd been washin' so hard. And he looked as if he wisht they'd run over him.

"'Oh, dear!' sighs Effie, lookin' scornful at the wheels. 'Not half clean, just as I expected. I knew by the looks of that—that *person* that he wouldn't do it well. Don't give him much, Albert; he ain't earned it.'

"They climbed into the cockpit, the shofer took the helm, and they was ready to start. But I couldn't let 'em go that way. Out I run.

"'Say—say, Effie!' I whispers, eager. 'For the goodness' sakes, what's all this mean? Is that your—your—'

"'My husband? Yup,' she whispers back, her eyes shinin'. 'Didn't I tell you to look out for my prophecy? Ain't he handsome and distinguished, just as I said? Good-by, Mr. Wingate; maybe I'll see you again some day.'

"The machinery barked and they got under way. I run along for two steps more.

"'But, Effie,' says I, 'tell me—is his name—?'

"She didn't answer. She was watchin' Sim Butler and his wife. Sim had stooped to pick up the quarter the Prince of Wales had hove at him. And that was too much for Susannah, who was watchin' from the window.

"'Don't you touch that money!' she screams. 'Don't you lay a finger on it! Ain't you got any self-respect at all, you miser'ble, low-lived—' and so forth and so on. All the way to the front gate I see Effie leanin' out, lookin' and listenin' and smilin'.

"Then the machine buzzed off in a typhoon of dust and I went back to Jonadab, who was a livin' catechism of questions which neither one of us could answer."

"So *that's* the end!" exclaimed Captain Bailey. "Well—"

"No, it ain't the end—not even yet. Maybe it ought to be, but it ain't. There's a little more of it.

"A fortni't later I took a couple of days off and went up to Wapatomac to visit the Van Wedderburns, same as I'd promised. Their 'cottage' was pretty nigh big enough for a hotel, and was so grand that I, even if I did have on my Sunday frills, was 'most ashamed to ring the doorbell.

"But I did ring it, and the feller that opened the door was big and solemn and fine lookin' and had side whiskers. Only this time he wore a tail coat with brass buttons on it.

"How do you do, Mr. Wingate?' says he. Step right in, sir, if you please. Mr. and Mrs. Van Wedderburn are out in the auto, but they'll be back shortly, and very glad to see you, sir, I'm sure. Let me take your grip and hat. Step right into the reception room and wait, if you please, sir. Perhaps,' he says, and there was a twinkle in his port eye, though the rest of his face was sober as the front door of a church, 'perhaps,' says he, 'you might wish to speak with my wife a moment. I'll take the liberty of sendin' her to you, sir.'

"So, as I sat on the gunwale of a blue and gold chair, tryin' to settle whether I was really crazy or only just dreamin', in bounces Effie, rigged up in a servant's cap and apron. She looked polite and demure, but I could see she was just bubblin' with the joy of the whole bus'ness.

"'Effie,' says I, 'Effie, what—what in the world—?'

"She giggled. 'Yup,' she says, 'I'm chambermaid here and they treat me fine. Thank you very much for gettin' me the situation.'

"'But—but them doin's the other day? That automobile—and them silks and satins—and—?'

"'Mr. Van Wedderburn lent 'em to me,' she said, 'him an' his wife. And he lent us the auto and the shofer, too. I told him about my troubles at the Old Home House and he thought 'twould be a great joke for me to travel back there like a lady. He's awful fond of a joke—Mr. Van Wedderburn is.'

"'But that man?' I gasps. 'Your husband? That's what you said he was.'

"'Yes,' says she, 'he is. We've been married 'most six months now. My prophecy's all come true. And *didn't* I rub it in on that Susannah Debs and her scamp of a Sim? Ho! ho!'

"She clapped her hands and pretty nigh danced a jig, she was so tickled.

"'But is he a Butler?' I asks.

"'Yup,' she nods, with another giggle. 'He's A butler, though his name's Jenkins; and a butler's high rank—higher than chambermaid, anyhow. You see, Mr. Wingate,' she adds, ' 'twas all my fault. When that Oriental Seer man at the show said I was to marry a butler, I forgot to ask him whether you spelt it with a big B or a little one.'"

The unexpected manner in which Effie's pet prophecy had been fulfilled amused Captain Sol immensely. He laughed so heartily that Issy McKay looked in at the door with an expression of alarm on his face. The depot master had laughed little during the past few days, and Issy was surprised.

But Captain Stitt was ready with a denial. He claimed that the prophecy was *not* fulfilled and therefore all fortune telling was fraudulent. Barzilla retorted hotly, and the argument began again. The two were shouting at each other. Captain Sol stood it for a while and then commanded silence.

"Stop your yellin'!" he ordered. "What ails you fellers? Think you can prove it better by screechin'? They can hear you half a mile. There's Cornelius Rowe standin' gawpin' on the other side of the street this minute. He thinks there's a fire or a riot, one or t'other. Let's change the subject. See here, Bailey, didn't you start to tell us somethin' last time you was in here about your ridin' in an automobile?"

"I started to—yes. But nobody'd listen. I rode in one and I sailed in one. You see—"

"I'm goin' outdoor," declared Barzilla.

"No, you're not. Bailey listened to you. Now you do as much for him. I heard a little somethin' about the affair at the time it happened and I'd like to hear the rest of it. How was it, Bailey?"

Captain Stitt knocked the ashes from his pipe.

"Well," he began, "I didn't know the critter was weak in his top riggin' or I wouldn't have gone with him in the fust place. And he wa'n't real loony, nuther. 'Twas only when he got aboard that—that ungodly, kerosene-smellin', tootin', buzzin', Old Harry's go-cart of his that the craziness begun to show. There's so many of them weak-minded city folks from the Ocean House comes pe-rusin' 'round summers, nowadays, that I cal'lated he was just an average specimen, and never examined him close."

"Are all the Ocean House boarders weak-minded nowadays?" asked the depot master.

Mr. Wingate answered the question.

"My land!" he snapped; "would they board at the Ocean House if they *wa'n't* weak-minded?"

Captain Bailey did not deign to reply to this jibe. He continued calmly:

"This feller wa'n't an Ocean Houser, though. He was young

Stumpton's automobile skipper-shover, or shofer, or somethin' they called him. He answered to the hail of Billings, and his home port was the Stumpton ranch, 'way out in Montana. He'd been here in Orham only a couple of weeks, havin' come plumb across the United States to fetch his boss the new automobile. You see, 'twas early October. The Stumptons had left their summer place on the Cliff Road, and was on their way South for the winter. Young Stumpton was up to Boston, but he was comin' back in a couple of days, and then him and the shover was goin' automobilin' to Florida. To Florida, mind you! In that thing! If it was me I'd buy my ticket to Tophet direct and save time and money.

"Well, anyhow, this critter Billings, he ain't never smelt salt water afore, and he don't like the smell. He makes proclamations that Orham is nothin' but sand, slush, and soft drinks. He won't sail, he can't swim, he won't fish; but he's hankerin' to shoot somethin', havin' been brought up in a place where if you don't shoot some of the neighbors every day or so folks think you're stuck up and dissociable. Then somebody tells him it's the duckin' season down to Setuckit P'int, and he says he'll spend his day off, while the boss is away, massycreein' the coots there. This same somebody whispers that I know so much about ducks that I quack when I talk, and he comes cruisin' over in the buzz cart to hire me for guide. And—would you b'lieve it?—it turns out that he's cal'latin' to make his duckin' v'yage in that very cart. I was for makin' the trip in a boat, like a sensible man, but he wouldn't hear of it.

"'Land of love!' says I. 'Go to Setuckit in a automobile?'

"'Why not?' he says. 'The biscuit shooter up at the hotel tells me there's a smart chance of folks goes there a-horseback. And where a hoss can travel I reckon the old gal here'—slappin' the thwart of the auto alongside of him—'can go, too!'

"'But there's the Cut-through,' says I.

"''Tain't nothin' but a creek when the freshet's over, they tell me,' says he. 'And me and the boss have forded four foot of river in this very machine.'

"By the 'freshet' bein' over I judged he meant the tide bein' out.

And the Cut-through ain't but a little trickle then, though it's a quarter mile wide and deep enough to float a schooner at high water. It's the strip of channel that makes Setuckit Beach an island, you know. The gov'ment has had engineers down dredgin' of it out, and pretty soon fish boats'll be able to save the twenty-mile sail around the P'int and into Orham Harbor at all hours.

"Well, to make a long story short, I agreed to let him cart me to Setuckit P'int in that everlastin' gas carryall. We was to start at four o'clock in the afternoon, 'cause the tide at the Cut-through would be dead low at half-past four. We'd stay overnight at my shanty at the P'int, get up airly, shoot all day, and come back the next afternoon.

"At four prompt he was on hand, ready for me. I loaded in the guns and grub and one thing or 'nother, and then 'twas time for me to get aboard myself.

"'You'll set in the tonneau,' says he, indicatin' the upholstered after cockpit of the concern. I opened up the shiny hatch, under orders from him, and climbed in among the upholstery. 'Twas soft as a feather bed.

"'Jerushy!' says I, lollin' back luxurious. This is fine, ain't it?'

"'Cost seventy-five hundred to build,' he says casual. 'Made to order for the boss. Lightest car of her speed ever turned out.'

"'Go 'way! How you talk! Seventy-five hundred what? Not dollars?'

"'Sure,' he says. Then he turns round—he was in the bow, hangin' on to the steerin' wheel—and looks me over, kind of interested, but superior. 'Say,' he says, 'I've been hearin' things about you. You're a hero, ain't you?'

"Durn them Orham gabblers! Ever sence I hauled that crew of seasick summer boarders out of the drink a couple of years ago and the gov'ment gave me a medal, the minister and some more of his gang have painted out the name I was launched under and had me entered on the shippin' list as 'The Hero.' I've licked two or three for callin' me that, but I can't lick a parson, and he was the one that told Billings.

"'Oh, I don't know!' I answers pretty sharp. 'Get her under way, why don't you?'

"All he done was look me over some more and grin.

"'A hero! A real live gov'ment-branded hero!'he says. 'Ain't scared of nothin', I reckon—hey?'

"I never made no answer. There's some things that's too fresh to eat without salt, and I didn't have a pickle tub handy.

"'Hum!' he says again, reverend-like. 'A sure hero; scared of nothin'! Never rode in an auto afore, did you?'

"'No,' says I, peppery; 'and I don't see no present symptom of ridin' in one now. Cast off, won't you?'

"He cast off. That is to say, he hauled a nickel-plated marline-spike thing toward him, shoved another one away from him, took a twist on the steerin' wheel, the gocart coughed like a horse with the heaves, started up some sort of buzz-planer underneath, and then we begun to move.

"From the time we left my shanty at South Orham till we passed the pines at Herrin' Neck I laid back in that stuffed cockpit, feelin' as grand and tainted as old John D. himself. The automobile rolled along smooth but swift, and it seemed to me I had never known what easy trav'lin' was afore. As we rounded the bend by the pines and opened up the twelve-mile narrow white stretch of Setuckit Beach ahead of us, with the ocean on one side and the bay on t'other, I looked at my watch. We'd come that fur in thirteen minutes.

"'Land sakes!' I says. 'This is what I call movin' right along!'

"He turned round and sized me up again, like he was surprised.

"'Movin'?' says he. 'Movin'? Why, pard, we've been settin' down to rest! Out our way, if a lynchin' party didn't move faster than we've done so fur, the center of attraction would die on the road of old age. Now, my heroic college chum,' he goes on, callin' me out of my name, as usual, 'will you be so condescendin' as to indicate how we hit the trail?'

"'Hit—hit which? Don't hit nothin', for goodness' sake! Goin' the way we be, it would—'

"'Which way do we go?'

"'Right straight ahead. Keep on the ocean side, 'cause there's more hard sand there, and—hold on! Don't do that! Stop it, I tell you!'

"Them was the last rememberable words said by me durin' the

205

next quarter of an hour. That shover man let out a hair-raisin' yell, hauled the nickel marlinespike over in its rack, and squeezed a rubber bag that was spliced to the steerin' wheel. There was a half dozen toots or howls or honks from under our bows somewheres, and then that automobile hopped off the ground and commenced to fly. The fust hop landed me on my knees in the cockpit, and there I stayed. 'Twas the most fittin' position fur my frame of mind and chimed in fust-rate with the general religious drift of my thoughts.

"The Cut-through is two mile or more from Herrin' Neck. 'cordin' to my count we hit terra cotta just three times in them two miles. The fust hit knocked my hat off. The second one chucked me up so high I looked back for the hat, and though we was a half mile away from it, it hadn't had time to git to the ground. And all the while the horn was a-honkin', and Billings was a-screechin, and the sand was a-flyin'. Sand! Why, say! Do you see that extra bald place on the back of my head? Yes? Well, there was a two-inch thatch of hair there afore that sand blast ground it off.

"When I went up on the third jounce I noticed the Cut-through just ahead. Billings see it, too, and—would you b'lieve it?—the lunatic stood up, let go of the wheel with one hand, takes off his hat and waves it, and we charge down across them wet tide flats like death on the woolly horse, in Scriptur'.

"'Hi, yah! Yip!' whoops Billings. 'Come on in, fellers! The water's fine! Yow! Y-e-e-e! Yip!'

"For a second it left off rainin' sand, and there was a typhoon of mud and spray. I see a million of the prettiest rainbows—that is, I cal'lated there was a million; it's awful hard to count when you're bouncin' and prayin' and drowndin' all to once. Then we sizzed out of the channel, over the flats on t'other side, and on toward Setuckit.

"Never mind the rest of the ride. 'Twas all a sort of constant changin' sameness. I remember passin' a blurred life-savin' station, with three—or maybe thirty—blurred men jumpin' and laughin' and hollerin'. I found out afterwards that they'd been on the lookout for the bombshell for half an hour. Billings had told around town what he was goin' to do to me, and some kind friend had telephoned it to the station. So the life-savers was full of anticipations. I hope they were satisfied. I hadn't rehearsed my part of the show none, but I feel what the parson calls a consciousness of havin' done my best.

"'Whoa, gal!' says Billings, calm and easy, puttin' the helm hard down. The auto was standin' still at last. Part of me was hangin' over the lee rail. I could see out of the part, so I knew 'twas my head. And there alongside was my fish shanty at the P'int, goin' round and round in circles.

"I undid the hatch of the cockpit and fell out on the sand. Then I scrambled up and caught hold of the shanty as it went past me. That fool shover watched me, seemin'ly interested.

"'Why, pard,' says he, 'what's the matter? Do you feel pale? Are you nervous? It ain't possible that you're scared? Honest, now, pard, if it weren't that I knew you were a genuine gold-mounted hero I'd sure think you was a scared man.'

"I never said nothin'. The scenery and me was just turnin' the mark buoy on our fourth lap.

"'Dear me, pard!' continues Billings. 'I sure hope I ain't scared you none. We come down a little slow this evenin', but to-morrow night, when I take you back home, I'll let the old girl out a little.'

"I sensed some of that. And as the shanty had about come to anchor, I answered and spoke my mind.

"'When you take me back home!' I says. 'When you do! Why, you crack-brained, murderin' lunatic, I wouldn't cruise in that hell wagon of yours again for the skipper's wages on a Cunarder. No, nor the mate's hove in!'

"And that shover he put his head back and laughed and laughed and laughed."

Chapter XVI
The Cruise of the Red Car

I DON'T WONDER he laughed," observed Wingate, who seemed to enjoy irritating his friend. "You must have been good as a circus."

"Humph!" grunted the depot master. "If I remember right you said *you* wa'n't any ten-cent side show under similar circumstances, Barzilla. Heave ahead, Bailey!"

Captain Stitt, unruffled, resumed:

"I tell you, I had to take it that evenin'," he said. "All the time I was cookin' and while he was eatin' supper, Billings was rubbin' it into me about my bein' scared. Called me all the saltwater-hero names he could think of—'Hobson' and 'Dewey' and the like of that, usin' em sarcastic, of course. Finally, he said he remembered readin' in school, when he was little, about a girl hero, name of Grace Darlin'. Said he cal'lated, if I didn't mind, he'd call me Grace, 'cause it was heroic and yet kind of fitted in with my partic'lar brand of bravery. I didn't answer much; he had me down, and I knew it. Likewise I judged he was more or less out of his head; no sane man would yell the way he done aboard that automobile.

"Then he commenced to spin yarns about himself and his doin's, and pretty soon it come out that he'd been a cowboy afore young Stumpton give up ranchin' and took to automobilin'. That cleared the sky line some, of course; I'd read consider'ble about cowboys in the ten-cent books my nephew fetched home when he was away to school. I see right off that Billings was the livin' image of Deadwood Dick and Wild Bill and the rest in them books; they yelled and howled and hadn't no regard for life and property any more'n he had. No, sir! He wa'n't no crazier'n they was; it was in the breed, I judged.

"'I sure wish I had you on the ranch, Grace,' says he. 'Why don't you come West some day? That's where a hero like you would show up strong.'

"'Godfrey mighty!' I sings out. 'I wouldn't come nigh such a nest of crazy murderers as that fur no money! I'd sooner ride in that automobile of yours, and St. Peter himself couldn't coax me into *that* again, not if 'twas fur a cruise plumb up the middle of the golden street!'

"I meant it, too, and the next afternoon when it come time to start for home he found out that I meant it. We'd shot a lot of ducks, and Billings was havin' such a good time that I had to coax and tease him as if he was a young one afore he'd think of quittin'. It was quarter of six when he backed the gas cart out of the shed. I was uneasy, 'cause 'twas past low-water time, and there was fog comin' on.

"'Brace up, Dewey!' says he. 'Get in.'

"'No, Mr. Billings,' says I. 'I ain't goin' to get in. You take that craft of yourn home, and I'll sail up alongside in my dory.'

"'In your which?' says he.

"'In my dory,' I says. 'That's her hauled up on the beach abreast the shanty.'

"He looked at the dory and then at me.

"'Go on!' says he. 'You ain't goin' to pack yourself twelve mile on *that shingle?*'

"'Sartin I am! says I. 'I ain't takin' no more chances.'

"Do you know, he actually seemed to think I was crazy then. Seemed to figger that the dory wa'n't big enough; and she's carried five easy afore now. We had an argument that lasted twenty minutes more, and the fog driftin' in nigher all the time. At last he got sick of arguin', ripped out somethin' brisk and personal, and got his tin shop to movin'.

"'You want to cross over to the ocean side,' I called after him. 'The Cut-through's been dredged at the bay end, remember.'

"'Be hanged!' he yells, or more emphatic. And off he whizzed. I see him go, and fetched a long breath. Thanks to a merciful Providence, I'd come so fur without bein' buttered on the undercrust of that automobile or scalped with its crazy shover's bowie knife.

"Ten minutes later I was beatin' out into the bay in my dory. All around was the fog, thin as poorhouse gruel so fur, but thickenin' every minute. I was worried; not for myself, you understand, but for that cowboy shover. I was afraid he wouldn't fetch t'other side of the Cut-through. There wa'n't much wind, and I had to make long tacks. I took the inshore channel, and kept listenin' all the time. And at last, when 'twas pretty dark and I was cal'latin' to be about abreast of the bay end of the Cut-through, I heard from somewheres ashore a dismal honkin' kind of noise, same as a wild goose might make if 'twas chokin' to death and not resigned to the worst.

"'My land!' says I. 'It's happened!' And I come about and headed straight in for the beach. I struck it just alongside the gov'ment shanty. The engineers had knocked off work for the week, waitin' for supplies, but they hadn't took away their dunnage.

"'Hi!' I yells, as I hauled up the dory. 'Hi-i-i! Billings, where be you?'

"The honkin' stopped and back comes the answer; there was joy in it.

"'What? Is that Cap'n Stitt?'

"'Yes,' I sings out. 'Where be you?'

"'I'm stuck out here in the middle of the crick. And there's a flood on. Help me, can't you?'

"Next minute I was aboard the dory, rowin' her against the tide up the channel. Pretty quick I got where I could see him through the fog and dark. The auto was on the flat in the middle of the Cut-through, and the water was hub high already. Billings was standin' up on the for'ard thwart, makin' wet footmarks all over them expensive cushions.

"'Lord,' says he, 'I sure am glad to see you, pard! Can we get to land, do you think?'

"'Land?' says I, makin' the dory fast alongside and hoppin' out into the drink. ''Course we can land! What's the matter with your old derelict? Sprung a leak, has it?'

"He went on to explain that the automobile had broke down when he struck the flat, and he couldn't get no farther. He'd been honkin' and howlin' for ten year at least, so he reckoned.

"'Why in time,' says I, 'didn't you mind me and go up the ocean side? And why in nation didn't you go ashore and—But never mind that now. Let me think. Here! You set where you be.'

"As I shoved off in the dory again he turned loose a distress signal.

"'Where you goin'?' he yells. 'Say, pard, you ain't goin' to leave me here, are you?'

"'I'll be back in a shake,' says I, layin' to my oars. 'Don't holler so! You'll have the life-savers down here, and then the joke'll be on us. Hush, can't you? I'll be right back!'

"I rowed up channel a little ways, and then I sighted the place I was bound for. Them gov'ment folks had another shanty farther up the Cut-through. Moored out in front of it was a couple of big floats, for their stone sloops to tie up to at high water. The floats were made of empty kerosene barrels and planks, and they'd have held up a house easy. I run alongside the fust one, cut the anchor cable with my jackknife, and next minute I was navigatin' that float down channel, steerin' it with my oar and towin' the dory astern.

"'Twas no slouch of a job, pilotin' that big float, but part by steerin' and part by polin' I managed to land her broadside on to the auto. I made her fast with the cable ends and went back after the other float. This one was a bigger job than the fust, but by and by that gas wagon, with planks under her and cable lashin's holdin' her firm, was restin' easy as a settin' hen between them two floats. I unshipped my mast, fetched it aboard the nighest float, and spread the sail over the biggest part of the brasswork and upholstery.

"'There,' says I, 'if it rains durin' the night she'll keep pretty dry. Now I'll take the dory and row back to the shanty after some spare anchors there is there.'

"'But what's it fur, pard?' asks Billings for the nine hundred and ninety-ninth time. 'Why don't we go where it's dry? The flood's risin' all the time.'

"'Let it rise,' I says. 'I cal'late when it gets high enough them floats'll rise with it and lift the automobile up, too. If she's anchored bow and stern she'll hold, unless it comes on to blow a gale, and to-morrow mornin' at low tide maybe you can tinker her up so she'll go.'

"'Go?' says he, like he was astonished. 'Do you mean to say you're reckonin' to save the *car*?'

"'Good land!' I says, starin' at him. 'What else d'you s'pose? Think I'd let seventy-five hundred dollars' wuth of gilt-edged extravagance go to the bottom? What did you cal'late I was tryin' to save—the clam flat? Give me that dory rope; I'm goin' after them anchors. Sufferin' snakes! Where *is* the dory? What have you done with it?'

"He'd been holdin' the bight of the dory rodin'. I handed it to him so's he'd have somethin' to take up his mind. And, by time, he'd forgot all about it and let it drop! And the dory had gone adrift and was out of sight.

"'Gosh!' says he, astonished-like. 'Pard, the son of a gun has slipped his halter!'

"I was pretty mad—dories don't grow on every beach plum bush—but there wa'n't nothin' to say that fitted the case, so I didn't try.

"'Humph!' says I. 'Well, I'll have to swim ashore, that's all, and go up to the station inlet after another boat. You stand by the ship. If she gets afloat afore I come back you honk and holler and I'll row after you. I'll fetch the anchors and we'll moor her wherever she happens to be. If she shouldn't float on an even keel, or goes to capsize, you jump overboard and swim ashore. I'll—'

"'Swim?' says he, with a shake in his voice. 'Why, pard, I can't swim!'

"I turned and looked at him. Shover of a two-mile-a-minute gold-plated butcher cart like that, a cowboy murderer that et his friends for breakfast—and couldn't swim! I fetched a kind of combination groan and sigh, turned back the sail, climbed aboard the automobile, and lit up my pipe.

"'What are you settin' there for?' says he. 'What are you goin' to do?'

"'Do?' says I. 'Wait, that's all—wait and smoke. We won't have to wait long.'

"My prophesyin' was good. We didn't have to wait very long. It was pitch dark, foggy as ever, and the tide a-risin' fast. The floats got to be a-wash. I shinned out onto 'em, picked up the oar that had been left there, and took my seat again. Billings climbed in, too, only—and it kind of shows the change sence the previous evenin'—he was in the passenger cockpit astern, and I was for'ard in the pilot house. For a reckless daredevil he was actin' mighty fidgety.

"And at last one of the floats swung off the sand. The automobile tipped scandalous. It looked as if we was goin' on our beam ends. Billings let out an awful yell. Then t'other float bobbed up and the whole shebang, car and all, drifted out and down the channel.

"My lashin's held—I cal'lated they would. Soon's I was sure of that I grabbed up the oar and shoved it over the stern between the floats. I hoped I could round her to after we passed the mouth of the Cut-through, and make port on the inside beach. But not in that tide. Inside of five minutes I see 'twas no use; we was bound across the bay.

"And now commenced a v'yage that beat any ever took sence Noah's time, I cal'late; and even Noah never went to sea in an automobile, though the one animal I had along was as much trouble as his whole menagerie. Billings was howlin' blue murder.

"'Stop that bellerin'!' I ordered. 'Quit it, d'you hear! You'll have the station crew out after us, and they'll guy me till I can't rest. Shut up! If you don't, I'll—I'll swim ashore and leave you.'

"I was takin' big chances, as I look at it now. He might have drawed a bowie knife or a lasso on me; 'cordin' to his yarns he'd butchered folks for a good sight less'n that. But he kept quiet this time, only gurglin' some when the ark tilted. I had time to think of another idee. You remember the dory sail, mast and all, was alongside that cart. I clewed up the canvas well as I could and managed to lash the mast up straight over the auto's bows. Then I shook out the sail.

"'Here!' says I, turnin' to Billings. 'You hang on to that sheet. No, you needn't nuther. Make it fast to that cleat alongside.'

"I couldn't see his face plain, but his voice had a funny tremble to it; reminded me of my own when I climbed out of that very cart after he'd jounced me down to Setuckit the day before.

"'What?'he says. 'Wh-what? What sheet? I don't see any sheet. What do you want me to do?'

"'Tie this line to that cleat. That cleat there! *cleat*, you lubber! *cleat*! That knob! *Make it fast*! Oh, my gosh t'mighty! Get out of my way!'

"The critter had tied the sheet to the handle of the door instead of the one I meant, and the pull of the sail hauled the door open and pretty nigh ripped it off the hinges. I had to climb into the cockpit and straighten out the mess. I was losin' my temper; I do hate bunglin' seamanship aboard a craft of mine.

"'But what'll become of us?' begs Billings. 'Will we drown?'

"'What in tunket do we want to drown for? Ain't we got a good sailin' breeze and the whole bay to stay on top of—fifty foot of water and more?'

"'Fifty foot!' he yells. 'Is there fifty foot of water underneath us now? Pard, you don't mean it!'

"'Course I mean it. Good thing, too!'

"'But fifty foot! It's enough to drown in ten times over!'

"'Can't drown but once, can you? And I'd just as soon drown in fifty foot as four—ruther, 'cause 'twouldn't take so long.'

"He didn't answer out loud; but I heard him talkin' to himself pretty constant.

"We was well out in the bay by now, and the seas was a little mite more rugged—nothin' to hurt, you understand, but the floats was all foam, and once in a while we'd ship a little spray. And every time that happened Billings would jump and grab for somethin' solid—sometimes 'twas the upholstery and some-times 'twas me. He wa'n't on the thwart, but down in a heap on the cockpit floor.

"'Let go of my leg!' I sings out, after we'd hit a high wave and that shover had made a more'n ordinary savage claw at my underpin-nin'. 'You make me nervous. Drat this everlastin' fog! somethin'll bump into us if we don't look out. Here, you go for'ard and light them cruisin' lights. They ain't colored 'cordin' to regulations, but they'll have to do. Go for'ard! What you waitin' for?'

"Well, it turned out that he didn't like to leave that cockpit. I was mad.

"'Go for'ard there and light them lights!' I yelled, hangin' to the steerin' oar and keepin' the ark runnin' afore the wind.

"'I won't!' he says, loud and emphatic. 'Think I'm a blame fool? I sure would be a jack rabbit to climb over them seats the way they're buckin' and light them lamps. You're talkin' through your hat!'

"Well, I hadn't no business to do it, but, you see, I was on salt water, and skipper, as you might say, of the junk we was afloat in; and if there's one thing I never would stand it's mutiny. I hauled in the oar, jumped over the cockpit rail, and went for him. He see me comin', stood up, tried to get out of the way, and fell overboard backwards. Part of him lit on one of the floats, but the biggest part trailed in the water between the two. He clawed with his hands, but the planks was slippery, and he slid astern fast. Just as he reached the last plank and slid off and under I jumped after him and got him by the scruff of the neck. I had hold of the lashin' end with one hand, and we tailed out behind the ark, which was sloppin' along, graceful as an elephant on skates.

"I was pretty well beat out when I yanked him into that cockpit again. Neither of us said anything for a spell, breath bein' scurce as di'monds. But when he'd collected some of his, he spoke.

"'Pard,' he says, puffin', 'I'm much obleeged to you. I reckon I sure ain't treated you right. If it hadn't been for you that time I'd—'

"But I was b'ilin' over. I whirled on him like a teetotum.

"'Drat your hide!' I says. 'When you speak to your officer you say sir! And now you go for'ard and light them lights. Don't you answer back! If you do I'll fix you so's you'll never ship aboard another vessel! For'ard there! Lively, you lubber, lively!'

"He went for'ard, takin' consider'ble time and hangin' on for dear life. But somehow or 'nuther he got the lights to goin'; and all the time I hazed him terrible. I was mate on an Australian packet afore I went fishin' to the Banks, and I can haze some. I blackguarded that shover awful.

"'Ripperty-rip your everlastin' blankety-blanked dough head!' I roared at him. 'You ain't wuth the weight to sink you. For'ard there and get that fog horn to goin'! And keep it goin'! Lively, you sculpin! Don't you open your mouth to me!'

"Well, all night we sloshed along, straight acrost the bay. We must have been a curious sight to look at. The floats was awash, so that the automobile looked like she was ridin' the waves all by her lonesome; the lamps was blazin' at either side of the bow; Billings was a-tootin' the rubber fog horn as if he was wound up; and I was standin' on the cushions amidships, keepin' the whole calabash afore the wind.

"We never met another craft the whole night through. Yes, we did meet one. Old Ezra Cahoon, of Harniss, was out in his dory stealin' quahaugs from Seth Andrews's bed over nigh the Wapatomac shore. Ezra stayed long enough to get one good glimpse of us as we bust through the fog; then he cut his rodin' and laid to his oars, bound for home and mother. We could hear him screech for half an hour after he left us.

"Ez told next day that the devil had come ridin' acrost the bay after him in a chariot of fire. Said he could smell the brimstone and hear the trumpet callin' him to judgment. Likewise he hove in a lot of particulars concernin' the personal appearance of the Old Boy himself, who, he said, was standin' up wavin' a red-hot pitchfork. Some folks might have been flattered at bein' took for such a famous character; but I wa'n't; I'm retirin' by nature, and besides, Ez's description wa'n't cal'lated to bust a body's vanity b'iler. I was prouder of the consequences, the same bein' that Ezra signed the Good Templars' pledge that afternoon, and kept it for three whole months, just sixty-nine days longer than any previous attack within the memory of man had lasted.

"And finally, just as mornin' was breakin', the bows of the floats slid easy and slick up on a hard, sandy beach. Then the sun riz and the fog lifted, and there we was within sight of the South Ostable meetin'-house. We'd sailed eighteen miles in that ark and made a better landin' blindfold than we ever could have made on purpose.

"I hauled down the sail, unshipped the mast, and jumped

ashore to find a rock big enough to use for a makeshift anchor. It wa'n't more'n three minutes after we fust struck afore my boots hit dry ground, but Billings beat me one hundred and seventy seconds, at that. When I had time to look at that shover man he was a cable's length from high-tide mark, settin' down and grippin' a bunch of beach grass as if he was afeard the sand was goin' to slide from under him; and you never seen a yallerer, more upset critter in your born days.

"Well, I got the ark anchored, after a fashion, and then we walked up to the South Ostable tavern. Peleg Small, who runs the place, he knows me, so he let me have a room and I turned in for a nap. I slept about three hours. When I woke up I started out to hunt the automobile and Billings. Both of 'em looked consider'ble better than they had when I see 'em last. The shover had got a gang of men and they'd got the gas cart ashore, and Billings and a blacksmith was workin' over—or rather under—the clockwork.

"'Hello!' I hails, comin' alongside.

"Billings sticks his head out from under the tinware.

"'Hi, pard!' says he. I noticed he hadn't called me 'Grace' nor 'Dewey' for a long spell. Hi, pard,' he says, gettin' to his feet, 'the old gal ain't hurt a hair. She'll be good as ever in a couple of hours. Then you and me can start for Orham.'

"'In *her*?' says I.

"'Sure,' he says.

"'Not by a jugful!' says I, emphatic. 'I'll borrer a boat to get to Orham in, when I'm ready to go. You won't ketch me in that man killer again; and you can call me a coward all you want to!'

"'A coward?' says he. 'You a coward? And—Why, you was in that car all night!'

"'Oh!' I says. 'Last night was diff'rent. The thing was on water then, and when I've got enough water underneath me I know I'm safe.'

"'Safe!' he sings out. '*Safe*! Well, by—gosh! Pard, I hate to say it, but it's the Lord's truth—you had me doin' my "Now I lay me's"!'

"For a minute we looked at each other. Then says I, sort of

thinkin' out loud, 'I cal'late,' I says, 'that whether a man's brave or not depends consider'ble on whether he's used to his latitude. It's all accordin'. It lays in the bringin' up, as the duck said when the hen tried to swim.'

"He nodded solemn. 'Pard,' says he, 'I sure reckon you've called the turn. Let's shake hands on it.'

"So we shook; and ..."

Captain Bailey stopped short and sprang from his chair. "There's my train comin'," he shouted. "Good-by, Sol! So long, Barzilla! Keep away from fortune tellers and pretty servant girls or *you'll* be gettin' married pretty soon. Good-by."

He darted out of the waiting room and his companions followed. Mr. Wingate, having a few final calls to make, left the station soon afterwards and did not return until evening. And that evening he heard news which surprised him.

As he and Captain Sol were exchanging a last handshake on the platform, Barzilla said:

"Well, Sol, I've enjoyed loafin' around here and yarnin' with you, same as I always do. I'll be over again in a month or so and we'll have some more."

The Captain shook his head. "I may not be here then, Barzilla," he observed.

"May not be here? What do you mean by that?"

"I mean that I don't know exactly where I shall be. I shan't be depot master, anyway."

"Shan't be depot master? *you* won't? Why, what on airth—"

"I sent in my resignation four days ago. Nobody knows it, except you, not even Issy, but the new depot master for East Harniss will be here to take my place on the mornin' of the twelfth, that's two days off."

"Why! Why! *Sol!*"

"Yes. Keep mum about it. I'll—I'll let you know what I decide to do. I ain't settled it myself yet. Good-by, Barzilla."

Chapter XVII
Issy's Revenge

THE FOLLOWING MORNING, at nine o'clock, Issy McKay sat upon the heap of rusty chain cable outside the blacksmith's shop at Denboro, reading, as usual, a love story. Issy was taking a "day off." He had begged permission of Captain Sol Berry, the permission had been granted, and Issy had come over to Denboro, the village eight miles above East Harniss, in his "power dory," or gasoline boat, the Lady May. The Lady May was a relic of the time before Issy was assistant depot master, when he gained a precarious living by quahauging, separating the reluctant bivalve from its muddy house on the bay bottom with an iron rake, the handle of which was forty feet long. Issy had been seized with a desire to try quahauging once more, hence his holiday. The rake was broken and he had put in at Denboro to have it fixed. While the blacksmith was busy, Issy laboriously spelled out the harrowing chapters of "Vivian, the Shop Girl; or Lord Lyndhurst's Lowly Love."

A grinning, freckled face peered cautiously around the corner of the blacksmith's front fence. Then an overripe potato whizzed through the air and burst against the shop wall a few inches from the reader's head. Issy jumped.

"You—you everlastin' young ones, you!" he shouted fiercely. "If I git my hands onto you, you'll wish you'd—I see you hidin' behind that fence."

Two barefooted little figures danced provokingly in the roadway and two shrill voices chanted in derision:

"Is McKay—Is McKay—
Makes the Injuns run away!"
"Scalped anybody lately, Issy?"

Alas for the indiscretions of youth! The tale of Issy's early expedition in search of scalps and glory was known from one end of Ostable County to the other. It had made him famous, in a way.

"If I git a-holt of you kids, I'll bet there'll be some scalpin' done," retorted the persecuted one, rising from the heap of cable.

A second potato burst like a bombshell on the shingles behind him. McKay was a good general, in that he knew when it was wisest to retreat. Shoving the paper novel into his overalls pocket, he entered the shop.

"What's the matter, Is?" inquired the grinning blacksmith. Most people grinned when they spoke to Issy. "Gittin' too hot outside there, was it? Why don't you tomahawk 'em and have 'em for supper?"

"Humph!" grunted the offended quahauger. "Don't git gay now, Jake Larkin. You hurry up with that rake."

"Oh, all right, Is. Don't sculp *me*; I ain't done nothin'. What's the news over to East Harniss?"

"Oh, I don't know. Not much. Sam Bartlett, he started for Boston this mornin'."

"Who? Sam Bartlett? I want to know! Thought he was down for six weeks. You sure about that, Is?"

"Course I'm sure. I was up to the depot and see him buy his ticket and git on the cars."

"Did, hey? Humph! So Sam's gone. Gertie Higgins still over to her Aunt Hannah's at Trumet?"

Issy looked at his questioner. "Why, yes," he said suspiciously. "I s'pose she's there. Fact, I know she is. Pat Starkey's doin' the telegraphin' while she's away. What made you ask that?"

The blacksmith chuckled. "Oh, nothin'," he said. "How's her dad's dyspepsy? Had any more of them sudden attacks of his? I cal'late they'll take the old man off some of these days, won't they? I hear the doctor thinks there's more heart than stomach in them attacks."

But the skipper of the Lady May was not to be put off thus. "What you drivin' at, Jake?" he demanded. "What's Sam

Bartlett's goin' away got to do with Gertie Higgins?"

In his eagerness he stepped to Mr. Larkin's side. The blacksmith caught sight of the novel in his customer's pocket. He snatched it forth.

"What you readin' now, Is?" he demanded. "More blood and brimstone? 'Vivy Ann, the Shop Girl!' Gee! Wow!"

"You gimme that book, Jake Larkin! Gimme it now!"

Fending the frantic quahauger off with one mighty arm, the blacksmith proceeded to read aloud:

"'Darlin',' cried Lord Lyndhurst, strainin' the beautiful and blushin' maid to his manly bosom, 'you are mine at last. Mine! No—' Jerushy! a love story! Why, Issy! I didn't know you was in love. Who's the lucky girl? Send me an invite to your weddin', won't you?"

Issy's face was a fiery red. He tore the precious volume from its desecrator's hand, losing the pictured cover in the struggle.

"You—you pesky fool!" he shouted. "You mind your own business."

The blacksmith roared in glee. "Oh, ho!" he cried. "Issy's in love and I never guessed it. Aw, say, Is, don't be mean! Who is she? Have you strained her to your manly bosom yit? What's her name?"

"Shut up!" shrieked Issy, and strode out of the shop. His tormentor begged him not to "go off mad," and shouted sarcastic sympathy after him. But Mr. McKay heeded not. He stalked angrily along the sidewalk. Then espying just ahead of him the boys who had thrown the potatoes, he paused, turned, and walking down the carriageway at the side of the blacksmith's place of business, sat down upon a sawhorse under one of its rear windows. He could, at least, be alone here and think; and he wanted to think.

For Issy—although he didn't look it—was deeply interested in another love story as well as that in his pocket. This one was printed upon his heart's pages, and in it he was the hero, while the heroine—the unsuspecting heroine—was Gertie Higgins, daughter of Beriah Higgins, once a fisherman, now the crotchety and dyspeptic proprietor of the "general store" and postmaster at East Harniss.

This story began when Issy first acquired the Lady May. The Higgins home stood on the slope close to the boat landing, and when Issy came in from quahauging, Gertie was likely to be in the back yard, hanging out the clothes or watering the flower garden. Sometimes she spoke to him of her own accord, concerning the weather or other important topics. Once she even asked him if he were going to the Fourth of July ball at the town-hall. It took him until the next morning—like other warriors, Issy was cursed with shyness—to summon courage enough to ask her to go to the ball with him. Then he found it was too late; she was going with her cousin, Lennie Bloomer. But he felt that she had offered him the opportunity, and was happy and hopeful accordingly.

This, however, was before she went to Boston to study telegraphy. When she returned, with a picture hat and a Boston accent, it was to preside at the telegraph instrument in the little room adjoining the post office at her father's store. When Issy bowed blushingly outside the window of the telegraph room, he received only the airiest of frigid nods. Was there what Lord Lyndhurst would have called "another"? It would seem not. Old Mr. Higgins, her father, encouraged no bows nor attentions from young men, and Gertie herself did not appear to desire them. So Issy gave up his tales of savage butchery for those of love and blisses, adored in silence, and hoped—always hoped.

But why had the blacksmith seemed surprised at the departure of Sam Bartlett, the "dudey" vacationist from the city, whose father had, years ago, been Beriah Higgins's partner in the fish business? And why had he coupled the Bartlett name with that of Gertie, who had been visiting her father's maiden sister at Trumet, the village next below East Harniss, as Denboro is the next above it? Issy's suspicions were aroused, and he wondered.

Suddenly he heard voices in the shop above him. The window was open and he heard them plainly.

"Well! *Well!*" It was the blacksmith who uttered the exclamation. "Why, Bartlett, how be you? What you doin' over here?

Thought you'd gone back to Boston. I heard you had."

Slowly, cautiously, the astonished quahauger rose from the sawhorse and peered over the window sill. There were two visitors in the shop. One was Ed Burns, proprietor of the Denboro Hotel and livery stable. The other was Sam Bartlett, the very same who had left East Harniss that morning, bound, ostensibly, for Boston. Issy sank back again and listened.

"Yes, yes!" he heard Sam say impatiently; "I know, but—see here, Jake, where can I hire a horse in this God-forsaken town?"

"Well, well, Sam!" continued Larkin. "I was just figurin' that Beriah had got the best of you after all, and you'd had to give it up for this time. Thinks I, it's too bad! Just because your dad and Beriah Higgins had such a deuce of a row when they bust up in the fish trade, it's a shame that he won't hark to your keepin' comp'ny with Gertie. And you doin' so well; makin' twenty dollars a week up to the city—Ed told me that—and—"

"Yes, yes! But never mind that. Where can I get a horse? I've got to be in Trumet by eight to-night sure."

"Trumet? Why, that's where Gertie is, ain't it?"

"Look a-here, Jake," broke in the livery-stable keeper. "I'll tell you how 'tis. Oh, it's all right, Sam! Jake knows the most of it; I told him. He can keep his mouth shut, and he don't like old crank Higgins any better'n you and me do. Jake, Sam here and Gertie had fixed it up to run off and git married to-night. He was to pretend to start for Boston this mornin'. Bought a ticket and all, so's to throw Beriah off the scent. He was to get off the train here at Denboro and I was to let him have a horse 'n' buggy. Then, this afternoon, he was goin' to drive through the wood roads around to Trumet and be at the Baptist Church there at eight to-night sharp. Gertie's Aunt Hannah, she's had her orders, and bein' as big a crank as her brother, she don't let the girl out of her sight. But there's a fair at the church and Auntie's tendin' a table. Gertie, she steps out to the cloak room to git a handkerchief which she's forgot; see? And she hops into Sam's buggy and away they go to the minister's. After they're once hitched Old Dyspepsy can go to pot and see the kittle bile."

"Bully! By gum, that's fine! Won't Beriah rip some, hey?"

"Yes, but there's the dickens to pay. I've only got two horses in the stable to-day. The rest are let. And the two I've got—one's old Bill, and he couldn't go twenty mile to save his hide. And t'other's the gray mare, and blamed if she didn't git cast last night and use up her off hind leg so's she can't step. And Sam's *got* to have a horse. Where can I git one?"

"Hum! Have you tried Haynes's?"

"Yes, yes! And Lathrop's and Eldredge's. Can't git a team for love nor money."

"Sho! And he can't go by train?"

"What? With Beriah postmaster at East Harniss and always nosin' through every train that stops there? You can't fetch Trumet by train without stoppin' at East Harniss and—What was that?"

"I don't know. What was it?"

"Sounded like somethin' outside that back winder."

The two ran to the window and looked out. All they saw was an overturned sawhorse and two or three hens scratching vigorously.

"Guess 'twas the chickens, most likely," observed the blacksmith. Then, striking his blackened palms together, he exclaimed:

"By time! I've thought of somethin'! Is McKay is in town to-day. Come over in the Lady May. She's a gasoline boat. Is would take Sam to Trumet for two or three dollars, I'll bet. And he's such a fool head that he wouldn't ask questions nor suspicion nothin'. 'Twould be faster'n a horse and enough sight less risky."

And just then the "fool head," his brain whirling under its carroty thatch, was hurrying blindly up the main street, bound somewhere, he wasn't certain where.

A mushy apple exploded between his shoulders, but he did not even turn around. So *this* was what the blacksmith meant! This was why Mr. Higgins watched his daughter so closely. This was why Gertie had been sent off to Trumet. She had met the Bartlett miscreant in Boston; they had been together there; had fallen in love and—He gritted his teeth and shook his fists almost in the face of old Deacon Pratt, who, knowing the McKay

224

penchant for slaughter, had serious thoughts of sending for the constable.

Beriah Higgins must be warned, of course, but how? To telegraph was to put Pat Starkey in possession of the secret, and Pat was too good a friend of Gertie's to be trusted. There was no telephone at the store. Issy entered the combination grocery store and post office.

"Has the down mail closed yet?" he panted.

The postmaster looked out of his little window.

"Yes," he replied. "Why? Got a letter you want to go? Take it up to the depot. The train's due, but 'Tain't here yit. If you run you can make it."

Issy took a card from his pocket. It was the business card of the firm to whom he sold his quahaugs. On the back of the card he wrote in pencil as follows:

"Mr. Beriah Higgins, your daughter Gertrude is going to meet Sam'l Bartlett at the Baptist Church in Trumet at 8 P.M. to-night and get married to him. LOOK OUTten dolla!!!"

After an instant's consideration he signed it "A True Friend," this being in emulation of certain heroes of the Deadwood Dick variety. Then he put the card into an envelope and ran at top speed to the railway station. The train came in as he reached the platform. The baggage master was standing in the door of his car.

"Here, mister!" panted Issy. "Jest hand this letter to Beriah Higgins when he takes the mail bag at East Harniss, won't you? It's mighty important. Don't forgit. Thanks."

The train moved off. Issy stared after it, grinning malevolently. Higgins would get that note in ample time to send word to the watchful Aunt Hannah. When the unsuspecting eloper reached the Trumet church, it would be the aunt, not the niece, who awaited him. Still grinning, Mr. McKay walked off the platform, and into the arms of Ed Burns, the stable keeper, and Sam Bartlett, his loathed and favored rival.

"Here he is!" shouted Burns. "Now we've got him."

The foiler of the plot turned pale. Was his secret discovered? But no; his captors began talking eagerly, and gradually the sense of their pleadings became plain. They wanted him—*him*, of all people—to convey Bartlett to Trumet in the Lady May.

"You see, it's a business meetin'," urged Burns. "Sam's got to be there by ha'f past seven or he'll—he won't win on the deal, will you, Sam? Say yes, Issy; that's a good feller. He'll give you—I don't know's he won't give you five dollars."

"Ten," cried Bartlett. "And I'll never forget it, either. Will you, Is?"

A mighty "No!" was trembling on Issy's tongue. But before it was uttered Burns spoke again.

"McKay's got the best boat in these parts," he urged. "She's got a tiptop engine in her, and—"

The word "engine" dropped into the whirlpool of Issy's thoughts with a familiar sound. In the chapter of "Vivian" that he had just finished, the beautiful shopgirl was imprisoned on board the yacht of the millionaire kidnaper, while the hero, in his own yacht, was miles astern. But the hero's faithful friend, disguised as a stoker, was tampering with the villain's engine. A vague idea began to form in Issy's brain. Once get the would-be eloper aboard the Lady May, and, even though the warning note should remain undelivered, he—

Issy smiled, and the ghastliness of that smile was unnoticed by his companions.

"I—I'll do it," he cried. "By mighty! I *will* do it. You be at the wharf here at four o'clock. I wouldn't do it for everybody, Sam Bartlett, but for you I'd do consider'ble, just now. And I don't want your ten dollars nuther."

Doctoring an engine may be easy enough—in stories. But to doctor a gasoline engine so that it will run for a certain length of time and *then* break down is not so easy. Three o'clock came and the problem was still unsolved. Issy, the perspiration running down his face, stood up in the Lady May's cockpit and looked out across the bay, smooth and glassy in the afternoon sun.

The sky overhead was clear and blue, but along the eastern and southern horizon was a gray bank of cloud, heaped in tumbled masses.

226

A sunburned lobsterman in rubber boots and a sou'wester was smoking on the wharf.

"What time you goin' to start for home, Is?" he asked.

"Oh, in an hour or so," was the absent-minded reply.

"Humph! You'd better cast off afore that or you'll be fog bound. It'll be thicker'n dock mud toward sundown, and you'll fetch up in Waptomac 'stead of East Harniss, 'thout you've got a good compass."

"Oh, my compass is all right," began Issy, and stopped short. The lobsterman made other attempts at conversation, but they were unproductive. McKay was gazing at the growing fog bank and thinking hard. To doctor an engine may be difficult, but to get lost in a fog—He took the compass from the glass-lidded binnacle by the wheel, and carrying it into the little cabin, placed it in the cuddy forward.

It was nearer five than four when the Lady May, her engine barking aggressively, moved out of Denboro Harbor. Mr. Bartlett, the passenger, had been on time and had fumed and fretted at the delay. But Issy was deliberation itself. He had forgotten his quahaug rake, and the lapse of memory entailed a trip to the blacksmith's. Then the gasoline tank needed filling and the battery had to be overhauled.

"Are you sure you can make it?" queried Sam anxiously. "It's important, I tell you. Mighty important."

The skipper snorted in disgust. "Make it?" he repeated. "If the Lady May can't make fourteen mile in two hours—let alone two'n a ha'f—then I don't know her. She's one of them boats you read about, she is."

The Cape makes a wide bend between Denboro and Trumet. The distance between these towns is twenty long, curved miles over the road; by water it is reduced to a straight fourteen. And midway between the two, at the center of the curve, is East Harniss.

The Lady May coughed briskly on. There was no sea, and she sent long, widening ripples from each side of her bow. Bartlett, leaning over the rail, gazed impatiently ahead. Issy, sprawled on the bench by the wheel, was muttering to himself. Occasionally he glanced toward the east. The gray fog bank was now half way to the zenith and approaching rapidly. The eastern shore had disappeared.

"Is! Hi, Is! What are you doing? Don't kill him before my eyes."

Issy came out of his trance with a start.

"What—what's that?" he asked. His passenger was grinning broadly.

"What? Kill who?"

"Why, the big chief, or whoever you had under your knee just then. You've been rolling your eyes and punching air with your fist for the last five minutes. I was getting scared. You're an unmerciful sinner when you get started, ain't you, Is? Who was the victim that time? 'Man Afraid of Hot Water'? or who?"

The skipper scowled. He shoved the fist into his pocket.

"Naw," he growled. "'Twa'n't."

"So? Not an Indian? Then it must have been a white man. Some fellow after your girl, perhaps. Hey?"

The disconcerted Issy was speechless. His companion's chance shot had scored a bull's-eye. Sam whooped.

"That's it!" he crowed. "Sure thing! Give it to him, Is! Don't spare him."

Mr. McKay chokingly admitted that he "wa'n't goin' to."

"Ho, ho! That's the stuff! But who's *she*, Is? When are you going to marry her?"

Issy grunted spitefully. "You ain't married yourself—not yit," he observed, with concealed sarcasm.

The unsuspecting Bartlett laughed in triumph. "No," he said. "I'm not, that's a fact; but maybe I'm going to be some of these days. It looked pretty dubious for a while, but now it's all right."

"'Tis, hey? You're sure about that, be you?"

"Guess I am. Great Scott! what's that? Fog?"

A damp breath blew across the boat. The clouds covered the sky overhead and the bay to port. The fog was pouring like smoke across the water.

"Fog, by thunder!" exclaimed Bartlett.

Issy smiled. "Hum! Yes, 'tis fog, ain't it?" he observed.

"But what'll we do? It'll be here in a minute, won't it?"

"Shouldn't be a mite surprised. Looks 's if twas here now."

The fog came on. It reached the Lady May, passed over her, and shut her within gray, wet walls. It was impossible to see a length from her side. Sam swore emphatically. The skipper was provokingly calm. He stepped to the engine, bent over it, and then returned to the wheel.

"What are you doing?" demanded Bartlett.

"Slowin' down, of course. Can't run more'n ha'f speed in a fog like this. 'Tain't safe."

"Safe! What do I care? I want to get to Trumet."

"Yes? Well, maybe we'll git there if we have luck."

"You idiot! We've *got* to get there. How can you tell which way to steer? Get your compass, man! get your compass!"

"Ain't got no compass," was the sulky answer. "Left it to home."

"Why, no, you didn't. I—"

"I tell you I did. 'Twas careless of me, I know, but—"

"But I say you didn't. When you went uptown after that quahaug rake I explored this craft of yours some. The compass is in that little closet at the end of the cabin. I'll get it."

He rose to his feet. Issy sprang forward and seized him by the arm.

"Set down!" he yelled. "Who's runnin' this boat, you or me?"

The astounded passenger stared at his companion.

"Why, you are," he replied. "But that's no reason—What's the matter with you, anyway? Have your dime novels driven you loony?"

Issy hesitated. For a moment chagrin and rage at this sudden upset of his schemes had gotten the better of his prudence. But Bartlett was taller than he and broad in proportion. And valor—except of the imaginative brand—was not Issy's strong point.

"There, there, Sam!" he explained, smiling crookedly. "You mustn't mind me. I'm sort of nervous, I guess. And you mustn't hop up and down in a boat that way. You set still and I'll fetch the compass."

He stumbled across the cockpit and disappeared in the dusk of the cabin. Finding that compass took a long time. Sam lost patience.

"What's the matter?" he demanded. "Can't you find it? Shall I come?"

"No, no!" screamed Issy vehemently. "Stay where you be. Catch a-holt of that wheel. We'll be spinnin' circles if you don't. I'm a-comin'."

But it was another five minutes before he emerged from the cabin, carrying the compass box very carefully with both hands. He placed it in the binnacle and closed the glass lid.

"'Twas catched in a bluefish line," he explained. "All snarled up, 'twas."

Sam peered through the glass at the compass.

"Thunder!" he exclaimed. "I should say we had spun around. Instead of north being off here where I thought it was, it's 'way out to the right. Queer how fog'll mix a fellow up. Trumet's about northeast, isn't it?"

"No'theast by no'th's the course. Keep her just there."

The Lady May, still at half speed, kept on through the mist. Time passed. The twilight, made darker still by the fog, deepened. They lit the lantern in order to see the compass card. Issy had the wheel now. Sam was forward, keeping a lookout and fretting at the delay.

"It's seven o'clock already," he cried. "For Heaven's sake, how late will you be? I've got to be there by quarter of eight. D'you hear? I've *got* to."

"Well, we're gittin' there. Can't expect to travel so fast with part of the power off. You'll be where you're goin' full as soon as you want to be, I cal'late."

And he chuckled.

Another half hour and, through the wet dimness, a light flashed, vanished, and flashed again. Issy saw it and smiled grimly. Bartlett saw it and shouted.

"'What's that light?" he cried. "Did you see it? There it is, off there."

"I see it. There's a light at Trumet Neck, ain't there?"

"Humph! It's been years since I was there, but I thought Trumet light was steady. However—"

"Ain't that the wharf ahead?"

Sure enough, out of the dark loomed the bulk of a small wharf, with catboats at anchor near it. Higher up, somewhere on the shore, were the lighted windows of a building.

"By thunder, we're here!" exclaimed Sam, and drew a long breath.

Issy shut off the power altogether, and the Lady May slid easily up to the wharf. Feverishly her skipper made her fast.

"Yes, sir!" he cried exultantly. "We're here. And no Black Rover nor anybody else ever done a better piece of steerin' than that, nuther."

He clambered over the stringpiece, right at the heels of his impatient but grateful passenger. Sam's thanks were profuse and sincere.

"I'll never forget it, Is," he declared. "I'll never forget it. And you'll have to let me pay you the—What makes you shake so?"

Issy pulled his arm away and stepped back.

"I'll never forget it, Is," continued Sam. "I—Why! What—?"

He was standing at the shore end of the wharf, gazing up at the lighted windows. They were those of a dwelling house—an old-fashioned house with a back yard sloping down to the landing.

And then Issy McKay leaned forward and spoke in his ear.

"You bet you won't forgit it, Sam Bartlett!" he crowed, in trembling but delicious triumph. "You bet you won't! I've fixed you just the same as the Black Rover fixed the mutineers. Run off with my girl, will ye? And marry her, will ye? I—"

Sam interrupted him. "Why! Why!" he cried. "That's—that's Gertie's house! This isn't Trumet! It's East Harniss!"

The next moment he was seized from behind. The skipper's arms were around his waist and the skipper's thin legs twisted about his own. They fell together upon the sand and, as they rolled and struggled, Issy's yells rose loud and high.

"Mr. Higgins!" he shrieked. "Mr. Higgins! Come on! I've got him! I've got the feller that's tryin' to steal your daughter! Come on! I've got him! I'm hangin' to him!"

A door banged open. Some one rushed down the walk. And then a girl's voice cried in alarm:

"What is it? Who is it? What is the matter?"

And from the bundle of legs and arms on the ground two voices exclaimed: "*Gertie!*"

"But where *is* your father?" asked Sam. Issy asked nothing. He merely sat still and listened.

"Why, he's at Trumet. At least I suppose he is. Mrs. Jones—she's gone to telephone to him now—says that he came home this morning with one of those dreadful 'attacks' of his. And after dinner he seemed so sick that, when she went for the doctor, she wired me at Auntie's to come home. I didn't want to come—you know why—but I *couldn't* let him die alone. And so I caught the three o'clock train and came. I knew you'd forgive me. But it seems that when Mrs. Jones came back with the doctor they found father up and dressed and storming like a crazy man. He had received some sort of a letter; he wouldn't say what. And, in spite of all they could do, he insisted on going out. And Cap'n Berry—the depot master—says he went to Trumet on the afternoon freight. We must have passed each other on the way. And I'm so—But why are you *here*? And what were you and Issy doing? And—"

Her lover broke in eagerly. "Then you're alone now?" he asked.

"Yes, but—"

"Good! Your father can't get a train back from Trumet before to-morrow morning. I don't know what this letter was—but never mind. Perhaps friend McKay knows more about it. It may be that Mr. Higgins is waiting now outside the Baptist church. Gertie, now's our chance. You come with me right up to the minister's. He's a friend of mine. He understands. He'll marry us, I know. Come! We mustn't lose a minute. Your dad may take a notion to drive back."

He led her off up the lane, she protesting, he urging. At the corner of the house he turned.

"I say, Is!" he called. "Don't you want to come to the wedding? Seems to me we owe you that, considering all you've done to help it along. Or perhaps you want to stay and fix that compass of yours."

Issy didn't answer. Some time after they had gone he arose from the ground and stumbled home. That night he put a paper novel into the stove. Next morning, before going to the depot, he removed an iron spike from the Lady May's compass box. The needle swung back to its proper position.

Chapter XVIII
The Mountain and Mahomet

THE ELEVENTH OF July. The little Berry house stood high on its joists and rollers, in the middle of the Hill Boulevard, directly opposite the Edwards lot. Close behind it loomed the big "Colonial." Another twenty-four hours, and, even at its one-horse gait, the depot master's dwelling would be beyond the strip of Edwards fence. The "Colonial" would be ready to move on the lot, and Olive Edwards, the widow, would be obliged to leave her home. In fact, Mr. Williams had notified her that she and her few belongings must be off the premises by the afternoon of the twelfth.

The great Williams was in high good-humor. He chuckled as he talked with his foreman, and the foreman chuckled in return. Simeon Phinney did not chuckle. He was anxious and worried, and even the news of Gertie Higgins's runaway marriage, brought to him by Obed Gott, who—having been so recently the victim of another unexpected matrimonial alliance—was wickedly happy over the postmaster's discomfiture, did not interest him greatly.

"Well, I wonder who'll be the next couple," speculated Obed. "First Polena and old Hardee, then Gertie Higgins and Sam Bartlett! I declare, Sim, gettin' married unbeknownst to anybody must be catchin', like the measles. Nobody's safe unless they've got a wife or husband livin'. Me and Sol Berry are old baches—we'd better get vaccinated or *we* may come down with the disease. Ho! ho!"

After dinner Mr. Phinney went from his home to the depot. Captain Sol was sitting in the ticket office, with the door shut. On the platform, forlornly sprawled upon the baggage truck, was Issy McKay, the picture of desolation. He started nervously when he heard Simeon's step. As yet Issy's part in the Bartlett-Higgins episode was unknown to the townspeople. Sam and Gertie had considerately kept silence. Beriah had not learned who sent him the warning note, the unlucky missive which had brought his troubles to a climax. But he was bound to learn it, he would find out soon, and then—No wonder Issy groaned.

"Come in here, Sim," said the depot master. Phinney entered the ticket office.

"Shut the door," commanded the Captain. The order was obeyed. "Well, what is it?" asked Berry.

"Why, I just run in to see you a minute, Sol, that's all. What are you shut up in here all alone for?"

"'Cause I want to be alone. There's been more than a thousand folks in this depot so far to-day, seems so, and they all wanted to talk. I don't feel like talkin'."

"Heard about Gertie Higgins and—"

"Yes."

"Who told you?"

"Hiram Baker told me first. He's a fine feller and he's so tickled, now that his youngster's 'most well, that he cruises around spoutin' talk and joy same as a steamer's stack spouts cinders. He told me. Then Obed Gott and Cornelius Rowe and Redny Blount and Pat Starkey, and land knows how many more, came to tell me. I cut 'em short. Why, even the Major himself conde-scended to march in, grand and imposin' as a procession, to make proclamations about love laughin' at locksmiths, and so on. Since he got Polena and her bank account he's a bigger man than the President, in his own estimate."

"Humph! Well, he better make the best of it while it lasts. P'lena ain't Hetty Green, and her money won't hold out forever."

"That's a fact. Still Polena's got sense. She'll hold Hardee in check, I cal'late. I wouldn't wonder if it ended by her bossin' things and the Major actin' as a sort of pet poodle dog—nice and pretty to walk out with, but always kept at the end of a string."

"You didn't go to Higgins's for dinner to-day, did you?"

"No. Nor I shan't go for supper. Beriah's bad enough when he's got nothin' the matter with him but dyspepsy. Now that his sufferin's are complicated with elopements, I don't want to eat with him."

"Come and have supper with us."

"I guess not, thank you, Sim. I'll get some crackers and cheese and such at the store. I—I ain't very hungry these days."

He turned his head and looked out of the window. Simeon fidgeted.

"Sol," he said, after a pause, "we'll be past Olive's by to-morrer night."

No answer. Sim repeated his remark.

"I know it," was the short reply.

"Yes—yes, I s'posed you did, but—"

"Sim, don't bother me now. This is my last day here at the depot, and I've got things to do."

"Your last day? Why, what—?"

Captain Sol told briefly of his resignation and of the coming of the new depot master.

"But you givin' up your job!" gasped Phinney. "*You!* Why, what for?"

"For instance, I guess. I ain't dependent on the wages, and I'm sick of the whole thing."

"But what'll you do?"

"Don't know."

"You—you won't leave town, will you? Lawsy mercy, I hope not!"

"Don't know. Maybe I'll know better by and by. I've got to think things out. Run along now, like a good feller. Don't say nothin' about my quittin'. All hands'll know it to-morrow, and that's soon enough."

Simeon departed, his brain in a whirl. Captain Solomon Berry no longer depot master! The world must be coming to an end.

He remained at his work until supper time. During the meal he ate and said so little that his wife wondered and asked questions. To avoid answering them he hurried out. When he returned, about ten o'clock, he was a changed man. His eyes shone and he fairly danced with excitement.

"Emeline!" he shouted, as he burst into the sitting room.

"What do you think? I've got the everlastin'est news to tell!"

"Good or bad?" asked the practical Mrs. Phinney.

"Good! So good that—There! let me tell you. When I left here I went down to the store and hung around till the mail was sorted. Pat Starkey was doin' the sortin', Beriah bein' too upsot by Gertie's gettin' married to attend to anything. Pat called me to the mail window and handed me a letter.

"'It's for Olive Edwards, 'he says. 'She's been expectin' one for a consider'ble spell, she told me, and maybe this is it. P'r'aps you'd just as soon go round by her shop and leave it.'

"I took the letter and looked at it. Up in one corner was the printed name of an Omaha firm. I never said nothin', but I sartinly hustled on my way up the hill.

"Olive was in her little settin' room back of the shop. She was pretty pale, and her eyes looked as if she hadn't been doin' much sleepin' lately. Likewise I noticed—and it give me a queer feelin' inside—that her trunk was standin', partly packed, in the corner."

"The poor woman!" exclaimed Mrs. Phinney.

"Yes," went on her husband. "Well, I handed over the letter and started to go, but she told me to set down and rest, 'cause I was so out of breath. To tell you the truth, I was crazy to find out what was in that envelope and, being as she'd give me the excuse, I set.

"She took the letter over to the lamp and looked at it for much as a minute, as if she was afraid to open it. But at last, and with her fingers shakin' like the palsy, she fetched a long breath and tore off the end of the envelope. It was a pretty long letter, and she read it through. I see her face gettin' whiter and whiter and, when she reached the bottom of the last page, the letter fell onto the floor. Down went her head on her arms, and she cried as if her heart would break. I never felt so sorry for anybody in my life.

"'Don't, Mrs. Edwards,' I says. 'Please don't. That cousin of yours is a darn ungrateful scamp, and I'd like to have my claws on his neck this minute.'

"She never even asked me how I knew about the cousin. She

was too much upset for that.

"'Oh! oh!' she sobs. 'What *shall* I do? Where shall I go? I haven't got a friend in the world!'

"I couldn't stand that. I went acrost and laid my hand on her shoulder.

"'Mrs. Edwards,' says I, 'you mustn't say that. You've got lots of friends. I'm your friend. Mr. Hilton's your friend. Yes, and there's another, the best friend of all. If it weren't for him, you'd have been turned out into the street long before this.'"

Mrs. Phinney nodded. "I'm glad you told her!" she exclaimed. "She'd ought to know."

"That's what I thought," said Simeon.

"Well, she raised her head then and looked at me.

"'You mean Mr. Williams?' she asks.

"That riled me up. 'Williams nothin'!' says I. 'Williams let you stay here 'cause he could just as well as not. If he'd known that this other friend was keepin' him from gettin' here, just on your account, he'd have chucked you to glory, promise or no promise. But this friend, this real friend, he don't count cost, nor trouble, nor inconvenience. Hikes his house—the house he lives in—right out into the road, moves it to a place where he don't want to go, and—'

"'Mr. Phinney,' she sighs out, 'what do you mean?'

"And then I told her. She listened without sayin' a word, but her eyes kept gettin' brighter and brighter and she breathed short.

"'Oh!' she says, when I'd finished. 'Did he—did he—do that for *me*?'

"'You bet!' says I. 'He didn't tell me what he was doin' it for—that ain't Sol's style; but I'm arithmetiker enough to put two and two together and make four. He did it for you, you can bet your last red on that.'

"She stood up. 'Oh!' she breathes. 'I—I must go and thank him. I—'

"But, knowin' Sol, I was afraid. Fust place, there was no tellin' how he'd act, and, besides, he might not take it kindly that I'd told her.

"'Wait a jiffy,' I says. 'I'll go out and see if he's home. You stay here. I'll be back right off.'

"Out I put, and over to the Berry house, standin' on its rollers in the middle of the Boulevard. And, just as I got to it, somebody says:

"'Ahoy, Sim! What's the hurry? Anybody on fire?'

"'Twas the Cap'n himself, settin' on a pile of movin' joist and smokin' as usual. I didn't waste no time.

"'Sol,' says I, 'I've just come from Olive's. She's got that letter from the Omaha man. Poor thing! all alone there—'

"He interrupted me sharp. 'Well?' he snaps. 'What's it say? Will the cousin help her?'

"'No,' I says, 'drat him, he won't!'

"The answer I got surprised me more'n anything I ever heard or ever will hear.

"'Thank God!' says Sol Berry. 'That settles it.'

"And I swan to man if he didn't climb down off them timbers and march straight across the street, over to the door of Olive Edwards's home, open it, and go in! I leaned against the joist he'd left, and swabbed my forehead with my sleeve."

"He went to *her*!" gasped Mrs. Phinney.

"Wait," continued her husband. "I must have stood there twenty minutes when I heard somebody hurryin' down the Boulevard. 'Twas Cornelius Rowe, all red-faced and het up, but bu'stin' with news.

"''Lo, Sim!' says he to me. 'Is Cap'n Sol home? Does he know?'

"'Know? Know what?' says I.

"'Why, the trick Mr. Williams put up on him? Hey? You ain't heard? Well, Mr. Williams's fixed him nice, *he* has! Seems Abner Payne hadn't answered Sol's letter tellin' him he'd accept the offer to swap lots, and Williams went up to Wareham where Payne's been stayin' and offered him a thumpin' price for the land on Main Street, and took it. The deed's all made out. Cap'n Sol can't move where he was goin' to, and he's left with his house on the town, as you might say. Ain't it a joke, though? Where is Sol? I want to be the fust to tell him and see how he acts. Is he to home?'

"I was shook pretty nigh to pieces, but I had some sense left.

"'No, he ain't,' says I. 'I see him go up street a spell ago.'"

"Why, Simeon!" interrupted Mrs. Phinney once more. "Was that true? How *could* you see him when—"

"Be still! S'pose I was goin' to tell him where Sol *had* gone? I'd have lied myself blue fust. However, Cornelius was satisfied.

"'That so?' he grunts. 'By jings! I'm goin' to find him.'

"Off he went, and the next thing I knew the Edwards door opened, and I heard somebody callin' my name. I went acrost, walkin' in a kind of daze, and there, in the doorway, with the lamp shinin' on 'em, was Cap'n Sol and Olive. The tears was wet on her cheeks, but she was smilin' in a kind of shy, half-believin' sort of way, and as for Sol, he was one broad, satisfied grin.

"'Cap'n,' I begun, 'I just heard the everlastin'est news that—'

"'Shut up, Sim!' he orders, cheerful. 'You've been a mighty good friend to both of us, and I want you to be the fust to shake hands.'

"'Shake hands?' I stammers, lookin' at 'em. 'What? You don't mean—'

"'I mean shake hands. Don't you want to?'

"Want to! I give 'em both one more look, and then we shook, up to the elbows; and my grin had the Cap'n's beat holler.

"'Sim,' he says, after I'd cackled a few minutes, 'I cal'late maybe that white horse is well by this time. P'r'aps we might move a little faster. I'm kind of anxious to get to Main Street.'

"Then I remembered. 'Great gosh all fish-hooks!' I sings out. 'Main Street? Why, there *ain't* no Main Street!'

"And I gives 'em Cornelius's news. The widow's smile faded out.

"'Oh!' says she. 'O Solomon! And I got you into all this trouble!'

"Cap'n Sol didn't stop grinnin', but he scratched his head. 'Huh!' says he. 'Mark one up for King Williams the Great. Humph!'

"He thought for a minute and then he laughed out loud. 'Olive,' 'he says, 'if I remember right, you and I always figgered to live on the Shore Road. It's the best site in town. Sim, I guess if that white horse *is* well, you can move that shanty of mine right to

Cross Street, down that, and back along the Shore Road to the place where it come from. *That* land's mine yet,' says he.

"If that wa'n't him all over! I couldn't think what to say, except that folks would laugh some, I cal'lated.

"'Not at us, they won't,' says he. 'We'll clear out till the laughin' is over. Olive, to-morrer mornin' we'll call on Parson Hilton and then take the ten o'clock train. I feel's if a trip to Washin'ton would be about right just now.'

"She started and blushed and then looked up into his face. 'Solomon,' she says, low, 'I really would like to go to Niagara.'

"He shook his head. 'Old lady,' says he, 'I guess you don't quite understand this thing. See here'—p'intin' to his house loomin' big and black in the roadway—'see! the mountain has come to Mahomet.'"

Mrs. Phinney had heard enough. She sprang from her chair and seized her husband's hands.

"Splendid!" she cried, her face beaming. "Oh, *ain't* it lovely! Ain't you glad for 'em, Simeon?"

"Glad! Say, Emeline; there's some of that wild-cherry bounce down cellar, ain't there? Let's break our teetotalism for once and drink a glass to Cap'n and Mrs. Solomon Berry. Jerushy! I got to do *somethin'* to celebrate."

On the Hill Boulevard the summer wind stirred the silverleaf poplars. The thick, black shadows along the sidewalks were heavy with the perfume of flowers. Captain Sol, ex-depot master of East Harniss, strolled on in the dark, under the stars, his hands in his pockets, and in his heart happiness complete and absolute.

Behind him twinkled the lamp in the window of the Edwards house, so soon to be torn down. Before him, over the barberry hedge, blazed the windows of the mansion the owner of which was responsible for it all. The windows were open, and through them sounded the voices of the mighty Ogden Hapworth Williams and his wife, engaged in a lively altercation. It was an open secret that their married life was anything but peaceful.

"What are you grumbling about now?" Demanded 'Williams. "Don't I give you more money than—"

"Nonsense!" sneered Mrs. Williams, in scornful derision. "Nonsense, I say! Money is all there is to you, Ogden. In other things, the real things of this world, those you can't buy with money, you're a perfect imbecile. You know nothing whatever about them."

Captain Sol, alone on the walk by the hedge, glanced in the direction of the shrill voice, then back at the lamp in Olive's window. And he laughed aloud.